"Now I am become Death, the destroyer of worlds."

- J. Robert Oppenheimer

1.

Hotel Moss.

Rjukan, Norway.

20th February 1945.

Otto Mortens put the cigarette from a fresh pack to his lips. As he struck the match, he knew Astrid would disapprove. After brief consideration, he shrugged, knowing that she was not with him, and therefore did not need to know.

With the cigarette lit, he waved the match out before he tossed it into the glass ashtray on the small marble slated table next to him. He relaxed in the low-slung leather chair. Picking a strand of tobacco from his teeth, he then proceeded to take a long leisurely drag. He worked his jaw slow and deliberate, trying to master blowing smoke

Also, by Rob Lofthouse

A Cold Night in June

Bazooka Town

Trouble at Zero Hour Trilogy

Trouble Ahead

The Sheer Nerve

The North Tower

The Few

Where Pilgrims Roam

Where the Fruit Hangs Low

To Matt,
I hope you enjoy the story
Best wishes
Rob

The Karma Ward

by

Rob Lofthouse

rings up towards the bleak off white ceiling of the hotel lobby. His attempts were in vain, for he could not get the hang of it. Other men in his security team were able to do it, but no matter how many times they demonstrated it, he never grasped it.

He was bored of the hotel, bored of Rjukan, bored of Norway, and most of all, bored of Jurgen Arens.

In his mind, Arens was a pretentious arse, who believed his genius to be the stuff of legend. The Heavy Water Scientist just so happened to be on leave for the birth of his umpteenth child when Norwegian terrorists raided the Vermork Hydroelectric Plant back in February 1943. The raid destroyed much of the means to create Heavy Water but was soon up and running again. At the time, Mortens was in Southern Russia, serving as part of the security team protecting the headquarters of Army Group South. After a reshuffle, Mortens was on the cusp of being reassigned to a fighting division when an old academy friend of his put in a good word for him to be reassigned back in Germany. Mortens could not believe his luck. Not long after he got back to Germany in early 1944, he was briefed to provide security for Arens in Norway after another attack by the Norwegians sunk a ferry carrying barrels of Heavy Water bound for Germany.

Mortens took another drag of his cigarette.

Arens was keen to continue his research back in Germany, but the powers that be felt that despite the sporadic, but effective insurgency in Norway, it was still safer to continue it there, and insisted he have a security team assigned to him, and the Vermork site reinforced with extra troops. Arens was most vocal, Mortens recalled, since Arens hated Norway as much as he did. The summers were about as good as a fresh spring day in Germany, and the winters were on par with Russia. The job was not difficult, save Arens and his habit to change his daily routine with little or no warning. Norway was just a boring assignment. Winters were long and bleak periods of soul crushing darkness, and the summers were cursed with long, exhausting periods of daylight, which played havoc with his body clock.

Putting out his cigarette, Mortens looked through the glass plated windows. His team shuffled around Arens official car, a Mercedes of all things. Its engine running, keeping the driver warm, but wasting fuel because as usual Arens felt the world should wait for him. He hauled himself to his feet and made for the doors.

His eight-man team, their greatcoat collars pulled up to their ears in the vain hope of keeping the evening wind from cutting through them, looked up the salt coated steps at him. Mortens face screwed up as the bitter cold hit him. He eyed the Mercedes and the second one sat idling two car lengths behind it, the driver of that one enjoying the warm interior.

'One of you stay with each car, the rest of you get in here. No point us all being cold. Take turns rotating through.'

Stamping their feet, the majority of his men trudged up the steps.

'Thanks boss,' the lead officer smiled, 'he likes to keep us waiting, doesn't he?'

'Yep,' Mortens held the door open, 'same shit, different day.'

With the two unfortunates stood with the cars, the others in the lobby shrugged themselves out of their coats. Draping them over the chairs, they dropped their hats unceremoniously on the small tables placed between each set of four. The lobby was spacious but austere. Where the Germans would showcase opulence, the Scandinavians were minimalists. The men rubbed their numbed hands together, when Paula, the receptionist leaned over the high desk.

'Coffee gentlemen?'

The plain clothed SS security team wrung their hands enthusiastically in response to the hospitality, except Mortens. Putting another cigarette to his lips, he managed to steal a seductive smile from the petite brunette. All the men in his team knew he was screwing her. Even Arens knew he was, despite his numerous attempts to dazzle her with compliments and anecdotes of his rebellious youth. He even tried to impress her with the fact that in SS circles he outranked the senior security officer, even in an honorary rank. Paula would smile and gasp in all the right places so to humour the insufferable man as she looked on at her lover, who knew to remain aloof. Mortens knew better than to begin measuring appendages with the scientist, it would only result in his reassignment, or his affair becoming known to Astrid. He did not put it past Arens to try such a stunt, so chose to keep his private life off Arens' radar as much as possible, and to do that in deepest darkest Norway, was to allow the scientist to think he was calling the shots.

Mortens felt Paula was dangerous too in her own right. Not long after he was assigned to the detail, he had heard a story among some of the town folk that she had been instrumental in having the Jews run out of there. The very hotel they stood in was apparently owned by a Jewish family. The local police arrived to arrest them, only to find that they were nowhere to be seen, the safe empty and the ledgers missing. Paula had apparently known where they were in hiding and put to them that unless they surrendered the ledgers to her, she would give them up to the police.

A cunning bitch, Mortens smirked with some satisfaction as he blew smoke from his nostrils. He would have to watch her. The sex was good, for there was almost nothing left to the imagination when he was in her bed, yet he made sure she had none of his home contact details. One ace that he played early with his men, was threatening them with a reassignment east if the woman come to know where his family lived. He knew then that he only needed to keep his own paper trail in order. Arens had connections back in Germany, but it was unlikely that his orders would hold much water with Mortens superiors. If all else failed, Morten could play the medieval card, and just have her arrested as an enemy of the state, or just take her into the woods and shoot her. He doubted the Gestapo office in Oslo would go out of their way to open an investigation.

Just another liquidated insurgent.

The men converged upon Paula as she brought a tray bearing a coffee pot and crockery out to them. Setting it down on one of the small tables, she stepped back as the suited men sought refreshment. Pulling her skirt straight, she looked up at Mortens with a warm, teasing smile.

'Would you care for coffee, Hauptsturmfuhrer?'

'Yes, please.' Mortens answered in Norwegian. He was not going to turn down the chance of a coffee before escorting Arens out to dinner.

Paula went to go for the coffee pot, but one of the men handed her a cup and saucer, with coffee already in it. Her pale petite hands, and their scarlet nails gently received the beverage before she sashayed around the men towards him. A good head and shoulders shorter than the SS officer, she beamed up at him as he accepted the drink.

'What time do you finish?' Paula asked at just above a whisper.

'Late.' Mortens muttered as he put the cup to his lips, 'He's not known for rushing about. You know that.'

Paula smiled as she nodded in agreement. She had come to know Arens well enough by now. Out here, away from Oslo, he was his own self-proclaimed Fuhrer.

She glanced over her shoulder at the other security officers enjoying the coffee, then back at Mortens.

'Coming over later?'

'Put him down, Fraulien, you don't know where he's been,' bellowed Jurgen Arens jokingly as he stood at the reception counter. Paula instantly blushed as the security men hurriedly finished off their coffees. Such overzealous pantomime no longer amused Mortens, who placed his cup and saucer on the table by his side. As he straightened up, the scientist, well wrapped for the shattering night air clipped over in very expensive leather shoes. Hat, coat, scarf, gloves in place, with his brief case held tight in his left hand, Arens made a show of embracing little Paula in his arms. As he did so, he cut Mortens a menacing leer, as if he too enjoyed the low hanging fruit of Norway. Mortens slid his hands into his trouser pockets and returned a tired expression.

Let the old fool have his fun.

Arens released his embrace of the woman, only to stand back and take all of her in.

'Paula, my darling,' he gushed, 'with each day that passes you grow more delicious.' Arens Norwegian was flawless. Paula knew when to bring in the harvest, and that meant whenever the sun was shining.

'Doctor please,' the brunette blushed, all for show. Arens took her tiny hand in his large, gloved paw, kissing it a little too long for Mortens liking.

'Paula?' Arens looked up at her, his thin rimmed glasses perched on the end of his nose, 'Would you join me for dinner tonight? I have a table booked at The Telemark.'

Paula placed her free hand on her chest apologetically as Mortens frowned with concern.

'Doctor,' Paula began, 'I'm flattered tha_ '

'That'll be three Sundays in a row.' Mortens blurted out in German, loud enough for his men to stop chatting among themselves and look up. Arens rolled his eyes as he released Paula's hand.

'I'm well aware of that, Hauptsturmfuhrer,' Arens responded sardonically, 'I know how to read a calendar.'

'We are already setting a pattern, Doctor.' Mortens stepped forward a pace, causing Paula to sidestep out of the way, 'I urge you to either dine here tonight or choose another venue.'

'The goulash at The Telemark is outstanding, Hauptsturmfuhrer.' Arens smiled at Paula as he countered back in Norwegian, 'Besides, they make it for me special, just like I have it at home.'

'Cancel the reservation please,' Mortens looked to Paula, who returned a concerned look, 'the good Doctor will be eating either here o- '

'Might I remind you Hauptsturmfuhrer,' Arens bellowed with slow blinking eyes as if he were above such pettiness, 'that as your superior officer, your only concern is to ensure that those who may wish me harm are not where I happen to be, whether it be planned well in advance or on the hoof, is that clear?'

'By not setting a pattern is exactly how I do that, Doctor.' Mortens was not going to concede without a fight.

'I have few vices in this frozen shithole, Hauptsturmfuhrer,' Arens nostrils flared, 'fewer than you I'm sure.' As Arens tailed off, he took in both Mortens and the brunette. The security officer frowned in challenge.

'Meaning?'

'Since our supposed betters in Berlin have exiled me here to continue my work, the least I can enjoy is dinner where I fucking well like.'

'You are no good to Berlin if you are dead, incapacitated or captured, Herr Doctor.'

'Then do your fucking job right Hauptsturmfuhrer, and that won't happen.'

2.

The optics bobbed as they tracked the well wrapped men leaving the hotel, before they descended the wide, shallow steps to the two Mercedes. The target stood back from the lead car, hugging his briefcase in his arms. The other men split up, three heading for the rear vehicle, joining the driver and the cold lone sentry, whilst the three that remained did the same with the lead.

With the men in place, the man overseeing the spectacle opened the door for the target, who acted like he had all the time in the world as he lowered himself into the back seats.

'The target is in the vehicle,' the observer, Paulie Nutt spoke to no one in particular.

'Yep, I see him.' Anton Rey, the resistance cell commander responded. 'Now we'll see if those Nazi bastards take him back to The Telemark for the third time.'

Nutt leaned into his binoculars, the security team were now in the cars, and creeping away from the hotel. He then focused on the glass doors at the top of the stairs. The brunette was there again.

'I'm gonna mount that traitorous bitches head above my fireplace.' Nutt hissed through his teeth.

'Later,' Rey spoke calmly, lowering his binoculars as he turned, 'we deal with the target first.'

Rey took in the hotel room. The bed was strewn with coats, hats, and gloves. On top were suppressed versions of the Sten sub machinegun. Spare magazines and Colt pistols were tucked into coat pockets. With Nutt peering through the heavy net curtains, the other three stood silent, or paced the room, smoking incessantly. They were nervous, Rey deduced, and rightly so. If they managed to get Arens, they would certainly kick the hornets' nest.

It is often said that pride would kill a man quicker than any other method, and in the breast of these Northmen, they owed much to those who went before them. Denying Hitler the means to create a weapon so devastating, he could have already won the war. Those Viking brothers, only the year before had sent the Hydro to the bottom of the fjord, which bought the Allies time. The Germans were nothing but predictable and efficient in getting production back up and running, but to keep it in Norway had been the topic of discussion many times for Rey and his men when they planned to strike in the name of Norway and the free world.

Why would the Germans not take production to Germany?

Rey summed up the reason and put it to his men. If their new weapon were to malfunction in Norway, the damaged could well be minimal in regard to German infrastructure and human casualties. Norway, however, would be sacrificed.

Nutt stood up as he moved from the netted window.

'We'll soon find out if the bastard goes where we think he'll go.'

If Arens was eating at The Telemark tonight, the phone in the room would ring. Rey would answer, the switchboard girl would connect him with Josef, who was watching The Telemark from another observation point, and be told a dinner reservation for one had been confirmed. They would then dress and arm themselves, meet up with Josef and his half of the cell and go into that hotel and kill Arens where he sat and any of his henchmen who dared to oppose them.

That was the plan anyhow. Until recently, Rey admitted to himself, nailing Arens down on any particular night was somewhat of a challenge. His security team were professional and imposing. Their routine hard to predict, their routes about the region varied. To mount an attack near the Vermork Hydroelectric Plant would only have the area swarming with German troops within the hour. Arens liked to eat out, and the eateries and restaurants, despite the harsh privations of occupation welcomed the man who was not shy in being lavish. In defence of the owners questioned by Rey's men, Arens always paid his bill, and tipped well.

Cracks, however, were beginning to show in the professional relationship between the security team and their principle. Despite getting pressure from London to eliminate or capture Arens, Rey had not sat on his laurels whenever they tried to predict Arens pattern of life. Through binoculars, he could tell by how animated Arens would become when speaking with one of the security team in particular. The scientist would pace about, his hands waving in agitation, whilst the bodyguard, hands in his pockets would keep his composure. Arens clearly did not like being restricted, and certainly did not like the bodyguard in question being in close proximity to the brunette on many an occasion.

Arens was jealous. Arens was threatened by the very man that was charged with keeping him out of the clutches of Anton Rey. Now however, the scientist was growing weary, and had got his own way two Sundays in succession. Rey just needed the phone call to confirm it would be the third and therefore last Sunday Arens would enjoy at The Telemark, never mind anywhere else.

To Mortens, the snow chains on the Mercedes made an awful crunching sound as they scrambled to get purchase on the main boulevard. It had not snowed in a few days, but the freezing temperatures at night delayed any melting until the sun was high and warm enough to begin the process. It was almost dark when they pulled in front of The Telemark. The snow around the car and along the pavements was blackened through human traffic, the apparent cleared areas dangerously slippery for the unwary. As the Mercedes crunched to a halt, Mortens opened his door, and the instant blast of Norwegian twilight air took his breath away. Refusing to show any form of weakness in front of Arens, he hauled himself out onto the pavement, his fellow team members doing the same, from his car and the Mercedes behind that carried the remainder.

With his team well drilled in their craft, they went about their security checks around the restaurant entrance before they nodded all was well to their commander. Mortens then pulled open the rear, nearside door. Arens hauled himself from his warm dwelling with not so much grace as when he climbed in. The pavement was yet to be salted, and his expensive, leather soled shoes let him know it too. Gripping the top of the car door, Arens rolled his shoulders as he took in the scene around his car. The street was as good as deserted. The occupation curfew was in full effect. The Norwegians were now well versed as to how the German authorities went about their business. Content all was well, Arens gave Mortens a smug grin.

'You see, Hauptsturmfuhrer. Nothing to fear here. Let's go eat.'

Pacing back and forth in front of the netted window, Rey was startled as the phone rang. All four men in the room froze, as if the first ring was just a figment of their imagination. They all looked at the vibrating object on the side table when it then rang again, and again, and again.

As Nutt paced over to it, the two men near the door straightened themselves up, one of them puffing out their cheeks as they ran the fingers of both hands through their hair. Rey swallowed hard as Nutt lifted the handset, putting it to his ear.

Rey observed a stern look from the man holding the handset. Nutt nodded slightly as he listened to the caller. He then replaced the handset, before fixing a determined look on his cell commander.

'Arens is at The Telemark.'

The tension lifted in Rey's shoulders as Nutt spoke. The other two cell members were wide eyed in almost disbelief since the long spells of observation and planning had now finally paid off. They were now in position to strike at Arens, and hopefully, kill off the

Nazis plans to create a super weapon. The British had also been patient to a point. They had furnished Rey with as much information as they could. Rey's cell knew what the target looked like, and what muscle he had in tow. The SS security team were not amateurs and would protect their principle if they were attacked. Rey knew they too would have to die if needs be. He also knew they would be hunted to the ends of the earth. What Rey struggled with was potential reprisals against the good people of Rjukan. They were simple folk, just trying to get through the occupation without drawing unnecessary attention from the German authorities.

Without being prompted, Rey's men loaded themselves with their suppressed Sten guns, their Colt Automatics before pulling on their large winter coats, hats, and gloves. It was not lost on Rey, that the next phase of the operation was not without risk. Norway was now under night curfew, with twilight giving way to dusk. Fighting aged males marauding Rjukan that were not German soldiers or Norwegian Police Officers under Nazi administration needed to be handled with care. The locals may well be submissive to those now in charge, but some could well be passive informers looking to win favour with the occupying force. Rey knew of those who had Nazi leanings, but he had thought better than to have them eliminated, for that would just push his fellow Norwegians into the Nazi fold. He could not vouch for the rest of Norway, but the Germans were rather good at playing the hearts and minds angle. Pregnant women were seen by proficient and highly trained medical staff from Oslo. Not soldiers, but actual medical staff drafted in from Germany. The elderly were treated with decorum, the German soldiers going out of their way to be approachable and reassuring when they visited the town for a little R & R from Vermork guard duties. Rey and his cell could have easily killed countless German soldiers, but all that would do is invite trouble when British support was so far away and slow to react.

Killing Arens was going to stir up serious trouble. But after all was said and done, Rey had to make sure what was about to befall the town in the form of reprisals was worth it. The Nazi Scientist must die tonight.

Mortens stood with his back to the restaurant doors, smoking almost constantly to keep out the cold night air. Rjukan was one of the few towns in occupied Norway that were exempt from blackout regulations. Streetlights blazed away, eateries and dwellings could enjoy having their lights on without reprimand from the wardens. The method to the madness was simple. With the hydroelectric plant lit up around the clock, the only real counter measure to confuse British bomber crews was to have neighbouring small towns and villages lit up too. Mortens acknowledged that the well-lit boulevard had its advantages: fewer shadows for the terrorist to hid in.

He had two of his men in the building with Arens, who preferred a booth to dine in, which irked Mortens since it afforded some cover for the principle, but it could be difficult to extract him should they come under attack. He had two men covering the rear of the building, leaving himself and the remaining three out in front, two of which remained in the cars that were running. Someone had to get the perk of a warm car. Dieter, the other standing sentry with him was far too professional to engage in small talk on a tasking, and patrolled back and forth, always looking outward for threats, and never looking in. Mortens always found it a little strange. The temptation to look inwards was always overwhelming for him, and he was meant to be the shining example. He had the elevated position of command and could always make out he was looking out for the rest of his men, but they were too seasoned to accept such an excuse. He had a good team working for him, and despite the shattering cold of the Norwegian night, it sure beat Russia, or Poland, or wherever the Red Army was now. Last he heard from Oslo, the Soviets were now on the Oder, not far from Berlin.

The Soviets were not in Norway, which was the main thing, Mortens accepted.

Rey and his men joined up with Josef and his men in one of the side streets not drowned in artificial light. Mindful of prying eyes overlooking their little gathering, Josef kept it brief.

'He's in the restaurant. In a booth on the right as you look at it.'

Josef then led Rey to the end of the alley leading onto the main boulevard. With caution, Rey peered around the corner. The street was void of any pedestrians, only the targets security men and their two cars sat out front. Rey could see exhaust smokes spiralling up, the engines still running. Driver in each. The boss of the team stood in front of the large plate glass window, minding the door whilst another patrolled back and forth, his collar up, shoulders hunched. It was without doubt a cold night.

Rey leaned back in. 'Where's the rest of them?'

'Four went in, but we've only picked up two still in the restaurant.'

'They are out the back,' Rey adjusted the silenced Sten under his overcoat. 'Let's get across this damn road.'

Mindful not to rouse those now at home keeping warm, Josef led the cell down a series of alleyways, in an effort not to cross the main boulevard until they were out of line of sight of the security team. Before committing to crossing a minor street, the cell would pause to take in the atmospherics before alerting the neighbourhood, thanks to a barking dog, or just stumbling into folks who were trying their luck after curfew. As Josef led them carefully down another alleyway, just before it merged with the main boulevard, they froze as two Kubelwagon buzzed past from left to right in the direction of The Telemark. With the canvas roofs buttoned up tight, whoever was in the vehicles would have had a limited field of view.

Taking a breath to compose himself, Rey looked to the others. Nutt shook his head.

'That was close.'

Peering around the corner, Rey was content that if they crossed at that point, those outside The Telemark would not see them. With a flick of his head, Rey beckoned the cell through, his Sten now in both hands, pointing down the boulevard, with Nutt covering the other way. The cell members made for what shadow they could find in the opposite alleyway before a click of fingers gave Rey and Nutt the signal that all was well. Walking with a purpose, the two men joined their comrades in the shadows.

Mortens frowned as the Kubelwagon slewed to a halt behind the rear Mercedes. With no snow chains fitted, the Kubelwagon almost shunted the sleeker, heavier car. With the headlights blinking out, Mortens witnessed a gaggle of eight soldiers tumble from within, the only soldiers who appeared remotely sober were the two drivers. As they giggled at each other's exit from their respective vehicle, they pulled themselves straight, their greatcoats adorning the rank titles of Oberleutnant. Most of them knew Mortens, and due to the fact they were all marooned far from home, both Mortens and the high-spirited Wehrmacht officers enjoyed a certain amount of banter. One of the young officers was unfamiliar to him. A new arrival perhaps.

The other drunk officers smiled and nodded knowingly at Mortens who returned the salutation whilst the new arrival was distracted with making himself look smart. His mischievous new comrades pulled him into a huddle and began whispering to each other before deliberately looking up at Mortens who was watching the whole spectacle before looking back into the huddle and chuckling away.

Mortens shook his head as he looked to Dieter, who returned an eye roll before he himself looked away.

Every time they do this to the new guy. Arseholes.

The huddle broke up, with the fresh-looking officer spinning on his heels, looking stern at Mortens, who knew to play along. The new arrival strode over to him as he pulled off his great coat, field cap, and gloves, revealing a tunic that did not have much colour in the way of decorations to speak of. Almost brand new out of the academy.

'What are you waiting for man,' hollered the young officer, 'get the fucking door open.'

Obediently, Mortens took one step to the side and pulled the door open in a well-practiced motion. As the young officer came up level, he pushed the greatcoat and field cap into Mortens chest, to which Morten received with his free arm. The young officer jerked a thumb over his shoulder.

'Be sure my drivers get something hot to drink. This country of yours is fucking freezing.'

As the young man turned to his giggling comrades, Mortens allowed the hat and coat to drop to the snow crusted ground. The young man flinched at the insolence as he squared up to the supposed valet.

'Who do you think you are?' the young brave officer sneered, only to have the hatted, well wrapped man before him respond in a calm tone.

'Hauptsturmfuhrer Mortens, SS Security.'

Face instantly ashen, the young officer crashed to attention, delivering his best party salute. In that instant, his comrades burst out laughing, some almost retching with the effort. Two were almost bent double, slapping their own thighs to try and compose themselves. Both Mortens and Dieter smiled at the joke.

Gets them every time.

Too afraid to move, the young man remained at attention as the SS officer before him retrieved his hat and coat from the ground. Mortens smiled as he pushed the garments into the owner's chest.

'Relax, Oberleutnant. A little joke we have going on.'

Feeling rather foolish, the young man smiled tight lipped. Even in the cold night air, he managed to bead with perspiration.

'Apologies Sir,' he nodded before sneering at his giggling brethren. Mortens ushered him in from the cold as the others followed on.

'Next time Otto,' one of them chuckled, 'we need you to go full rage, okay?'

'You bet. 'Mortens smiled, as they filed in.

As the last one staggered across the threshold, Mortens gripped him by the bicep. The drunk man blinked repeatedly at him.

'Tonight Erik, no shooting up the place, do you hear?'

Erik suppressed a beer fused belch away from the SS officer, nodding as he did so.

'Sure thing, Otto. Thanks for not writing me up last time.'

Erik was a competent officer when sober but was social dynamite when he was full of beer. It was Mortens slight editing of the facts to an incident he witnessed a little while back that kept Erik from a reassignment back east.

Mortens smiled as he released Erik, patting him on the shoulder.

'Enjoy tonight and stay off my shit list.'

3.

Hugging the shadows, Rey and his men picked their way through the alleyways and side streets. Boisterous laughter carried on the bitter night air, giving Rey pause to try and establish where it had come from. He slowly pirouetted round, eyeing the man behind him.

The cell member nodded in the direction of the boulevard that ran on their right side. Rey nodded as he turned back and carried on. Ensuring he kept his men in shadow, Rey led on back towards the boulevard, waving his men down.

'Wait here.' He hissed before heading on.

Not more than two hundred yards from where he peered was the rear of the two Kubelwagon. Exhaust smoke spiralling up in the still frigid air. The presence of the one he considered the boss stood well wrapped at the top of the broad, shallow steps. Movement caught Rey's eye as a second, well wrapped security man appeared from around the front Mercedes. Easing himself back into the side street, Rey could not be sure if the Kubelwagon were manned. If they were manned by at least one soldier, that would mean they were armed. He had no idea how many had travelled in them, which meant he had no idea how many were now in the restaurant. Officers would perhaps have a pistol each at best. It was unlikely for soldiers to dine there. They were more inclined to drink and whore, whereas their officers, just as prone to the very same vices, but felt a little more refined dining out.

Mindful of his footing, Rey returned to his men. Nutt was at the head of the column, a lit cigarette hanging from his lips. Rey pulled the cigarette from him, taking a long pull for himself.

'Well?' Nutt hissed, 'what's the matter?'

Rey handed back the cigarette as he exhaled through his nostrils.

'More Germans have turned up.'

'What do you mean?'

'In the restaurant. Two Kubelwagon, can't see if the drivers are still in them. Engines are running mind.'

'Fuck!' Nutt spat, stomping out the unfinished cigarette. Rey looked down the column. He had enough men to carry out the mission, but it could get messy, very quickly.

'What do you wanna do?' Nutt asked. Rey waved the men kneeling in line forward. He did not want to repeat himself. As they gathered in, he looked about the side street.

'We have more Germans in the restaurant. Could be as many as ten. Plus, up to four out front.'

A low whistle emitted from one of the men. Rey took a breath.

'We stay on mission. We've waited too long for this.'

The men huddled before him nodded. Some looked nervous, the others just looked cold.

'I will take care of Arens. I want Rudy and Kam with me as we go in the back. I want you and the remainder to take care of those out the front. Only open fire once you hear shooting inside. We can't have Arens escape. Understand?'

They all nodded. Kam, a young volunteer, eager to please Rey nodded tight lipped. His knuckles white as he wrang the Sten is his big paws. Weak in the chin and cursed with acne, Kam rolled his broad shoulders as if warming up for a fight. Rudy on the other hand, was round in the face to the point of chubby and looked petrified. Throughout the rest of the cell, the shivering from cold now replaced by pre match adrenaline. With their instructions delivered, Rey turned and headed off, across the narrow side street towards the rear of The Telemark. With Kam and Rudy following on, he glanced over his shoulder as Nutt and the remainder of the cell made for where he spied the new arrivals. Nutt understood what needed to be done.

At least Rey thought Nutt understood what was required.

Eyeing the rear of the restaurant, Rey was suspicious as to why it was not guarded. The security team looking after Arens were usually sticklers for protocol, which unnerved him. The light emitting from the kitchen access out into the waste cluttered alleyway gave away the fact that the door was of stable design, only the top half open. As Rey went to begin his approach, a shadow appeared in the light. Tucking in instantly, the sudden movement had Kam and Rudy concertina into the back of him with a clatter. Flashing to anger, more out of nerves if anything, Rey glared at them before checking himself.

 They did not mean it.

Nutt peered around at the front of the restaurant. He confirmed that the Kubelwagon were indeed still running, but he could not tell if the two Mercedes were likewise. Stepping out slowly, whilst keeping low, Nutt could see one security officer by the front door, plus the head and shoulders of another beyond the farthest Mercedes, facing away from him.

Two Security officers, Nutt concluded, *at least four drivers, all armed.*

The driver of the nearest Kubelwagon climbed out and began walking to the rear of his vehicle. Well wrapped, he began to fumble with gloves as he pulled the engine compartment open. Nutt ducked back in, his heart leaping, for he was certain the German may have noticed him. Pressed in tight against the side wall, Nutt and the men held their breath, waiting for the alarm. Which did not come.

Exhaling slowly, Nutt looked to the next man tucked in behind him.

'Get ready.'

Pushed flat against a wrought iron gantry that served as a fire escape for the apartments above them, Rey watched as the head and shoulder shadow cast onto the snow moved a limb up and down, from head to then out of sight behind the stable door.

Was it one of the security team? Rey thought. The shadow then moved away, but not before it flicked the remains of a cigarette out into the alley.

Probably kitchen staff, Rey deduced to himself. Glancing at his two comrades, he flicked his head as a signal to follow on.

With his Sten pulled tight into his right shoulder, he paced deliberately, his leg movements tight at the knee, so only the lower limbs shuffled forward, keeping his crunching footsteps to a minimum. With his heart pounding in his ears, Rey swallowed hard as he prepared to enter the kitchen.

Shuffling along, shadows then appeared in the alley as the bottom half of the stable door was opened. The shadows lengthened as two, well wrapped men of the SS Security Service stepped out. Both men were too embroiled in trying to light their cigarettes to notice their assassins were crunching their way towards them. Rey's heart leaped into his mouth as he drew closer, eyeing any possible cover to his right.

There was none, they were now committed.

Marcel, the newest member of the security detail got the fright of his life as he stood straight to take a long pull of his cigarette, only to see three dark profiles bearing down on them. Before he could alert his colleague, the Norwegian terrorist cut them down in a long burst of rippling whacks. Both SS men erupted in a pink mist as the suppressed Sten did its job, both letting out wailing belches as they dropped like sacks of coal on the blood-spattered snow.

The purpose-built suppressor fabricated to the Sten gun was silent in name only. It still gave off a loud whack as it fired, the confines of the alley amplifying the shots and the cries of the SS men. One of them lay still as the other, the one that spotted Rey writhed in agony, the blood of his comrade pooling under them. As Rey cast an eye over them to ensure they were no longer a threat, the wounded SS man held up his hands in wide eyed terror as Kam fired another burst, killing him outright. The rippling whacks buffeted their ears again. Rey shot the young volunteer a look but knew there was no point reprimanding him. They were committed and needed to just get on with it.

As Rey entered the kitchen, the kitchen staff in their pristine whites gasped and flinched as they stepped back from going to investigate the noise in the alley. Pots and pans clattered as the Head Chef and his porters were pushed aside by three armed men eager to get into the dining room. It was as Rey drew close to the service hatch which gave him a panoramic view into the dining room, a young waitress taking hold of a tray of soup bowls and sundries yelped in panic as the armed men approached. Instantly ducking down out of sight, the tray and its contents crashed to the floor, the hot soup coating her back and hair.

Mortens stamped his feet at the exact same time as the crashing crockery startled him. Spinning around, he peered through the large plate glass window to see the pristine looking waitress now coated in a dark fluid writhing on the floor before curling up into a ball. Movement through the service hatch also caught his attention. Before he could register what it was, an alarmed cry came from his left as rippling whacks and muzzle flashes strafed the rear Kubelwagon and its driver who crumpled to the floor instantly.

Mortens dashed for the front of the very same vehicle, eager to get the solid mass of its engine mounted in the rear between himself and the incoming fire, for it could absorb some punishment before the body work and interior was shredded. With the vehicle length separating him from the attackers, Mortens fumbled for his Luger as return fire came from Dieter and his own drivers, well trained in anti-ambush drills. The driver of the front Kubelwagon tumbled out of the passenger door, his MP40 clattering out after him. With the rear Kubelwagon rocking and bursting from the fusillade of incoming fire, Mortens beckoned the Wehrmacht driver to keep low and join him. As he crawled up, Mortens snatched the MP40 from him, tossing him the Luger in return. With a lull in the firefight, Mortens stood up, keeping most of his profile out of sight of the muzzle flashes rippling from around the corner of the building and fired two short bursts, resulting in a pink mist and a yelp. Squatting down to compose himself, Mortens caught sight of the dead driver, lying on his back, his face nothing but smashed pulp and hair. As he held out a hand for more magazines, he caught movement in the restaurant in his periphery.

All of those seated in the restaurant flinched at both the crashing of crockery, the yelp from the waitress and the eruption of punctured metal and popping glass outside. The security officers standing over Arens booth instantly pulled their Lugers, with one of them trying to push the principle lower in his seat. The drunk Wehrmacht officers roared obscenities as they tried to stand, unsure what was happening. The now not so sober Oberleutnant spotted Mortens and his man firing back at the threat outside. It was as the besieged Hauptsturmfuhrer Mortens looked into the restaurant, did the commotion in the kitchen draw his attention.

Rey leaned through the service hatch as both Kam and Rudy blundered their way through into the dining room. He let off a long chugging burst into both security men who fell instantly before emptying the remainder of his magazine into the booth. As he ducked down beneath the service hatch to change his magazine, the distinct rippling whacks from both Kam and Rudy's Stens made short work of the drunk Wehrmacht officers, their cries as they were strafed whilst trying to pull their own pistols. With the kitchen staff and the poor girl in the dining room wailing in terror, Rey stood back up to put another burst into the booth, only to see a number of plain clothed and uniformed soldiers aiming through the large plate glass window. No sooner had Rey ducked back down did his world implode around him.

The screaming of the girl and the cries of the kitchen staff were drowned out as multiple hornets snapped through the service hatch and the thin partition wall that made the threshold between the kitchen and the dining room. Crockery, pots and pans, ingredients, not to mention plasterboard, tiles and kitchen fittings burst around him as the incoming fire punched through all that stood in its way. Not brave or foolish enough to make a stand against overmatching firepower, Rey slewed around on his belly and crawled as fast as he could for the splintered, limp stable door. As the strafing eased, the kitchen staff too were making for the door, crawling as fast as terrified civilians could, trying their best not to make themselves a target.

With the ringing in his ears easing off, he could hear the whimpering girl caught in the dining room. With guilt beginning to wash over him, Rey tumbled out into the alley landing against the two men he had cut down less than two minutes before. The Head Chef and his porters scrambled to their feet and made off into the cold frigid night. Rey hauled himself away from the dead SS men, leaning against the wall to catch his breath, uncertain if Arens was also dead.

4.

MP40 pulled tight into his right shoulder, Mortens crunched his way into the dining room through the now wide-open window frame. The carnage that greeted him took his breath away. The drunk officers now lay dead or writhing on the ground, the waitress had managed to make it into the booth nearest the kitchen, her sobs gave her away. His two officers were crumpled together at the threshold of Arens booth. They were both dead.

'Doctor…Doctor?' Mortens called into the booth, which was punctured and splintered. Slumped on the ruined seating was Arens, groaning. The dark crimson upholstery made it difficult for Mortens to identify blood, but he had a feeling the man had been hit.

'Doctor Arens, can you move?' Mortens asked as he slung the MP40 across his body. Movement and the crunching of glass underfoot distracted him for a moment as Dieter and one of the drivers moved through, weapons up, to clear the kitchen. Looking back into the booth, Arens was trying to sit upright, but was clearly in pain. Clutching his right wrist, the cuff of his shirt and jacket ragged and bloodied, perhaps shattered. The man gasped as he spoke, blood on his teeth.

'Breathing…it feels weird,' was all Arens could manage.

Suspecting a punctured lung, Mortens needed to get Arens out of Rjukan. He had no idea how many terrorists were in the area. Mortens needed urgent medical attention, and Oslo was the best place for it. Driving him there would take an age, and prone to further attacks. He would put Arens on the Navy launch at Mael. Out on the water, the terrorists could not get at him again.

Dieter and their driver returned from the kitchen. Mortens looked to them. Dieter's expression was one of loss and anger.

'Karl and Marcel are dead.'

'What?' Mortens gasped. Dieter nodded as he looked to his other two comrades slumped on the floor. Mortens went to say something, when one of the drivers called out in the street.

'Blood. We've got a blood trail.'

Dieter and the driver were about to set off when Mortens grabbed the former by the arm.

'No. We need to get Arens out of here. Help me.'

As they hauled the wounded Arens out of the booth, both SS men grunted under his dead weight. Only once he was out of the booth, did he put weight onto what appeared to be his good leg. Limping prominently, the officers helped him out to the front Mercedes.

'Bobby and I will get him to Mael,' breathed Mortens under the weight, 'get the army and their dogs down here. They can follow the blood.'

'Okay.' Dieter acknowledged.

Cursing under the weight of the gravely wounded Arens, who wheezed and gurgled with every step, the three of them managed to get him into the back of the lead Mercedes. With Arens slumped on the back seat, Mortens scrambled for the substantial first aid kit under the front passenger seat. He grabbed a handful of dressings before climbing in after the wounded man. As he went to pull the door after him, he leaned back out to holler at Dieter as he went back to the shot-up restaurant.

'Call ahead to Mael. Tell them our principle has been attacked and we need to evacuate him immediately to Oslo.'

Dieter returned a thumbs up as he turned back to the scene of the restaurant. Bobby slid into the driver's seat, pleased he had kept the car running, and the interior warm. With snow chains already fitted, he was more confident driving out of the valley down to the ferry terminal. Chains or not, he could not go too fast. As he pulled away, he could see a melee of activity in his rear-view mirror.

With his own hat, coat and warm clothing around his feet, Mortens wrestled with Arens outer garments. The wounded man wheezed, gurgled, and groaned as he was pulled about by the SS man trying to save his life. As he pulled Arens upright, he could see he was clutching his shattered wrist.

That's one wound he could identify, but it was not going to kill him. As the heavy Mercedes rocked on the high cambered road, Mortens looked to Bobby in the rear-view mirror, their eyes meeting.

'Please don't put us in the ditch Bobby.' Mortens implored, to which his man nodded.

'Yes Sir. How is he?'

As he carefully pulled Arens arms apart, he gave his driver a rundown of what he knew, more to keep himself from sinking into panic if anything.

'He's been hit in the right wrist and right buttock; I spotted that as we pulled him out of the booth.'

'Is that bad?' Bobby asked, his eyes flicking up to the mirror. Mortens opened the coat, to be greeted with a wheezing sound coming from the man's chest. The shirt speckled with some blood, but enough for Mortens to investigate further. Ripping the shirt open, Mortens found two small entry wounds, one under the left nipple, the other further down at his left hip. Wrestling the man's neck tie clear, Mortens unceremoniously hauled the clothing off the man's shoulders, which had him yelp, before coughing and wheezing, blood bubbling through his teeth and lips. Pulling the coat, jacket, and shirt past the shoulder blades, he could not find an exit wounded for the top entry point, but he found the exit wound for the shot to the hip. Hand glazed in blood, Arens flinched and whimpered as Arens felt for the exit wound. Aware Arens was in a world of pain and fever, Mortens was tentative with his fingers. The exit wound felt about the size of an acorn.

With the car rocking, the road the Mael treacherous, and the prospect of another ambush on the way to the ferry very real, Mortens dressed the exit wound as best he could, given the confines of the car. The coppery tang of blood hung in the air, with Arens coughing and wheezing as he tried to take a full intake of breath. With Arens pulled upright, Mortens main priority was keeping the man from falling asleep. He hardly felt it could be possible because he had failed to get the morphine from the medical pack. As Arens fought for breath, he spoke to him calm and methodically, whilst using another dressing to clean the blood off his own hands.

'Doctor, you have possibly a hit to your left lung, and a definite wound to your left hip which has gone straight through.'

Arens gasped again for breath, blinking wildly. Mortens steadied him in his seat as he peered through the window, which was misting up with all the heat exerted by all those within. Mortens wiped the window clear to a point with the dressing he used to clean his own hands. It was a poor choice, for all he had managed to do was smeared Arens window with the man's blood, to whichced the wounded man turned back to Mortens, his eyes wild at the evidence of his mortality.

Mortens mouthed an apology.

It did not take much for Rey to find Nutt and the rest of his cell. The blood on the snow was easy enough to follow. Rey looked to the upper floors of the dwellings dominating the alley, for many lights were coming on, the occupant no doubt curious as to the gunfire so near their homes. He'd yet to see shutters open, or a curtain open to investigate, but he could hear hushed voices of people stood at their rear doors. As he drew near, the young volunteer standing guard challenged him, but soon relaxed when he recognised his leader. As Rey moved past, he could see the others huddled around someone lying on the ground. Peering in he could see his men tending to who could only be Nutt.

He was in a bad way.

Many dressings had been wrapped around his head, face, and chest. All of them failing to keep the blood from seeping through. The men looked up at him, their lips tight, their eyes shot and raw from trying not to let the situation overwhelm them. With blood caked all over both hands, one of the men felt for a pulse.

Nothing.

'We need to get out of here.' Rey stated, matter of fact, 'They'll come after us with dogs, so we need to get as much distance from here as we can.'

'Sweden?' One of the young men asked to which Rey nodded. The young man looked down at Nutt, shaking his head.

'We can't carry him all the way to Sweden.'

'We're not.' Rey answered deadpan, 'We'll leave him here for their dogs to find. Besides…'

Rey eyed the blood trail in the eerie light of the alleyway.

'They won't need dogs to find us if we stay here.'

'Are we really going to leave him here?' The young volunteer asked as the others stood, cuffing their faces. Rey shrugged as he nodded.

'He'll still be dead when we get to Sweden. If we get to Sweden.'

'Won't the British help?'

'They will,' Rey countered, 'but only when we get to Sweden.'

The men stood silent for a moment, all taking in Nutt, less the young sentry facing back the way they had come. Nutt was a son of Norway. Rey just hoped he would be welcome in the halls of Valhalla, and now drinking mead from curved horns. He had served his country and its people well, and it cost him his life. Rey knew that Nutt would be most annoyed if they chose to stay out of sentiment. They needed to flee and hopefully fight another day. Gathering up their weapons and equipment, Rey and what was left of his cell of freedom fighters crunched away into the darkness, making the for imposing sanctuary of the hills and in time, the Swedish border.

Swooning from blood loss, Arens swayed over, collapsing against Mortens as they entered the small, unremarkable ferry port at Mael. Mortens pushed the wounded man back to the upright position with enough vigour to disturb him from his slumber.

'Stay awake, Doctor, we're at the ferry. Come on, stay with me.'

Bobby creeped the Mercedes through the sparse port towards the small ferry moored up. Mortens peered through the windshield, for he could see sailors climbing all about the vessel, some even hopping onto the jetty and jogging towards them. He nudged Bobby on the right shoulder.

'Get as close as you can, he can't walk now.'

Bobby drew the large heavy car as close as he dared to the jetty. The Kriegsmarine sailors stood back a little, waiting for the car to stop. As it became stationary, one of the sailors stepped forward, trying to peer through the blood smeared window. Mortens waved a hand, beckoning the man to open the door.

'Get him onto the ferry, quick.' Mortens implored.

The nearest sailor pulled the door open, the sudden draft of cold took the occupants of the cars' breath away. Initially, the gathering sailors were somewhat ginger with the wounded man, who groaned and yelped as he was lifted from the blood-soaked leather interior. Bobby joined his leader as they climbed from the Mercedes, feeling the need to help. Mortens came around the front of the car, directing the sailors.

'Onto the ferry quick men. The good doctor has lost a lot of blood. We need to get him to Oslo.'

Under the dead weight of Arens, the sailors grunted and cursed as they tried to keep a purchase on the icy, snow crusted jetty. Between them, they managed to get Arens aboard, taking him below. With Bobby waiting at the car, Mortens followed them aboard.

'Captain?' Mortens hollered, 'Captain?'

The captain of the vessel emerged from the wheelhouse, his cap perched on a shock of salt and pepper hair that much like his beard was certainly not the regulation length for the Kriegsmarine. His off-white roll neck woollen jumper looked like it had never seen the inside of a laundry. The man himself looked as if he had just returned from a 60-day U-boat war patrol and smelled like it too. Clearly a man of function, not style, the mariner was not about to get ruffled by the presence of the SS.

Mortens held out his hand, before realising it was caked in Arens blood. The captain frowned at the hand offered. Embarrassingly, the SS officer withdrew it before wiping it on his suit trousers.

'Otto Mortens, Captain. Thank you for coming to our aid.'

The captain tipped his cap.

'Hans Lepp, anything to help. How is he?'

Mortens puffed out his cheeks as he shook his head.

'Lung shot, hence his struggle to breath. Hip shot went straight through. Wrist and buttock. It's not pretty, but it's the lung I'm worried about.'

'Terrorists?' Lepp offered, to which the SS man nodded. The mariner looked down into the hull, his men already changing Arens dressings whilst he coughed up frothy blood into a towel. Lepp looked up at Mortens.

'It's gonna take us a couple of hours to get to Haugen. Will he make it?'

'We have to try.' Mortens shook head, crestfallen, 'I have to try.'

'Okay,' Lepp patted the bloodied security officer on the shoulder, 'I'll not spare the horses, just have an ambulance waiting for when we arrive.'

'Thank you.' Mortens smiled, 'I must head back. Lots to do.'

Bobby and Mortens stood on the jetty as the ferry chugged away. The captain was true to his word, for he was already pushing the craft to really make good time.

'Do you think he'll make it, Sir?' Bobby asked. Mortens turned to his subordinate.

'I hope so, Bobby. I do hope so.'

As they both crunched back to the car, Mortens took notice of his own appearance. His hands and shirt cuffs were encrusted with blood. Peering in the back of the Mercedes, the leather upholstery was smeared, with the packaging of the dressing flickering in the footwells. Closing up the car, Mortens joined Bobby in the front.

'Let's keep the heating on shall we?'

5.

Opel army trucks, both troop carrying and ambulance variants were parked along both sides of the boulevard outside The Telemark. As they pulled up, both Mortens and Bobby could see bodies under blankets being removed and put into the ambulances. A small sense of relief washed through Mortens as he noticed Erik, the drunken belching Wehrmacht officer sat in the back of another ambulance, getting a dressing pulled around his neck. With their eyes meeting, Erik gave Mortens a thumbs up.

One survivor at least, Mortens thought as he returned the gesture whilst making for the restaurant.

Dieter met him at the threshold, both men side-stepping to allow another body to be removed. Mortens could see Dieter's eyes were raw and shot. Full of sorrow and rage,

Dieter knew better than to allow his instincts to get the better of him and just collect the facts and save the wounded. Before Dieter could speak, Mortens turned to Bobby who was walking up behind them.

'Get back to Vermork and get onto the ferry port at Haugen. Tell them what they are to expect, and also get an ambulance dispatched from Oslo. We'll meet you back there later.'

'Sure.' Bobby clicked his heels before returning to the Mercedes.

Mortens fumbled for a cigarette. Putting it to his lips, his hands, now dried and crusted in gave off a familiar coppery tang that invaded his nostrils. With the cigarette lit, he stood just outside the threshold, stealing a moment for himself before he entered the butchers' shop that was The Telemark dining room. Dieter loitered just inside the threshold, allowing his boss a moment to enjoy his cigarette before subjecting him to the post attack formalities. Mortens, grateful that his man had let him enjoy his cigarettes, spun on his heels, and leaned on the doorframe. A few seconds later, medics carried out another blanket covered body on a stretcher, followed on by Dieter. Watching as the stretcher was carefully hauled aboard the ambulance, Dieter spoke.

'That's the last one.'

'Who?'

'Marcel, the new lad.'

'Shit.'

'Know him?'

Mortens shook his head as he exhaled cigarette smoke, a ring surprising him as it drifted skywards. A bitter sweet victory.

'I knew his older brother. I think he was killed in France last year. Either that, or the Americans captured him, I know it's one or the other.'

'Well…' Dieter tailed off, stealing a glance into the restaurant before looking back to his boss. Mortens frowned, intrigued.

'What?'

Dieter gave off a devilish smile.

'Come and see.'

Faces glazed in fever, their pain evident in their screwed-up faces, Mortens looked down at the two wounded terrorists slumped against the pockmarked service hatch wall. With their Wehrmacht guards uninterested in their bloody, oozing, untreated wounds, both men tried their best not to writhe in agony. Confident they were now unarmed; Mortens told the guards to go and have a cigarette. Without question, the two soldiers happily stepped away.

Mortens eyed the two men inquisitively. He was surprisingly calm given that they had just tried to kill him and had been successful at killing most of the Germans caught in the attack. In his periphery he noticed Dieter kick the suppressed Sten guns on the floor.

'Probably had British help.' Dieter mumbled.

'No doubt, 'Mortens responded, deliberately in Norwegian. Dieter smiled as he knew what his boss was up to.

'Certainly, British help.' Dieter responded in kind. The two terrorists winced as they knew exactly what their captors were saying. Mortens eyed the wounded men.

'Do you know who I am?' He put to them. They both looked to each other, sheepishly, neither wanting to respond first. Mortens rolled his eyes.

'Fine, let me refresh your memories. My name is Hauptsturmfuhrer Otto Mortens. I'm the head of the S.S Security Team assigned to the close protection of Doctor Jurgen Arens. I'm sure this is nothing new to you, for you would have spent enough time planning tonight, would you not?'

The wounded men looked to each other, then back up at Mortens, who returned a sardonic leer.

'I'm going to make you an offer for cooperation, a one-time offer in fact. Tell me where your radios are, your weapon caches and by what name your British handlers go by in Oslo.'

The wounded men only sneered back at Mortens. Dieter, hands in pockets looked down at them, an uninterested look on his face. Mortens squatted, keeping their focus on him.

'Gentlemen, I have no intention of taking out reprisals against the good people of this little town. Give me what I want, I can then ensure that when Gestapo officers arrive, they will be armed with the facts, and you will be treated better for it. As for your friends tonight, I already have troops and dogs hunting them down. They won't get far.'

'We are not traitors!' roared the terrorist sat on his left, before his outburst reduced him to a wheezing, bloodied, coughing fit. A lung had been hit.

Mortens stood, unimpressed.

'Well then. I guess we are going to see how tough you Vikings really are. You did well tonight, I'll give you that, but we will now see how well you do in Gestapo custody.'

Mortens turned to address the troops stood in the threshold, indicating the terrorists as he spoke in German once more.

'Have these two taken to the Guardroom at Vermork. Gestapo officers will arrive within the hour. Separate cells.'

'Yes, Hauptsturmfuhrer.' The troops responded as they stomped into the room. Both S.S men stood aside as the Wehrmacht troops hauled the terrorists unceremoniously to their feet, their injuries making them howl in agony. Both unable to walk properly, they were dragged, punched, and kicked by the troops as they were bundled out of the restaurant, with Mortens and Dieter following on, unconcerned.

Back in the officers' mess accommodation, it felt like it had taken an eternity to remove Arens blood from his hands. The shower was long, hot, and most welcome. With his suit in laundry, and the shirt in the bin since it was far from saving, Mortens settled in his low-slung leather chair, mulling over the events of the evening. He thought through the evening that led to the attack, all of which could have been potentially avoided if Arens had not been so arrogant and changed his dinner venue. As he enjoyed a cigarette, he thought about how he would compose his report to Berlin. Arens had been badly wounded, the assassins were hell bent on getting him, and in the pursuit of their ultimate goal, had killed others in the process. His men were good at what they did, but they could not withstand a hail of bullets. The army officers they had killed, and wounded were good men too, drunk but proficient when sober anyhow.

The terrorists that fled would be tracked down by dogs, and as for the two now in Gestapo custody, it would only be a matter of time before they broke. They always broke eventually.

He thought of Paula. He could have easily sought comfort in her bed that very night but was not in the trusting mood.

Was she genuine in her affections? Mortens wondered. Or was she another British plant that led to the attack on his principle? He was not sure. He needed to take a breath and draft his report before he considered what to do next. With his principle on his way to Oslo, and no doubt Germany in due course, there was no reason for him and his surviving officers to remain in Norway, so why spend any more time with Paula?

Mortens promised to call Astrid once he had made his report. Selfishly, he had seldom called or had written to her as often as he should. Up until that moment, he had taken her for granted, so far away and out of mind whilst he sought comfort in the bed of another. Now, he admitted, he missed Astrid, for he now felt very far away from home.

6.

Spean Bridge.

Scotland.

30th March 1945.

The two commandos set off their timing pencils simultaneously before dashing into cover. The small amount of explosive set at the base of the large oak had taken only seconds to prepare. What made demolitions a rudimentary waiting game was the pencils, for they were mass produced and notoriously inaccurate and unpredictable. The first pencil went off with a loud crack that echoed across the Scottish countryside, buffeting Captain Fynlay Jones' ears as he looked through his binoculars. With the stark contrast of the dark, leaf void copse and the fleshly laid snow, he observed with ease the old oak begin to list to one side under its own weight but refused to go over. The second pencil then went off, splintering what remained of the base, sending the centuries old oak crashing to the ground, taking small trees clustered nearby with it.

As the echo rolled through, Company Sergeant Major Tristan Montgomery lowered his own binoculars. A fresh flurry of snow cartwheeling around them.

'Bloody pencils will be the death of us, Sir.'

'You're telling me,' Jones responded as he observed through his own lenses the demolition men, plus others leaping from cover armed with axes and saws before setting about the mighty fallen oak, 'we have to use different batches on the same job, or else we could find ourselves with a bunch of duds, or pencils that go off too early.'

Jones was the company commander of a restless bunch of commandos who had been kicking their heels in Scotland for most of the winter. Their last mission being on The Scheldt in northern Belgium, where they raided a German strongpoint which denied access to the deep-water port of Antwerp. The mission was a success, but the price high, since many of Jones's men fell victim to pre-prepared machinegun positions whose casements could not be cracked due to lack of explosives and the cursed timing pencils, some of which went off prematurely, taking the hands of some of their handlers. Others did not go off at all. Jones and his men had to resort to flame throwers to overwhelm the stubborn defenders, a job not for the faint hearted.

Since that mission, Jones had an obsession with mastering demolitions. He had the boys work again and again with the timing pencils to increase their confidence handling them, plus proving the contraptions were more dangerous to the user than they were to the intended target. He would constantly lobby with the Quartermaster to order different batches, because if one of the pencils were faulty, there was a good chance the entire batch was likely to fail. He had managed to get his way and witnessed the result of a two-batch attack when the mighty oak fell. Getting explosives was easy enough, for you were then restricted to how much you could carry, it was mastering the temperamental pencils which was the tricky part.

As his men energetically turned the fallen oak into firewood for their billets, Jones looked to Montgomery.

'Who is coming to see us today?'

'The C.O, and some guy from London. Probably got a job for us.'

Puffing out his cheeks, Jones put his binoculars back in his smock, before fishing out his cigarette case and lighter. Putting a cigarette to his lips, he clicked the case closed, rubbing his thumb over the Royal Norfolk Regiment cap badge embossed on the front of it. Putting the case away, he knew Montgomery was a non-smoker. He lit the cigarette before pulling up his collar to keep the brisk Scottish wind from biting the back of his neck. He then sliding the lighter into a trouser pocket. An olive drab woollen headover rolled into the classic ridge cap had substituted his green beret which was tucked within his smock. Formal military dress regulations were seldom enforced in Jones's company. They did not need to be, for everyman was a professional. In the harsh Scottish winter when out in the field, the headover was the stalwart of commando headwear.

'Could certainly do with one right now. The boys are getting fat and bored. Hiking Ben Nevis just to keep them busy is starting to get a little mundane, I think you'll agree.'

'Yes Sir,' Montgomery nodded, 'I think we could all do with getting back into the thick of it.'

Cigarette hanging from his lips, Jones turned to see that the men had made short work of the oak. Others were backing up Universal Carriers with trailers so they could load the chopped wood. They knew it would be too soon to use the wood for fuel, as they already had batches from previous demolition sessions to use. The estate manager was a decent guy, so providing his men did not lay waste to the land, dropping the odd tree was overlooked. Besides, that winter had been brutal, and the insatiable thirst for firewood was evident in the billets.

Despite his gloved hands, Jones rubbed them together enthusiastically. Commando or not, cold was cold, and any fool could be cold. The faint whine of an engine got both men's attention. Turning to see what it was, they spotted the American lend-lease jeep leave the metalled road and begin to gingerly pick its way along the track that led up to the two observers. The jeep was a simple, yet reliable design, up to most of the terrain and demands the British Commandos had placed on it in the harsh terrain of Scotland. With the canvas flip-top roof in place, Jones did not envy the occupants who still needed to be wrapped up to fend off the cold. Both men watched as the jeep slewed left and right as it found purchase on the well-worn, deep rutted, yet frozen track, until a final roar of its engine limped it just short of the captain and sergeant major. No sooner had the driver switched off the engine, the yapping of a dog carried on the din.

Jones closed his eyes in irritable resignation, muttering aloud.

'Why does he insist on taking that bloody dog everywhere?'

Montgomery chuckled, as he too had almost tripped over the off-white Maltese, Shih-tzu, Yorkie cross more than once in the company offices. Oskar, the little fellows name was handsome enough, but he just needed to sit in his master's office and not chew the furniture.

His master being Captain Matthew 'W-W' Walsh-Woolcott. W-W clambered out from behind the steering wheel, whistling to bring Oskar to heel as he scampered about Jones and the sergeant major, but all was in vain. The dog did as it well pleased. W-W strode up to his superior, glancing back at the two men clambering from the jeep. W-W was six foot if an inch, with a full head of swept back black hair. A cavalry officer in a former life, having volunteered to join the commandos after his light tank unit was decimated by Stuka dive bombers in Greece, 1941. A large crow foot scar on his left cheek was the result of his own tank exploding as he left the Squadron HQ tent to mount up and fend off German paratroopers going for the Corinth Canal Bridge. Waking up in Gibraltar, his head was covered in bandages and the pain unbearable. His second morphine induced purgatory saw him all the way back to Gosport Hospital in Hampshire. W-W had not seen the inside of a tank since.

Jones was appointed Officer Commanding of the company, with W-W as his deputy, despite both being of the same rank. Jones was senior by about six months, with the finalities of his promotion to Major being ironed out at Regimental Headquarters. As W-W drew up to Jones and Montgomery, it was the sergeant major who nodded his compliments to the dashing, yet scarred captain. W-W smiled in return as he pulled his smock collar up around his ears.

'Bloody fresh this morning, eh?'

'Who's the suit?' Jones asked, flicking his head at the passengers trudging through the snow to join them. W-W turned, shrugging his shoulders.

'Some chap from London. Must be serious, whatever it is. Trudging out here in them shoes.'

'Didn't you ask?' Jones cocked an eyebrow. W-W gave a tight-lipped smile.

'The C.O gave me his 'don't ask' look, so I didn't.'

W-W rolled his shoulders higher to fend off the cold as the two passengers came into his periphery. Both Jones and Montgomery pulled themselves to attention, yet neither saluted.

The first passenger was none other than their Commanding Officer, Lieutenant Colonel Paul Hook DSO. Hook was a legend in the commando community, having led the audacious and bloody raid on the U-boat pens at La Rochelle back in the spring of 1943. Using a captured U-boat as a trojan horse, Hook, then only a captain himself, and his company poured off the U-boat within the facility and caused enough damage to put the facility out of action until well after D-Day in the June of 1944. The other U-boats moored in the pens were written off, but Hook took heavy casualties in the raid and the subsequent withdrawal from La Rochelle into the French interior, where he continued to cause havoc amongst the Germans hunting them. Wounded twice in the raid, one of them being from a German shepherd, Hook was awarded the Distinguished Service Order. A man amongst men. Jones tossed away what remained of the cigarette.

'Good morning Colonel.' Jones forced a smile as snowflakes stung his face. Hook held out a hand, to which Jones accepted.

'Great to see you, Fyn. You've certainly picked a day for it. What are you guys up to?'

Releasing their embrace, Jones jerked a thumb over his shoulder.

'Collecting firewood. We've got some new timing pencils to test. A constant thorn in my side.'

Hook nodded and smiled as he turned to bring the well wrapped and hatted gentlemen into the circle. The man offered his hand to Jones.

'Good morning Captain, Timothy Lewis, MI6.'

Jones shook the man's hand slowly, a little put out that MI6 would send someone out into the cold Scottish mountains to speak with soldiers. Lewis then shook Montgomery's hand. The sergeant major put on a polite smile as he always did. With the introductions over, Hook jerked thumb at the jeep.

'Fyn, need to speak with you. W-W, you may as well come too.'

As Hook and Lewis headed off, Jones and W-W cut each other and intriguing frown. Montgomery was seasoned enough to know that it was 'officers chat' and took interest in Oskar yapping and pouncing about his feet.

Both captains set off after Hook and Lewis. W-W nudged Jones with an elbow.

'What do you reckon?'

'Reckon what?'

'You reckon we are deploying?'

'I hope so,' Jones nodded, 'we are all getting restless.'

7.

Huddled around the front of the jeep, Hook got straight to the point.

'Fyn, you and your men are going into Germany to grab a High Value Target.'

'High…Value…Target?' Jones repeated. Both Hook and Lewis nodded.

'That is correct, Captain,' Lewis replied, 'but in order to brief you on all that we have, we need you and Captain Welsh – Woolcott to come to Edinburgh Castle.'

W-W winced at the mispronunciation of his name but could not be bothered to correct him at that time. It was not the first time it had happened, and no doubt the last.

Jones rubbed his chin. 'When do we deploy?'

'As soon as you are ready, but don't take too long about it,' Lewis responded in earnest, 'we only have one shot at it, and the Soviets are already at the Oder.'

'Okay,' Jones nodded as he shrugged his shoulders. He knew enough about Germany to know that if the Soviets were sat on the Oder, they were very close to Berlin.

'What shall I tell the men for now?'

'Warn them off for a deep penetration raid,' Hook offered, 'that'll fire them up whilst we go through the finer points in Edinburgh.'

'Two of my troop commanders are on leave.' Jones confessed. Hook frowned.

'Who?'

'Claxton is on his honeymoon and Barrett is on paternity leave. Given that we had nothing going on, I granted them leave.'

Hook looked to Lewis, who merely shrugged. The colonel then cocked a smile back at Jones.

'You'll just have to go with what you've got. In the meantime, brief up the CSM and your Troop Sergeants, for we leave for Edinburgh after lunch.'

Despite the journey to Edinburgh being long, cold, and uncomfortable, Jones sat in the passenger seat of his jeep, nursing a cigarette between his fingers, deep in thought. W-W tapped away on the steering wheel, cigarette hanging from his lips, with Oskar sound asleep on his lap. Jones was pleased with the boy's reaction when he delivered them the warning order. Since The Scheldt operation, they had sat in Scotland waiting for another mission. Unlike most of the other commando units, Hooks commando unit, six hundred strong on paper, was kept out of the fray when not needed. The other commando units were being employed as regular infantry as the Allies bludgeoned their way deeper into Nazi Germany. Jones could only assume that Hook had the clout to lobby for his men to not be employed as regular infantry. He clearly got his way. The La Rochelle raid, not to mention grabbing the U-boat in the first place had given the man kudos. Jones was pleased to have Hook as his Commanding Officer, for the man was relaxed with the usual military bullshit, and cared only for operational matters, and the welfare of his men.

It was long after dark once they finally arrived at Edinburgh Castle. The short winter days dominated by long cold nights. Once all concerned were checked by those at the security gate, both jeeps were waved through to the courtyard before being ushered into the Governors House where many of the rooms had been converted into offices and accommodation. Behind heavy blackout curtains, the business of the day, whatever they happened to be doing in the castle was still in full swing. The offices heaved with desks loaded with papers, typewriters, ashtrays piled high with dead cigarettes, and manned by a combination of fresh and exhausted uniformed personnel from all three-armed services, whether coming on shift or due to go off.

'Busy for a castle.' Jones murmured as he took in the organised chaos. Hook pulled off his beret and smock as he spoke.

'It's a hospital. For the time being anyhow. The Governor and his wife have lodgings elsewhere and leave these guys to keep the place running.'

Handing his smock to one of the stewards, Hook then led all three men into the drawing room. Hot refreshments awaited them. All four of the half-frozen men swooped in on the silverware, eager to warm themselves after their long journey. Oskar skipped off to be a nuisance elsewhere. With their China cups full of sweet tea warming their hands, Hook led them into a huge adjoining room. Jones took the opportunity to light a cigarette, only to have to surrender it to W-W as he beamed a smile in his direction. As Jones lit another one, he gave W-W a nudge.

'I'm all out now. You'd better have some.'

A large oak table dominated the room with chesterfields lining the walls facing inwards, a roaring fire at the far end. Jones and W-W took in the opulent, high-ceilinged room, with its impressive chandelier and framed pictures of men who had come long before them looking heroic and magnificent on canvas. In front of the fire stood a tall, serious looking, gentlemen. Tailored in his suit, W-W, always a cavalryman at heart could only assume this man was an account holder on Saville Row. Jones eyed the man who returned the compliment. With swept back silver hair, a little thin in the middle, the hawkish look on the man was one of confidence, and he was not going to be cowed by a room full of commandos. Both captains flinched as Lewis shut the oak double doors heavily behind them.

With the room warming up quickly, those that had not already done so shed their coats and headwear. W-W fetched a small glass ashtray from one of the side tables. Lewis took a leather satchel from under his end of the table, along with a thick cardboard tube. The soldiers in the room had been in that game long enough to know what it contained: maps.

Hook stood back; arms crossed as Lewis fixed a serious look on both the captains.

'Gentlemen, you are to deploy deep into Nazi Germany and grab a much sought-after SS Scientist.'

Lewis allowed a moment for the bold statement to sink in. He was pleased when the two commando captains kept a poker face as they too folded their arms.

'Go on.' Jones responded, smoke from his cigarette lingering slowly towards the ceiling. With a tight-lipped smile, Lewis put the tube on the table before opening the satchel, pulling out a large manilla envelope, the top flap sealed in wax. Jones could see the envelope was not particularly thick nor heavy in the agents' hands. He watched as Lewis allowed it to slap hard on the table. He then dropped the satchel out of sight. The tall, suited gentleman remained silent as he moved to the nearest chesterfield, taking a seat. Jones watched as the man appeared aloof to what was taking place.

Lewis then shoved the envelope across the table in Jones' direction.

'It's your mission, Captain,' Lewis grinned, 'only proper that you open it.'

Putting the cigarette out, Jones took up the envelope. It felt somewhat rigid. Turning it over in his hands, he could see the royal coat of arms embossed on the wax. Very official. Cracking the seal with both hands, he opened the envelope and pulled from it the contents which were within another thin card file. On the front was typed text.

Operation FLATIRON – UK EYES ONLY

'Flatiron?' Jones cocked an eyebrow at Lewis, who kept a poker face.

'Flatiron,' Lewis confirmed, 'believe it or not, this is an American sponsored mission, but the United Kingdom has been asked to execute it.'

'Why?' W-W asked.

'Let's just say at political level, the United States is calling in a favour.'

Hook, in an attempt to remain aloof, looked to the suited gentleman, who he could see was squirming a little in his seat. Hook folded his arms tighter and remained mute, for he was just as curious as his subordinates were as to why Brits were having to do Yank work. He knew Jones would not go quietly.

'So why aren't the yanks doing this job?'

Lewis waved dismissive hand, in an attempt to move things along.

'I'm afraid that's above all our paygrades, Captain, now if you please...'

'I suggest,' Jones interrupted, 'you give us a little more to go on, if you think I'm jumping into Germany to grab this scientist.'

Flushed in the cheeks, Lewis went to speak when the suited gentleman got to his feet.

'Captain Jones,' the man spoke in an authoritative tone, which drew the attention of both its intended and W-W, 'this individual you are to grab for us is of much interest to the Americans, and in exchange for his safe passage into American custody, the United Kingdom will be included in their plan to rebuild Europe after this bloody war is over.'

'You are?' Jones challenged, not intimidated by the bullying house master tactic. The man pulled himself straight, putting his hands behind his back.

'Andrew Cowen. Private Secretary to the Prime Minister.'

After a few rapid blinks, Jones cut a glance at the stern face of Lewis before turning to Hook, who, now with hands on hips had a stern expression which indicated to Jones that he had no idea the conversation was about to go the way it did. He looked back at Cowen, his elevation and posture worthy of a commission in the Brigade of Guards.

'Mr. Cowen,' Jones measured his tone, 'I'm not in the business of picking fights with my superiors, and I dare say, by default, you certainly fall into that category. But you must understand a soldier's need for context if he is expected to deliberately go into the teeth of the enemy.'

'Of course,' Cowen smiled warmly, 'that's why I am here so you are fully aware of the gravity this mission brings. Mr. Lewis will answer your questions candidly, well... as candidly as is allowed.'

Jones knew the intelligence agent would only give him so much, but judging by the company he was in, it was not the usual 'hit and run' kind of mission. Jones nodded that he understood as Cowen returned to his seat. Hook relaxed also now that he was in the picture a little more.

Lewis cleared his throat.

'The H.V.T is Jurgen Arens. He is a Heavy Water Scientist that is of interest to the Americans.'

He pointed to the file in Jones' hand, 'we have some photos of him in the file.'

W-W stepped in closer to Jones as he thumbed the file. Inside was two photographs, both rather grainy. One was of a man smoking outside what looked like a restaurant or café, whilst the other was of him, in better focus, in full SS regalia among others all cheering at what Jones could only speculate was a Nazi rally.

'SS officer?' W-W looked up at Lewis, who merely shrugged.

'It's an honorary title we believe, he served in the last war as a staff runner, nothing grand or as reckless as what you gents get up to.'

Both Jones and W-W cut a sly smirk, Lewis continued.

'His officer status in the SS is purely for administration purposes. Our Norwegian friends have reported that he is somewhat of an arse and likes to order people around as if he is actually an officer.'

'Imagine that.' Jones smirked at Cowen, who returned a disapproving frown.

Rotating through the two images, Jones held up the one of Arens in uniform.

'I need this mass produced. Enough for one per man.'

'Why?' Lewis challenged, but Jones knew he would.

'I'm not spending my time on target looking for him myself, so I need all my guys to know exactly who they are looking for.'

Lewis looked at Cowen for approval, who merely sighed as he rested his elbows on the high arms of the chesterfield, steepling his fingers. The agent smiled at Jones.

'Fair enough, we can do that.'

Jones held up the other image, 'How old are these photos?'

'The one in uniform is from '38, and the other is more recent, say last summer. The former was taken by a Nazi party photographer, hence the better quality, whereas the latter was taken by one of our guys in Norway.'

'So why Germany, if he's clearly in Norway?' W-W asked.

'A Norwegian resistance cell was tasked by us to kill him. Arens is key to the development of a super weapon that could devastate a city. Over the last two years, we've had your Viking counterparts going out of their way to disrupt its development. Should Hitler obtain such a weapon, we estimate that he will raze Paris, in order to shatter the Anglo-American alliance. Political pressure will force us to negotiate with him as he then turns his attention to the Soviets as they close on Berlin.'

Jones remained tight lipped, for the rationale for the mission was not without merit. Lewis however, had still not answered the question.

'Why are we not going to Norway to grab him?'

'Arens survived the assassination attempt. Reports are that he was badly wounded, but his security team managed to rescue him from the ambush and get him back to Oslo. He was then flown back to Berlin, where he was transferred to a hospital for SS troops north of the city. You have air recce photos in the file.'

Jones flipped through the file until he came across some aerial photographs of what looked like a lakeside resort. With the lake long and wide, and the complex of various sized building gathered in the grounds on the west bank. The photo indicated the reconnaissance flight came in low, and that it could well have been taken in the summer as the trees lining the bank and throughout the complex were in full bloom, making it difficult for Jones to identify all of the buildings should they be hidden under canopy. He held it up facing Lewis.

'How old is this?'

'Taken in the summer. Given the time of year, we have another scheduled for tomorrow. The trees would have dropped its leaves, so we can confirm how the complex looks under the canopy.'

'Tell us about this complex.' W-W asked of the agent. Lewis slid his hands into his trouser pockets as he cleared his throat, more out of habit than necessity.

'Hohenlychen Sanatorium is a hospital where SS personnel convalesce. It sits on the west bank of the Zenesee, just south of the village of Lychen, fifty miles north of Berlin. We have tracked Arens to this hospital, were he continues to recover from his wounds.'

'Why do the Americans want him so bad?' Jones looked up from scanning the photographs. Lewis flicked a cursory glance at Cowen before answering.

'Arens is crucial to the Nazis development of this wonder weapon. That's as much as we have been told. A conference took place at political level some time ago, where they discussed the future of post-war Germany.'

Jones eyed Cowen, who remained passive, so decided to push. 'Go on.'

Lewis rolled his shoulders.

'The hospital will fall within the Soviet zone of occupation. The Americans, and our Prime Minister in fact are most eager that Arens is not lifted by the Soviets in a similar operation to this one.'

Jones broke into abroad grin.

'So, the Americans are building their own super bomb.' Lewis pulled his hands out of his pockets abruptly, his face flush.

'I said weapon, not bomb.'

'Whatever.' Jones waved a dismissive hand. The cat was out of the bag now. He looked to Cowen for a response to the revelation. There was none. Jones glanced over at Hook, who approached the table before looking back to Lewis.

'Right then, since we now know what all this is about, we can now get on with planning this mission. Wouldn't you agree gentlemen?'

The tension in the room lifted now that the rationale for the mission was established. As Hook drew up next to his subordinates, Cowen lifted himself from the chesterfield and approached Jones, pulling an envelope from inside his blazer.

'Captain Jones, would you please join me at the fire?' Cowen's tone was softer, more cordial. Jones frowned with intrigue as he stepped around Hook to join the man in front of the fire. Cowen then handed him the envelope. The handwriting addressed it to *Major Fynlay Jones.* He looked up at Cowen before looking to his Commanding Officer. Hook, hands in pockets returned a broad smile.

Jones, flipped over the envelope, waxed sealed again with the Royal coat of arms. Breaking the seal, he then slid out the single sheet of folded paper. Unfolding the note, he began to read the scratchy and scruffy handwriting.

Major Jones,

The sanatorium will fall within the proposed Soviet Zone of Occupation.

Grab your man and destroy that nest of vipers with extreme prejudice.

God speed.

'Firm'

Winston Churchill

Jones looked up at the Prime Ministers private secretary. Cowen held out his hand for the return of the letter. Jones, numbed at the personal note from the Prime Minister himself handed it back without protest. Sliding the note back into the envelope, Cowen spoke as he did so.

'Major Jones, has the Prime Minister made himself clear?'

Jones, for the first time in a long time was lost for words. All Cowen got in reply was a nod.

'Good.' Cowen responded as he tossed it into the fire. Both men watched the envelope blacken and curl in the flames. Satisfied the note was destroyed, Cowen pulled himself guardsman straight as he buttoned up his tailored blazer.

'Congratulations on your promotion, Major, and I was never here.'

The man offered his hand to Jones, who took it, still a little shocked at what he had just read yet returned a manly handshake all the same. Cowen then moved away, nodding to the others around the table.

'I'll see myself out.'

As Cowen politely pulled the door closed behind himself, those remaining in the room just looked at each other. W-W noticed Jones steadying himself against the fire surround.

'You okay?'

Lost in thought, Jones looked up, 'What?'

'Look like you've seen a ghost.'

8.

'Firm'

Le Paradis

27th May 1940

Filthy, thirsty, and exhausted, Lieutenant Fynlay Jones huddled in a crudely dug trench as another mortar round crumped nearby, setting fire to an ammunition cart, its horses long dead having been caught in a blizzard of machine gun fire coming from German positions in the woods.

Jones' men, that of C Company, Royal Norfolk's, along with a mixed bag of men from Headquarters Company tried their best to find cover wherever they could as the Germans swept their positions with continuous machinegun fire. Mortars kept their heads down as the

Germans broke from their cover in the woods and advanced quickly in their mechanised halftracks.

Jones caught sight of two of his lads hauling the cumbersome 'Boys' anti-tank rifle up on to the rim of their trench. He watched in awe and a fair helping of terror as German tracer bullets snapped and peppered about them. Their aim steady, they fired, causing the lead halftrack to stop dead, a neat hole punched through the driver's cab. Jones was unsure as to the result of the shot, but it was enough for the troops occupying the halftrack to bail out and continue their advance on foot. Smirking, more out of nervousness than amusement, Jones looks to the lads who fired at the vehicle.

His heart sank, for both were dead. One was missing his head, whilst the other remained in the aim behind the weapon, his posture inviting more bullet strikes from Germans eager to remove the threat. A very close mortar impact snapped Jones out of his trance, his ears ringing. Slumping back into the trench, he watched Private Parks, his radio operator shouting into his handset, but the ringing in his ears dominated all that was going on about him. Just as his hearing became acute once more, Parks pounced on him, knocking the wind out of him in the process. The ground shook as a number of large impacts rocked their position. Spoil tumbled in over them as Parks grunted but remained where he was. As the bombardment eased off, the muffled shouting in his ears became more animated.

'We gotta go, we gotta go!' someone shouted. Jones was pinned down under the weight of Parks. Jones was no weakling but being caught in a sitting position had him at a disadvantage. All of a sudden, Parks lifted himself off of his platoon commander. Jones looked up to see his Platoon Sergeant, Dicky Barton hauling the very dead Parks off of him, laying him to one side.

'Boss, we gotta go. We've lost the farmhouse, let's go.'

Shocked that Parks had given his life to protect him from the shelling, he pushed himself to his feet as Barton reached into the trench and grabbed the radio set. Beyond Barton, he watched men throwing smoke grenades before running back towards him, with just their weapons in their hands. Standing over him, Barton placed the radio down before clapping his hands in front of Jones' face.

'Boss. Grab your shit, let's go.'

Still stunned at the whole spectacle, Jones followed Barton's orders and hauled himself out of the trench, taking his rifle with him. Following on after the heavily laden Barton, Jones was shocked to see the farmhouse they had set their defensive perimeter around now just a burning shell. The bombardment had found its target, hence their withdrawal. Giving the farmhouse a wide berth, he followed Barton and many of his men towards the rear of the farm complex. The men looked desperate as halftracks over took them around the outer limits of the farm, only to have them all jog into a half circle of halftracks and German troops waiting for them at the rear of the buildings.

Before Jones could resume any position of command, he watched his men lay their weapons down and put their hands up. Dicky Barton carefully put the radio set down before accepting the inevitable. Realising he was the only one still holding his weapon, he noticed the German troops shouting at him, pointing their weapons at just him.

Jones put his rifle down and put his hands on his head.

Filthy and exhausted looking, in his baggy green mottled smock, the SS trooper searching Jones was rough, methodical, and thorough. Jones remained with his hands on his head as the German took from him his wristwatch, what French Francs he had, his lighter and the cigarettes from their slender case. The German eyed the emblem on the front of it.

Jones remained mute, as he was not about to try and explain the emblem was in fact the cap badge of the Royal Norfolk Regiment. Losing interest quickly, the SS trooper handed it back to him. With his search over, he risked a glance around the courtyard. Some of his men were still being searched. What stunned Jones was the number that had been captured. At least one hundred men. Not all were from his company. Some of them were from Headquarters Company.

Once all the men were searched, one of the SS men, his demeanour led Jones to assume he was an officer beckoned for them all to follow him. At first, the men looked sheepish at each other before Barton took the lead and they fell into single file behind him. As the men filed out, Jones merely tagged on at the back. With no pistol on his hip at the point of capture to give him away as an officer, he could not help but feel that the SS thought Barton was in command. With his head thick from the bombardment, and the shock at the death of Parks, he had certainly not portrayed to the Germans at least, any position of command. He followed on nonetheless, their hands now permitted to be lowered as they filed through the war wrecked farm, and past their own trenches. The men could only look on as the Germans searched them. Shuffling past his own trench, Jones winced as the SS men roughly searched Parks. Taking his watch and cigarettes.

As they passed through the gates of the farm out onto the main road, their captors made little effort to veer the column clear of the burning horse drawn cart that crackled violently. The horses, peppered with bullet and shrapnel holes remained in their harness. The men that had ridden the cart lay in macabre poses alongside the horses. Jones went to shuffle over to try and identify the men, when one of the SS men nearby shoved him back in line. No sooner as he turned to look at the soldier, did the cart explode, the blast cartwheeling Jones into the roadside ditch opposite.

Head swimming, his hearing gone once more, Jones lay on his back, staring up as the ash grey sky as what remained of the cart came tumbling in towards him. Instinctively rolling into a foetal position, the debris just missed him on impact, but rolled on top of him as it come to rest. His muffled hearing gave him a sense of confusion up on the road. He could make out shouting and cries in both English and German. After time, the commotion faded as his hearing returned.

All was quite.

Stiff from the sudden assault on his body, Jones eased himself out from under the cart wreckage. The ditch he was in, was purposely dug for drainage, but given how warm the spring had been, it was dry. Peering up to look onto the road, he noticed one body lying face down. Peering right, the cart was now scattered all over the place, the backsides of the two dead horses stripped to the bone from the explosion. The two dead cart riders were now lying by the farm gates. Unsure there were no Germans loitering about, Jones moved along the ditch on his hands and knees until he was level with the new body on the road. He could make out it was in British uniform, now minus a head. Saddened, Jones took a breath. The man without a head would remain unknown to him. He could not tell who it was, or which company he had served in. Jones tried to take comfort in the fact that the man was dead, and that it had been quick.

Jones flinched as machinegun fire rippled off to his left. Ducking back into the ditch, he could not help but hear screaming and wailing over the gunfire. After a few seconds, the firing stopped, yet wailing and crying remained. Peering over the lip of the ditch, he flinched as short sharp cracks of pistol fire quietened those wailing and begging for their lives. No sooner had it started, it was quiet again. German voices shouted to each other, only to have closer voices call back. Fearing he would be discovered, Jones scrambled back along the ditch and crawled under the debris that had covered him in the explosion. As he pulled his feet in behind him, he was horrified to see the very SS trooper that had shoved him back into line sat in the ditch no more than ten yards from him.

Minus helmet and his entire lower jaw, the German stared sightless straight back at Jones. The man's green mottled smock almost ripped from his torso. Only his equipment prevented it from coming away completely. Frozen in fear, Jones could hear footsteps crunching louder on the road behind him. Unarmed and alone, he could do nothing more than pray that the debris he was under would not be moved.

Not daring to move or breath too heavy, Jones could hear numerous German voices above him. They sounded sad. Jones witnessed three SS men climb into the ditch, covering their dead comrade in a green mottled poncho before hauling him out and away. With the crunching of their boots fading. Relief washed over Jones, for should he have been discovered, they would have probably shot him where he lay. Composing himself, he made the decision to wait until nightfall.

For Jones, the remainder of the long spring day was nothing more than an assault on his senses. Every unfamiliar sound filled him with fear. The long bouts of silence played havoc with his emotions. He could not help but think of his men being executed as he lay in the ditch. Dicky Barton constantly filled his thoughts. Dicky was a career soldier, and a great platoon sergeant for the young subaltern to serve his unofficial apprenticeship with. Barton was firm but fair with the men in his platoon. The man was not without his own problems. Barton was in the midst of a messy divorce because his estranged wife had taken to the bed of a man that was around more often and would give her the attention she demanded. Her soldier husband gave all his energy and attention to his mistress, the Army.

Jones made the decision, that after nightfall, he would at least investigate what had become of his men. If they had been shot, he needed to confirm it before making for Brigade Headquarters in L'Epinette. If they were still there.

At twilight, Jones made his move. Cautiously, he climbed from the ditch and made his way through the polder in the direction of what he could see was a farm building that had a large stonewall leading off to its right. As he approached, he could make out clusters of what looked like broken earth at the base of the wall. Very soon, the broken earth revealed what it actually was.

Dead bodies.

Mown down by the machineguns he had heard; they had not fallen as he expected. Some were slumped against the wall. Others slumped together, holding each other up in a macabre kneeling position. The SS had shot them and literally left them where they had fallen. Looking about the scene, Jones could see that there was about one hundred bodies. His men. As he went to confirm if Barton was among them, he caught the sound of French voices coming from behind the wall, accompanied with torch beams bobbing and swaying. Jones dashed away from the wall and lay prone in the broken polder. Emerging from the far end of the wall was a group of what he could assume was men, all carrying torches and shovels. They came to a standstill at the first body in their path.

The Germans had sent their burial party. French locals.

Jones kept low on the polder as he watched the party break up and orbit his side of where the men had been cut down. His stomach turned as the men dragged quiet unceremoniously the bodies into a neat orderly line. In pairs, the Frenchmen searched the dead, taking items from them. In the gloom, and so low to the ground, Jones struggled to make out what they were taking, until the beam of a torch highlighted the men's identity tags.

Jones took the opportunity to count the dead as they were searched, for the night was only getting darker and if he remained perfectly still, there was every chance he would not be detected. He had got to forty-seven when both Jones and the Frenchmen got a fright when one of the dead men raised their hands of their own accord.

There was a survivor.

The Frenchmen gathered around the wounded man, who still hand his arms up, hands open palmed in a vain attempt to defend himself. Not sure which side the French were on, Jones lay motionless as the group got somewhat loud and animated. What Jones could make out, was one of the older men waving away two much younger ones, who at a jog disappeared behind the wall. Jones' heart sank, for he feared they were heading off to inform the SS that they had missed one. The Frenchmen continued searching the others, whilst one man knelt with the survivor. Jones could see he was holding the man's hand in both of his. His French was strong enough to order a beer or a coffee, but the young Lieutenant could not understand what the kneeling man was saying to the soldier. The tone in which he spoke was quiet and soothing, as if there was no point in chastising a dying man. Jones wanted to go to him, but the risk of suffering the same fate was too great. He was torn between the rational thought of self-preservation, and that of cowardly guilt.

The Frenchmen searching the bodies burst with excitement. They had found another. So far, two of those mown down by the SS were still alive. The group were too far for Jones to even guess at who it could be. As they huddled around the second survivor, the two young men returned with a horse pulling a cart, and thankfully, no German soldiers. Jones watched as they gingerly lifted the two survivors into the cart before the young men who brought it in the first place led it away, behind the wall once more.

As Jones watched the remaining Frenchmen begin to dig, he could only hope that those who had survived were taken to a hospital. There was every chance they would end up as prisoners or finished off if the SS troops come to hear that they had survived, but there was nothing Jones could do about that. With a count of ninety-seven dead, and two survivors, Jones crawled backwards, through the polder until he could scramble unseen back into the ditch.

It was a dark night, and the only ambient light afforded to him was the glowing embers of what remained of the ammunition cart. Jones took a moment to compose and orientate himself. He had no map or compass, no torch or weapon. He needed to get back to Brigade Headquarters, for they were less likely to move as much as his Battalion would.

If his Battalion still existed that is.

Striking north, Jones took the most direct route to L'Epinette, where he hoped to find friendly forces. Wracked with thirst and feeling totally exposed as he shuffled at a crouch, the open farmland seemed endless. He had no idea if the Germans were already in L'Epinette, or if his own side would shoot him down rather than challenge him. In the gloom, he could just make out clumps of trees, with the rooftops of dwellings sat beyond. Out of nowhere came a challenge.

'Who goes there?' The voice gruff, but English. Jones put his hands up.

'Lieutenant Jones, C Company, Royal Norfolk's.'

There was a long pause. Jones winced through fear of getting shot. Instead, out of the murk came a lone figure. The silhouette looked menacing, ready to shoot. As the profile got closer, Jones could make out the soldier was of stocky build, and correctly dressed for battle. The figure stood still in front of him, leaning in to speak at a low hush.

'Mr. Jones? Why are you out here on your own, you flaming lunatic?'

Jones squinted at the face under the helmet rim. A filthy face revealed a toothy smile.

'It's Butcher, Sir. A Company.'

A wave of euphoria washed over Jones as he bent down, hands on the top of his thighs.

'Thank fuck for that,' he gasped. Butcher stepped away a little, fearing the subaltern would vomit.

'Sir?'

'Billy, please tell me the battalion is here?'

'Yes Sir,' Butcher confirmed, 'what's left of it anyway.'

Private William Butcher was a C Company man, until a pub brawl he started put him in the Guardroom for twenty-eight days without pay. Butcher was then sent to A Company, despite Jones going in to bat for the man, as he was a likeable character in the company and not a shirker. After putting a case to the Commanding Officer for Butcher to be his runner, his pleas were ignored. Butcher was a solid soldier, just a nightmare on the beer.

Butcher led them both through the defensive perimeter on the south side of L'Epinette. In the darkness, he could make out the crude trenches that had been dug, the men sat in pairs, one dozing whilst them other remained alert, or so it seemed anyhow. As they made their way into the hamlet, Jones noticed a flurry of blacked out activity in and around what he could see was a boutique.

'Battalion Headquarters, Sir.' Butcher indicated, before turning to look at the exhausted young officer.

'I think I can leave you here, Sir.'

'Thanks Billy,' Jones squeezed the man's shoulder as he headed off towards the boutique, 'Is the C.O here?'

'Not sure,' Butcher shrugged, 'I think the Adjutant is in charge at the moment. We're all over the place.'

With a tight-lipped smile, Jones patted him on the shoulder and headed towards the melee of activity. With his meeting with the Adjutant, Captain Bertie Franks imminent, he weighed up his chances with the Germans. Franks could be prickly, and no fan of Jones.

Inside the blacked-out boutique, it had a medieval setting. The thick heavy curtains allowed those within to use copious amounts of candles. They were everywhere. Jones looked about the main room, which would have been used to sell the owners' wares. Men huddled over maps, some waving their hands in big gestures, explaining how their sub unit was going to this and that. Behind the orators perched their radio operators, their handsets wedged between cheek and shoulder as scraps of paper were thrusted at them, the message to be sent to whom it was concerned. As Jones picked his way though, he could see a doorway leading into a room at the rear of the property. Another curtain screened him from seeing through the threshold until it was suddenly whipped to the side by a soldier sporting a thick bloodstained bandage around his head. It was Bertie Franks.

'Jones?' The Adjutant croaked, 'What the fuck are you doing here?'

Before he could answer, Franks cut him off.

'C Company will act as rear guard, so we can break out of here and make for Dunkirk. What's your manpower strength right now?'

Jones swallowed hard.

'Just me.'

'What?' Franks pulled a face, to which Jones returned a shrug.

'I'm all that's left of C Company, Sir.'

'Major Butler? Captain Steele?' Franks enquired after the Company Commander, and the Company Second in Command. Jones just shook his head.

'We got overrun at Le Paradis,' Jones chose not to mention the shootings, 'grenade knocked me flat. I woke up alone.'

Franks bit his lip, his face reading that he was not sure whether to doubt the Platoon Commander or console him. He flicked his head.

'Get in here. I need to show you what were are doing next.'

The map sprawled over the kitchen table was speckled in what looked like blood, with chinagraph pencil scrawled all over it. Franks used one of the pencils to point out various features.

'We are here. A Company are providing security whilst the other companies move in to rally with us. Before first light we will be striking north for Dunkirk, here.'

Everyone, Jones included did whatever they needed to so they could see the port town for themselves. Having come ashore at Cherbourg, the terrain they were about to navigate was new to them. Franks cleared his throat.

'We have been informed that were are being recovered back to England from there. But we need to get out of here sooner rather than later. The Reconnaissance Platoon are already on task, proving the route. Once they have picketed as far north as they can with what men they have left, they will then send guides back to lead us along the route. Everyone with me so far?'

All those around Jones nodded. Franks continued.

'Order of march will be walking, and stretcher wounded. Headquarters Company will assist in getting them along the picketed route, with B and D company combined following on for they are both low in numbers. C Company…'

Franks tailed off as he looked up at Jones, forcing a wince.

'Sorry Fyn, my bad.'

Jones was a little shocked, since Franks was usually an arse to subalterns, and to call him Fyn was something he never expected from the man. The other officers stood around him looked a little confused. Franks felt the need to put them all in the picture.

'Gentlemen, C Company has been destroyed. Mr. Jones is all that remains.'

There was a noticeable gasp from those around him. Jones felt a hand squeeze his shoulder; another patted him between the shoulder blades. Jones jaw ached as emotion was beginning to overwhelm him. Franks, not famous for caring about the plight of young officers nodded to the crestfallen man.

'Mr. Jones will join the B and D Company group.'

Jones gave off a tight-lipped smile, as Franks resumed his business-like demeanour.

'Our right flank will be guarded by the Machine Gun Platoon, our left, the Anti-Tank Platoon. A Company will act as a rear guard. They will have their work cut out come first light as I'm sure the Germans will try and press their advantage. Any questions?'

'What German forces are we up against?' A voice came from behind Jones' right shoulder. Franks tapped the pencil on the map.

'Infantry, with horse drawn artillery in support. As far as our latest reports show.'

Jones was stunned at how way off Franks information was. The look on his face was not lost on Franks, who returned a stern look.

'Something you wish to add, Mr. Jones?'

Jones nodded slightly as he placed both filthy hands on the table.

'We were overrun by SS troops, with halftracks. Panzer Grenadiers.'

The room was silent, Jones could feel the pull on him for more information, he looked to Franks, jabbing a finger at their current location.

'We need to bolster A Company with the Anti-Tank Platoon. It's the only chance they will have of halting the halftracks. Make the SS dismount, then A Company stand a better chance of keeping them at arm's length.'

To the left, a stocky, burly captain with a thick floppy moustache shook his head.

'I have very few rounds left for any real impact if they come at us with a mounted company.'

'But you have rounds left?' Jones eyed the anti-tank officer. Captain Matthew Wood was a very experienced officer, having come up through the ranks, and lethal on the rugby pitch. The glare he delivered to Jones put the subaltern on edge, having forgotten himself as he countered his senior. Instead of apologising, Jones held his nerve and glared back. Tight lipped, it was Wood that conceded.

'Yes, of course.'

Jones rolled his shoulders, for the tension had built so quickly, he was sure to cramp.

'We just need to punch their halftracks in the face hard enough to discourage them from trying to overrun us. Their troops will have to dismount, slowing the rate of advance.'

'Their halftracks will just stand off and hammer us with their machineguns.' Franks challenged, only to receive a resigning shrug from Jones.

'Yes they will, but we can get out of their line of sight more easily at distance.'

All those about the table fell silent. Only the static from radio sets kept up a continuous white noise. As Jones went to speak, a series of thudding crumps rolled through the building, causing all those within to flinch.

'Mortars!' came a cry from outside. As more came crashing into the village. The clattering of glass, rooftiles and masonry rung loudly against the building they stood in. With everyone except Jones making for the door, Franks ripped the map from the table.

'Get to your sub-units, stand-to!' bellowed the adjutant.

Unsure where to put himself, Jones looked to the man stuffing his crudely folded map into his battledress jacket. As Franks stood straight, he noticed him.

'Don't just look at me Jones, make yourself useful. Help A Company.'

Jones nodded that he understood as he made for the door. In the near darkness outside, he fought to avoid the drifting red orbs in his vision. As he got use to the darkness, flares popped under their parachutes high above the village, drowning where he stood in brilliant light. The shadows cast by the buildings grew longer and swirled as the flares drifted to earth. Taking advantage of the artificial light, he made his way to where Butcher had encountered him. He knew he would come across the positions of A Company before that.

Picking his way through the outbuildings, he soon found what could most likely be their trenches. In the flare washed glare, he could make out tin helmets bobbing about in the crude holes. At a crouch, he made for a trench picketed by a sparse forest of radio antennas. Looking within, he found it empty. Confused as to where its occupants were, he scanned the area, mindful not to stand too tall in the open ground of what appeared to be gardens. As another cluster of flares burst above him, he was horrified to see the front end of several German halftracks edging their way into the footprint of light. No sooner had he identified the Germans advancing on A company's position, did the air around crackle and fizz with incoming fire as the machine gunners, sat high on their halftracks strafed the area with tracer. Jones dived into the command trench as men around him shouted and hollered to each other, their return fire pathetic in response. Off to his left came the steady drumbeat of a Vickers machine gun. Jones peered high enough to see the chugging stream of tracer bullets flicking and sparking off the protective shields of the SS machine gunners. As the flares got lower, the flickering shadows revealed their infantry comrades dismounting the halftracks and begin to fan out as they launched into the assault. Numerous helmets from British trenches bobbed and weaved as they lobbed grenades at the German infantry. Most dashed behind their vehicles, the grenades detonating with little result, whilst others, not so quick on their feet were punched flat by the concussion. The chugging beat of the Vickers ceased as the flares fizzled out.

Blinded by darkness, all Jones could do was hear British and German voices scream at each other in the confusion of the blacked-out assault. As more flares popped above them, Jones got the fright of his life as the lumbering profile of Butcher came crashing into his trench, cradling a sizzling Vickers. In the artificial light, Jones could make out a soaked empty sandbag draped over his forearm like a waiter, the hot machinegun on top of it, causing it to sizzle and steam. With belt ammunition wrapped around him like a Mexican bandit, Butcher looked the shell-shocked officer up and down.

'We're getting overrun, Sir. I'm going right to cover you lot as you break clean and get the fuck out of 'ere.'

'Okay.' Jones nodded. 'I'll call it as you start firing.'

'Right,' Butcher hollered as he hauled himself from the trench, 'see you in Dunkirk, Sir.'

In a flash, Butcher was gone. Jones tried to track his progress as the dull thud of a Boys anti-tank rifle cause his ears to ring. The firer scored a frontal hit on one of the centre halftracks resulting in a flurry of sparks. The stricken vehicle rocked to a halt. Jones could not be sure if the vehicle were damaged, or the driver lost his nerve. As the shadows grew longer, two more halftracks were hit by unseen members of the anti-tank platoon, both resulting in a flurry of sparks and immediate loss of enthusiasm from both crew and its infantry.

The Vickers fire Jones had been waiting for spluttered back into life, with Butcher strafing the infantry trying to use their halftracks as cover from his murderous fire. Cupping both hands around his mouth, Jones gave it all that he was worth.

'Break clean, break clean!'

As he went to shout it again, he was pleased that the men in the trenches nearest him, repeated his order at the top of their lungs also. The order soon echoed all over the position despite the blistering incoming fire, and Butchers steady drumbeat of fire going back at them. Braving the fire, Jones hauled himself from the trench as the flares fizzled out. With darkness consuming them once more, Jones could make out the men climbing from their trenches and jogging on into the village. The scarlet stream of tracer bullets arcing right to left all over the German attackers confirmed Butcher was indeed covering the withdrawal. Quietly confident that Butcher would pick his moment to join them, Jones jogged on after the men as more flares burst above them. No sooner had he picked his way between the first dwellings did mortars begin to burst all about the rooftops and outbuildings. At a half crouch, Jones made for the bustling boutique housing Battalion Headquarters. As he drew near, he was punched flat my a near miss.

Jones regained consciousness, head throbbing under a swathe of blood crusted bandages. He squinted and shuddered like a vampire in the brilliant light. As his eyes adjusted, he found himself looking up at a drab, grey clouded sky. He fought to move his arms, but they were bound tight to his sides. Lifting his head, he could make out helmets and bandaged heads bobbing about him. Unsure what was going on, he rested his head back, only to see the glistening walnut exterior of a motor launch. A lap of seawater washed over him, giving him a shock.

'Sorry about that, Sir.' A voice chuckled, as he was hauled aboard. The stretcher he was bound to soaked as much as he was. Jones squinted only to see the grimy, unshaven grin of Franks looking down at him.

'Let's go home, Fyn.'

Jones blinked rapidly; his throat parched.

'What the fuck is going on?'

'Were at Dunkirk, Fyn. We're going home.'

9.

31st March 1945.

Hohenlychen Sanatorium

50 miles North of Berlin

Otto Martens exhaled long and slow, the cigarette smoke spiralling lazily over his swept back hair. The Zenesse was calm as it too lapped lazily against the jetty he stood on. As crisp as the morning March air was, he thought it would not hurt to break out his fishing gear once he had settled into his new command.

Only a month had passed since Doctor Jurgen Arens attempted assassination. Only a month since he was covered in the man's blood whilst fighting to keep him alive as he put him on the ferry to Oslo. Only a month since he had command of a small, well trained security team. Only a month since he was stomping his feet to keep warm in the frozen purgatory that was Norway.

Only a month.

In less than a month, he had been pulled from his Norwegian duties and thrown back into uniform. Fearing an eastern deployment for his failing to keep the scientist safe, he had received an unexpected reprieve.

Arens was an arrogant, egotistical arse in Mortens eyes, but the man had kindly put in a good word with his superiors in Berlin. Instead of the expected criticism in Arens report to Berlin, the man had actually been very complimentary regarding his immediate evacuation from the danger. The medical attention he had received at the hands of Mortens was crude, almost battlefield standard in the midst of combat, yet it was effective enough to prevent considerable blood loss. Arens recommended that Mortens be spared combat duty, for he had indeed saved the scientists life. Mortens masters in Berlin took Arens report into consideration and chose to assign the crestfallen Hauptsturmfuhrer to the SS sanatorium at Hohenlycen as Head of Security.

The sanatorium sat on the Zenesse, north of Berlin, in a sleepy collage of lush forests and lakes. The facility housed wounded SS officers and men from not just the eastern front, but from wherever they had been fighting at the time. Germany was being pressed on all sides, the boundary lines between the different fronts were nothing more than lines on a map. Most of which were already out of date. The facility was not very big, for it was nothing more than a handful of large, turn of the century wards with smaller administration offices dotted about the site. The officers convalesced in the five-storey ward nearest the shore, whilst the soldiers were housed in the larger complex further inland. The men enjoyed the relaxing grounds, plus the indoor spa and pool attached to their own five-storey ward. With all the rooftops in the facility white washed with a large red cross in pride of place, the recovering soldiers and officers enjoyed relative peace as they recovered from their warfighting ordeals. Whilst a few were ardent Nazis and put on a good show of being eager to return to the front and serve their Fuhrer and the Reich, most for the main were content for the war to play out without any more involvement from them.

Mortens attention was captured by the barking of his German Shepherd, Tommy, who bound onto the jetty with a long, damp branch that had fallen in the shattering winter they were now coming out of. Mortens turned to Tommy, deliberately named so, just to irritate his superiors. He grabbed the branch, which Tommy was reluctant to release.

'Of all the sticks you could have picked up, boy.'

Tommy refused to let go, not until his master knelt and offered his bribe. An army issue biscuit. Mortens revealed the prize, and as predicted, Tommy gave up the branch and sat patiently for his treat. There was no shortage of ration biscuits for Tommy, for when the men arrived bloodied and torn from the front, they still had their equipment with them. With the food considerably better at the sanatorium, they were happy to donate their biscuits to the dog. Mortens was pleased Tommy was there, along with Astrid, for they had been allowed to take lodgings in the village just outside the facility. Mortens reflected on the news of sudden relocation he had given Astrid. She had been staying with her parents, along with Tommy. Her parents old and frail, they found the dog too boisterous for their liking, and given the rationing they all had to endure, the upkeep of a dog was beginning to tell. Astrid leapt at the opportunity to be with Mortens again and brought the restless Tommy with her.

Their lodgings were modestly furnished, and the village was clean and rather peaceful. Many of the SS officers stationed at the sanatorium were in fact doctors and medical staff, and they also enjoyed living in the village. The soldiers assigned for the security of the facility were from a camp at Ravensbruck, ten miles to the west. Mortens remained on site, whilst companies of SS men, one hundred and twenty all told would rotate through from Ravensbruck every two weeks. The company on site at present was due to be rotated out in the next few days, and the cycle would start again.

When Mortens began his takeover of the facility, he noticed that the SS troopers were in good spirits, as they too had the opportunity to fish, relax between guard shifts and also use the pool and spa facilities. Mortens was pleased with not having been posted to Ravensbruck, for it was dull, drab, and overcrowded with female inmates. The sanatorium, as ominous as it sounded was, in his mind, the better assignment of the two.

With Tommy giving up the branch for the biscuit, Mortens lobbed it into the lake as he followed the dog off the jetty. On land stood a number of medical orderlies, all at attention as Mortens drew near. Frowning at the small group, one of the NCOs pointed out over the Zenesse. Mortens turned just as a relentless drone registered in his ears. The dark bird on the horizon grew bigger, the drone louder. Its profile morphed into that of a BV-222, a Luftwaffe flying boat.

The aircraft had all the markings of the Luftwaffe but was now tasked with getting wounded SS men out of the battle and at Hohenlychen in quick time, for it would land on the lake and make for the northern jetty. They were coming in at a rate of at least two a day for the battlefront was edging ever closer, so the flying time was reducing accordingly. Bored of the spectacle he turned and followed on after Tommy.

Facing him as he walked was the Officer Ward. The terrace, for which the patients could relax in the sunshine, faced out over the lake whilst stewards in their white tunics fetched them refreshments. Everything about the facility was designed to be calming, clean and refreshing. The broken fighting man could leave the blood and mire behind and return to a peaceful setting, until they were ready to be launched back into the fight anyhow.

It was not long after breakfast, and the terrace was empty. Mortens knew it would not be long before the officers would take their coffee outside and converse as if they were still in a position to plan their next attack. Only the other day, Mortens was invited to join some convalescing officers who had been evacuated from the Ardennes just a few months prior. They asked for his advice on various situations. A little embarrassed, he explained that he lacked the tactical acumen to offer any advice. He was not from a fighting division, but fresh form a security assignment in Norway. Intrigued, they then pressed him on the sudden change of scenery. He admitted that one of the newly admitted to the ward was in fact Doctor Jurgen Arens and explained what had happened to him. The officers tittered some, before mocking Arens for already ruffling feathers in the ward. Mortens owed the man his gratitude, so chose to just smile and went about his rounds.

Making his way through the leafy grounds, he approached the Soldiers Ward, which loomed long and large compared to that of the officers. A few of the men, with cigarettes hanging from their lips, were already playing with Tommy as he bounded excitedly about them. As he drew closer, they clocked the uniformed Hauptsturmfuhrer before pulling themselves to attention.

Those with the ability to do so, delivered a crisp party salute. Mortens returned the salutation before removing his cap and wedging it under his left armpit. After running his free hand through his hair, he fished out the cigarette case from his trouser pocket.

As he put the cigarette to his lips, one of the soldiers presented a book of matches. Accepting them, he lit his cigarette, and for a few silent seconds joined the men in the ritual that is smoking.

Picking a loose flake of tobacco from his bottom lip, he was about to engage the soldiers in polite conversation when he picked up the faint warbling of an air raid siren. As it grew in pitch, both he and the men instinctively looked to the skies through the naked branches arching over them. Out of nowhere, the distinctive soundtrack of a Rolls Royce Merlin thundered through as a British Supermarine Spitfire streaked overhead along the Zenesse before barrel rolling over and out of sight.

'Arrogant bastards!' one of the soldiers spat. Mortens could only smirk as he nodded. He turned to the offended soldier.

'Don't worry. I've requested flak guns for this place.'

'Really, Sir?' Another asked. Mortens nodded.

'This might be a hospital, but I still need to be able to defend the patients and staff that occupy it, no?'

The soldiers shrugged and nodded to each other, as Tommy continued to be a pest as he tried to sniff out more biscuits from his master. As Mortens ruffled the ears of the German Shepherd, he could not help but speak his mind.

'Question is, why the sudden interest?'

10.

Edinburgh Castle

Same day.

Arms folded, nursing a cigarette which was burning ever closer to the fingers holding it, Jones stared blankly out of the window, giving him a grandstand view of Princes Street and the panorama beyond, picketed with barrage balloons, high and low. In his own world, the beauty of the view was lost on him.

So deep in thought, he had failed to noticed W-W raiding his breakfast plate for the sausage and bacon, before spiriting them away under the table for Oskar. Realising that his newly promoted friend was, on this occasion, a terrible breakfast companion, W-W made a bold, exaggerated show of pouring tea for them both.

Jones just continued to stare out over Edinburgh. Bored at the lack of conversation, W-W allowed himself to bring the teapot down with a crash, resulting in Jones flicking his cigarette ash all over what remained of his breakfast. Oskar yapped loudly as the other diners and mess staff all looked in at them. Flushed with embarrassment, Jones looked about the room before frowning at the captain.

'What?'

'You've not said two bloody words since that Cowen fellow buggered off back to London. Are you gonna tell me what's up?'

'What?' Jones was a little confused. W-W glanced sheepishly about the room as he leaned in closer.

'After Cowen left, you were just stood there, half struck and dumb. We just called it a night because you were not in the room as it were. What was in the letter?'

'Letter?' Jones frowned.

'You read it before he threw it in the fire. What did it say?'

Jones took a swig of tea before cuffing his lips.

'It was a note from the Prime Minister, wishing us well.'

'Bullshit!' W-W hissed, 'You wouldn't have gone quiet just because Winston is seeing us off, what did it say?'

Jones glanced about the room, leaning on the table, he looked W-W in the eyes.

'The facility they want us to hit, is going to fall to the Soviets. I, say we, have been instructed to raze it to the ground.'

'Really?' W-W frowned, glancing over shoulders. Jones nodded.

'Grab this Arens guy and destroy the facility as we leave.'

W-W could not help but give away a mischievous grin.

'Awesome.'

Sitting back in his chair, Jones was pleased at the captain's response. What then soured his mood was the fact that his breakfast plate was missing sausage, bacon and the remainder was covered in cigarette ash. Tight lipped, he pushed the plate away.

'That bloody dog!'

Back in the briefing room, W-W, Tim Lewis, and Colonel Hook poured over the map and referred to what aerial photographs they currently had. Jones stood behind them, fighting indigestion from his crudely made sausage and bacon sandwich he had pulled together as they left the dining room. With breakfast consumed, Jones joined the others as they spoke aloud.

'When will we have the latest photos?' Jones looked to Lewis, who glanced at his watch in response.

'We had an overflight of the facility this morning. Providing they get out okay, we should have them with us just after lunch.'

'Okay.' Jones nodded, 'Whilst we wait for them to come in, we can iron out other issues.'

'Such as?' Lewis responded. Jones pointed to the target on the map.

'Like how the hell we get there, and back is a good start.'

Jones, W-W and Hook all looked to the MI6 man, who realising they were waiting for his lead shrugged.

'What are you looking at me for? That's your bag, old man. Let me know what you need, and I'll accommodate.'

'Okay then.' Jones wrang his hands enthusiastically. 'Parachuting in. yay or nay?'

Before W-W could speak, Hook waved a dismissive hand.

'I'd rather you didn't Fyn. Take it from me, you'll have no friends in Germany to help you. You need a solid out.'

'Okay then,' Jones offered again, 'how do we get out, once we've grabbed this Arens chap?'

Hook leaned over the map, tracing the Zenesse with a finger before looking up at Lewis.

'138 Squadron taking us in?'

'Yes, of course.'

'Do they have Catalinas?'

'Cata-what?' Lewis was lost.

'Catalinas. Flying boats.'

'I'm not sure, why?'

Hook beckoned Jones and W-W to look at what he was pointing at. Without a word between them, all three smiled mischievously at each other before they all looked up at Lewis.

'Call 'em.' Jones instructed the MI6 man. 'Ask them if they have Catalinas.'

Whilst Lewis was away making the call, the three commando officers wasted no time as they continued to plan their mission. With fresh cups of tea in hand, they poured over both maps and aerial photographs, building a picture of the target and the surrounding terrain in their minds. On the photo, giving them a general view of the sanatorium, Jones pointed out the large and small buildings that were scattered throughout the complex.

'We will number the buildings. We can then save time when it comes to target identification, and if we have the Catalinas, fire control.'

W-W smiled as he nodded.

'We can save weight by not taking Bren guns if the aircraft can provide us fire support.'

'Exactly.'

'I wonder how much they can carry?' Hook murmured as he scrutinised the photos. 'I know they have great range, but if they can't lift much, we might have to go with the parachute option.'

'We, Colonel?' Jones smiled to his senior. Paul Hook, used to planning his own raids, stepped back, his hands out in capitulation.

'Fair cop, Fyn. Old habits and all that.'

The three men snorted as Hook folded his arms.

'Besides, you know what you can do with that parachuting lark…I never did like it.'

'Word on the street is, Colonel…' W-W flashed a cheeky grin, 'you weren't much of a submariner either.'

Jones winced mockingly as Hook feigned offence.

'I'll let you have that one. In the meantime, Captain,' Hook held out an empty tea cup, 'this thing won't fill itself.'

It was past lunch when Lewis returned from making enquiries about the Catalinas. The three commando officers, fresh back from lunch themselves were greeted by a smiling Lewis armed with a cardboard tube.

'They have four Catalinas, but one is in workshops.'

'Okay, we'll have to go with the three.' Jones nodded as he looked to both W-W and Hook for approval. Hands in pockets, Hook nodded to the tube under Lewis' armpit.

'That for us?'

Lewis frowned before he realised his still had hold of it. He pulled it out, slamming it down on the table.

'Ah, yes. I've been told the quality is excellent.'

Breaking the seal at the end of the tube, Jones pulled the contents out onto the table. The black and white collection of images were blown up as much as they dared without losing quality. The Photo Reconnaissance Pilot had done their work, and had done it well, for they had provided Jones with crisp images of not just the sanatorium and all that was in the grounds, but also the run in from the southern tip of the Zenesse, through the facility and over the village of Lychen to the north, before heading for home. Among the rolled-up images was a slim, rectangular cardboard box holding a stereoscope. W-W pulled the contraption free of the box before unfolding the thin wire legs that were designed as such so the observer could scrutinise the photo image and enjoy the features as they were lifted from the photograph to provide a three-dimensional image. Lewis flipped onto the table a separate, thick brown envelope.

'The photo of Arens you wanted mass producing. One per man.'

Taking in the facility laid out before them, it had been an excellent run by the pilot, and an ideal time of year. The trees that would have concealed the facility buildings from the air in lush summer months were void of leaves, and the photographs revealed all of them, with their off-white rooftops and large dark red crosses in place. A Luftwaffe flying boat on the Zenesse. Lewis joined the three officers as they marvelled at the quality of the images.

'Case of beer for that pilot, Lewis old man.' Hook gushed, 'He certainly earned his pay today.'

'She earned her pay. I'll let her know you like what you see.'

'She?' W-W cocked an eyebrow, to which Lewis nodded.

'Squadron Leader Dawn Hadnett. It's her handy work.'

As both Jones and W-W went back to looking at the images, Hook pulled himself away, over to the window that gave him a grandstand view of the city below. Lewis noticed the Colonel roll his shoulders as he took in the view.

'You okay, Colonel?' Lewis enquired, which caused both Jones and W-W to look up and take notice. Jones frowned at the back of Hooks head.

'You okay, boss?'

Hook turned around, his face beaming a wide smiled, his eyes glistening to the point of tears.

'She's still flying, the crazy bitch.'

With that, he cuffed his eyes as he returned to the window to compose himself.

The significance of Hooks reaction was lost on Lewis, who looked to the other officers for clarity. Jones tilted his head toward Hook.

'Hadnett got shot down outside La Rochelle in '43. The boss got her out.'

Now in the picture, Lewis relaxed a little, feeling the need to add comment.

'Well, kudos to you Colonel. That's why chaps like you are just the right fellows for the job.'

Cuffing his eyes once more, Hook turned and re-joined them at the table.

'Let's get on with this, shall we.'

It was whilst W-W was peering through the stereoscope, he noticed something rather familiar. Standing up, he invited Jones to peer in.

The area he was looking at was among the sparse trees. Jones could clearly see a cluster of figures stood together outside the larger building in the complex. Jones nodded.

'People.' He summarised, 'about a dozen or so.'

'What else can you see?' W-W challenged. Jones cut him a sidewards glance before looking again.

'What have you seen that I haven't?'

W-W pointed to what appeared to be a smudge in the image, but through the stereoscope revealed its true form.

'A dog.'

11.

'Now that we have the three Catalinas at our disposal,' Jones looked to Lewis, 'I need them to rehearse with us before we deploy. They have their own flying boats coming and going, so our engine noise won't spook them too much. Just more arrivals, doubt anyone will tumble out of bed to investigate.'

'Okay,' Lewis nodded approvingly, 'when and where?'

'Tomorrow and here.' Jones pointed at the map that highlighted most of Scotland. Lewis and the other officers leaned in. Blackwater reservoir.

'Why Blackwater?' Lewis enquired. Jones ready with his rationale.

'It's remote, and we can rehearse with live ammunition. The north bank has wooden jetties much like the

Zenesse, so we can also rehearse getting on and off the aircraft. We will build targetry, so the Catalina gunners can practice fire control whilst we get slicker getting on and off. We will be at our most vulnerable during those phases.'

'Okay,' Lewis looked to both Hook and W-W, who judging by their faces, were very much onside with Jones' wishes, who then continued.

'We will accommodate ourselves at the western end by the dam. We have the tentage and means to keep ourselves fed and warm whilst we prepare. Once ready, we can deploy direct from the reservoir to the target.'

'Very well,' Lewis agreed, 'our American friends want Arens taken to Sweden, once you have him that is.'

'Sweden?' Hook jumped in, 'Why Sweden?'

'Ours is not to reason why, Colonel.' Lewis shrugged. 'Once you have our man, you are to fly him to Sweden.'

'Do the Swedes know what the Americans have in mind?' Hook challenged, only to receive another shrug.

'I have no idea. We wanted him brought back here, but they insisted he be delivered to them in Sweden. They love your Catalina idea by the way.'

'Who?'

'The Americans, in fact, they thought the parachute option in the first place was risky.'

'The Americans appear to be rather intrusive in our business, considering they don't want to get their hands dirty.' Hook frowned at the agent.

'Colonel,' Lewis slowly headed over to the tea tray, 'this Arens fellow is clearly a big deal to the Americans, hence why they want him handed into their custody in Sweden instead of here.'

Hook folded his arms as he looked to his junior officers.

'They're scared we might keep him for ourselves, aren't they?'

Lewis returned an exaggerated shrug, 'You tell me.'

'Okay,' Jones cuffed his nose, 'where is this Arens guy?'

'What do you mean?' Lewis frowned, tea pot in hand. Jones pointed to the image of the sanatorium.

'What building will we find him in?'

'No idea.' Came the short, and somewhat lacklustre response. Jones looked to his peers, who also held stern looks towards the man more preoccupied with refreshing himself with tea.

'You have no idea?' Hook tried his hardest not to sound agitated. He was failing in that regard. Lewis, cup in hand turned to answer.

'We know he is at the Hohenlychen Sanatorium. That's it.'

'That's pretty fucking vague,' W-W countered, 'we can't spend our time on target going house to house. They'll have SS troops all over us within the hour.'

'We've tried to get someone in there. To report back that is.' Lewis spoke apologetically, 'But it's a closed shop, and difficult to infiltrate.'

Jones puffed out his cheeks as he ran his fingers through his hair. With hands on hips, he surveyed the facility on the blown-up photograph. He then traced a finger along the eastern bank of the Zenesse. The image revealed dense forest all along the bank opposite the leaf sparse sanatorium on the west bank.

'We may have to send in a team ahead of the main force.' Jones murmured, loud enough to hear. 'Set up an O.P.'

An Observation Post was a means for soldiers at ground level to gather information on the enemy whilst remaining concealed. Well camouflaged, well-armed and with the means to communicate with a larger force, an O.P team could report on the enemy in a timely fashion, allowing planners behind the lines to build a picture of what the enemy is doing, and plan accordingly. What could shape the plan was enemy strength, weapons and equipment, routine, and morale.

Jones looked to W-W.

'Fancy doing some recce work?'

W-W shrugged, 'Sure.'

With two of his troop commanders away, Jones did not have much of an officer pool to choose from. W-W was good at what he did, and seldom complained, officially that is.

'I have one demand.' W-W looked to both Hook and Jones, respectively. Jones lifted his chin a little, awaiting the demand.

'Sergeant Mould.' W-W spoke, 'I need a solid NCO with me on this.'

'Done.'

Sergeant Ian Mould was a solid operator. Short, stocky with a flair for Rugby, Mould was not one for showboating. He clocked in, got the job done, and clocked off. No fanfare, no bravado, just a soldier through and through. Unflappable in a tight spot, a connoisseur of demolitions and respected by the men.

Hook leaned in pointing at the map.

'I'm glad you want him along, because you might want to do something about that.'

The other men, Lewis included, looked to what he was referring to on the map of the target and the village to the north of the same name.

'There is a road bridge there. You might need to blow that if you don't want their reinforcements coming in.'

Both Jones and W-W looked to the map before conferring with the photo image of the same terrain. The photograph showed the road bridge Hook had highlighted, plus a narrower footbridge running from the bank in which the target sat on into the dense woods on the opposite bank.

'I'm thinking that if we jump in off to the east, we walk in and set up our O.P on the bank somewhere.'

'Okay.' Jones nodded as W-W traced a finger over both the road and footbridges.

'We prep the road bridge for demolition and use the footbridge when the time is right to join the rest of you on the target.'

Jones and Hook eyed each other. What W-W had in mind was certainly workable. Jones turned to the mapping and began to scan the ground off to the east of the Zenesse.

'You need a drop zone.'

With only the maps to go on, both W-W and Jones discussed possible drop zones. Without any photographic confirmation, they were going on faith that the maps were up to date and accurate. As they conferred, Hook took the opportunity to recharge his cup. As he tended to his refreshments, he noticed in his periphery that Lewis had joined him. Forcing himself to be cordial, Hook turned with tea pot in hand.

'Top up?'

'Oh, yes, thank you.' Lewis smiled, cocking his head over to the two officers leaning on the table.

'Good men.' Lewis offered, not that he had much interaction with commandos before.

'The best.' Hook confirmed, 'I'm not one for sitting out missions, but I've now got more companies under my command to keep on a leash.'

'Sound like quiet a handful.' Lewis put the cup to his lips. Hook shrugged a little.

'They fear being sent back to their original units more than tangling with the Germans, let me assure you.'

'Really?' Lewis was surprised. Being a civilian, he seldom understood the motivations of the soldier. From what he had seen, it was not for the glory, and certainly not the money that allured the men to volunteer for such missions. Sensing that he now had an 'in' with the revered and much respected Lieutenant Colonel Paul Hook, he chanced his arm.

'So, what's with Hadnett?'

'I'm sorry?' Eyebrows raised; Hook put the cup to his lips. Lewis flicked his head at the others.

'You appeared to have a moment, when I mentioned she was the pilot that took these images.'

Hook snorted as he lowered the cup.

'Long story.'

Knowing better than to push the issue, Lewis kept it polite.

'A story for the grandchildren, eh?'

Tight lipped, Hook looked out of the window. His thoughts taking him to the severely wounded SS trooper he had left for the locals to find back in '43 whilst extracting from La Rochelle. He had asked the young German to do the same.

'Tell your grandchildren this story.'

Looking out over Edinburgh, he echoed the very same response from the dying SS trooper.

'Let's hope so.'

12.

Both Jones and W-W were content with their method of insertion, and the deployment of an advance party. The two officers then briefed their commanding officer. W-W would lead the advance force, with Sergeant Ian Mould as his Second In Command. Their drop zone was to be on the open polder between the small villages of Steinrode to the north and Rosenow to the south. To the west lay the large forest that backed on to the Zenesse. Their plan was to march cross country, using the canopy of the forest to conceal them from the air during a daylight move to save time. They would then stop short of the eastern bank of the Zenesse and locate an ideal position in which they would then establish their O.P to observe the sanatorium. Whilst obtaining information, they would also, under cover of darkness scout the footbridge that leads into the northern end of the facility and the road bridge connecting the facility and the village of the same name. They would then rig the road bridge for demolition to prevent reinforcements coming from the west.

'I like it.' Hook nodded, 'I don't have much faith in communications, given the distances involved. How do you plan to rectify that?'

'The assault force and I will sit in Swedish waters, whilst W-W feeds us information.' Jones informed Hook. 'The Catalinas will allow us to do this.'

With a tight-lipped smile, Hook looked to Lewis.

'How will the Swedes feel about that?'

Lewis puffed out his cheeks as he folded his arms.

'They have form for taking any belligerent into custody who crosses their sovereign borders. Even the Germans tread lightly. I'm not one to make assumptions, but I can certainly speak with our American friends regarding this matter.'

'Please do.' Hook smiled, as the other two nodded. As Lewis went to speak again, there was a loud knock at the door.

'Wait!' Lewis bellowed as all the men flipped over mapping and photographs. Content all sensitive material was now covered, Lewis called for whoever it was to enter. The door eased open to reveal a thin, acne scarred mess steward. He raised a small sheet of paper, reading whatever was on it.

'Sorry to interrupt you gentlemen, but there is a call from Sergeant Major Montgomery for Captain Woolcott.'

W-W closed his eyes as he pinched the bridge of his nose. The curse of the double-barrelled surname. If it was not one, it was the other, or it was mispronounced altogether. Even Kaila, his wife misspelled it when they were preparing to get married. With Stepanic being her maiden name, the Canadian native would chuckle embarrassingly as she embraced her new surname. As W-W stepped off to follow the mess steward, both Jones and Hook eyed each other disconcertedly.

'Are you expecting a call?' Jones called out after him. W-W turned shrugging his shoulders as he stepped out of the room. Turning back to the map table, Jones spoke to no one in particular.

'Let's discuss our route to the target.'

Both Hook and Lewis joined him at the table. With pencil in hand, Jones pointed out the Blackwater Reservoir.

'I trust the Catalinas have the range to get us there and back?'

'Yes,' Lewis nodded, 'I would say it would be wise to skirt around the northern end of Denmark, keeping

Gothenburg on your left before coming ashore at Bastad and move south east, avoiding Malmo before moving out over open water to a position where you can sit tight and await the call from the Captain.'

Jones scoured the map, looking for ideal inlets and bays for which he could sit with the Catalinas. He traced a finger between Ahus and Nogersund on the Swedish coast.

'Plenty of hiding places between them. We cannot afford for German naval patrols to see us.'

'Agreed,' Lewis smiled as he nodded approvingly, 'I will put this suggestion to the Americans.'

As Lewis went to leave the room, he almost bumped into W-W returning. Jones noticed the captains face was ashen, his eyes raw and shot as they glistened. With a trembling hand rising to cuff his chin, Hook walked over to him.

'What?'

The Nazi V-2 ballistic missile pulverised Kaila Walsh–Woolcott's street at two thousand, five hundred miles per hour. Returning home from sleeping at a girlfriends after a night out, Kaila got off lightly compared to many who were still at home. A burst eardrum and concussion were enough to put her in Roehampton Hospital for a few days, but she was spared the agony of seeing the faces of the children returning home to neither homes nor their parents. The attack occurred late morning, the school aged children spared. Their infant siblings, however, were not so fortunate.

Jones saw W-W and little Oskar to Edinburgh Waverley station. They were far from ready to deploy on the mission, so the almost widowed captain could get down to London and be with his wife. As he slammed the carriage door, W-W leaned out of the window.

'I'll be back up as soon as I can.'

'Don't rush Matt, seriously,' Jones squeezed his forearm, 'just see to Kaila.'

The shrill of the whistle, the hissing of steam and the final commotion of passengers shuffling onboard prompted Jones to stand back, giving his deputy the thumbs up. All he got in return was a light-lipped nod. As the train pulled out of the station, Jones meandered back up to the castle, taking in the early afternoon air. As he climbed the steps of Advocate's Close, he summarised in his own mind where they were right now.

He had been given his mission, and he was confident it was certainly achievable. He was, as of that moment, three officers light. His troop sergeants would have no issue stepping up for the mission that was for sure. He had yet to meet the pilots and crews of the Catalinas. He needed to have his company rehearse before they even attempted the mission, for to neglect such a critical step in their battle preparation would most definitely result in disaster. He needed to get the company to Blackwater

Reservoir and set up camp, along with the mock-up of the sanatorium, so they could practice getting on and off the aircraft, not to mention gunnery and fire control measures should they require it.

Jones had a plan. It was vague, but he had a plan.

13.

1st April 1945

Hohenlychen Sanatorium

Otto Mortens placed the handset down, trying his hardest not to curse out aloud as he did so. With his clerk typing away just outside his office door, he knew she could sense all was not well. Her sixth sense had already picked up on the atmosphere building in the boss' office. With the door always open, she nervously stood at the threshold, as she deliberately cleared her throat to get his attention. Mortens looked up.

'Coffee, Hauptsturmfuhrer?'

Mortens blinked hard as he leaned back in his chair. He shook his head slowly as he turned to look out of the window.

'No thank you, Lucy.'

The plain German girl returned to her own desk as Mortens looked out over the Zenesse. He could only do so given the time of year. Come summer, the canopy would be too thick with leaves. It was the resumption of Lucy's typing that brought him back to the present. She was a nice, polite girl, not in the SS, but the daughter of one of the physicians that worked with the soldiers in their recovery. Tommy, forever the flirt when it came to the girls, would loiter or sleep under her desk for he knew a good thing when he saw it. Lucy was terrible for bringing him treats.

Mortens meanwhile tried his hardest not to lose his temper.

Not with sweet Lucy, or his greedy Tommy, but the overripe pheasants that would lord it from their high perch at Ravensbruck. Since taking over as the Security Officer for Hohenlychen, the lack of actual defensive measures for the hospital worried him. No perimeter fence, no watchtowers, a lacklustre security force, and even more lacklustre support network at Ravensbruck. He had lost count how many times he had to phone the Quartermaster and ask for what he felt were reasonable resources. Mortens had to be fair to the man, for the Quartermaster was onside, but Mortens requests to make improvements to the hospital's security measures were always vetoed by someone who worked at the very hospital Mortens was trying to make safer.

SS-Gruppenfuhrer Karl Gebhardt.

Mortens had met Gebhardt on his first day in post as he strutted about the officers' terrace in his pristine white lab coat, his small wire rim spectacles perched on the end of his nose, delivering crisp party salutes to those his senior as they took in the crisp morning air in pyjamas and bathrobes. Mortens instantly took a dislike to the man, whom he had already labelled an opportunist and charlatan. Gebhardt would dismiss his concerns with an arrogant flick of the hand, stating that it was a hospital, not a barracks. He would then bore Mortens with how the soldier's recovery would only stall if they were consumed by all things military, their mental health as vital as the physical. Gebhardt's rationale was not without merit, Mortens conceded, but he feared that the enemy, whomever sought to overrun the facility, needed to be held at bay whilst the patients, staff and their families were evacuated. Enclosing the village of Lychen behind the wire along with the facility was also on Mortens agenda. After screwing up in Norway, he could not afford for something to go wrong again. His masters in Berlin would give him no quarter next time.

Feeling the need for some air, Mortens got to his feet and pulled his field cap from the coat stand. He would walk home and take coffee with his wife. Given how laissez-faire everyone else appeared to be at Hohenlycen, Mortens sneered, why should anyone care?

He sauntered after Tommy, who always liked to follow the water's edge back home. The German Shepherd would hopefully enjoy chasing off the birds in the summer but given that they were coming out of one of the most brutal winters on record, the birds were still enjoying warmer climates further south. With his field cap wedged under his left arm, Mortens, quiet unusually, since he knew that he should always be correctly dressed when out in the grounds of the sanatorium, strolled with his right hand in his pocket. With a deep sigh, he thought through his current situation.

He was essentially home with his wife and beloved Tommy. He was not assigned to a combat posting and should therefore perhaps accept that he should not ruffle the feathers of his superiors in Ravensbruck. He had approached them more than once already, demanding security enhancements to the Hohenlychen facility, but most to no avail. He had however been given some concessions. He was to receive from the Ravensbruck garrison three, twenty-millimetre anti-aircraft guns. He could only assume enough ammunition and crews would accompany them, since they were not much good to him otherwise. Given the role in which they were designed, he could not be certain if the crews would be from either the SS or the Luftwaffe. He did not care one way or the other. He just needed them to come with crews.

Looking up, he could see Tommy making a fuss among the officers who took in the morning air with coffee on their terrace overlooking the Zenesse. Those convalescing from their combat wounds appeared and sounded good hearted as Tommy sniffed about them. Mortens took out his hands and placed his field cap on, knowing better than to not encourage those more senior than him to raise the issue of his turnout. Arriving before the throng of garden furniture and the recovering, battle scarred officers of the Waffen SS, Mortens pulled his heels together as he delivered a party salute. Some of those who could manage it got to their feet and returned the salutation. The seated remainder, less those more interested in Tommy, returned a lacklustre flick of the hand. At the rear of the group, in a vain attempt to remain aloof of all the fuss over the dog, sat Jurgen Arens. Mortens nodded in his direction, only to receive the gesture in return.

Content that Tommy was not too much of a nuisance, Mortens orbited around the terrace and headed over to Arens. As he pulled up, he pulled off his field cap before running his free hands through his hair.

'Good morning, Obersturmbannfuhrer. I trust you are well?'

Arens took a deliberate long sip of his coffee before responding with a broad smile.

'I am, thank you, Hauptsturmfuhrer. I must say, the uniform does you credit. Far more handsome than the suit you lived in up in Norway. Please.'

Flushed in the cheeks from the unexpected compliment, Mortens took a seat. He peered over to ensure Tommy was not running off with anyone's toast, before looking back to Arens, who sat wrapped tight in a dressing gown over pyjamas. The scientist refilled his cup from the silver coffee pot.

'Coffee?'

'No, thank you. I'm off home to have coffee with my wife.'

'Ah, wonderful.' Arens bellowed, a little louder than he probably intended, for the officers sat away from them all looked over. Arens raised a friendly hand, which had them all go back to talking among themselves, or ruffling Tommy's ears. Arens shook his head subtly.

'Just trying to be friendly. Tough crowd. Anyways, how is the lovely Astrid?'

Mortens instantly recognised the mischievous smile on Arens face. He knew better than to make a thing of it. Arens knew he was screwing around in Norway, so allowed him the win.

'She is well, thank you. Pleased to be up here with me.'

Putting the pot back down, Arens adjusted in his seat. Mortens read that the wince Arens gave away meant he was not yet fully recovered.

'Still healing?'

Arens pulled face as he adjusted the pillow he was sat on.

'I will certainly leave out of my memoirs the part where I got shot in the arse.'

Both men snorted. Mortens was a little surprised that Arens could do humour, especially at his own expense. Cupping his coffee in both hands, Arens sighed deeply as he looked out over the Zenesse.

'I should not be here, Otto.'

Mortens flinched at the familiarity.

'What do you mean?'

'I'm a scientist, not a soldier. These guys barely give me the time of day. It is all rather lonely here if I'm honest.'

Mortens slowly glanced over his should before responding.

'Doctor, you are an Obersturmbannfuhrer in the SS. So, what if you are not from a combat command? Half of those in this place have come from all manner of duty. Take it from me.'

Arens nodded some as he took a mouthful of coffee.

'Yes, I suppose you are right.'

Mortens leaned in a little.

'Have you had the pleasure of meeting the Chief Surgeon?'

'Pah!' Arens snorted, causing the other officers to look over again, a look of irritation on their faces. Tight-lipped, Arens eyed them as he leaned in towards Mortens.

'Insufferable man. I thought I could be an arse, but my goodness…'

'Did he treat your wounds?'

'Who?' Arens frowned in a hush, 'Gebhardt?'

Mortens nodded as Arens sat back waving a dismissive hand.

'Did he hell. He saunters about here in his lab coat, saluting anyone he feels he can cosy up to. I don't think he's a surgeon in that respect.'

'What do you mean?' Mortens was intrigued. Arens, coffee cup to his lips, shrugged.

'There must be something in the cellar of this building, for he keeps going down there, along with other white coated staff. I've tried to see what it is, but the cellar stairs are guarded by the fire piquet.'

'Really?'

'Yes.' Arens nodded. 'They come and go in the middle of the night. Ambulances come and go. I have no idea what they do down there.'

Mortens, now mute, sat back in his seat.

No wonder Gebhardt was always countering his requests to improve the security measures at Hohenlychen. With fences and barriers comes security checks. Security checks would potentially uncover whatever Gebhardt, and his staff were up to. If Mortens pushed too hard, he could find himself reassigned to the Oder front. He did not want that. He had managed to get flak guns approved, that was one thing. In a shameful sense of self preservation, Mortens knew he would have to approach further security concerns with care. Arens got his attention, which snapped him out of his thoughts.

'Go and have coffee with your wife, Hauptsturmfuhrer. Enjoy the fact that you can.'

Mortens smiled at the prospect as he got to his feet.

'I'd like to thank you, Obersturmbannfuhrer for speaking highly of me after what happened in Norway. I'd be a liar if I did not expect the contrary.'

Arens smiled up at the younger man, who was putting his field cap on.

'You saved my life, Otto,' the scientist spoke sincerely. 'We may have not always seen eye to eye, but I always knew you just wanted to keep me and your men safe. I am truly sorry for the officers you lost that night.'

Mortens nodded a little. He had made an official report to Berlin regarding the attack, but he had yet to sit down and write letters to the families. He promised to himself that he would do that whilst at Hohenlychen, for the assignment allowed him the time to do so.

'Enjoy your day, Sir.' Mortens saluted Arens, who nodded with a smile.

'And you, Hauptsturmfuhrer. And you.'

Mortens left Arens to his coffee, shepherding Tommy out from among the terrace furniture and further along the Zenesse. As he reflected on his conversation with his former principle, he noticed medical staff coming and going from some external cellar steps at the northern end of the officer's ward. All were clad in lab coats, armed with clipboards, with a sense of urgency as if daylight would turn them all to dust. As Mortens raised a mocking eyebrow, he was suddenly surprised to see one of the white coated staff double over and vomit. He could not help but stand and look on.

The man wretched his guts up noisily as his colleagues rallied around him and try and return him to their subterranean domain. The chastised, sickly man fought them off and slumped against a tree before crumpling to the ground. Mortens felt the need to assist, and as he stepped off to approach, one of those stood over the fallen man turned to face him.

'Go about your business, Hauptsturmfuhrer,' the order was curt. Mortens frowned at the man.

'I'm Head of Security at this facility.'

'You'll be a company commander on the Oder front if you don't go about your day, young man.'

Mortens eyed the shorter, older man. The lab coat he was wearing gave nothing away with regards to his rank and knew better than to pursue the issue. The older man glanced at his fevered colleague at the base of the tree.

The other men tended to him. The man that challenged Mortens looked back at him.

'Our colleague here is not well. Too much schnapps perhaps.'

'Perhaps.' Mortens eyed the sickened man as he was hauled to his feet and led away. The older man took his leave and followed on after them. Mortens watched them until they were out of sight behind the Soldier Ward. Pushing his cap onto the back of his head, he puffed out his cheeks as Tommy glided past his right thigh. Looking to the cellar doors, he shook his head.

'What on earth is going on down there?'

14.

3rd April 1945

Blackwater Reservoir

Scotland

13 Miles south of Spean Bridge

With W-W still in London on compassionate leave, Jones was left to write the Administration Instruction for his own Company Quartermaster. Such a document would have usually been in the remit of his Company Second in Command, but without another Troop Commander to assign it to, he was lumbered with the task. His Commanding Officer, Paul Hook chuckled as he happily provided the newly promoted Major with coffee as he composed the document. As Jones' superior, he certainly was not going to write it, but he remained on hand to assist with its creation, should Jones overlook an issue. Jones did have one thing going for him, he was able to write it in the comfortable setting that was Edinburgh Castle.

Chilled to the bone, Jones looked down from the dam at the far western end of the reservoir. At the base of the dam, the fruits of his literary labours were budding. The Company Quartermaster, Colour Sergeant Phil Gorman had received the Admin Instruction in good time and ensured that all the logistics required for the next phase of the mission planning were taken care of. With their overloaded convoy setting off from Spean Bridge, Company Sergeant Major Tristan Montgomery set the men off in patrols of four via the summit of Ben Nevis to the very location they were in. It served a number of purposes. They did not have enough trucks to take men and material in one lift, plus the fact that they could polish up their navigation skills whilst having a workout. At the dam, wrapped up warm from their exertions, they then went about building the tented camp that would serve as home until it was time to deploy.

Once their rudimentary barracks was built, Jones could then deliver his orders for the coming mission. Stood up on the dam, he awaited the arrival of the most important equipment of the operation. The three Catalina flying boats. Wrapped up for the weather, Jones watched as Montgomery climbed up to join him, a cup of hot, sweet tea in each hand. The slightly older man, a seasoned veteran of commando operations puffed and cursed as he fought to not slip over in front of his boss. Once up on the dam, he puffed out his cheeks as he offered a cup. Jones nodded his thanks as he took it.

'How's the feet?' Jones enquired, given that the sergeant major had too scaled Ben Nevis on the way to the dam. Montgomery rolled his shoulders.

'Fine. A little tender, but fine.'

'Can't believe you made them walk here.' Jones chuckled into his mug. Montgomery shrugged.

'They've been getting fat and bored and needed the exercise.'

Both men's shoulders bounced as they savoured their tea. The lads were tough. Very tough in fact. The long winter in Scotland had certainly taken the rough edges off those who had joined the unit recently. Commandos by right, they were quickly accepted by their more seasoned peers, for there was no room for measuring appendages since they could be called to action with little or no notice. This operation certainly qualified in Jones mind, and given the target, it would be a little more exotic than they were used to.

Enjoying the steam from the tea warming his chapped cheeks, Montgomery spoke.

'How was Edinburgh?'

'You'd hate it, Sarn't Major.' Jones smiled mischievously, 'Log fires and fine dining, and the rattle of typewriters.'

'Ha!' Montgomery scoffed, 'I'll be sure to let the boys know how rough you had it.'

'It was good to have Colonel Hooks input in the initial planning, I must say.' Jones admitted, to which his sergeant major shrugged and nodded a little.

'Aye, he's been a round the bazaars in the last couple of years. I bet he spoke as if it was his mission he was planning.'

Jones gave Montgomery a sly side glance as the man put his cup to his lips. Jones had no counter, for the seasoned soldier was right on that count. Montgomery cuffed his chin with his sleeve as he pointed with his free hand to something in the distance.

'These for us?'

Jones looked to where the man was pointing. Squinting a little, he could make out three specks on the horizon. The light grey cloud bank gave them away, the drone of engines faint but growing louder.

'Yes they are.'

The three Catalina flying boats from 138 Special Duties Squadron dipped their port wings as they flew east over the dam before banking to starboard for a long arching swing to port which allowed them to touch down one at a time on the water. With their speed drastically reduced, they taxied over towards the dam before dropping anchor, their engines fluttering out. The commotion up on the water had some of the company scrambling up to see what it was. The crew launched small rubber boats, each carrying three men before paddling to the jetty further down the bank. Both Jones and Montgomery walked down to meet them. As they clambered ashore, Jones could see their fleece lined leather gear denied him any indication as to their ranks. Since all were minus head wear, they all pulled themselves to attention. At the front was a broader, older looking man, the others, despite their thick clothing were trimmer, all looking about the same age, give or take a year.

The broad, older airman offered his hand as he introduced himself.

'Warrant Officer Richard Monk, Sir. Pilot.'

Both Jones and Montgomery shook his hand, respectively.

'Sarn't Major,' Jones smiled, 'pleasure to finally meet you guys.'

Monk introduced all the others. It quickly became apparent that Monk was the most senior of all the airmen. Jones frowned with intrigue.

'No officers hiding out on the water?'

Monk returned a tight-lipped smile as he looked to his comrades, all of whom shrugged, whilst some folded their arms. Monk looked back at the commando officer.

'Let's just say that the brass doesn't want any of them captured. So, you've got us.'

Jones pulled a face that read nothing but bewilderment. Montgomery too fared no better. Monk pushed a polite smile.

'What can I say gentlemen. We can fly and shoot straight, so you'll be just fine with us.'

'Ah well,' Montgomery snorted, causing Jones to look at him, 'not the first time we've had to piss with the cock we've got.'

With the Catalina crews ferried to shore, Jones led them down to their makeshift canvas tented barracks, with Montgomery and some of the other commandos following on. Jones could see the airmen had the means to keep warm at altitude but were lacking sleeping bags. Montgomery, in his remit as Company Sergeant Major, would liaise with the Company Quartermaster to ensure their newly arrived guests had what they needed. In the meantime, Jones led them to the large olive drab tent that served as their Cookhouse. With the lunch meal in preparation, the best Jones could offer was hot drinks. As all thirty airmen took care of their beverages, Jones ushered Monk off to one side. The RAF Warrant Officer gave one of his boys the thumbs up for a brew when it was ready. Jones folded his arms as he spoke.

'I had no idea you would be bringing so many crew.'

Monk gave off a warm smile.

'We'll share sleeping bags if we have to, Sir.'

'No, I mean… can you lift us all to the target…and back?'

'How many are you thinking?'

Jones shrugged as he was not exactly sure at that point.

'I guess, all in…Ninety men, plus our kit for the task.'

The RAF pilot puffed out his cheeks, shaking his head a little.

'Not a chance, Sir. Weight isn't the issue, it's literally the lack of space for all your men and equipment.'

Jones bit his bottom lip at the revelation.

'What can you lift?'

Monk looked about the cookhouse, eyeing those stood about the brew area before looking back at the major.

'It'll still be a little tight, but we can do twenty men plus crew.'

'Per aircraft?'

'Per aircraft.'

Jones stewed on the information as one of his men came over armed with a cup in each hand. He offered the first to Jones, who surprised at the gesture, accepted it with a smile. Monk accepted his as the airman returned to his colleagues stood chatting and smoking. Savouring the tea, Jones felt the need to address another issue he had.

'Sarn't Major, I'd like to make a rather radical request.'

'Go on.' Monk sipped at his tea.

'I want my guys to be the gunners on your aircraft.'

Monk frowned, a mouthful of tea yet to be swallowed. After he did so, he cuffed his chin.

'Why Sir?'

Running his free hand through his hair, Jones came clean.

'We've been given a rather juicy mission, deep in their back yard as it were. I'd like as many of my guys on that mission as I can. Those sixty you will be bringing in for us will be assault troops, and I want my men manning your gunner stations as fire support.'

'Oh…' Monk tailed off, a concerned look growing on his face. Jones read this and added context, for reassurance if anything.

'Should the mission all go to pot, I'd rather walk out of there with as few airmen under our wing as possible, if you get my drift?'

Tight-lipped, Monk nodded, cupping his mug in both hands.

'I see what you mean, Sir. I have no issue with it, and if I'm honest, I'm sure the lads won't be too devastated either.'

'Really?' Jones was surprised. Monk smiled.

'It's nearly over Sir. You can almost taste it.'

'You really think so?'

'I do Sir. They can't hold out much longer. We've been lifting out agents and all sorts up and down the line. So deep into Germany they are. It's on the cards.'

'All sorts?'

Monk's face was deadpan.

'Nazis Sir. Nazis.'

Jones snorted as he finished his tea.

'Somewhat of a theme going on right now.'

15.

With the canvas tent city established at the base of Blackwater Dam, there was little else for the men to do but strip wash, change and grab hot food. Once fed, they settled in the cookhouse tent with tea, a book, or a chessboard. One of his signallers managed to get some music on the go. Jones was eager to get on with further planning so he could then direct how he wanted his rehearsals to go. Colonel Hook was travelling up from Edinburgh with the Pilot and Navigator for the advance force drop. They too were seconded from 138 Squadron. Until he had all those required for the mission, he just sat and touched up his current plan.

It was late afternoon when Hooks jeep arrived at the dam. Well wrapped against the elements, Hook and his passengers clambered out, one of the men pointing them in the direction of the tent that served as an Operations

Room. Having seen the jeep arrive, Jones made his way from the cosy Cookhouse to join them. Inside the tent, with a backdrop of radio sets and men manning them, Jones shook hands with the cold, weary travellers.

'Flight Lieutenants Jack Lewens and Luke Stagg.'

Their hands warm from many hours deep in their pockets, Jones welcomed them to their rather rudimentary home for the next few days. Hook, rubbing his hands together, looked about for the kettle which he then gravitated towards.

'I'll stick around until you've delivered your orders, Fyn. I'll need to get these guys back down to Glasgow so they can prepare their crews and aircraft.'

'Sure, no problem.' Jones smiled at his guests. As he went to speak, W-W, wrapped for the weather stepped into the tent. With their eyes locked, both men acknowledged each other before Jones excused himself from the new arrivals to speak with his Company Second in Command. Walking over, he offered W-W his hand, who took it with both of his.

'Wasn't expecting you back so soon.' Jones spoke apologetically, 'How's things?'

Releasing their embraced, W-W slid his hands into his pockets.

'She's going back to Canada. My folks are taking her to Liverpool right now.'

With a straight face, Jones was not quite sure what to say next. In Canada, she would certainly be safe, and with family.

'Are you okay with that?'

'I guess.' W-W shrugged. 'She's taking Oskar with her.'

'Oh dear,' Jones responded, trying not to smirk too much, 'the Germans are in trouble now.'

W-W pulled a face.

'Let's just get on with it.'

Into the late evening, Jones, W-W and Hook in support put to all of the pilots and navigators their proposed route to the target. Over a map spread on the large table in the operations tent, range was not the issue, but the sticking point came when to avoid any Luftwaffe interference over Denmark, they would have to fly through Swedish airspace.

'Our ambassador in Stockholm will probably get a dressing down, but that's about it.' Hook smiled. 'I'm sure our man Lewis in Edinburgh will in turn get dragged over the coals for it too, buts that's what he's here for.'

'Are the Swedes hostile?' Lewens asked to which Hook replied.

'Going by what Lewis has said, they are no friend to any belligerent. If we end up having to land within their sovereign border, we will be taken in to custody.'

'Will they hand us over to the Germans?' Monks asked, a little concerned. Hook shook his head.

'No, they are straight down the middle most of the time. They probably have German airmen and sailors in custody, along with whoever from our side fell afoul.'

'Most of the time?' Stagg countered. Hook looked to him with a shrug.

'Lewis says the Americans are stroking Swedish egos, so they don't get too excited if we end up in their back yard. Let's put it that way.'

With the initial reservations dealt with, Jones took his cue to offer some lying up options for the Catalinas. His pencil drifted about Sweden's southern coast.

'If we hide the Cats in these inlets, between Torso Bay and Nogersund, the Halifax will continue on to the proposed drop zone for the advance force.'

Jones eyed W-W, who returned a nod. Jones looked back to the map.

'We wait for the call to come in and land on the Zenesse right next to the target. Judging by the flying boat in the latest air photos, in the dark, that will hardly rouse them. Once we come back aboard after our little visit, we return via the same route, but we RV here with the Americans. Torso Bay.'

The Catalina pilots leaned in, nodding a little with approval.

'They will then take the prisoner from there to heaven knows where. All we know is that we are to deliver him.'

All those about Jones stood straight, some puffing out their cheeks whilst others scratched heads. Jones knew the information at present was somewhat vague to them, but all would be revealed when he delivered his orders to everyone involved. He looked to them.

'What do you think? From a flight perspective.'

It was at this time, Monk looked to the commissioned pilots for their thoughts. With arms folded, Jones could tell by the looks on their faces that the flight could be straight forward. German fighter activity had greatly diminished since the Normandy battles the summer previous, and if anything, many of what remained of German airpower would most likely be off to the east to take on the Soviet army massing on the Oder. Lewens nodded his approval at Jones.

'I trust after we've dropped the advance party; we take the same route home?'

'Yes please.' Jones nodded, 'Let's keep this simple.'

He cleared his throat as he addressed the Catalina airmen.

'We will do the same once we've finished with the Americans.'

'That poor ambassador,' W-W sniggered, 'two rollockings in succession.'

Jones smiled.

'Lewis may as well stay outside the Foreign Secretary's office too.'

16.

The Cookhouse tent was the only tent big enough to get all the men in. With the tables stacked off to one side, the sergeant major and company quartermaster had laid out all the chairs, as W-W placed a photograph of Arens face down on each of them. The chefs, seconded from Edinburgh garrison for the tented camp carried on in their designated kitchen tent next door, ensuring the breakfast meal would still be ready bright and early in time for mission preparations to carry on in earnest the following morning. Operational security was not an issue, for the chefs, and the Catalina gunners replaced by his own men would be quarantined in the tented camp until after the operation. The sergeant major would be deploying on the mission, so the company quartermaster would run the camp in his absence.

As the men filed in, they began filling up the seats from the third row backwards. The two front rows were for the Troop Sergeants and NCO's who would be commanding their respective groupings, not to mention the Pilots and Navigators of each aircraft. It would be a bit of a squeeze once everyone was in the tent, but it sure beat giving the brief outside.

Naturally, the men were looking at the photographs placed on their seats. Each image numbered in the bottom right corner with a chinagraph. Jones, proofreading the orders in his notebook knew what was coming. The boys were anything but predictable.

'Not for me boss. I'm taken thanks.'

'Boss, you don't quite understand this dating lark, do you?'

The jibes brought sniggers and chuckles from the boys sat around the hecklers. Jones smiled in return, for they were in good spirits, and certainly wished it to continue. The orders he was about to deliver to them, could well spoil that, but that would be too bad. They had a job to do. He glanced to his left, W-W scanned the mapping and blown-up aerial photographs he had pinned to the wall of the tent, facing the men. He too glanced down at his notes, for he was now very much back in the game, and part of the planning cycle. His wife, her hearing ruined from a V-2, was on her way back to her native Canada, and to make it worse, she was taking Oskar with her. W-W was angry, and therefore had no intention of missing the opportunity to get some payback.

With the last of the men now seated, Company Sergeant Major Montgomery closed the flap and gave his company commander the thumbs up. Just as Jones cleared his throat to begin, he noticed Lieutenant Colonel Hook slip in and stand besides Montgomery, who nodded an acknowledgement. Hook gave Jones a reassuring nod and smile, which indicated to the major it was time to get down to business.

'Gentlemen, you are about to receive orders for a prisoner grab behind enemy lines.'

The low hum of conversation among the men faded out. He now had their undivided attention. Jones held aloft the photograph of Arens.

'The photograph you have is of our intended target. Obersturmbannfuhrer Jurgen Arens. Between now and when we fly, you are to keep looking at this man. You'll be handing these photographs back in before you depart. He is a key Scientist involved in German weapons development. We have been charged by the Prime Minister himself with taking him into custody, alive.'

Jones held a deliberate pause for effect. He could see the men looking at their photographs, before glancing at each other, shrugging. So far, so good.

'We are to have him in custody before he is well enough to continue his work.'

All the men nodded their approval for the rationale behind the plan. To remove people like Arens from weapons development could certainly slow the Germans down before they developed something truly horrifying. Jones looked to W-W as he fetched a long, thin stick leaning against the canvas.

'Let's talk Task Organisation. Two groups. The Advance Force, under the command of Captain Walsh-Woolcott, Sergeant Mould as his second in command, plus the eight men they have already assigned. The Assault Group, commanded by myself, with the sergeant major as my deputy, plus sixty men and those already chosen to act as gunners for the Catalinas.'

The men murmured and nodded among themselves, seemingly content with their roles on the mission. Jones looked to those not deploying, especially the aircrew now relegated to the bench.

'Apologies for those not coming with us, but space on the aircraft is limited. So, there you have it.'

As those being left behind accepted their lot, Jones looked to W-W. for it was his turn to speak to the masses.

'Gentlemen,' W-W called for their attention, 'let's go over the ground.'

The men looked up as W-W, stick in hand, pointed at the map showing Nazi Germany in its entirety.

'The location of Arens is fifty miles north of Berlin, here.'

W-W paused as low whistles emitted from lips. He then sidestepped to the right and pointed at the blown-up image of the Zenesse and the cluster of buildings under sparse trees on the west bank.

'Arens is current convalescing at Hohenlychen Sanatorium. A hospital exclusive to the SS. It sits on the west bank of the Zenesse lake and comprises of a number of buildings. We have numbered them for ease of orientation and fire control, which we will discuss later in these orders. With only these photographs to go by, we have estimated the purpose of the buildings.'

W-W paused to consult his notes before continuing. Jones looked on as NCOs sat ready, pencils poised over their notebooks. W-W then continued.

'Building one is a rail station, notice the rail line running north to south.'

W-W traced along where is was on the image.

'Building two, Guardroom. Building three, Soldier Ward. Building four, Officer Ward, where Arens will most likely be, but I will confirm that on the ground.'

He paused again, to allow the NCOs to catch up with their note taking.

'Building five, headquarters slash administration offices. Building six, a church.'

He scanned his notes again before continuing.

'Other areas of note, to the north of the facility, Lychen village. Between the village and the facility is a road bridge, which will be key on this operation due to a barracks located ten miles off to the west, which could be where their reinforcements will most likely come from.'

Jones eyed the audience, all of whom were serious in their demeanour as they all scribbled notes. W-W continued to give his ground brief.

'There is a footbridge that runs east-west across a bottleneck as it were, from the northern end of the facility to the east bank of the Zenesse. That will be crucial, and this will be explained in more detail in the execution phase of these orders. In addition, which will certainly be of use to the main assault group, two jetties which allow us to disembark the Cats and get onto the target. Any questions before I hand back to the OC?'

There were none. Just a faint scrape of pencil on paper. Content that all those looking up at him were ready for the next load of information, W-W looked back to the photograph.

'Hohenlychen Sanatorium sits amid lakes and forests, which makes it ideal for Catalina insertion and extraction, plus plenty of cover for the advance force. There are numerous small hamlets in the area, but none appear to be garrisoned. However, given the very nature of the target facility, there will be a security element we will have to contend with.'

W-W took the opportunity to hand the stick back to Jones who would orate the next phase of the orders. Clearing his throat, Jones got the men's attention.

'Situation enemy forces.' Jones announced, prompting note takers to begin a fresh paragraph.

'The sanatorium is lightly garrisoned. Given the lack of what appears to be a perimeter fence, or any air defence measures, we estimate perhaps a security force of no more than Platoon strength.'

This estimation caused a confident stir among the men. To outnumber the enemy in any situation was ideal, and they were doctrinally aware that they would always like to have the odds three to one in their favour. That rationale only really worked if a full company was going to attack the sanatorium. The Catalinas could only lift perhaps half that. Jones knew that on a good day, providing all the aircraft arrived and his men were in a fit state to fight when they arrive, it would be two to one at best, with the Cats providing fire support. He called for attention as the chattering among the men grew louder.

'Gentlemen, the sanatorium is most likely supported by the larger garrison to the west. So, we must not take too long grabbing our man. The enemy troops on site will have personal weapons, perhaps a couple of MG42 at best. Anyone coming to reinforce them however could bring in halftracks, which will make our job more difficult.'

Jones was losing the audience now as the men were now in conference with each other. NCOs interacted, both between themselves and their men sat directly behind them. Jones was up against it time wise and looked up at his sergeant major to call order.

'Settle down boys!' Montgomery bellowed from the back, which had an immediate positive effect on the audience. With a smile and a nod, Jones continued.

'The morale of the enemy could be mixed. They are not on a combat assignment which could mean their morale is high, but with news spreading about the Soviets gathering on the Oder, this could now begin to be somewhat detrimental to them. Fighting quality is questionable, given that the Germans will always want their best eleven at the front.'

This caused another conference to ferment in the ranks. Jones just had to get on.

'Be under no illusion, gentlemen.' He bellowed, calming the audience.

'They are well rested and fresh, so we must not take them for granted. Please keep that in mind as we embark on rehearsals after these orders, so let us press on…friendly forces!'

The audience has his attention, which had Jones spread his arms wide, like a priest addressing his congregation.

'Look about you. This is what we have. We will be out on a limb to say the least. This is a prisoner grab, not a set piece battle. We do not have the means to wage a lengthy operation. In and out.'

The men looked about at their neighbours, some throwing a mocking jab into their friends' shoulders. Jones looked to his notes. Now was the time for his mission statement.

'Our mission…' Jones opened in a loud, measured tone which calmed the audience, 'is to take Jurgen Arens into custody, alive. Be prepared to engage and destroy enemy forces within the facility, in order to halt German weapons development.'

The silence hung thunderously as Jones absorbed many pairs of eyes looking back at him. He repeated his mission statement.

'Our mission is to take Jurgen Arens into custody, alive. Be prepared engage and destroy enemy forces within the facility, in order to halt German weapons development.'

Many eyes in the audience blinked as they touched up their notes. Their mission statement had now been officially given. Jones glanced over his notes before he delivered the next phase of his orders.

'Execution...' He announced, prompting the note takers, mainly those sat in the first two rows to turn a page.

'Upon completion of our rehearsals, which will be day and night live rehearsals, we will then deploy. The Advance Force will move with all their weapons and equipment to Glasgow Airport, where they will board their aircraft. Once they are ready to taxi, we will board the Cats and taxi into a position where we can then take off and join them in formation over this location before we make our turn east and on towards the North Sea.'

On cue, Flight Lieutenant Luke Stagg got to his feet, his notebook in his hands. He turned to address the audience. Jones handed him the stick which he traced on the map, highlighting the flight route they would take. As the lead navigator in the formation, he dictated to the Catalina navigators the route. Speed, altitude, time of each leg, bearing of each turn, physical description of what they should see, cloud permitting, especially when tracking south along Sweden's coastline.

Stagg eventually got to the Final Rendezvous, where the Catalina group would break off and descend to seek refuge in the secluded coves of Nogersund. Stagg explained the run south to the Drop Zone for the Advance Force, before explaining in less technical vernacular the return journey. With Staggs oration now concluded, he handed the stick to W-W, who would command the Advance Force.

With the tip of the stick circling the proposed Drop Zone, W-W began to speak.

'Once we have rallied, we will move into the forest here before we bury our 'chutes.'

He paused, allowing the men, especially his own group to get their mind on the job at hand.

'We will then advance west, through the forest until we are just shy of the eastern bank of the Zenesse. We will then scout out the best place to establish our O.P. Once the O.P is established we will occupy and then observe the facility throughout the day. At last light, we will message the Assault Group our findings via Morse pad. We will then, after dark, scout the footbridge and the road bridge, taking our demolition charges with us. It is my intent to prepare the road bridge for demolition on the first visit. We will initiate the timing pencils only once the Assault Force are on their way to the target. Any questions?'

There were no questions. A wave of dread turned in the pit of Jones' stomach. He hated the unreliable timing pencils, hence the need for two different batches. W-W continued.

'Once contact is made, and the shooting starts, we will move to a position covering both bridges, the aim of which to prevent reinforcements coming into the facility via the village of Lychen at the northern end, here. Only upon receiving the order to withdraw, we will move into the facility and rally at the northern jetty.'

W-W circled the tip of the stick at the northern jetty on the aerial photograph. Jones took the stick from him to continue the narrative.

'Let us rewind a little to before the shooting starts. Once each Troop have disembarked from the southern jetty, we will make our way along the bank of the Zenesse for ease of navigation. I don't want you guys wandering among the buildings, because we increase the risk of fratricide, especially if we encounter roaming sentries and the likes. Once we have eyes on the target building identified by the Advance Force, 1 Troop plus my headquarters group will enter the building. We will be taking a few crow bars and sledgehammers should we need to bash our way in, either way, we will be going in. 2 and 3 Troop will provide all round defence outside.'

Jones allowed a pregnant pause for the men to absorb his plan. One of his NCOs in the second row of seats raised a hand. Corporal Mark Rider, 1 Troop.

'What's the layout inside Sir?'

'That's the tricky bit,' Jones confessed, 'we have no idea.'

The rumble of conversation immediately reverberated through the tent. Jones was not in the habit of bluffing his men. He had absolutely no idea what the layout entailed inside whatever became the target building. Jones called for calm.

'The buildings throughout the facility are four to five stories high, not including a cellar, which the Germans are rather fond of. We deal with the ground floor before moving up. We will leave a small team at the foot of the stairs, just in case we need to come back down in a hurry. But let's consider this…'

Jones tailed off just long enough to keep the men engaged.

'It is a hospital ward. Patients as a rule are most certainly unarmed. Even the SS doesn't want wounded personnel waving weapons everywhere. Armed opposition within the building will be minimal. We will be the ones waving weapons around.'

Jones could see the men were somewhat reassured. In his own mind, he felt his rationale had merit. It was a hospital after all. They would have security teams wandering about the facility if anything, but unlikely in the wards at night. Jones need to press on.

'We find our man, and confirm it is him. Intelligence reports state he received gunshot wounds to the lung, hip, and buttocks. Be sure you check him over before we haul him out of there. No doubt he will make a fuss, so be prepared to deal with him and whoever tries to come to his aid. Remember, we are the ones holding the weapons.'

Jones could see the men smirking at the condition of the man.

'We then leave the building and make for the northern jetty. This is where it will get rather tricky, hence my eagerness to get this rehearsed as soon as possible.'

The boys now had their notebooks closed and were all ears. Jones looked to the photograph, highlighting the north jetty.

'Each Troop will be carrying a flare gun, plus a number of different coloured flares. White for illumination, red for fire control and green for the signal for the Cats to approach the jetty one at a time, whilst the other two provide covering fire. The CSM will set up shop in the area of the north jetty and provide illumination should we come under contact either before we enter the target building or as we extract. With the area lit up, the Cat gunners can do their work. Everyone understand so far?'

Jones received a sea of nodding heads.

'Should any of us require fire onto any particular target or area, you will fire a red flare at the target. The Cat gunners will pour fire into that area or building. Only on a green flare will the aircraft taxi in towards the north jetty. I don't care which aircraft comes in what order; I'll leave that to the pilots to fight over. I just want a slick extraction with Arens bundled onto any aircraft. We just need to leave with him. Understood?'

The men answered with nodding heads. Content that the finer detail could be ironed out in rehearsals, Jones summarised the plan, jabbing the photos and map with enthusiasm as he narrated. The mission was bold, but that's what they were trained to undertake. Bold missions. With the men beginning to look fidgety, he looked to Montgomery as he spoke.

'Let's grab something to drink, and take a leak if you need it, before we continue.'

The men did not need any further encouragement, for they almost rose as one, all making for the tea making facilities. Those sat near the front stood, some letting out a stretch, whilst others touched up their own notes. Jones took the opportunity to light a cigarette, quietly hoping one of the boys would bring back a cup of tea for the boss. W-W, hands in pockets sauntered in close. Blowing out smoke, Jones looked up at him.

'You okay?'

'Yeah. Just eager to get on with this.'

'Me too.'

Montgomery arrived with a cup in each hand, the steam of the welcome content spiralling lazily. He offered both cups to the officers.

'There you go, gents.'

Both officers thanked the sergeant major as he went back to herd the troops into some kind of orderly queue. With the warm cup in both hands, Jones gave W-W a concerned look.

'If you'd missed this one out, Matt, I wouldn't blame you.'

W-W frowned at the concern.

'My wife is buggering off back to Canada, she's taking my dog, and my street is wrecked. What would be the bloody point?'

Jones straightened, for his deputy's response was rather spiteful. W-W, flush in the cheeks sighed deeply before seeking refuge in his tea.

'Sorry. I didn't mean to bite your head off.'

Jones smiled, reaching up to pat him on the shoulder.

'I asked for it, don't fret.'

After ten minutes, Montgomery had the men back in their seats, all nursing mugs of tea, some still with cigarettes hanging from their lips. Some officers would consider the men rude, but Jones was not offended by such trite issues. If they were smoking and drinking tea, that meant they were not falling asleep. Being the narrator, he ensured his own cigarette was extinguished before he let out an exaggerated cough. The men settled.

'Let's talk 'Actions On.'

Jones then embarked on discussing contingencies for any issues that could occur on the mission. He addressed them in chronological order. The issues ranged from one of the aircraft having to turn back due to malfunction, conduct should Swedish authorities take them into custody, what if Arens is killed in the operation to capture him? Jones left no stone unturned until both he and the men, who also had the opportunity to contribute and challenge the plan had addressed all that could go wrong with the mission. Once they had dealt with the issues facing them, the officers and men of Major Fynlay Jones' Commando Company were content. Jones looked to the rear of the tent and could see Montgomery approaching. Now it was his turn.

The CSM picked his way around the audience, pulling his notebook from his smock. Given his kudos as the most senior soldier in the company, the men fell silent. Anyone armed with a notebook opened it, for they would need to take notes.

'Service Support,' Montgomery announced, 'pin yer ears back.'

Jones looked on as Montgomery went about delivering his logistical requirements for the operation. He addressed a number of issues, such as weapons, their ancillaries. The ammunition required for each type. Regarding the latter, he gave instruction that he would supply the Advance Force with their ammunition at the reservoir before they headed for Glasgow to board their aircraft. He would then distribute ammunition to the main group. Ammunition, casualties, and prisoners was very much in the remit of a Company Sergeant Major, not to mention discipline when in barracks. He then spoke of rations and water to be carried by each man. Rations would be light since the operation was to be a raid and not an enduring task. As for water, the men would carry at least one full bottle on them, with the means of sterilising any water they refill with from the many lakes that surrounded the target location.

He then spoke of each man carrying two empty sandbags on their person. The plan was to have Arens taken into their custody and hooded for the return trip back to where they would RV with the Americans. What the Americans did with him once they handed him over was their business.

Each eight-man Section was to have one sledgehammer and one crowbar, should they have to break into the target building. Jones and his men had no idea as to whether or not they were locked down at night, so had to have the means to overcome the problem. Radio sets were to be, as usual, packed in their bergens, with the Advance Force having the means to rig up an antenna should they have issues speaking with the main group moored off the Swedish coast. It was vital both parties could speak to each other.

Medical kits were to be carried one per section. Tourniquets and morphine would be carried in the same smock pocket on every individual. The method to the madness was so that no time was wasted looking for those items on the man that was bleeding to death. Field dressings would be carried in another nominated pocket, the reason being much the same.

Flare guns plus cartridges would be carried by Section Commanders. Montgomery questioned the men regarding what coloured flare was for what purpose. The men answered as one, all having paid attention, which pleased Montgomery and the officers that flanked him. With his concerns taken care of, the sergeant major raised his hand as he closed his notebook, the men beginning to chat amongst themselves.

'Listen up boys.'

The men looked to him, their chatter falling away. He nodded as he spoke.

'We leave no wounded behind. Understand?'

'Sir!' the men answered as one.

'Make no mistake, they will not take kindly to us upsetting their lakeside resort. So, we haul everyone out. The dead, however, are dead. Make of that what you will.'

Silence hung heavy in the tent as Montgomery looked to W-W for he would deliver the next instalment, Command and Signals. In the absence of an artillery officer to call the time check, W-W called it, so every watch carried on the company was to the second in tandem with everyone else. He directed radio issues to the Yeoman of Signals, who would issue out frequencies once they were published to him. With the orders wrapping up, Jones then spoke of another issue.

'Gents, just a quick one if I may.'

The men calmed down from conversing to look in at him. Jones cleared his throat.

'A situation that applies to all of us deploying in the next few days is regarding what happens if we have to walk out of there.'

The topic had the men rendered mute as Jones looked to the pilots in particular.

'Should we find ourselves not in a position to fly out, we still need to get Arens out. So, I suggest we make our way to the drop zone where the Advance Force came in and rally there. We can call for our London friends who will let the Americans know where to collect him. After that, we will lay low in the forest until they can recover the rest of us. If anyone has any other suggestions, I'm all ears.'

Jones received no alternative suggestions as he looked to Hook stood at the back. Content the backup plan was basic, but could work, he briefed the men up on a rather sensitive issue on his agenda before they were dismissed for the evening.

'Make no mistake, we will certainly be kicking the hornets' nest when we grab Arens. I demand that all of you only take identification discs and your paybook to prove who you are should you come to be in their custody. No photographs of Arens will be taken onboard aircraft, as the Company Quartermaster will be collecting them in. In addition, no photographs of family, or your wedding rings for that matter. We will go behind enemy lines as sterile as we can be. Any questions?'

There were none, since for most, it was not their first mission behind enemy lines. Content the men understood what was at stake, he forced a smile and a nod.

'Alright then, tomorrow morning we will build targetry for us to rehearse on. Once they are built, we will then begin working with the aircraft. Dismissed.'

As the men rose and began shuffling out of the tent, Hook picked his way down the side towards where Jones and W-W remained standing, along with the pilots. Jones was pleased to see him smiling.

'Should you have to get Arens lifted out, I'll be in Edinburgh monitoring radio traffic. I'll get the yeoman to issue a standalone frequency should you need to get him lifted via the drop zone. Lewis will remain with me also, so he can keep whoever needs to know in the picture, and by that I mean Americans.'

'Thank you.' Jones nodded reassured.

17.

In the early morning Scottish mist, wrapped up well and with bellies full, thanks to the chefs seconded from Edinburgh garrison, both Jones and W-W looked on as the men got on with the business of the day. The men nominated to be Catalina gunners were already aboard with their instructors, and the pilots had taxied to the far end of the reservoir so they could get some early morning shooting in. The CSM, assisted by the company quartermaster had put in some regulation targetry against the slope of the northern bank. Nobody would get hurt, the place was as remote as it could get. Automatic gunfire reverberated through the shallow valley, but that was to be expected. Jones doubted anyone would come to investigate, since farmers tended to have the common sense to keep themselves and their livestock well away from trouble. From their elevated position, the two officers could see streams of tracer bullets arcing into the target area, the odd round deflecting skywards upon contact with a rock, whining as it disappeared from view. Both found it impressive to watch, given the distance.

'Some decent fire support.' W-W murmured, blowing into his bare hands, before stuffing them back into his smock pockets. Jones, shoulders hunched as he resisted a chilling gust of wind across the back of his neck, merely nodded.

Further towards the dam, on the northern side of the reservoir, the remainder of the company, including those not deploying on the mission were busy constructing the targetry that would represent the buildings within the facility. After much time consulting the maps and aerial photographs, the scale of the wooden framed, hessian target screens were huge. In a Scottish winter, to have the creaking frame pitched vertical would be a non-starter, for they would just act as a giant sail and keep falling over. The men, with little prompting from their seniors, thought it better to build them so they looked like a series of large, long single ridge tents. The apex of the structures orientated the way the actual buildings would be in the sanatorium. Give or take a yard, the men had the targetry built and pitched where they felt the buildings would be. Both officers were impressed.

Jones looked over to the old wooden jetty that would act as the southern jetty on mission. It was sturdy enough for the men to climb on and off the aircraft, but they had nothing to replicate the northern jetty. He had no Royal Engineers to build one in time, so would, for the sake of rehearsals use just the same jetty. It was not ideal, but he had to go with what he had.

The men were now fitting the large hessian sheeting to the timber frames. The wind howling through the valley was kind enough to allow the men to get most targets finished, the hessian tacked onto the frames. In large white font, the men had painted numbers on both sides of the apex, for the benefit of aerial gunnery practice later on. With the men battling the wind to get the last targets covered and tacked down, the mock-up of the sanatorium was finished, excluding trees for there were none around the reservoir.

Walking through the target area, Jones could now see what the men had achieved. The targets were like a series of large, long tent roofs, minus legs, and sides. They would not replicate the height of the actual structures but allow for target indication and gunnery practice. They did not have the information to practice moving through the buildings, which would just have to be dealt with on the day. Studying the map and photographs with W-W, the boys had got it bang on. Content with the mock-up, Jones allowed the men to return to camp and grab a well-earned late lunch. The men puffed out their cheeks as they looked to their watches. The better part of the day had already gone. Both Montgomery and Gorman joined the officers as the men jogged back to camp.

'That Admin Instruction you sent me, Sir.' Gorman scoffed, 'You weren't kidding about how much hessian and timber I had to get my hands on.'

In return, Jones gave the man a mischievous smile.

'I'm sure the Quartermaster at Spean Bridge was most accommodating when you handed it to his staff.'

'At first he had a bit of a moan, but soon came around.' Gorman confirmed as they walked on.

'How did you manage that?' Montgomery, once in the job Gorman now had asked. Cuffing his nose, Gorman said two words.

'Single malt.'

W-W let out a long sigh.

'And that gentlemen, is how shit gets done around here. I think we should try that tact in London.'

Back in the cookhouse tent, Jones, W-W, and the sergeants nominated to lead their respective Troop in the absence of their Troop Commanders sat together so they could address what needed to be covered during rehearsals. The faint echo of machinegun fire rippled over them as the newly appointed Catalina gunners were put through their paces. With the light beginning to fade,

Jones knew they would soon call it a day and come back to camp.

It was Montgomery that spoke first, licking his thumb as he turned to a fresh page in his notebook.

'I need to speak with the QM at Glasgow. Given the amount of ammo the boys are getting through up there, they'll need to restock before we deploy anyhow.'

'Agreed.' Jones nodded. 'Same will go for fuel too no doubt.'

'I'll chat with him about that too.' Montgomery scribbled on the small page.

'He knows the Catalinas have been stood up for tasking,' W-W attempted to reassure the sergeant major, 'so, in theory you shouldn't get any push back on what we require.'

Montgomery nodded as he stood, stuffing the notebook back into his smock pocket.

'I'll break bread with him right now, so I can gauge when he'll have what we need in time for our deployment. Sirs!'

As Montgomery took his leave, Jones looked up at him, a mischievous smile on his face.

'Play nice Sarn't Major, you might want to try the Single Malt approach yourself.'

'Yeah,' Montgomery scoffed as he pulled his smock a little straighter, 'flowers and a box of chocolates too.'

As the man left the tent, Jones looked to the sergeants who would be leading their men on the mission.

'Right, before we start shooting the targets to bits, we need to master getting on and off the Catalinas without anyone hurting themselves. We only have one jetty to practice on, and we can't be ferrying men to the bank in rubber boats. So that will be our first order of business in the morning. We'll load the men, us included onto the aircraft and taxi around practicing it until it can be as slick as it can be. Agreed?'

W-W and the others nodded. Jones then addressed the next point.

'We need to be able to reboard the aircraft under covering fire, should the whole bloody facility wake up and take offence at our removal of Herr Arens. We'll get this done right in the daytime, but we will have to make sure we can do it in the dark. White light will be provided by the sergeant major, for he will be by the jetty throughout. My main concern is if the Catalinas firing into the facility will be able to steer clear of us as we leg it back to the jetty with Arens.'

A silence fell among the group, for Jones' concerns certainly had merit. The last thing they needed was their own fire support cutting them to ribbons as they extracted from the facility. It would have to be approached with care. The daylight rehearsal could iron out the issues. Jones got their attention once more.

'What we do inside the target building will certainly require a little creative licence. We will guard our entry and exit point whilst the remainder of the group stay as one as we search the wards. I plan to be in the wards with you to confirm Arens identification. Keep studying the photographs you have and be sure to keep on at the boys to do the same.'

Jones had said all he wanted to say at that point, for he felt the rehearsals would give them the confirmation they needed. With the Troop sergeants' content with what needed to be done for the time being, Jones allowed them to return to their men and brief them accordingly. Jones, now alone with W-W nudged his elbow.

'You okay?'

'Sure.'

'Is there anything I've missed?'

W-W frowned. 'What do you mean?'

'Have I missed anything? The plan I mean.'

W-W shrugged.

'Fyn. Keep the plan simple. If it's simple, it's easier to remember. With that Lewis fellow dealing with the grown-up stuff, we're gonna fly in, find this Arens guy, drag him back to the plane, and get the hell out of there.

If anyone tries to stop us, we have three Catalinas plus our own guys to shoot the shit out of the place. Keep it simple.'

Jones could only agree with his friend. He also need not remind himself that most of his men were used to deploying with basic information, because in some fashion or another, the plan would always have to change once the shooting started anyway. He had a basic plan, so he just needed to back his own horse and have thorough rehearsals. W-W returned the nudge as he got to his feet.

'Tea?'

'Great, thank you.'

As W-W made for the teapot, Jones noticed Hook had entered the tent. The man appeared to be searching for someone. Jones raised an arm, to which Hook acknowledged and made his way over. Before he got to the table, W-W got the Colonel's attention and held up an empty cup, to which Hook gave a thumbs up. He sat himself down in front of Jones.

'You okay?' Hook enquired, a look of concern on his face.

'I'm fine, Colonel.' Jones forced a smile. 'What we are about to do is becoming a little overwhelming if I may say so.'

Hook returned a shrug.

'Keep it simple. It's always worked for me.'

Jones pulled a face at his superior.

'Keep it simple?' Jones scoffed,' You attacked a U-boat pen with a fucking submarine.'

Hook shrugged again.

'I wasn't driving it, I had others to do that for me. I just dealt with what happened when we got off the thing. Let the pilots and navigators get you there and back. The gunners to give you fire support, and just focus on getting Arens out of bed and onto the bloody aircraft. That's it.'

'Your extraction from France was hardly simple, Colonel.' Jones was mindful of the company he was in. Hook accepted the observation with a light nod.

'Well, yes, that's the part that you have to make up on the fly. The Germans won't make it easy for you, that's for sure.'

As W-W made his way back over with three mugs of steaming sweet tea, Jones leaned in to Hook, who sat a little straight in response.

'So why did you push further inland and link up with that SAS squadron?'

Hook looked up to W-W accepting the mug. The captain then settled in beside him as he carefully rearranged the mug in his hands as he spoke.

'Before La Rochelle, I was second in company of a company raid on a port in Tunisia. No sooner had things started blowing up thanks to us, the Germans, instead of getting into a shootout with us made for the waterline instead and waited for us there. We had a hell of a time extracting, resulting in us losing good men, including Major Phil Bird who was leading the mission. His death was the very reason I ended up commanding the La Rochelle mission. I did not want a repeat of Tunisia, so I opted to push into the French interior and link up with the SAS. I knew we would not be welcome, but I needed extra manpower and to try and throw the Germans off the scent.'

Hook paused long enough to enjoy the tea. He then gave Jones a wry smile.

'So, once you've got Arens on the plane and out of there, you might find yourself walking to Berlin. The Germans won't expect that.'

Jones eyed his superior over the top of his own mug.

'Not a fucking chance, Sir.'

18.

The following morning, after breakfast, Jones and his men got to work mastering how to board and disembark the Catalina flying boat. With the aircraft moored against the sturdy jetty, each aircraft group went about clambering in and out of the aircraft. To begin with, Jones had all involved in the mission go about the drill in just what they were wearing, minus weapons and their fighting equipment. He saw no point in risking men falling into the frigid water fully kitted, as that would not only risk the life of the unfortunate who was now very wet, but also those who would have to haul him back to the surface. Only once Jones was satisfied that they could carry out the basic function without getting hurt or prematurely wet, did they up the ante and go through the drill again with what they would take into battle.

The equipment was certainly a handicap. The pilots and their chief engineers winced as they stood overlooking the jetty as heavily armed commandos clattered and cursed in and out of the fuselage. The drill was taking longer, and that could pose a real problem when under fire. After a considerable period of time, Jones called a halt to the drill and had the company quartermaster bring up urns of well-earned tea. With plenty of sweet tea consumed, Jones now wanted the assault group to carry out more dynamic evolutions, namely bringing aboard a reluctant scientist, and casualties. The appointed principle who would refuse to come aboard was probably the biggest built commando in the company. The lads assigned to take him aboard looked to their commander, a little perplexed.

Jones merely shrugged.

'If you can get Dobbs to bend to your will, I'm sure a middle aged, scrawny Nazi official should not present a problem. He'll be hooded and will have to be put on the aircraft, so get to it.'

One of the NCO's pulled the two sandbags from his smock and shoved one inside the other, making it double lined. Before Dobbs, the muscular man could react, the NCO had it over his head before a jab in the gut jack-knifed the stunned Dobbs as the lads about him went for his arms now wrapped around his own midriff. In a matter of seconds, Dobbs recovered from the cheap shot and began to fight back. Jones, W-W and Montgomery looked on with interest as the men wrestled with the increasingly angry hooded man. Clenched meaty paws connected with chins and cheekbones as they tried to wrestle him aboard the slightly bobbing Catalina. A well-connected right hook from Dobbs sent the very same NCO that hooded and jabbed him off the pier into the water. With two men breaking away to shed their fighting equipment and weapons in a bid to rescue the weighed down NCO, Dobbs was now getting the upper hand. Unable to keep hold of his preferred punching arm, Dobbs managed to rip off the sandbags and now face his assaulters. His challenge fell flat as the lads were now more preoccupied with getting the heavily laden NCO out of the cold water. W-W looked to Jones, who returned an unconcerned look.

'They'll have darkness and gunfire to contend with too.'

The NCO, free of the frigid water coughed and spluttered his breakfast on to the ground in front of him. Relieved that he had not drowned, the men patted him on the back before he was offered the huge hand of Dobbs who hauled him to his feet. Dobbs held hold of him until he was steady. Both the NCO and Jones eyed each other.

'You okay?'

'Yes, Sir.' The NCO belched, bringing up more breakfast and reservoir water. Dobbs stepped away as the man bent double, hands on his knees, his Thompson swinging down his right side. Jones joined the men on the jetty.

'I'm not gonna labour the point lads, but come the day of the race, we may have to deal with this kind of thing in the dark, and plenty of shooting going on. Know what I mean?'

The men nodded. Jones looked to the NCO.

'Get back to camp and get out of that wet gear. It'll be a long day for you in we keep you up here soaking wet.'

Jones then looked to Dobbs.

'Go with him, just in case the cold gets the better of him on the jog back.'

'Yes sir.'

With Dobbs and the NCO jogging away back to camp, Jones had the men continued practicing getting on and off the aircraft. This time he had the men carrying 'wounded' men onto the jetty prior to boarding. It was an intricate, time-consuming operation, in daylight never mind at night. He now brought into the rehearsals the RAF crews. With each aircraft's allocation of commandos, he had the pilots taxi the Catalinas in a methodical fashion so whilst one was loading its troops the other two would be stood off, providing covering fire. No live firing would take place until the drill was good enough to progress on to that. Jones wanted to address each rehearsal chronologically.

Once all concerned were satisfied that getting on and off the aircraft was dealt with, Jones then moved them on to fire control measures. With the aircraft manned with aircrew and gunners, Jones and one NCO at a time occupied the jetty, armed with a flare gun and plenty of red flare cartridges, whilst the remainder of the company moved back to the dam so to avoid any potential ricochets. With the Catalinas bobbing in a loose triangle formation on the water facing east, their ports side blister gunners could all engaged any of the numbered targets that represented buildings on the actual target.

With the three aircraft loitering menacingly on the water behind them, Jones and the NCO agreed that they should carry out the new drill on their bellies. Given that the real operation would be done in darkness, and with the real prospect of incoming fire, they would want to make themselves as small as possible in the potential crossfire between the Germans and the Catalinas. The drill would be carried out in the form of two methods, the first would be via radio communication, where the caller would call out the number of the structure that required strafing, or enough to orientate the gunners to enemy troops nearest the building in question. It was not an exact science. The second would be that of red flares, should communications be difficult or the need for fire support was grave. Jones, who had form for leading by example, called the Catalinas.

'Charlie-Charlie Alpha Callsigns, Building Six, Building Six, Over.'

The double call of Charlie to the Alpha Callsigns indicated that all aircraft listen in to the call. Only one however would be required to respond.

'Charlie Three, roger! Building Six, Out!'

As both Jones and the NCO remained prone on the jetty, streams of red tracer bullets reached out and splashed through and around the target screen, which represented the Hohenlychen church, furthest to their left. Jones wanted assurance that his gunners could identify the target called before calling fire in closer. With the tracer bullets slicing through the hessian screens, some howling as they deflected off hard surfaces beneath, Jones called a halt to the fire.

'Check fire, check fire!'

Without a vocal response from the aircraft gunners, the firing ceased. The echo of the cacophony rolling out over the hills. Jones then had the NCO call in fire onto Building Five, which represented what they deduced to be the administration offices within the actual facility. The snapping of the tracer bullets cutting close to their left side made both men, seasoned to incoming fire flinch all the same. The NCO, satisfied that the hessian screen had been strafed sufficiently, called a halt to the firing.

Both men on the jetty then wriggled lower, before the NCO called for fire onto Building Four, the supposed Officer Ward, which sat slightly off centre to the left of the jetty. They braced, for what would be very close fire support. The gunners, aware of how close their fire would be, kept their burst short and controlled. The tracer bullets buffeted the ears of the two men hugging the jetty. It was most certainly close. The gunners ceased firing of their own accord before calling the jetty men on the radio.

'Boss… upper floors won't be a problem, but ground floor fire will certainly be tight.'

Both men on the jetty nodded to each other as Jones responded.

'Yeah, roger that. We certainly got a haircut with that lot.'

Jones dismissed the NCO to have another join him on the jetty. The fire control rehearsal was certainly beneficial. It gave the gunners more range time, and also gave the NCOs calling in the fire an appreciation of how tight things would be on the jetty for real. Jones put as many men through the daytime rehearsal as he could before the fading light would make it too dangerous for the gunners to shoot without artificial light from white flares. As the day became twilight, Jones had the company plus the Catalinas crews take their evening meal at the dam. A hearty thick meaty stew, with plenty of bread, butter and tea was in order for the night grew even more bitter. Once the men were fed and watered, they went out to the next, rather dangerous phase of their rehearsals.

Fire control at night.

19.

'Otto darling, shall I run your bath?'

Mortens did not hear Astrid's offer. He was far too engrossed in what he witnessed earlier that day outside the Officer Ward when the ashen faced man staggered from the cellar before collapsing. He recalled how his apparent colleagues were quick to come to his aid, and even curt with him as he came to offer assistance. The threat of an Oder assignment irked Mortens for he only wished to help the troubled man.

'Otto?'

Astrid's call had him flinch from his reverie.

'What?'

'The goulash not to your liking?'

'What?'

Mortens looked to the meal before him, now cold. Astrid was an excellent cook, and they were thankful that the army cooks that fed the Soldier Ward were generous with what they could offer in return for cigarettes and recommendations that they remain in Hohenlychen. In his initial tour of the facility, when he took over as Head of Security, the Chief Cook asked rather bashfully if he and his kitchen staff could remain since they preferred the lakeside facility to the drab and foreboding Ravensbruck facility. Mortens had made no promises, but he assured the Chief that he would put in a good word with his superiors. The Chief was more than happy with that. Since then, Astrid was amazed at some of the food stuffs and sundries her husband had managed to bring home. The quantity certainly outweighed what she would have had to cook with if she had remained at with her parents. There was even enough left over after the evening meal for Tommy to enjoy the leftovers.

Mortens pushed the plate away.

'I'm not hungry.'

As Astrid shook her head and returned to clearing the dishes, Tommy looked up at his master, with his beautiful chestnut eyes fixed on him. In his periphery, Mortens knew Tommy was waiting for his dinner. Without so much as a ruffle of his ears, Mortens scooped up the plate and passed it down. Before he could release the plate, the German Shepherd was scoffing away at the meat chunks in the thick gravy, the boiled potatoes tumbling away onto the wooden floor.

'Really, Otto.' Astrid clucked as she shook her head. 'He has a bowl; I don't want him eating off our plates.'

'Stop crowing woman!' Mortens responded curtly, only to regret it the moment she turned open mouthed. Sheepishly, he got to his feet.

'Sorry, my love. I'm out of sorts.'

'Manners too, I would say.'

Pulling the well licked plate from the floor, Mortens strode over, placing it in the hot, soapy water.

'Sorry.'

Astrid pointed a soapy finger at her cheek.

'Kiss me and make coffee. I might find it in myself to forgive you.'

He did as she commanded before turning his attention to the stove. As he lit the hob, he spoke over his shoulder.

'I'm going back into work.'

'Whatever for?'

'There's something I need to do.'

'Can it not wait till tomorrow?'

'Not really. This work takes place at night.'

'What work?'

Mortens turned to his wife, who dried her hands as she faced him.

'I'm not entirely sure.'

Astrid draped the tea towel over the drying crockery.

'Otto, what troubles you so?'

Mortens leaned against the sink next to her, arms folded.

'Something is not quite right here.'

'What do you mean?'

Mortens breathed deeply before going on.

'Ever since I took over this assignment, I have this feeling in my guts that all is not what it seems here.'

Astrid turned to face him.

'It's a hospital, Otto. No one is asking you to be a surgeon.'

'I know, I know,' Mortens responded, 'but it feels like I'm not welcome here at all.'

'You're Head of Security Otto,' Astrid scoffed, 'you're here to keep them safe, and they've clearly had a good run of things without you till now.'

'Do you not feel welcome here?' Mortens asked her. Astrid turned back to the sink, shrugging.

'The other wives are pleasant enough. They say hello when I go shopping, but I've yet to get to know them. Their husbands are of a medical profession I would assume, so I could be made to feel a little like an outsider.'

'Does that bother you?'

'A little. At home, it was a little crowded with Tommy in with us, but I had my friends. Here, it's just another posting I must get used to.'

Mortens stood behind his wife, sliding his arms around her waist as he kissed her neck.

'I'm sorry if you feel out of sorts here. I was just grateful not to get shipped out to the Oder front.'

Astrid stroked his bare forearms, as she peered through the slim gap in the blackout curtains.

'Will the Soviets come here?'

'What do you mean?'

'The Oder is not far from here. Are we safe?'

Mortens planted a long, lingering kiss under her right ear. She smelled of soap.

'We are safe, Astrid.'

Astrid rolled her head against his. Hohenlychen was certainly a place to get used to, but she had Otto with her, and that was all that mattered to her. She patted him on the forearms.

'Right, Otto Mortens, if you're going back into work, get on with it. I don't want you out all night, and that's an order.'

He stepped back, clicking his heels.

'Understood, Fraulien.'

Coming to the boil, he finished preparing her coffee before rolling down his shirt sleeves and fetching his tunic. Astrid frowned a little.

'Do you have to be in uniform?'

Pulling his right arm into the tunic, he pulled a face.

'I'm going back to work, not drinks with the Commandant.'

Astrid shrugged as she put the cup to her lips. Mortens whistled for Tommy as he buttoned himself up. Astrid snorted.

'I swear you spend more time with him than you do me.'

'Hey,' Mortens gave off a frown, 'Tommy is my partner in crime, you know that. Besides, he warns the lads when I'm coming. What I can't see, I can't grieve over.'

Astrid raised an inquisitive eyebrow.

'Isn't that the very thing that troubles you?'

Tommy arrived at his master's side. Mortens teased his ears as he looked to his wife.

'You have a point there.'

After last light, the village of Lychen was blacked out, according to regulations. The imposing sanatorium too was cloaked in darkness. Tommy panted and trotted ahead unleashed as Mortens strolled behind. The Head of Security nodded greetings to those coming home late from the facility, their torch beams bobbing as they walked. It was too dark to see rank, so he just ensured he kept the salutation polite, to which they replied in kind. As he crossed the road bridge into the open site of the sanatorium, it still irked him that the security measures in place were lacklustre at best. On the slim wooden footbridge to his left, Tommy loitered about, sniffing at something that interested him. The footbridge spanned a narrow bottle neck of water that allowed patients and their minders to venture out and explore the other side of the Zenesse. Mortens wondered if there had been any security patrols over there of late.

Calling Tommy back to him, to which the German Shepherd complied, Mortens turned his head in time to catch two roaming sentries flicking away their cigarettes. The glowing tips giving them away. Mortens snorted as he shook his head a little. As he drew close, the helmeted sentries pulled themselves to attention. They knew the Head of Security had a dog.

'Good evening Sir.' One of them offered. No salutes, which pleased Mortens, for they were outside, and he could never be certain who was watching. He knew that honey always worked better than vinegar, so he had to play his next move wisely if he was to get any information out of the soldiers. He fished out his cigarette case, offering the sentries before taking one himself. Both looked to each other. They both shrugged in unison, after all, if the boss offers, you cannot get in trouble for accepting. With his own cigarette now lit, he cupped his lighter under the chin of each of them as they drew in air to get the tobacco glowing. All three men savoured the first inhale before any of them spoke.

'Thank you, Sir.' The broader of the two responded. Mortens nodded as he lingered on his a little longer. He had plenty of time, and if they were fresh on duty, so did they. With him finally exhaling, he watched as the ash grey smoke climbed lazily in the still night air. He removed his field cap, tucking it up under his right arm, very casual. The sentries, a little nervous at first soon relaxed in his presence, especially when Tommy snaffled at their trouser pockets for treats. With a sharp snap of his masters' fingers, Tommy came to heel before losing interest and sauntered off into the darkness.

All three men looked after him. Mortens broke the silence.

'I swear children would be more obedient.'

The sentries snorted in response. Mortens looked to them.

'Either of you have children?'

Both looked to each other embarrassingly before shaking their heads.

'No, no Sir.' The slimer sentry answered, 'I'm not long out of High School.'

Surprised at the response, Mortens stepped in closer. In the low light, he had failed to identify the ages of the men. The slimer one was indeed childlike, and the other, broader one not much older.

Just kids, Mortens confirmed. The situation at the facility was now all the more farcical. It now mattered little. They were in uniform, serving the Fatherland, when they should have still been in some kind of apprenticeship. Mortens knew that the war had certainly robbed the youth of their innocence, especially in Germany.

He took another pull of his cigarette before speaking again.

'Is this your first posting?'

Both soldiers nodded.

'Yes Sir.' The broader one answered, 'We were initially assigned to Ravensbruck, but the Commandant didn't want kids in the main facility, so had us shipped here.'

'Does it bother you?' Mortens challenged. Both glanced inwards at each other slightly.

'What do you mean, Sir?'

'That he referred to you as 'kids,' or that he sent you here?'

In the gloom, Mortens could see their shoulders relax as they pulled on the own cigarettes.

'No Sir.' The slimer one responded. 'This place beats the main camp, hands down. Guard shifts here are pretty straight forward, and we can go swimming in the soldier ward pool.'

'Do you only work nights?'

'Sir?'

'Guard duties. Do you only patrol at night?'

'It depends. The duty Scharfuhrer sets the roster. We rotate through as fairly as he can make it.'

'Nice.' Mortens nodded as he looked about for Tommy. He looked over at the wooden footbridge, pointing as he did so.

'Ever patrol that side of the water?'

'We have done, but not recently, Sir.' Broader man spoke.

'Why not?'

'Just speaking personally, Sir. No doubt patrols go out there all the time.'

Mortens cut them both a friendly smile.

'Let's hope so. When did you last go over there?'

'A month ago, maybe. Can't be sure, Sir.'

Mortens folded his arms as he nodded slightly. He observed the Zenesse. The thick forest dominated the far bank, almost touching the waterline in places. Mortens thoughts wandered to the fact that not only was his facility open planned, but he probably had a lacklustre patrol programme taking in the area beyond the footbridge. Another item to address on ever growing list of concerns. He knew it would be unfair to reprimand the young soldiers stood with him, or the Scharfuhrer in charge of them for that matter. He would take it upon himself to implement changes to the security regime first thing in the morning. He would no longer run them by his superiors in Ravensbruck, for they would no doubt come to hear of them from one of the clucking hens in their white coats soon enough.

Turning slowly to the two sentries, one of whom was now ruffling Tommy's ears, Mortens indicated the Officer Ward.

'The men in white coats. Who are they?'

'Sir?' Slimer man asked, not being chastised by the German Shepherd.

'Earlier today, I saw a group of men in white coats leave via the cellar access. One of whom was not at all well. What's down there?'

'Not sure, if I'm honest, Sir.' Slimer man shrugged. Broader man stood up straight as Tommy took off, hoping the soldier would play with him.

'Have you seen them come and go?' Mortens challenged. Both soldiers looked to each other, as they both nodded in return.

'Most days.' Broader man answered. 'But the trucks only come at night.'

Now we were getting somewhere, Mortens checked himself.

'Trucks?'

'Stretcher cases mostly.' Slimer man offered. 'Females from Ravensbruck.'

'Females?'

'Yes Sir. Poles mostly. I think they bring Gyps here too.'

'Gyps?' Mortens cocked an eyebrow. Slimer man cleared his throat as he rubbed out his cigarette with his boot heel.

'Gypsies. Begging your pardon Sir.'

'Why would they bring them here?' Mortens question was rhetorical as he put his hands on his hips as Tommy pestered around him.

'No idea Sir. They come and go at night.'

'How many trucks?' Mortens demanded as he tossed the spent cigarette away.

'One Sir. One a night.'

'A night?'

'Yes Sir.'

'Do any of them leave?'

'Who Sir?'

'Those on the trucks?'

'I think so. Only stretcher cases.'

Mortens turned his attention to the broader man.

'Don't they all come on stretchers?'

'Not all Sir.' Broader man answered, brushing Tommy's snout from his crutch. Mortens snapped his fingers again, sending Tommy into the darkness once more.

'Some arrive on foot.'

'But none walk out?'

Both soldiers shook their heads.

'Not the ones we've seen, Sir.'

Mortens puffed out his cheeks as he ran his free hand through his hair. Many thoughts ran through his head as he looked up at the imposing blacked out buildings. The very fact that he was unaware of some of the activities taking place in a facility where his main duty was to ensure he knew everything that was going on troubled him. He glanced at his watch. The night was young, so there was every chance he could witness the arrival of this lone truck from Ravensbruck.

'Is there anything else you require of us, Sir?'

Mortens was oblivious as he looked in all directions, even up at the clear starred studded sky.

'Sir?'

'Yes?' Mortens snapped out of his thoughts. Both soldiers were looking in at him.

'Do you require anything more of us, Sir?' Broader man asked.

'Erm, no.' Mortens responded, looking for Tommy. 'Thank you, gentlemen. If you see me wandering about this evening. Just doing my rounds.'

'Very good Sir.'

As the two sentries moved away, Tommy appeared from the direction of the footbridge, taking Mortens by surprise, for he was fixated on the buildings. He ruffled the dogs' ears in reassurance.

'Let's get you to the office. Can't have you giving me away.'

If there was anything good about owning a dog, particularly in the job he was in, it was the fact that whoever was up to no good got plenty of warning that Mortens was coming thanks to Tommy. True to form, the German Shepherd would dash into the headquarters building and make a nuisance of himself with whoever happened to be in there. He was always received well, not just for the fact that his owner was the head of security, but as a welcome relief to what could be a rather mundane duty.

Given the late hour, Tommy scoured the offices for someone to chastise. As Mortens followed him in, he could hear commotion from one of the rooms.

'Tommy, shit! Get dressed!'

No sooner had Mortens entered where the commotion was coming from, was he surprised to see Lucy, his clerk, very flushed in the face stood next to a bare headed Scharfuhrer, just as flushed, his tunic open and his shirt caught in his trouser zip. The Scharfuhrer pulled himself to attention, whilst Tommy sniffed about his crotch. Not taking his eyes off the SS Officer stood at the threshold, the dishevelled young man pushed the dog away.

Tommy was not taking the hint.

'Good evening, Sir.' Lucy offered, her right hand sweeping a stray lock of hair from her face, tucking it behind her ear. 'I didn't think you'd be in tonight.'

'Clearly.' Mortens smirked, before clicking his fingers which brought the energetic Tommy to heel at his side. The young Scharfuhrer flinched a little as he was not sure what to do. Deliberately, Mortens spoke to him whilst paying attention to the dog.

'Scharfuhrer, I trust you are on duty this evening?'

'Yes Sir.'

'May I suggest you return to the Guardroom, where your talents would be put to better use.'

'Yes Sir.'

The Scharfuhrer dressed himself as Lucy planted him a generous kiss on the lips. They had been caught bang to rights, so why try to hide her feelings now. Mortens noticed it in his periphery and chose to remain where he was just to toy with the forlorn young man. He was not going to send the young man to the Oder front for screwing his girlfriend in her office, after all, her boss was supposed to be at home by this hour. He doubted it was the first time such a liaison had taken place on her desk. As the Scharfuhrer shuffled passed the officer and dog, Mortens held up a hand to get his attention. Now dressed to a standard befitting an NCO in the SS, Mortens smiled.

'Scharfuhrer, how long have you been stationed here?'

'Sir?'

Mortens spoke on, indicating both the young man and Lucy.

'Are you two exclusive?'

'Yes Sir.' The Scharfuhrer raised his chin a little, proud of the fact. Mortens glanced at Lucy, who too was smiling.

'One can only assume that taking her to barracks, or you to her home is out of the question?'

'Yes Sir,' Lucy answered, 'my parents would go mad, and I'm not sharing his bunk surrounded by the idiots he calls comrades.'

'Fair point.' Mortens smiled, 'Wait here.'

Mortens left the couple as he went to his own office. From a key press behind his office door, he fetched a long, tired looking key. He returned, handing it to Lucy.

'Duty officers' bunk. It's not the Adlon, but from what I've seen so far is that the officers return to their lodgings in the village once they have done their rounds, so I doubt you'll be disturbed in future.'

Lucy frowned a little before looking at the key in her small hands. It then dawned on her the gesture made by her boss. She returned a warm smile, her eyes a little glazed.

'Thank you, Sir. We really appreciate it, don't we Paul?'

'Err, Yes. Yes we do. Thank you Sir.'

'Right then,' Mortens nodded to the pair of them, 'piss off the pair of you, I've got shit to do.'

Lucy and her beau needed not a second order as the girl gathered up her coat and handbag from the coat stand by the door. As they both stepped off, arm in arm down the corridor, Mortens called to the Scharfuhrer.

'Scharfuhrer?'

'Yes Sir?' the couple halted, looking back at the officer. Mortens was rubbing the end of his nose, a frown on his face.

'How often do patrols go out over the footbridge before I arrived?'

'Sir?'

'The woods on the far bank of the Zenesse, how often are they patrolled?'

'I've been here a while Sir, and I've only been over there once.'

Mortens bit his lip as he waved a dismissive hand. As the couple disappeared into the darkness, Mortens looked to the curled-up, dozing Tommy.

'We need to change that.'

20.

Unfortunately for Mortens, his own office did not allow him line of sight to the main entrance of the Officer Ward. He knew from his many walks through the sanatorium grounds with Tommy that there were a set of double doors to the right of the main entrance that led into the cellar of the structure. Perched on the window ledge in Lucy's office, he wished now he had asked the two sentries which side did the apparent truck park. He could always wander in plain sight, torch in hand. He doubted if anyone would challenge him. He just preferred to be indoors as long as he could, for the nights were still very cold.

After his umpteenth cigarette, and numerous cups of coffee, Mortens had yet to see the illusive lone truck arrive. Tommy, no stranger to sleeping in with Lucy during the day had not moved, which was ideal for

Mortens. He would lock the dog in the building, so not to betray his presence. After a few hours, Tommy stirred a little as Mortens returned from a much-needed toilet. Putting on his field cap, he fetched a torch from the filing cabinet behind the door before heading out into the blacked-out grounds, pulling the door shut as he went.

As much as he wanted to be subtle, he could not afford for sentries to apprehend him for sneaking about beneath the trees, so he opted for the bold approach. Torch on, cigarette lit. He orbited the barracks in a wide clockwise fashion, acknowledging the salutes of soldiers he encountered. Nothing out of sorts in that regard. Given the relaxed atmosphere of the facility, he doubted if the soldiers paid any attention to the comings and goings from the Officer Ward. After all, soldiers seldom cared for the affairs of their officers at the best of times. Why pay any attention to a truck turning up in the middle of the night?

Mortens paced slowly out as far as the rail tracks that led to the small and unremarkable train station, where the line terminated. The sanatorium sat at the end of a main branch line that ran from Berlin out north to Rostock. By rights you could alight the train and just hop off the platform and make a direct line for whatever building you wished. Not that a German soldier would ever do such a thing. Running parallel to the rail line was a road that took you north into Lychen village or right into the sanatorium grounds via the Guardroom. Mortens made his way slowly to the Guardroom, hoping to appear genuine in his reason for being there.

As predicted, the SS troopers crashed to attention upon his entering the building, the sentries outside the only ones to remain unfazed, for they now put on a good show of looking vigilant. Unsure how long he would have to wait for this truck to arrive, he went about questioning the soldiers about patrols on the far side of the Zenesse. Out of the twelve he spoke with, only two, one of which was the Scharfuhrer he had come to meet earlier. Mortens did not want to wander the grounds all night, so diverted the topics away from the facility. He engaged the men in talk of women, beer, pay and leave. They all professed that they always enjoyed the Hohenlychen duties, for they were relaxed, they could go swimming when off duty, and in the summer, the facility was in bloom and could almost be mistaken for a lakeside resort. None of them enjoyed working in Ravensbruck. Now relaxed in each other's company, Mortens spoke of Norway. The endless daylight in the summer which played havoc with your body clock, and then the endless darkness of winter that sapped your soul. Scandinavia offered no middle ground.

'No wonder the Vikings ventured overseas,' he put to the men in good humour.

It was just after midnight when a lone truck rattled up to the sentries on the road outside the Guardroom. Excusing himself from the conversation with the

Scharfuhrer, Mortens stepped out of the Guardroom and casually walked on behind the truck as it chugged away into the facility. With the truck confined to the road network that meandered around the buildings, Mortens cut across the grass under the sparse trees to ensure he could observe what came out the back of the truck. After skirting clockwise around the large, imposing Soldier Ward, he found himself on the south eastern corner of the building, with an unobstructed view of the main entrance of the Officer Ward and the truck now reversing up to it.

The Opel engine cut out with a rattle, an indication to Mortens that the truck had seen too much mileage and not enough servicing. True to form, the men manning the cab climbed out without the interior light betraying blackout regulations. Mortens could make out three individuals stood at the back of the truck as they slowly lowered the tail gate. The canvas flap that would prevent you from seeing in to the cargo bay suddenly flipped up. That made at least four soldiers in the truck. As the first walking individual was lowered down from the cargo bay, Mortens noted a number of white coated individuals emerging from the cellar entrance. The white coats clustered together made it difficult for him to count how many there were. At least three of them. A hunched frame, covered in a blanket shuffled among them and was then ushered down into the bowels of the building. Two more walkers followed in the same manner. Mortens them observed the first stretcher case being slowly removed from the high cargo bay. The soldiers did the heavy lifting, whilst the white clad men looked on. Slowly, three stretchers in total came off the truck. As the last one went out of sight, Mortens noticed the truck was now unattended. For how long he could not be certain. For a moment, he toyed with the notion of casually walking over, torch on as if he were just conducting his rounds. He would no doubt be given the same warm reception he had be subjected to earlier that afternoon. He decided to remain where he was and let the transaction play out.

After what felt like a lifetime, but was in fact only a few minutes, Mortens observed the soldiers emerge from the cellar with a stretcher between them. This time, they lifted and shoved the stretcher into the cargo bay without much care. Mortens knew by how cumbersome it was that it held a body. The men went about fetching three more stretchers, the last requiring two of the men to climb aboard and no doubt, make room. With the last stretcher aboard, one of the soldiers remained in the rear, whilst the remaining three lifted and slammed the tailgate shut, whilst the soldier in the rear leaned up, pulling the canvas flap back down. As they mounted up in the cab, one of the white coated men emerged from the cellar to watch it leave. As the Opel chugged away, the man in white stepped back out of sight, pulling the doors closed behind him.

Approaching the building as if he were going about his duties, Mortens stopped just short of the broad, shallow steps that led to the main entrance. The dark oak double doors were high, their Reich eagle mounted top centre on each. He leaned right to where the cellar access doors sat in their sunken position. Just dark and plain, no insignia, no signage. Given the blackout regulations, Mortens could not tell if the interior lights were on. Ascending the steps, he thought it would not hurt to try and gain access, after all, he was the head of security for the sanatorium.

The lights within the foyer were turned down, giving off an eerie glow. As he closed the door behind him, the foyer echoed with this boots on the polished parquet flooring. In front of him stood the first flight of stairs that spiralled to the right as they climbed the structure, a large stained-glass window dominating the top of the first flight. The pattern was bright and full of colour. Nothing party orientated, just refreshing to look at. An open door to the left of the stairs led into a room that emitted the faint trace of steam. Mortens had yet to see inside the very wards he was assigned to provide security for, so deduced that they were the showers. Sat at the base of the flight of stairs on the right side sat someone behind a desk, too embroiled in eating something whilst reading a book, for their back was to the main door. As the individual took another bite, the crunch echoed around the foyer. Mortens looked about himself. The walls were bare, save for a fire regulation poster to his left, detailing the occupants as to which muster point they should attend in the event of a fire.

Mortens returned to looking at the chewing slob now cuffing his face, and advanced.

The chewing man was slow to react to the clicking of boots approaching him. Mortens could see the man wore the rank of Scharfuhrer on his collar. The SS man glanced in Mortens direction, and as he went back to his book, his senses became acute to the impending reprimand. The Scharfuhrer spun in his creaking chair before crashing to attention, both book and apple cartwheeling out of sight. As Mortens pulled up at the desk, the SS man delivered his best party salute in the vain hope that the verbal lashing he was about to receive would lessen. Aware that he could pick his own time when to strike, Mortens returned a lacklustre salutation as he pulled off his field cap. Running his free hand through his hair, Mortens gave the impression that he was in the building on urgent business.

'Scharfuhrer. Give that door a knock will you.'

The SS man frowned as he lowered his salute.

'Door, Sir?'

Mortens rolled his eyes as he exaggerated pointing beyond the man. Another pair of plain, metal drab grey doors.

'That door.'

The Scharfuhrer looked sheepishly about the contents of his desk. A wrist watch, Army issue chocolate, a half-drunk cup of whatever, a deck of smutty playing cards plus the lamp perched at the corner. His book and half eaten apple were under the desk somewhere.

'I'm afraid that's not permitted, Sir.'

'Not permitted?' Mortens blinked rapidly at him. The Scharfuhrer nodded with tight lipped smile.

'Besides, I don't have a key for it, Sir.'

'Who does?'

'The Live Tissue Training Team, Sir.'

'The…what?' Mortens asked with raised eyebrows.

'The Live Tissue Training Team, my dear Haupsturmfuhrer.' Another voice answered. Mortens snapped left to see Jurgen Arens stood at the threshold of the shower room. Wrapped in a bathrobe, stood in slippers, his stern face and swept back hair glistening from his ablutions. Pressing his washbag to his hip with one arm, he leaned heavily on a cane with the other. He shuffled into the foyer pulling close to the desk, the Scharfuhrer still at attention. Arens greeted Mortens with a friendly smile.

'From what I've been told,' Arens flicked his head at the plain metal doors, 'great advances are being made regarding getting our wounded soldiers back in the fight sooner than before.'

'How so?' Mortens pressed, to which Arens merely shrugged as he turned to shuffle away.

'How the hell do I know? Not my field of expertise.'

Mortens stepped off after him.

'Is Gebhardt running it?'

Arens stopped to peer over his shoulder, his face no longer friendly.

'Would that be Gruppenfuhrer Gebhardt you speak of, Haupsturmfuhrer?'

Mortens held his tongue and composure as the man sneered at him. He was not about to be dressed down over rank. Arens nodded as he shuffled on.

'The Gruppenfuhrer leads the Live Tissue Training, yes.'

'Why was I not informed of this activity?' Mortens demanded, only to have Arens turn on his heels and shuffle right back at him.

'For heaven's sake, Otto,' Arens hissed, 'the only reason you are here is because I could not bear to have you sent to the Oder front. Do not jeopardise what you have here.'

'What I have here?' Mortens stepped back a pace. Arens nodded enthusiastically.

'Yes, yes. You have Astrid keeping your bed warm, no doubt a beautiful yet humble home, your pest of a dog, plus you happen to be far from the fighting. Don't test their sense of humour Otto, for your own sake.'

'Why do you care?'

'I'm sorry?' Arens flinched at the challenge. Mortens stepped in closer, his fists rising up onto his hips.

'Why would you give a second thought to what I'm trying to achieve here?' He hissed, glancing over Arens shoulder to ensure no one was approaching. 'The facility has all the characteristics of a lakeside holiday resort. It just so happens to have a bunch of soldiers wandering about, pretending to give a shit, just to avoid pulling guard duty at Ravensbruck.'

'My dear Otto,' Arens reciprocated Mortens awareness by ensuring the Scharfuhrer had gone back to his book and apple, 'the whole set up here is to allow those convalescing to relax and not be harangued with military protocol.'

'How am I as head of security supposed to operate in keeping everyone here safe if no one supports me. Is this place just a tethered goat for the Soviets?'

'What do you mean?'

'The Oder front is very quiet right now. I'm not a tactician, I'm a bodyguard by trade and even I know the Soviets won't just sit on their side of the Oder for much longer. We are not that far away.'

Arens knew all too well the geography involved. A determined Soviet thrust through the woods and lakes that surrounded them would be without much resistance. Anyone that could so much as handle a rifle was drafted into the Berlin garrison. Hohenlychen thankfully was an exception. He nodded subtlety at Mortens.

'If it comes to that, will you do something for me, Otto?' Arens voice was low and sincere.

'What's that?'

'Get yourself and Astrid west as quickly as you can. As an SS officer, I don't fancy your chances, or Astrid's for that matter if the Soviets get you.'

Mortens pulled a face.

'I must say, Herr Doctor, I can never tell what you're about to say next.'

'I only me- '

'First you tell me to basically mind my own business, despite the position I hold here,' Mortens spat, 'then you implore me to desert. Not what I was expecting from an Obersturmbannfuhrer.'

'Please.' Arens dismissed, 'You hold more kudos in that regard. At least your security credentials justify your rank and salary. The rank given me merely helps me lobby for what I require to continue with my research. It just looks impressive when written on documents. Why do you think I seldom interact with my battle-scarred peers? I'm a civilian, and they know it.'

'I'm sorry to hear that.' Mortens conceded. Arens gestured for him to follow on.

'Let me show you what I mean.'

The Scientist led Mortens along the wide corridor. The parquet flooring gave of an echo as the slippered man shuffled and the booted officer followed on. As they walked, Mortens could not help but peer into rooms that branched off either side. The rooms were large, high ceilinged with six beds in each. Additional furniture included low slung chairs and a large table clustered at the far end in front of an unlit fire hearth, with side cabinets next to each bed. The occupants were either slouched in bed, or at the table either playing cards, reading correspondence or newspapers. Tobacco smoke hung heavy in each room, pipes being the trend.

'Mine is at the very end.' Arens offered over his shoulder, 'Don't forget your manners.'

'My what?'

As they entered Arens room, he saw that there were only four beds in the same sized room as the others. The omitted beds were now clusters of chairs and coffee tables. By the fire hearth a large easel held situation map boards, with older men, in their bed attire jabbing at it with pencils. Mortens could not help but roll his eyes at the patients' apparent sense of self-importance. Still planning operations as if the Fuhrer would care to listen.

As Arens leaned his cane against what appeared to be his bed, those reading reports through glasses perched on the end of their noses, and those making big gestures over the maps stopped as one to look at him and the uniformed arrival. Mortens took this as his cue to clip his heels to attention and deliver a party salute. The pipe smoking elders, no doubt the same rank of Arens or above nodded their approval of the salutation and went back to their grand plans.

'See.' Arens beamed a smile. 'Tough crowd.'

Feeling a little out of sorts, Mortens wrung his hands.

'Is there anything you need, Doctor?'

Arens eyed his not so friendly peers before waving Mortens closer. He then spoke in a low voice as he sat on the bed.

'Why are all the patients armed?'

'I'm sorry?' Mortens frowned. Arens gave a subtle jerk of his thumb, indicating the bed next to him.

'They all have pistols. Is this normal?'

Tight-lipped, Mortens nodded a little. He knew officers were allowed to keep their side arms, more out of prestige than practicality. Another issue for him to address.

'Are you armed?' Mortens asked, to which Arens puzzled a face.

'Why on earth would I be armed? I'm a scientist.'

'Has there been issues?'

'Two nights ago, we were all woken by gunfire.'

'Really?' Mortens was stunned. Arens nodded.

'One of the fellows on one of the upper floors apparently lost his reason and fired off an entire magazine into the ceiling.'

Mortens stood straight, his free hand pinching the bridge of his nose as he took a long, deep breath. He was unaware of the whole incident. Was there to be no end to the lunacy in which the whole place was run?

He opened his eyes to see Arens peering either side of him. Mortens frowned at the activity. Before he could enquire, Arens looked up at him.

'Are you not meant to be armed?'

Mortens instinctively rubbed a hand on his right hip. He then smiled reassuringly at Arens.

'I leave it in my desk when I go home. I must have forgotten to put it back on.'

Arens appeared a little concerned but chose not to pursue the issue. Instead, he forced a smile.

'I'm sure you have things in hand, Haupsturmfuhrer. Enjoy what remains of your evening, and don't be a stranger. As you can see, I'm not part of their headquarters.'

The chill of the night air cut through Mortens as he stepped out onto the steps. The building, especially Arens room was warm, cosy and welcoming. He put a cigarette to his lips, the placebo of warmth about to fill him once he had it lit. As he savoured the cigarette, he thought on Arens predicament. The man was alone. His peers loathed to interact with a man that was SS in name only. He checked himself to visit the man more often. They were hardly friends, but Arens had certainly assisted in his assignment to the facility. Perhaps he could bring Arens home for a meal one evening. It was risky since Arens knew enough about Paula in Norway, and a little too much wine and cognac could have something slip. Mortens would think on it.

It would not be the only thing Mortens would need to think on. He had some kind of experiment being conducted in the bowels of the very building beneath his feet. Officer patients were armed and shooting the ceiling whilst embroiled in a nightmare. He was not happy with any of it but had to appear proficient in his duties of guarding the facility. From whom, he could not be sure, given that the very men enjoying the facilities were waving pistols around in their sleep. He had to challenge that policy. The white coated experiments were one thing, but he did not need patients running about, shooting at their own shadows.

With his cigarette exhausted, he made off back to his office. As he picked his way by torchlight under the sparse canopy, the faint drone of aircraft filled his ears. As the drone grew to its loudest, he looked up through the leafless branches to see what aircraft it was, but it had no lights on until it banked over the Zenesse. Intrigued since it had come over very low, Mortens made for the jetty opposite the Officer Ward. The aircraft was out of sight to him at the southern end of the lake, but he heard a change in engine pitch as it touched down on the water. A flying boat. With lights on, it taxied around the short headland and appeared to head for where he stood on the jetty. Given how loud the engines buffeted his ears, Mortens turned to see if any hospital staff were coming to greet them.

Nothing. Just him.

Mortens stepped back off the jetty, keen to see what action was to take place upon the aircraft's arrival. As the huge aircraft drew up alongside, Mortens identified it as a Blohm and Voss 222. The wash from the three propellers on the port side chastised Mortens as he grabbed his field cap before he lost it. The spindly branches above him whined and swirled as the aircraft gingerly perched its nose at the end of the jetty before the engines cut out. Straightening himself once more, Mortens observed the port side nose door open with a member of its crew hoping out with a coil of rope, quickly mooring the aircraft to the jetty. Once the aircraft was braced, the crewman strode along the peer, pulling of their helmet and headset as they went, shaking their head as they ran their fingers through their hair. Mortens made himself known.

'You there?'

The crewman stopped, not sure where the voice had come from. Mortens stepped forward from under the canopy. The crewmen peered at him, the darkness not helping. It was not until Mortens stepped onto the jetty, did the crewman pull himself to attention.

'Apologies Sir. Didn't see you there.'

Mortens waved a friendly hand.

'No problem, just taking in the night air. Where are you going?'

'To be honest Sir, I was hoping you'd know.'

'I'm sorry?'

'I don't normally do this run. I'm looking for the Guardroom.'

'Why?'

'Got casualties, Sir.'

'Where from?'

'Tempelhof, Sir. They were brought in from all over. Mustered at Tempelhof.'

'What ranks are they?'

'Officers mainly. I've been told to get porters from the Officers' ward. If you could point me in their direction, Sir. That'll save me a load of hassle.'

Mortens indicated the very building he needed, and with that, the Luftwaffe crewman jogged off into the darkness. He looked back at the enormous aircraft, all its interior lights on, all blackout regulations discarded in the effort of unloading their human cargo. Once again, another shortcoming was highlighted in the running of the facility. Those delivering the wounded had to find the means to get them off the aircraft and on to their respective wards.

Mortens had seen quiet enough and chose to go fetch Tommy and return home. As he lowered himself into bed, a warm, naked, silky-smooth Astrid rolled in to kiss him. Stroking his chest, he pulled her in tighter, for the night was growing colder.

21.

Night rehearsals were certainly not for the faint hearted. With ears ringing and the need to replace the canvas screens set ablaze by overzealous flare firing made the rehearsals cold and longer than was planned. Jones and his men carried on through till the early hours. Every man in the company had fired flares at various 'buildings' from the very exposed and precarious jetty. Throughout the night however, Jones was with them. The boys needed to be able to see him where the danger would be. That was his style. To add a little realism to the evening, Sergeant Major Montgomery and his radio operator, Private Melvin hunkered down, just off the jetty ramp, providing white illumination of the target area. By the time Jones was satisfied they had rehearsed all that was in their control, the infiltration, firing onto marked and radio-controlled targets, and the hazardous extraction, he called a halt to the proceedings.

Before they retired to their beds, the men gathered in the cookhouse tent. One part of the mission that was a grave concern for Jones was the very fact that they had no idea as to the layout inside the buildings. They would essentially be going in blind. After conferring with the other troop sergeants, along with W-W, they agreed that once they had gained access to the target building in question, they would secure the foyer on the ground floor and head for the top floor to begin searching for Arens. Everyman would have a torch, plus their weapons. If they have interior lights on, all the better. They doubted if patients tucked up in bed would give them any trouble. If any made a fuss, they would be shot.

Jones thought about the letter Cowen had handed him. He had the blessing of the Prime Minister to kill with extreme prejudice. The SS were to be given no quarter. As much as Jones had no problem with the implied order, he knew his men would have mixed feelings. He was not about to order them to kill unarmed men in their beds. If the situation warranted the shooting to start then so be it, but he was not about make murderers of them. The SS were more than proficient in that regard, and he loathed to have to stoop to their level. The were after Arens. If they had to go in and out guns blazing, fine, but if they could pluck him from the Hohenlychen Sanatorium without a shot fired, even better.

'Listen up!' called the Sergeant Major, the chattering among the men then petered out. Montgomery looked to Jones who nodded his thanks.

'Gentlemen. Thank you so much for your patience and professionalism tonight. It has been long and certainly cold, so please fill yourselves with hot tea, and I believe Chef has soup and bread for you all.'

Jones could smell the delicious soup, and hoped he had not promised something he could not deliver.

'Before you grab some sleep, I want to let you know now, that we go at last light tonight, and there is much to do before that. We will rouse at noon, and then we must get on. We've burned through a lot of ammunition tonight, so we must restock. The Catalinas will return to Glasgow to refuel and rearm taking Captain Walsh-Woolcott, Sergeant Mould and their band of merry men with them.'

Jones paused so his bleary-eyed men could process what he was saying.

'Ensure you only take what is critical on the mission. Space is of a premium, certainly on the Catalinas. Once the Advance Force are aboard their Halifax and taxiing, we will board our aircraft. Colour Sergeant Gorman will take from you as you board the photograph I have asked you to study. You have the remainder of today to get to know Jurgen Arens, for we will all be looking for him under torchlight soon enough. Any questions?'

There were none.

Jones dismissed the men, who sought out the promised soup and bread before heading for their sleeping quarters. Some loitered about, smoking, drinking tea, lost in their own thoughts. As Jones savoured his own tea and cigarette, he liked to people watch. His men come from all backgrounds, extravagant to humble. Most were single, which pleased Jones for they would naturally have less to think about when about to put themselves in harm's way. The married men, or those in steady relationships with a girl were somewhat difficult to pick out, for they dealt with their inner thoughts in their own way. He noticed W-W taking a wander, and he had every reason to. His wife had nearly been killed and had now left for Canada. Jones quietly hoped that his friend and deputy would keep his cool on the mission. Full of anger, a man can make mistakes that could cost everyone dear. Jones checked himself. He knew W-W would keep his cool, lesser men would or could.

In the tent he shared with W-W, Montgomery and Gorman, Jones eased himself onto his cot bed. The wood burning stove provided for each tent by the enterprising Company Quartermaster was blazing away, fending off the Scottish cold. Easing himself into his sleeping bag, Jones knew sleep would struggle to seduce him. So much to think about. Lying on his back, fingers interlocked on his chest, he just looked at the unremarkable canvas roof above him. Content he had dealt with every operational issue within his control, he could not help but think on the Prime Ministers letter. He had been given the authority to massacre the entire garrison. He doubted his men, or the aircraft could carry enough ammunition onto the target if they wanted to raze the place to the ground. He knew his men would fire on targets that posed a threat, but the deliberate act was just something he could not put to them. With the warmth of the tent making his eyelids heavy, Jones fought to put the issue out of his mind.

Jones flinched as he felt a hand squeeze his right shoulder. Eyes open, the figure above him slowly swam into focus.

'Hey.' W-W smiled. 'Your snoring is fucking atrocious by the way.'

Blinking hard, Jones propped himself up on his elbows. As everything around him came into focus, he noticed the cot beds of both Montgomery and Gorman were missing. He looked up at W-W pulling on his smock. His deputy spoke matter of fact.

'After a few choice words for you in the night, they moved to the C-Q's stores tent.'

'How dare they.' Jones mocked as he hauled his legs off the cot. Not yet ready to pull his aching frame from the warmth of his sleeping bag, Jones rubbed his raw eyes. As he did so, he asked W-W for the time.

'Just before noon. The C.O and that Lewis chap are in the cookhouse tent.'

Both Jones and W-W entered the tent a little bleary eyed. Hook and Lewis were sat at one of the centre tables, whilst a few of the company shuffled about getting cups of tea and bacon sandwiches. Before Jones could advance, Hook smiled at him, miming a cup to his lips before finishing with a thumbs up gesture. He had time to get tea and bacon.

Both newly awakened commandos eased themselves down next to Hook and Lewis. With arms crossed on the table, Hook smiled at Jones who was sipping the hot tea.

'You guys ready?'

All Hook got in response was a nod as Jones placed the cup down. W-W, with a mouthful of sandwich cuffed his greasy chin as he spoke.

'Aircraft are refuelling and rearming this afternoon. My team will be returning with the Cats to Glasgow where we will get aboard the Halifax.'

'Good.' Hook nodded. 'Mr. Lewis and I will monitor the situation in Edinburgh. We'll set off back when you guys' head to Glasgow.'

As Jones pulled a stretch, he glanced about the tent.

'Sarn't Major? C-Q?'

'Ammo delivery from Edinburgh came in early this morning.' W-W spoke between mouthfuls of bacon. 'No rest for the wicked. C-Q is dishing out rations, torch batteries and what not.'

The officers, plus their esteemed MI6 associate sat in silence for a short while as the tent slowly filled with sleep drunk men. Chatter was to a minimum. With the breakfast inside them, operational business would resume in earnest.

As Jones and W-W finished their breakfast, Hook got their attention.

'Had Mountbatten on the phone last night.'

'Really?' Jones was surprised. Both Hook and Lewis nodded.

'Yes.' Hook smiled. 'He wishes you all the best in this endeavour. He mocked me however for sitting this one out, but that's politics for you.'

Jones pulled a menacing grin at W-W, before looking back at his commanding officer.

'You want to come along, don't' you, Sir?'

Hook stole a glance at the MI6 man before responding.

'Too bloody right.'

By mid-afternoon, W-W, his team, along with the Halifax men climbed aboard the Catalinas bound for Glasgow. As Jones and Montgomery waved them off, Jones enquired on Hook and Lewis.

'Did the Colonel and Mr. Lewis get away alright?'

'Yes Sir. The C-Q even ensured they went away with a flask and sandwiches for the long drive back.'

Jones snorted at the due care and attention of Gorman. Always going above and beyond to make everyone comfortable.

As the Catalinas taxied out into open water, Jones gave instruction.

'We should see them back just before last light. I want the men kitted up waiting at the jetty.'

'Yes, Sir.' Montgomery responded, shuffling photographs of Arens as if they were playing cards. The slick hand movements, which were croupier standard without doubt caught the eye of the major.

'Did they hand them all in?'

'All accounted for.'

Late in the afternoon, with the light fading quickly, Jones finally got the call that the Catalinas were on their way back to Blackwater Reservoir. Already a little anxious, Jones was curt.

'They're bloody late.'

'Ventral gun hatch needed a new seal apparently.' Montgomery shrugged.

'What the hell is a ventral gun hatch?' Jones frowned, only to have his sergeant major shrug. Jones rolled his eyes as he puffed out his cheeks.

'Right then. Let's go.'

22.

Glasgow Airport.

Scotland.

'I forgot how much all this shit weighs.' W-W cursed as he adjusted the straps pulled tight up into his groin. Sergeant Mould and the rest of the men smiled in agreement as they too fought with their equipment to get more comfortable. Only once they were ready, could they then check each other over. Given the weight, and the restricted movement, thanks to their parachute harness, they could just about stand up straight as they went about their business.

In addition to their parachutes, their weapons, water, and rudimentary rations, consisting mainly of biscuits and chocolate, they also had to jump with leg bags containing radio equipment, spare batteries, antennas, morse pads, plus additional ammunition, grenades, demolition equipment and their own flare gun and cartridges. Not to mention medical kits, considering they were not only about to go parachuting, which has its own set of hazards, but they could well come under fire from the enemy. The life of the soldier.

Sergeant Ian Mould did his checks and was content all was in order.

'I've never liked parachuting.' He confessed to the captain.

'Why on earth did you join?' W-W pulled a face, to which Mould gave a suppressed shrug under his harness.

'I thought that's what Para's did, hence why I didn't join them.'

Both men managed a smile as RAF ground crew waved them toward the Halifax. Lewens and Stagg, along with the remainder of the crew were at their stations going through their checks, business as usual. One at a time, the ground crew assisted the heavily burdened commandos aboard. Amid the curses and grunting, along with sweat dripping from heavily camouflaged faces, W-W and his men were finally aboard. Comfort was not on offer. The men crammed in where they could fit. W-W was laden down too much to be able to get forward and converse with the pilots. He was a passenger until they were over their drop zone, and the red light was flicked on. From then on, once the green light had him drop through the crude opening in the fuselage, it was his show.

As the commandos shuffled and heaved themselves into some kind of comfortable sitting position, the Halifax was cleared for taxi. The aircraft creaked forward under the deafening roar of the engines as they increased in pitch. To W-W, it felt like an age as they taxied to the far end of the runway. As a passenger, all he could do was just get as comfortable as he could and be with his own thoughts. He thought of Kaila. She would soon be safe with her family. Oskar too. In the cold light of day, he knew her going home was the right choice, for the mission he was embarking on was not without risk. In addition, given what Kaila had been through of late, staying home was proving dangerous too.

The Halifax rolled to a stop; its taxi complete. Whilst it remained stationary, the din no less horrendous, W-W felt a firm bash on his parachute. Instinctively, he turned his head as far as his cramped confines would allow, only to see one of the crew offering him a headset. Pulling his helmet off, he accepted the headset with a nod before placing it over his ears. The din of engines reduced to a low continuous hum the moment the cups were over his ears.

'Captain Woolcott? If you can hear my voice, give the crewman a thumbs up.'

W-W did as he was instructed by the mystery voice crackling through.

'Alright Captain, I'm afraid you will have to listen to our mumbo jumbo during the flight, but it'll at least keep you in the picture a little better. We are just waiting for clearance, and we'll be on our way.'

W-W nodded enthusiastically for the benefit of the crewman. Whilst they waited for clearance, all he could do was give a thumbs up to Mould and the men, with the confident chatter of the crew back and forth from their final checks. After a few minutes, the drone of the engines once again changed pitch as the whole aircraft lurched, its brakes releasing. With the aircraft accelerating, the ground noise of the huge tyres on the metalled runway penetrated his headset. Before long, the nose lifted, allowing the rumble of wheels to cease immediately. As they gained altitude, the Halifax bobbed a weaved as it clambered upwards. W-W noticed the mixture of facial expressions shown by his men under their camouflage cream. They ranged from mild fear to nonchalant boredom as their heads bobbed as one with the aircraft. The latter was that of the imposing Dobbs, who threw the NCO into the reservoir. With the undercarriage closing up under them with a clunk, W-W shifted a little, for the meantime, his small force was in the hands of those flying the aircraft. The purpose-built hole in the fuselage floor did little to keep the cold air out, but there was nothing the commandos could do about that now. They had warm clothing in their jump bags, but to have it on under their parachute harnesses would have made their cramped conditions all the more challenging. As their sweat dried from their exertions boarding the aircraft, a chill began to creep in.

Enduring the cold night air was all they had to concern themselves with for the time being. Before long, the cold would be the least of their concerns.

With the Catalinas recently returned from their rearming and refuelling run to Glasgow, word was soon transmitted to Jones and the remainder of the company that W-W and his men were airborne. Those not going on the mission assisted their comrades as they climbed from the camp to the top of the dam. Their fighting gear was heavy enough, and Jones' men were certainly fit enough to carry it. The additional help was welcomed however regarding sledgehammers and crowbars. Two in each section ensured that if the plan had to change on the ground, each troop had the means to gain access to the Officer Ward, once identified. One Catalina at a time, the men assigned to each aircraft boarded. The crew, save the pilots and flight engineers went through their pre-flight checks, assisted as the commandos climbed carefully into the aircraft. Leg room was certainly at a premium as they filled each aircraft from the rear. The commandos assigned as gunners chastised their comrades to make room so they had unrestricted movement should enemy aircraft be a factor. It was a tight fit, and certainly uncomfortable, but all of the men came aboard and had a place to sit if nothing else. On the jetty remained Jones and Montgomery, the former constantly looking at his watch. Montgomery looked to him.

'Don' fret, Sir. All is well. Captain W-W will find our man and call us in. When they get here we'll get airborne and follow on.'

'I know.' Jones resigned. 'Pre-match nerves is all.'

After what felt like an age waiting for the Halifax to arrive overhead, Jones could make out the drone of engines. With the pilots receiving a call from Lewens, they began to spin up their engines, giving the Major and his Company Sergeant Major their cue to climb aboard. As Jones assisted Montgomery aboard, the other two Catalinas began taxiing out into the middle of the reservoir facing east. One at a time, the Catalina pilots accelerated away before lifting their heavily loaded aircraft off the surface of the reservoir, before joining the Halifax as it orbited above. With all four aircraft in formation, the Halifax leading, their struck east for the North Sea, and onwards towards Sweden.

23.

The Drop Zone

Western side of Steinrode

6 miles North East of Lychen

W-W touched his battered nose gingerly. With his nostrils full of dried blood, and a fat top lip to add to his troubles, all he could do was sit and wait in the pre-arranged rendezvous point. Far to the south of his position, the horizon glowed and occasionally flashed. The relentless rolling thunder of Aerial bombardment the soundtrack. After consulting his map under reduced torchlight, he deduced Berlin was still taking a pounding. Quietly confident he was where he was meant to be, all he could do was stay alert and scan the gloom for his men as they came to join him. As he waited, he reflected on his shocking arrival.

The Halifax was going too fast, he was sure of it. Being first in the stick out of the belly of the aircraft, W-W was reminded in short order the very physics that accompany slipstream and objects leaving from fast moving aircraft. On the green light, he was first through the hole. He was in command, so would always go first. As his legs and accompanying leg bag were exposed to the air ripping past at a rapid rate of knots, he was dragged out the rest of the way, causing him to smash his face on the aircraft as he went. Thankful for the static line that allowed his chute to open automatically upon clearing the aircraft, he dangled senseless for a few seconds before he regained himself in time to prepare for the ground coming up to meet him. It was only a matter of seconds before he hit the ground when he managed to release the leg bag, for to land with it attached would certainly cripple him. In the gloom of night, his warning his descent was almost over was the dull thud of the bag hitting the ground before he too hit the ground hard, knocking the wind from him. With his chute collapsing all over him, he rolled onto his back and gave himself a minute to gather his senses and regain some air in his lungs. As he calmed down, he heard the thud of men and material hitting the ground, cursing, and grunting in various fashions. With the drop phase over, W-W clambered from his silk tomb to orientate himself. After gathering his equipment, he made for the rendezvous.

After a time, W-W could make out lone figures coming out of the gloom. Tactical awareness was sacrificed due to having to carry their leg bags full of mission vital equipment over their shoulders, plus their parachutes in their arms like a huge bundle of laundry. Not a very impressive sight, W-W conceded, but they could not afford for their chutes to be discovered the next day by a farmer or enemy patrol. The first man out of the gloom happened to be Sergeant Mould. A short way off, Mould paused before carrying on as the captain waved him in. Breathing hard as he passed by, the sergeant snorted and spat as he dumped the chute yet slipped the leg bag from his shoulder carefully, placing it onto the ground with care. W-W watched the man with interest, nodding with satisfaction.

Explosives and the infamous timing pencils were sensitive in ideal situations, and they had already taken a battering in the parachute drop. Mould knelt as he checked his Thompson submachinegun.

'How you doing Sir?' Mould whispered.

'Busted my nose I think.' W-W responded; his blocked nose had his hushed words sound very loud in his ears. Mould, forever mother, leaned in to examine his face. With his head bobbing side to side, he then patted the officer hard on the shoulder.

'You'll be fine. Your boyish looks will survive I'm sure.'

'You're all heart, Sergeant.'

'If it makes you feel any better,' Mould continued, 'I thought I'd knocked my bloody teeth out as I fell out of that crate.'

'Really?'

'Yeah. Swear they were going too fast for the green light.'

W-W shrugged, satisfied that he was not alone in his assessment.

It was over half an hour when the next two men arrived in the rendezvous. Nearly two hours before all but one, Dobbs arrived to join their comrades. All complained at how fast they were going when they jumped. In the gloom, they check each other over. Some limped, others had actually lost a tooth or sported an impressive fat lip or black eye. Parachuting, W-W concluded was not for the feint hearted. The issue now concerning them all was the absence of Dobbs, for he also had in his leg bag explosives and pencil timers. W-W checked his watch. They had only a few hours of darkness remaining to locate Dobbs and get him to the rendezvous. He thought over a plan to search for him.

He had the compass bearing the Halifax had taken over the drop zone, so he knew the general direction in which to search. He knew Dobbs was the penultimate man in the stick to jump, the last being Mould, so it was confirmed that he had left the aircraft. Mould confessed that he lost sight of him in the gloom as he descended to earth, which was not the man's fault.

W-W was now faced with a dilemma. He had a man and equipment to be found, and a lot of parachutes to bury in the forest before they could proceed. Dobbs was also in possession of vital equipment. Should by chance his equipment be found by locals or German troops, they will know of British intent in the area, which would result in the area being flooded with troops hunting them. Time was precious, and they needed to get on. W-W made the decision based on the fact that Dobbs was a large man and may be a stretcher case. His equipment and chute would also need to be carried. He turned to his men, who huddled around him.

'We drag our chutes three hundred yards into the forest, and we all look for him. He's a big lad, so we need all hands for this. Any questions?'

'Our leg bags?' Mould asked. W-W bit his lip before answering.

'Fuck it. We'll stash them under the chutes. So long as we are back before first light, I doubt the Germans will find our kit before then.'

With himself patrolling slowly on the compass bearing, W-W had his men in extended line off to his left, with Mould on the end. Given how dark it was, the men were spread out to the limit of visibility. Concerned their sweep would not cover enough ground, W-W intended to search as far south as the unremarkable village of Rosenow. Given the hour, he doubted if they would stumble into anybody, but he could not rule out either the village insomniac, or farmers beginning their work early.

Not less than two hundred yards short of the dwellings on the northern edge of Rosenow, W-W called a halt by way of hand signal. The commandos knelt as they surveyed not only the blacked out, sleeping village, but their immediate surroundings. W-W had done enough parachuting both day and night to appreciate that under canopy, your descent was not always under your control. He would rather deal with the issue of cutting Dobbs down from a chimney stack than to not have him at all. With Dobbs yet to be discovered, W-W gave the signal for the men to turn around. Remaining kneeing, W-W counted the men through as they formed up on the opposite side for the return sweep. Mould followed on at the rear, giving the thumbs up to the captain as he walked by. As W-W waited for the men to spread out, he could not help but keep looking over his shoulder into Rosenow. He felt exposed with an enemy village to his rear. The occasional yap of a dog, and the commotion of a chicken coop was nothing out of the ordinary. What intelligence they did have of the area did not reveal any particular interest in the area by German forces, who would most likely be massing in the Berlin region, given the Soviets were now at the Oder. Still, he could not afford to be complacent, and having a missing man was not helping.

The return sweep was slower due to a number of small yet tall tree clusters. The commandos scoured them thoroughly, up in the thin canopy and the deadfall gathered at their base. Neither Dobbs nor his equipment were to be seen. With heavy hearts, they continued their sweep. Just as the rendezvous location came out of the gloom, W-W noticed commotion to his left as some of his men crouched before getting onto their bellies and crawling forward. Instinctively, he followed suit.

Was the enemy already onto them?

Pulling binoculars from his smock, W-W peered through them. He could just about see movement under the dark canopy. Had German troops already discovered their parachutes, not to mention what lay beneath them? Commotion and heavy breathing to his left distracted him. He looked over to see a dark figure scrambling up the line of troops towards him, on hands and knees, cradling a Thompson in the crook of his right arm. The camouflage scrim flapping about on his helmet. The soldier crawled in besides him. Sergeant Mould.

'Movement.' Mould managed, catching his breath. 'In the RV.'

'Dobbs?' W-W hoped.

'Could be.'

W-W checked his Thompson before getting up onto his haunches. Mould looked up at him, sweat dripping from his blackened face.

'We need to approach and be sure.'

As W-W went to stand, Mould grabbed him by the smock sleeve, pulling him back down.

'Boss don't be a dick. That's Privates work.'

W-W checked himself. Mould was right. He was so eager to get on with what they had come for, be it at the expense of a well thought of member of the company, he was putting himself at unnecessary risk. The captain looked on as Mould crawled over to the two nearest men, Neame and Crossland. Both were seasoned men, cutting their teeth at Saint Nazaire. With their instructions clear, the two commandos got to their feet and advanced at a half crouch on the movement under the canopy. Mould re-joined his commander, who winced at the prospect that both men could be cut down in a hail of bullets at any moment. Through their binoculars, both W-W and Mould observed as the two commandos grew fainter in the gloom. Both men looked to each other, Mould puffing out his cheeks.

'Let's see.' W-W murmured.

No sooner as he spoke, Mould frowned as he propped himself higher on his elbows.

'Hold up.'

W-W looked to where the sergeant was concerned. Out from under the canopy came a lone figure walking towards them with purpose. Both men eyed each other. No shooting had been heard, and W-W doubted any soldier was that skilled and swift with dagger to defeat two armed and very capable men. All they could do was get up on their haunches and receive the lone walker. The dark profile and gait revealed it to be that of Neame. Stopping short, he jerked thumb over his shoulder.

'Dobbs is here Sir.'

A wave of relief washed over both W-W and Mould as they relaxed. Neame looked to where the other men maintained their position in the sweeping line. He waved them in.

'Silly sod is stripped to his under crackers.'

'Why?' Mould snorted.

'Went up to his tits in water. Drop bag nearly took him under. Everything he has is soaked.'

In just his underwear, stood on top of his bundled parachute, Dobbs used his brawn, though chilled to wring out his clothing. As his comrades gathered around him, they let out muffled chuckles. Dobbs shook his head as both the captain and Mould looked in at the unlucky man.

'Of all the bloody farmland,' he hissed,' and I end up in a poxy water filled ditch.'

'Well, that settles it then.' Mould spoke matter of fact. Dobbs frowned.

'What?'

'You're going under the bridge to place the charges. As you're already wet.'

'Wow, thanks.'

W-W smirked somewhat as the men sniggered, only to be given suggestive hand gestures by the half-naked man. Whilst Dobbs shook himself back into his very damp attire, the men got on with the business of digging a hole big enough for the parachutes. With the hole dug, the huge bundles of silk were pulled and kicked in, followed by W-W's helmet, favouring the familiar woollen cap comforter, a rolled up crude balaclava. With their commander ditching his helmet, the remainder followed suit. As W-W and Mould stood watch, the men pulled their canvas packs from the top of their jump bags and packed the remaining contents into the former. As the bags were empty, they too went in the hole. Content nothing vital had been left in the bags, the men got on with burying it all. With hands and the only two picks and shovels brought on the flight due to weight, the men feverishly filled in the hole, eager to get away from the area. As the men adjusted their weapons and equipment for the march towards the target, W-W studied his map under torchlight, the glare reduced by splayed fingers over the lens. After a few minutes he whispered for Mould to join him.

'Given the vast forest we have to move through, which does in fact take us right up to the eastern bank of the Zenesse, I vote we leave at first light.'

'Okay.' Mould responded a little bemused, to which W-W nodded.

'We leave here once we are certain we've hidden the 'chutes properly. Navigation and keeping quiet is also made easier if we can actually see what's ahead of us. I doubt enemy aircraft will detect us in this lot. We mind the tracks unless we have to cross them. We will make the Zenesse in good time before we start to lose the light again.'

At first light, after ensuring the digging had left little evidence of their passing, largely thanks to deadfall getting dragged over the site, W-W gave the order to move out. With Corporal Fletcher, a short, tough man from the Wirral leading, the remainder of the advance force patrolled away, some limping due to the hazards associated with parachuting. W-W held a place in the column five men in, with Neame acting as signaller in tow. Neame had the unenviable task of not just hauling the radio set, but also the antenna mast that would be required to ensure they could speak with those awaiting their call on the Catalinas. Mould brought up the rear. The sergeant was relieved that Dobbs had not only survived the jump and nearly drowning, but the fact he had managed to retain his jump bag. With himself carrying one batch of timing pencils, and Dobbs the other, the last thing they needed was not to be able to blow the road bridge.

24.

Torso Bay

Sweden

As dawn broke, the early to work fishermen native to the unremarkable village stood smoking their pipes on the breakwater, their attention fully on the three Catalinas bobbing in the bay. Aware their arrival had certainly not gone unnoticed in the night; Jones could do little more than give a casual wave as he stood up on the parasol wing of the rather conspicuous aircraft. Given the fact that they were now in the sovereign waters of a neutral country, Jones thought it wise to have anyone stretching their legs up on the wing do so unarmed. He knew the Swedish authorities had form for taking warring belligerents into custody should they cross their frontier and prayed that Lewis' tradecraft had taken care of any potential entanglements with them. With the fishermen now bored of the new arrivals, they appeared to Jones to be going about their day. As some of the men clambered up to join him, he nodded their arrival as he looked to the other two Catalinas. They had followed suit, nursing cups of something hot, smoking or stretching their cramped limbs. Thankfully, they had left their weapons below.

In the wake of the fishermen chugging out from behind the breakwater, Jones noticed someone in a small rowing boat bobbing about in the wake of the fishing boat. As they rowed on, they appeared to be towing another empty small boat. Jones looked to his men who were also intrigued as to what was developing. They caught his eye, only to return a shrug. As the commandos looked on, another rowing boat appeared, crewed by a person also towing a second boat. This prompted Jones to lean into the aircraft and have someone pass him his binoculars. Putting the sling around his neck he looked to the other aircraft. NCOs already had their binoculars up and scanning the small flotilla. Jones peered through his optics.

The lead boat was manned by a man, and the follow-on pair was rowed by a woman. No sooner had he lowered his binoculars, the men stood about him pointed as one. A third pair of small boats came out from behind the breakwater. Using his optics once again, Jones confirmed it was a younger man rowing towards them. Lowering the binoculars, Jones just looked to his men, now joined by the sergeant major.

'Are we about to be arrested?' murmured Montgomery. Jones let out a giggle, the men already finding the episode rather amusing.

'Shortest commando raid ever.'

The lads laughed aloud at the absurdity of it. Jones beamed a smile at Montgomery, who was never short of quips.

'They'll be fucking knackered rowing us all to shore.'

The men stood on the wing chuckled away. Jones tried his hardest not to join in, but it was all too much.

'I think we've been rumbled lads.'

As the lead pair of boats sloshed past, the commandos peered down as the gentleman rowing them puffed and cursed red faced under his breath. His bald head glistened with the exertion but sported an incredible moustache. He looked up at the intrigued British commandos and gave them a friendly wave before correcting his course for the middle aircraft. Jones looked back to the middle pair of boats, piloted by a woman. As she came up alongside, she stowed the oar nearest the aircraft and grabbed a coil of rope attached to her small boat. Two of the men up on the wing clambered down to meet her, her intentions clear. They caught the thrown rope and held the rowing boat steady. As the two men secured her to the aircraft, she manoeuvred herself to the rear of the boat and began to pull in the second, repeating the process of throwing the rope to the men above her. As the second boat was secured, the woman readjusted her sitting position and looked up at the commandos peering down at her. From Jones' vantage point, the woman was early middle age, her hair was fair, almost straw like and tied in an untidy ponytail. Void of any make up, but not unattractive. He noticed she projected a warm smile.

'Good morning gentlemen,' she offered, to which most of those up on the wing returned the salutation. 'Which of you handsome devils are Major Fynlay Jones?'

Jones flinched as everyone around him, with the exception of his loyal sergeant major, pointed him out without hesitation. Jones frowned as the men gave him a mischievous grin. The major shook his head as he stepped forward.

'I'm Major Jones.'

The woman beckoned him to join her in the boat.

'If you would, Major.'

Unsure, Jones looked about him before challenging her.

'Your name?'

'Freya. Happy now?' The women's demeanour appeared to be turning to sarcasm. Jones cocked an eyebrow.

'Is that your real name?'

'Of course not.' Freya scoffed, beckoning him once more to join her in the boat. 'Bring Sergeant Major Montgomery with you. He can do the rowing.'

Jones looked to Montgomery, who held a stunned expression before looking back down to the woman in the boat. Before he could muster anything in response, she rolled her eyes.

'I work for Tim Lewis. Now if you please, we have much to do, and I fucking hate rowing.'

As both men clambered down, chortles of laughter followed them. Not even a cutting glance from their sergeant major could quash the rebellion.

'Gotta hand it to you, gentlemen,' one of the men offered after them, 'you sure know how to pick 'em.'

This brought about open laughter from all around. As both Jones and Montgomery gingerly clambered into the small boat, Freya addressed those looking on, indicating the other empty boat before turning a little to point out a feature in the village.

'See that blue tined roof hut on the quayside?'

She looked up to see they were nodding. 'That's where you piss and shit. Anyone hanging their arse over the side will be arrested by the police. Not even the King will get you out of that cell you'll be sitting in, understand?'

The men nodded, not wanting to try their hand at further comedy. She flashed them a smile before turning her attention to the sergeant major as he got to grips with the oars.

'Back into port, if you please.'

As Montgomery got them back behind the breakwater, Freya, sat tight against the commando major pointed to the olive drab chalet next to the hut she had pointed out to his men. Smoke drifted from its small chimney stack.

'You are welcome to use the chalet for further planning and eating if you wish. I've swept it for listening devices. The Abwehr are not that smart, but you can't be too careful.'

Far be it for Jones to criticise the abilities of German Military Intelligence, he just took her reassurances at face value. They were in a neutral country after all. He was more inclined to think that the Swedes were eavesdropping if anything.

'I'd have thought the Swedes would be more interested.' Jones offered, in hope of a nibble. Freya scoffed.

'Ha yes. Your endeavours would interest them greatly, but our American friends have smoothed the way for your stay to be hopefully without interruption. Besides…'

Freya tailed off. Jones sensed a change in tone. She adjusted herself to look at him more squarely.

'From a strategic perspective, the Germans are no longer our main concern. The Soviets are.'

'Really?'

Freya nodded.

'We've had over the last few weeks here and all along the coast to be fair U-boats coming into port and surrendering. Police cells are full of bored and homesick German sailors. We have more Enigma machines than we can cope with now. The sailors know the game is up. We interviewed their officers and asked why they had not made for South America or some other exotic location.'

'Their response?' Montgomery chimed in, pulling a stroke. Freya smiled tight lipped.

'They are low on fuel but don't want to risk docking in Germany and get caught by the Soviets or sunk by the Royal Navy going for the Atlantic. Some are already damaged one way or the other and cannot dive.'

'Self-inflicted?' Jones proposed to which Freya shrugged.

'Perhaps. Who knows?'

As they came alongside a long wooden jetty, other fisherman preparing for sea stopped to take in the new arrivals. In flawless Swedish, Freya conversed in a relaxed manner with the men as the two British commandos clambered up onto the wooden structure.

With tight lipped smiles, both Jones and Montgomery followed the impatient woman off the jetty up onto the road that ran around the lip of the quay. They crossed the road before ascending wooden steps up to the chalet. As Freya entered, Jones turned to see if the fishermen were watching. They had gone back to whatever they needed to do before heading out to sea. Last in the chalet, Jones pushed the door shut behind him.

Stood in what could best be described as the living room, it was clear to the major that Scandinavians lived an austere existence. There was enough furniture to be comfortable, but certainly not opulent. The building was nice and warm, the fire crackling away. Jones deduced that Freya was expecting them and had lit the fire in time. Both men followed her into the basic kitchen. On the hob of a stove that looked a hundred years old if a day sat large copper pots. On the table sat crates of produce, ranging from peaches to ham. Bread and bananas were stacked neatly next to lemons and oranges.

'Haven't seen one of them in a while, may I?' Montgomery marvelled at the fruits on the table before him before going for a banana.

Jones pulled a face at their host.

'Where on earth did you get them?'

'The Germans actually. One of the U-boats that came in the other day was full of them. They'd rested in The Azores before trying for home. Shame to waste them.'

Jones cocked an eyebrow at his sergeant major chomping his way through his second banana.

'Indeed.'

Freya walked over to a table covered in a white sheet. Under it bulged a large, box like mystery. Pulling the sheet off, the mystery turned out to be a radio set, complete with morse key, log books and stationery.

'Save the batteries on your aircraft.' Freya offered, 'This set can suffice when your advance team report in. No need to camp out on the water if you don't have to. Just an idea.'

Jones and Montgomery looked at each other, impressed with the set up.

'Thank you.' Jones smiled. Freya returned the smile whilst holding her arms outstretched, emphasising the room they stood in.

'Not exactly the Ritz, but you and your men can sleep here. The locals won't give you any trouble. Just be sure to leave your weapons on the aircraft.'

'That's very kind. Thank you.' Jones was pleased he did not have to try and sleep on the crowded Catalina. 'Will you be stopping with us?'

Freya nodded.

'I've got the kids room upstairs, but you and your men will have to sleep where they find a space.'

'The owners?'

'What owners?' Freya pull a broad smile. Jones knew she worked for the intelligence services and liked to be vague. He knew better than to press her, despite their short acquaintance.

'Fair enough.' Montgomery smiled, to which Freya returned the gesture as she pointed out of the window to the three aircraft on the water, their broad parasol wings cluttered with men. The old man and boy were now back behind the breakwater making for the same jetty in which they moored up.

'When you guys leave, I'm to man the radio as a rebroadcast, should range back to Edinburgh be an issue. If you can't call direct, call me.'

'That's good to know.' Jones nodded reassuringly. He noticed the kettle stood among the copper cooking pots.

'Tea?'

25.

6 miles East of Hohenlychen Sanatorium

Nazi Germany

Captain Walsh-Woolcott crawled forward slowly, his heart beating like a bass drum in his ears, sweat dripping from his nose, his eyes stinging. Any abrupt movement could get their attention and the game would be up. He did not want to have them killed, for that would just make their predicament even worse. Hiding the bodies would not be so much of a problem but taking them captive was impossible.

Edging ever closer to his lead men, who also lay prone, their movements slow and deliberate. Their going through the large forest was fairly easy up until that point. Vast amounts of deadfall had to be circumnavigated, which frustrated forward progress, but they were well hidden, the canopy generous enough to let in light, but also generous enough not to expose them to enemy aircraft, not that there were any.

All was well on their approach march to the east bank of the Zenesse until his lead scout, Corporal Fletcher halted the march before slowly getting down on his belly. The other men after him did the same, enticing W-W and the remainder of his force to do likewise. The whole team, including Neame who hauled the radio set, worked a practiced hand, slipping a shoulder strap as they rolled out of their heavy packs, instantly freeing them of their loads. With only the actions of Fletcher to go on, W-W thought it best to sit tight and keep his eyes open for subsequent hand signals to come down the column. After a minute or so, a hand signal was passed down, and it was not one W-W wanted to see. It was the thumbs down gesture. Instantly, his stomach turned.

Enemy seen.

W-W duly passed the signal on before he began his exhausting move forward to see the enemy for himself. He was almost upon the next man forward when whispers came back from Fletcher to greet him.

'Boss…up front.'

Nodding that he had got the message, he continued on passed Private Bobby George on the left and onwards to where he would hopefully find Fletcher. With Privates Tam Bambury and Paul Talbot respectively marking the route to Fletcher, W-W finally caught sight of the rubber soles of Fletchers boots. The boots issued to the commandos were somewhat lighter than the standard issue hobnailed combat boot suffered by the rest of the armed forces. After what felt like an age, W-W hauled himself along Fletchers left side. Composing himself, for the effort of the crawl was exhausting not so much as the physical activity itself, for W-W was in good shape. It was the sheer energy and effort expended not to make any noise as he did so. After a few seconds, he looked as to where Fletcher was pointing.

Before them lay a large heap of rotting deadfall. W-W squinted as he focused on what lay beyond. Through the twisted limbs of the deadfall, he caught movement. As he continued to observe, he picked out various features. Not more than one hundred yards beyond the deadfall was a break in the forest. A prominent track cut across their frontage from left to right. As his eyes adjusted to the backdrop, he picked up the flicking head of a lone horse. He then picked up that it was attached via harness to a large, overloaded wooden cart. Movement up on the cart caught his eye. A lone person, an old man, roughly dressed clambered aloft the pile of deadfall limbs loaded on the cart.

A wave of relief washed through the captain as he let out a long breath. He thought to reprimand Fletcher for the undue panic but was just pleased it was not an enemy patrol. As he looked to the NCO, the blackened face shook his head.

'Not the old man,' Fletcher hissed as he stretched out his hand once more, 'the kids.'

Flicking back to the man on top of the cart, W-W scoured beyond the deadfall for the illusive children. He noticed movement forward left. A head. A girls head. As the rest of her profile came into view, she had in her arm's small limbs of deadfall. She stood at the rear of the cart, dropping the load. As she passed the limbs up to the old man, W-W assessed she was mid-teens if a day. Nothing menacing. Long brunette hair tied back. Rough looking, possibly homemade clothing. Certainly, a country girl. As he rested on his elbows, W-W sensed movement behind him. Peering over his shoulder, he watched as Talbot and Bambury crawled up to join them. Both moving left and right respectively until they were level with the captain and NCO. A little uneasy at the impromptu muster behind the deadfall, W-W looked inquisitively at the two recent additions. Their faces were stoney, full of purpose. Fletcher winced, catching W-W attention.

'Shit.'

All but W-W hunched down lower, their eyes locked on the old man and child beyond the deadfall. He peered through at the old man, now stood high on his overloaded cart. He was calling out to the girl pointing in the direct of where ten British commandos lay still watching them. W-W could feel his stomach tighten, but eased a little when he noticed the girl still stood at the rear of the cart. It was the sudden shrill of another, much younger voice closer to them that sent a flutter of panic through him.

Another child.

Without so much as a word uttered between them, Fletcher, Talbot, and Bambury carefully placed their Thompsons in front of them and pulled their Fairbairn-Sykes knives slowly from their sheaths. All the while they carried this out not one of them took their eyes off the old man and the girl. W-W' heart raced as he tried to get eye contact with the men either side of him. The young, excitable German voice grew ever closer. Aware that now was not the time to dress the men down, W-W remained mute, and concentrated on both the old man and girl whilst trying to locate the second child somewhere on the far side of the deadfall. It was the sudden movement of the deadfall that had all four commando's flinch.

The child was merely feet away.

With the deadfall in front of them sitting considerably higher than they were, it would not take much for the unsuspecting child to find themselves looking down on four, knife wielding foreign soldiers. W-W silently prayed for the child to lose interest and return to his elders. He knew that if they were seen they would have to take robust action, for the success of the mission was at this point hinged on their successful infiltration of the target area and identification of which building to breach. To have it all go to hell because of a wayward child bordered on the absurd. Killing civilians, especially children was not the way they did business. Granted, civilians had been caught in the midst of direct action on previous missions, and no doubt some were also slain in reprisals by the Germans in the aftermath, but it was not a deliberate act to involve them. As the unseen child's chatter back and forth with the girl and the old man grew to fever pitch, Fletcher and the two men slowly clambered into a kneeling position. W-W closed his eyes and took a deep breath.

It was the girl calling out to the child that came to his ears. W-W peered through the deadfall to see her waving whoever it was back to the cart. The deadfall shuddered as the excitable young voice chirped away but then began to quieten. Eager to see the second child, W-W leaned forward a little, leaning right through the thicker limbs. A small boy, ten years old if a day jogged back before walking up to what could be assumed as his older sister. The old man clambered forward on to the cart bench, taking hold of the reigns, before snapping them enough to prompt the tired looking nag to begin hauling the prospective firewood away. Both children skipped and shoved each other as they followed on. With the cart creaking and groaning as it rattled away, the three commandos brandishing knives rolled onto their backs, clearly relieved.

None was more relieved than their commander.

It was the perfect opportunity to take on water and enjoy some ration chocolate whilst the old man and the children made their way slowly out of the area. Children had quick reflexes, were unpredictable and the small boy appeared to be darting all about the place. W-W decided to rest his men until the civilians were out of sight before they crossed the trail.

With the trail crossed, W-W and his men continued on their original compass bearing. Sticking to it was a challenge for their route was blighted with huge heaps of deadfall. Meandering around them burned precious daylight for sometimes the deadfall obstacles happened to be in a natural choke point between random lakes of various sizes, making the commandos take considerable detours, only exacerbated by civilians fishing for their supper. W-W grew frustrated at the apparent lack of forward movement but knew the Zenesse was long enough for them to eventually encounter its long eastern bank.

After what seemed an age, the British could recognise the long glimmering sliver that was the Zenesse glinting back at them through the trees. After a short period of check navigation and rehydration, the British concluded they had arrived on the Zenesse further to the south than they originally planned. It was not of concern, providing any deadfall did not channel them down towards the water's edge and potential exposure to anyone on the far bank as they patrolled north. The idea was to go firm opposite the sanatorium, and then go about choosing a suitable location for their observation post.

By the time they were opposite the sanatorium, the clear skies presented a western sun low in the sky. Observing the facility which sat on the far bank at a range of almost four hundred yards was difficult for the sun had the men squinting, and to use binoculars would only encourage glint that may have attracted attention. Ensuring they were far enough inside the forest, W-W ordered the men to shed their loads and rest. In all round defence, the British commandos sat on their packs, collecting their thoughts. Content he was where he was meant to be, W-W ordered the radio be established, just so they could report to Jones sat out in Swedish waters that they had indeed arrived at the target. At twilight, W-W and Neame would go about siting where the observation post would be. Neame and the radio where vital in the next phase, for the captain could well pick a very suitable physical location in which to observe the sanatorium and defend his own position in the event of attack, but if they had no signal in which to speak to Jones, the position was as good as useless. In the meantime, W-W took in the panorama of the sanatorium with the naked eye.

From his current vantage point, the facility looked vast to him. The clusters of buildings made confirming with his own mapping and sketch map of the facility a challenge to translate. He could easily make out roaming pairs of German sentries. They hugged the western shore. Without his binoculars to scrutinise them in more detail, he could not make out if they were alert and looking his way, or just chatting among themselves. The buildings, a drab red and brown for the main part where far taller than the imagery he had seen had led him to believe. One of the larger buildings was five storeys, not including a cellar. He knew the Germans were fond of a cellar.

Squinting into the setting sun, he could make out white clad personnel walking about, in pairs mostly, but the occasional loner moved between the buildings. He was glad the groves of trees standing about the facility were still void of leaves, for if they were in full bloom, he would not see much of the target area, with or without binoculars. As they waited for twilight, Sergeant Mould produced a flask from his pack, filling the accompanying cup almost to the brim. The aroma of the fluid was instantly recognisable to the men.

Tomato soup.

Mould offered the cup around the men, who took it in turns to take a mouthful of the now tepid contents. It did not matter, for it was a nice surprise. W-W enjoyed his turn, savouring the unexpected offering. Working in pairs, without prompting from their seniors, the commandos ate chocolate and hard tack biscuits from their meagre rations or gave their weapons a wipe down.

'Radio set up, Boss.' Neame informed the captain. Adjusting his seating position on his heavy pack, W-W took the Morse key on top his right thigh, composed himself and began.

26.

Grateful for the opportunity to get off the Catalinas, including their own crews, Jones and his men relaxed in and around the chalet. As the final streaks of daylight faded over the western horizon, the men dozed, whilst others read and smoked. Those that wanted to ensure their weapons and equipment was good to go for the umpteenth time remained on board. During the day, the food was enjoyed by all, with a couple of the men showcasing their kitchen talents. Despite the increasingly raucous banter between the self-appointed chefs and their diners, Jones looked on with interest as they prepared whatever they planned to feed everyone. Jones considered himself a knowledgeable and competent man, but in the kitchen he was a lost cause. Egg on toast was about his limit. In the large copper pots, the chefs had prepared a stew of sorts, heavy with potatoes and chopped up yet chunky vegetables. The meat on offer in the coal store was in fact deer meat, already butchered and prepared. All the men had to do was chop it down further for the pot. The delicious aroma of hot food hung heavy in the chalet, to the point where Jones suddenly had a rush of consciousness for the locals and their own privations.

'Relax, Major,' Freya reassured him as she liberated a chopped carrot from the strainer, 'Sweden doesn't go hungry, I can assure you.'

Jones smiled as he checked himself, the war had been long and he was in the grand scheme of things, weary of it. As well read as he considered himself, he would forgive any of his men if they forgot their current host nation was neutral. The locals, namely the adults, kept their distance as they went about their business. The three Catalinas in distinct RAF markings bobbing about in the bay hard to miss. By now, Jones half expected local law enforcement to make themselves known, but they did not. Not in uniform anyhow. Jones deduced that Freya and her associates had taken care of any such event.

One thing that no amount of tradecraft or back channelling could keep at bay was children. The men who rested in the pleasantly warm Scandinavian sun were preyed upon by children, big and small for what soldiers always appeared to have on them in tales of old besides bullets…sweets. The rations provided by

American sponsors ensured chocolate and other sweet delights were in abundance. As the men dished out the booty to the children, a football appeared out of nowhere. Before long, soldiers played against the much smaller and faster Swedish internationals. With smocks and children's coats as rudimentary goal posts, the heavy-footed commandos put up a respectable resistance against the Swedish onslaught. The match lasted long enough for Jones and Freya to take coffee on the front step and witness England's humiliation against Sweden's under 18's. As the light faded, the game petered out and the belligerents shook hands. The kids jogged away, pockets crammed with chocolate, leaving their ball for the commandos to knock about during their undetermined stay.

Now enveloped in darkness, save for street lights and dwellings about the village spilling their light into the gardens. Jones spoke into his cup as he finished the now tepid contents.

'Is this Arens fellow worth all this effort?'

Freya tossed the dregs of her own cup onto the grass before answering, her voice low.

'What do you know about heavy water?'

'Not much' Jones confessed, shrugging. 'I just know that America is calling in a favour to grab this guy before he completes his work for a Nazi super bomb or something. This heavy water is a key ingredient.'

'That's part of the reason.' Freya scanned the area about them. 'The powers that be feel that if Hitler gets his super bomb, he will flatten Paris with it.'

'Why Paris?' Jones cocked an eyebrow. 'Why not London, Washington, Moscow even?'

'Smash Paris, the western armies are neutered. With western powers reeling from the attack, Hitler can turn all his attention to the Soviets.'

'Pretty bold chess moves there.' Jones puffed out his cheeks. Freya smiled.

'The other part is more threatening.'

'More threatening?'

'If Arens gets taken alive by the Soviets, this very same threat remains, but this time Washington could be the target in the near future.'

'I'm sure the Soviets are still on our side.' Jones scoffed. Freya remained deadpan.

'For now.'

Jones went to challenge Freya's last comment when a call when out inside the chalet.

'Boss?' Montgomery hollered, unsure where the major was. 'Message from the Advance Team.'

Freya followed Jones into the chalet, heading for where the radio set was stationed. Taylor, his signaller handed his log book up to the major, his decoding in upper case pencil.

ARRIVED ON TARGET.

ALL MEN AND EQUIPMENT ACCOUNTED FOR.

OCCUPYING OSCAR PAPA TONIGHT.

BEGIN TARGET IDENTIFICATION AT FIRST LIGHT.

HOPE YOU ARE WELL.

Jones smiled as he handed the log book back to Taylor, squeezing the man's shoulder in approval. He looked to Montgomery, already reading the room.

'Gather the men.'

After a brief chirp on the Morse Key by Taylor, those that remained on the Catalinas, aircrew included, made their way to join those already mustered at the chalet. After the men had charged cups with tea and opened notebooks for what was about to come their way, Sergeant Major Montgomery called for order. As the men quietened down, Freya looked about the dark street before closing the door, giving Jones a thumbs up. The Company Commander looked to his men, clustered in the one room.

'The Advance Team have arrived on target, all men and equipment accounted for.'

He allowed a moment for the news to soak in. The men were all smiles in response, some even bumping fists with those sat next to them. Jones continued.

'There is every chance that they will identify the target building before last light tomorrow evening, so we must be ready to fly at last light. As we go into night time routine this evening, please ensure Taylor is not the only fellow manning the set. Fight among yourselves, but just ensure there is enough people to keep a radio watch through the night.'

Faint murmurs at Taylors expense carried across the room, resulting in tittering amongst his comrades. It was Warrant Officer Rich Monk, the senior Catalina pilot who raised his hand. Jones acknowledged him.

'My guys will hold the fort on the aircraft, if that's alright with everyone?'

Jones looked about the room for any objections. There were none. It made resting his troop even easier as they would be consolidated around the chalet, whilst Monk and his colleagues manned their respective aircraft, and their own radios, plus all the weapons and ordnance on board.

'No problems with that, Sarn't Major.' Jones returned a smile, before looking up at his men. 'Right then. Eat well, rest well, and we'll see what develops over the next day. Dismissed.'

As the melee of men fought their way out of the now cramped chalet living room, Freya made her way over to Jones, who was in conference with Montgomery. As Jones looked to her, she pointed apologetically at Montgomery.

'It's the sergeant major I wish to speak with, actually.'

Jones, flushed in the cheeks, stepped aside, as she turned her attention to the inquisitive looking warrant officer.

'The lads can crash in my room if you need the space. I doubt I will rest much tonight. Pre-match nerves and all that.'

'Oh, that'll be great, thank you.' Montgomery beamed. Freya nodded.

'Also, put me down for a stint on the radio. If I'm not going to sleep, why keep another man up just for appearances?'

27.

The first night hunkered down under the trees hugging the east bank of the Zenesse was long, cold and without incident for Captain Walsh-Woolcott and his team. Fearing roaming patrols their side of the lake, four men at a time remained awake, ready to do battle. Those that had the opportunity to sleep found it a challenge. They were deep inside enemy territory, and in a short period of time, the sheer geography of where they were in the world come home to them. Give or take fifty miles north of Berlin, they could not have been more in the enemy's back yard. Arriving by parachute, they would be walking out of trouble one way or another if the main assault group could not arrive, or they were discovered before they got a chance to identify the building where Jurgen Arens would most likely be staying in.

A huge risk, so far from help or home.

It was this fact that kept W-W awake throughout the night. His sleeping bag kept the worst of the cold at bay, his body shivering through nerves and anticipation of what they needed to take care of as soon there was enough ambient light to begin setting their observation post correctly. With the radio set and antenna in a proven spot, given that Jones sat far away on the Catalinas in Swedish waters had responded in kind, he was loathed to moved it. If he needed to, they could run a remote line to where they would finally set up their physical position. With the morse key in their location along with their weapons and equipment, the radio set could be concealed with deadfall, and the antenna run up the side of one of the numerous trees that covered them from the air, and to a lesser degree, those who may peer in their direction from the grounds of the sanatorium.

Activity in the sanatorium grounds was minimal. Not placing his trust entirely in the photographs available to them, W-W made the effort to scan the facility as best he could. No watchtowers were evident. No sweeping searchlights to assist the two pairs of roaming sentries that revealed themselves at any given time. Their discipline appeared poor to W-W. They were correctly dressed, but were over reliant on torches and constantly smoking, or in the motions of lighting their next cigarette. Sparks of matches or lighter forever striking the darkness. They walked about their prescribed route without any real purpose. To W-W, they appeared in deep conversation or looked plain bored. Nothing new to any soldier on that score. During the course of the night, W-W noticed the absence of dogs accompanying the roaming sentries. He recalled seeing one through the stereoscope back in Edinburgh, but that could have just been a personal pet of one of the staff. As a dog lover, he was rather loathed to harm one, and hoped the Germans would not bring them into the fray should it unfold.

A little after midnight, a pair of headlights got the attention of the commandos. Nudged awake by Neame, W-W looked across the lake. Thin slitted headlights bobbed and vanished behind buildings in the facility before appearing again, be it briefly before disappearing for what felt like for good behind Building Four on his sketch map. With little else to observe except the bored, wandering pairs of sentries, W-W settled back down to try and sleep. After an hour or so, the creak and rattle of an engine had him raise his head and squint at a faint white convoy light as the vehicle returned back the way it had come in.

Nothing untoward, just logistics during a blackout protocol.

As dawn made itself known in the east, W-W and his commandos, less those on sentry duty went about building their observation post. With folding saws fished from their packs, they fought with the deadfall, trying to remain as quiet as possible. Their footing deliberate and slow, for the snap of a branch underfoot would still carry on the early morning air. Under the canopy, the echo would sound deafening. So, haste, not speed was the order of the day.

It was Sergeant Mould that found what he considered a suitable position where to actually establish the observation post. A generous dip in the forest floor, without surface running tree roots lining the bottom, which would only make their long hours of inactivity uncomfortable. With deadfall lining its rim like a crude corral of sorts, the whole team could occupy it and still observe generous arcs of fire and more importantly, the entire panorama of the west bank in which the sanatorium sat. The radio would have to remain where it was, forward left of their position, but only on a remote line of twenty yards. Concealed under deadfall of its own, the frequency would only be changed in an emergency, and that task would fall to Neame, who if in daylight would have to crawl forward slowly and deal with it. Not ideal, but most situations in war rarely where.

As the light of dawn gave way to morning, the commandos put the finishing touches to their position. Unless already made in flasks, hot food and drinks would be out of the question for the foreseeable future. Smoking too would be forbidden. The British could not afford to give their position away with so much as the aroma of cooking, coffee, or tobacco. Toileting would be into either a bottle or a plastic bag depending on the function required. Such ablutions were not for the bashful. There would be no wandering off to find a private spot, for it would all take place in the position. Shaving and the brushing of teeth was also forbidden. Water was too precious to waste on such activities. After last light, they could make their way back to one of the numerous lakes to replenish water bottles and bury toilet waste away from water courses, but until that time of the day presented itself, the British commandos would just have to rough it.

With binoculars perched on the lip of the position, W-W knew that come the late afternoon, with a setting western sun, his optics would glint, so to counter such an event, he fashioned a hessian sandbag so he could cover the optics and observe through the hessian. Sergeant Mould copied the idea. With men, weapons, equipment, radio and camouflage in place, the observation post was set. Now began the waiting game. At a range of almost four hundred yards to the nearest building on the western bank, identification of Arens would be impossible, but if they could deduce what building officers convalesced in, that would be the target building. Arens may not have been a full bloodied officer, but he held the rank that would have him accommodated with them. W-W just needed enough to go on to call in Jones and the Assault Group.

The sooner they found Arens, the sooner they could have him out of there before any heavy reinforcements arrived. It was not lost on W-W that the only fire support they had would be the Catalinas. Their .303 Vickers machineguns could pour devastating fire into a target, which their rehearsals could confirm. The issue would be that the Catalinas would be literally sitting ducks on the water until Arens was located. Any German reinforcements worth their salt would neutralise the aircraft, denying the attacking force their fire support and means of escape. The knowledge of a large camp facility not more than ten miles to the west was certainly a cause for concern. The enemy could have reinforcements joining them within the hour.

W-W wished he had prepared the road bridge linking Lychen village to the sanatorium for demolition the night just passed, but there was little he could do about it now. Mould and his small band of determined men would just have to deal with that once darkness returned. Even if they identified the target building before lunchtime, the main group would not arrive until the early hours anyhow. It would not hurt to soak in all that went on at the sanatorium, establish pattern of life, sentry routes and routines before calling in the big guns. W-W had to be right, for they would not have the time to search every building for the scientist.

As the light improved, the commandos hidden in their position ate cold rations and chocolate bars before settling down for the long day ahead. At first, the morning revealed a drab and overcast sky, threatening rain. With W-W taking the first watch of the day, along with Neame as his co-observer and radio operator, he slowly and meticulously scanned the entire panorama of the sanatorium from left to right. He quietly commended the Germans for their neatness in almost everything that they did, particularly in a barracks setting. At first glance, all the buildings sported a similar Teutonic theme, red tiled rooftops, black and white facades, the windows bordered in dark timber, with window shutters either locked up tight, or locked in the fully open position. The interior of the latter far too dark for any meaningful observation within. Some of the taller buildings had cone roofed turrets on the corners, giving them a castle like appearance. Lawns were neat, bushes trimmed, paths clear. The few sentries he has initially spotted walked in ankle deep leaf litter when not on a path or road, given the abundance of trees that dotted the facility. The tree canopies were indeed sparse but would bud soon enough as spring finally emerged from a most brutal winter. He lingered on each building that came into his field of view, only glancing down to his crude sketch of the facility to confirm the identification of the buildings. The building identified as the church was a neat affair, everything he expected as churches went. It was void of any human activity, but that was to be expected, given the hour.

The larger building that came into his field of view next was in stark contrast to that of the church. Its open shutters, certainly on what would be designated as the ground floor, gave away all manner of human activity. Figures moved to and fro, whilst W-W and Neame observed more personnel arriving outside the building either in large staff cars, or on bicycles.

'The cars.' Neame murmured, intent of trying to identify the calibre of passenger that would arrive in such splendour.

'Seen.' W-W responded, switching his focus to the very same cars. Two cars, both the same shape, gave the commandos observing cause to confirm they were in fact Mercedes. In addition, they were flanked by two Zundapp outriders, with sidecars, armed with what W-W identified to be MG34 machineguns. The rider and sidecar occupants were adorned in helmet, goggles, and long leather greatcoats. The soldier on the motorbike had what appeared to be a submachinegun strapped across his chest, whilst the sidecar occupant had control of the MG34. Drivers were observed climbing out of the Mercedes before only the rear driver opened their rear door. Other personnel came out from the building to greet them in a shower of party salutes, only to stagger a little as a huge built officer clambered out. The giant returned the salutation before being ushered into the building, both W-W and Neame rested their eyes.

'Bloody size of him.' Neame scoffed, thumbing his nose free of something irritating him. 'Anyone we know?'

The captain shook his head slowly.

'Couldn't really tell. Could do with some stronger binos.'

Conscious of weight and lack of space in their jump bags had forced W-W and his men to omit other optics for long range observation. Their binoculars were standard issue and could easily be tucked into a smock when not in use.

'Would be a good number if we could bag us some top brass when we grab our man later.'

Neame nodded his agreement before movement to his right, along the shoreline caught his attention. After a quick glance through his binoculars, he gave the captain a gentle nudge with his elbow.

''Ere you go Boss, something that'll entertain you.'

'What?' W-W frowned, looking out over the water. Neame pointed a finger to what he was referring to.

'Dog. North jetty.'

28.

Tommy paced the jetty whilst his master caught up. Mortens enjoyed the slow walk into work. Apart from sentries going about their duties, he pretty much had the world to himself. Astrid would of course see him right first thing with coffee whilst he showered and dressed. She would feed Tommy, but not too much for she was well aware that he had a way of getting treats out of pretty much anyone he encountered. Tommy was a popular member of the establishment, and they had not been stationed there for long. Breakfast for Mortens was little more than coffee and cigarettes. He seldom had an appetite first thing in the morning, and depending on how well the day progressed, it would determine if he ate at all until he finally returned home. The administration staff had acquired a small grill in which to make toast from the overzealous chef in the Officer

Ward kitchen. The delicious aroma of toast would hang in the air throughout the offices in the late morning, and Mortens could be forgiven for being seduced by it once or twice since he arrived.

As he passed the north jetty, Tommy fell in beside him. A cigarette pinched between thumb and forefinger on his left hand, he could shield from most the fact that he was smoking as he strolled. Anyone approaching would have him flick it into the water, no harm, no foul. The laid-back atmosphere at the sanatorium was not beginning to contaminate him, but he could feel himself getting somewhat tardy. He found it hard to be on point, on his game in all of his duties when those about him seemed to not care one way or the other. His tardiness quickly leaped from his demeanour when he spotted the Zundapp outriders and two staff cars outside the offices.

He quickly dived into his thoughts. Had he an appointment with top brass today? He could not remember. Had his staff briefed him on such a visit? He could not remember. As Tommy pranced about the drivers and troopers stood about the entrance to the offices, Mortens asked who was here. A capless driver pulled himself to attention.

'Haupsturmfuhrer Roche, Sir.'

Roche was Adjutant at the Ravensbruck facility. Mortens frowned at the staff cars and those that had accompanied them.

A little over the top for a glorified captain, Mortens thought. Upon entering the offices, all appeared to be business as usual. As he removed his cap, Lucy, armed with cup and saucer clipped over to him, a flushed smile for him too. Taking his cap, she then handed him the cup and saucer. She knew how he liked his coffee.

'Haupsturmfuhrer Roche is in your office.'

'Just him?'

'Just enough room for him,' Lucy smirked.

Walter Roche stood at six feet; four inches barefoot. With high cheekbones, chiselled jawline and thick black sweepback hair, his broad athletic shoulders under an immaculate tailored tunic gave him an aura of invincibility. Originally from the 10th SS 'Frundsberg' Division, Roche sported a web of scars across his left cheek and chin due to wounds sustained in Holland the September gone. Initially to be assigned to the Fuhrers premier unit, the 1st SS 'Leibstandarte Adolf Hitler' Division, it was decided that he was not ideal to feature in the formation due to his 'Jewish' looks. The black hair, thick eyebrows and oversized nose would have forgiven most for thinking his heritage to be that of a Jew. Roche endured the relentless teasing from both superiors and peers. Mortens had heard through the faceless and more so nameless grapevine that Roche was sacked from a unit designed to infiltrate Jewish resistance groups because he was just too damn tall. Far too bulky for parachute operations, and Jewish males were not known for their height, Roche was drafted from the special forces to command a Panzer Grenadier company instead. After recovering from his wounds, he was offered the job of Adjutant at the Ravensbruck facility. After his company was decimated at Nijmegen, he would not have a combat command again. Sitting at five foot, ten inches, Mortens could not help but acknowledge the man's presence in his now seemingly small office.

Turning to receive Mortens, Roche flashed him a toothy smile as he stepped forward, offering a huge paw.

'Walter Roche.'

Mortens accepted his peer's hand.

'Otto Mortens. Just you visiting?'

'Yes, just me. Apologies for imposing myself on you this early in the day.'

'Not at all.' Mortens smiled as they released their embrace, ushering the huge SS officer to one of the chairs in front of his desk. 'What brings you out here at this hour anyways? What's with all the cars?'

Roche gingerly lowered himself into the leather chair, placing his field cap on Mortens desk.

'Not my idea. Allied planes have been chased off over Ravensbruck, and I'm not sure if I'm either bait or decoy.'

This revelation irked Mortens internally. Roche could well have brought Hohenlychen to the attention of Allied aircraft. He had no idea if the sanatorium had the protection of the Red Cross. In the presence of equal rank, Mortens noticed the huge Roche relax in the chair.

'I've been sent by the Commandant to speak with Chief Surgeon Gebhardt, but I felt it only proper to speak with Head of Security in the meantime.'

'How so?' Mortens was most intrigued as he leaned on the front of the desk, coffee cup at his lips, saucer held underneath. Roche eyed him seriously.

'SS-Reichsführer Himmler is coming to Hohenlychen.'

Mortens swallowed more coffee than he intended, coughing instantly as a result. As he composed himself, he could see the beginning of a smirk growing on Roche face. Face flush, Mortens managed to croak his response.

'Why the hell is he coming here?'

'Under orders from the Fuhrer, he is to rest before the coming battle.' Roche response was laced with sarcasm, which was not lost on Mortens, sensing the absurdity of the situation, but it was the fact that Himmler was coming to stay and not just visit that had him captivated.

'He's coming to stay?'

'Yeah.'

'How long?'

Roche merely shrugged, leaning over to fetch his coffee cup from Mortens desk. 'I'm just the messenger, Otto.'

Cuffing his chin, Mortens frowned at his peer.

'I've been beating the drum for security upgrades since I got here. How is the Reichsführer going to feel when he comes and sees for himself how exposed this place really is?'

Roche shrugged once more as he put the cup to his lips. Mortens puffed out his cheeks as he looked out of the window.

'For fucks sake.'

'I know,' Roche snorted, 'hardly the time for a vacation.'

Mortens looked to Roche, 'What battle?'

'Huh?' Roche sipped coffee. Mortens stepped away from the window.

'What battle?'

The cup now empty, Roche returned it to the desk before answering.

'Ravensbruck security is getting stripped to the bare minimum and getting sent into the Berlin garrison. The inmates are getting relocated further west.'

'Really?'

'Yeah. Your guys here won't be touched thanks largely to Himmler's visit. Just don't be surprised if you have to let men go into Berlin.'

'Right,' Mortens tailed off, then had to ask the question, 'what about you?'

'What about me?' Roche frowned.

'Are you getting transferred?'

'Not that I'm aware. Why?'

Mortens shrugged, feeling a little ashamed that self-preservation was now on his mind, not the defence of his nation's capital. Roche leaned forward, eyeing the office door before looking up at Mortens, his voice hushed.

'Otto, I know you are head of security here, but do yourself a favour.'

'What?' Mortens responded in a low tone, leaning in a little. Roche fixed his eyes on him.

'Get the hell out of here at the first opportunity.'

Mortens blinked hard at Roche, who kept his composure.

'What do you mean?'

'Go west, Otto. The British are not that far away now. Hand yourself into them.'

Mortens stood straight, a little shocked to hear such talk. Roche glanced at the door before continuing.

'The Soviets will give you no quarter, and you have to be sure you meet the right Americans. The British are a safer bet.'

Mortens kept quiet as he absorbed what Roche was saying. He would rather have Astrid move west and take her chances with the British but could not guarantee how he would be received. He had heard enough horror stories from the east to not have her among the Soviets. Roche hauled himself from the seat, standing straight as he pulled down the bottom of his tunic.

'Just think about it, Otto. It's nearly over, don't you see?'

Tight lipped, Mortens could only nod at what Roche was saying. He was right. With a friendly smiled, Roche fetched his coffee cup.

'Anymore coffee going?'

29.

'No fucking way.' W-W hissed as he stared through his binoculars. Neame flinched as he looked to the captain.

'What?'

'The fucker on the bike.'

Neame peered through his own binoculars across the lake to where the motorcade sat. The nearest Zundapp rider was looking back that them with his own binoculars. Neame's heart leaped.

'Shit.'

'Yep.'

'Surely not.'

'Well,' W-W paused, 'we'll soon know about it if he can see us.'

Keeping his eyes fixed in his optics, W-W spoke calmly to the rest of his men, huddled down behind him.'

'Lads?'

'Boss?'

'Keep still will you.'

'Huh?'

'Some fucker is looking right at us.'

'What?'

'Just keep still.'

Fearing their own movement would confirm the Germans suspicions, all W-W and Neame could do was keep stock still and see what developed. After what felt like an age, the German began to scan to the south. He would then lower his binoculars and converse with the sidecar gunner. Their demeanour, at least to W-W, appeared jovial. It was as the two rolled their heads back in laughter did W-W begin to relax. It was just a rather stressful coincidence.

'He hasn't spotted us.' W-W exhaled, his shoulders relaxing. Noticeable sighs could be heard as the remainder of his team relaxed in response. It appeared that the curious German was not looking at anything in particular. W-W felt the presence of someone on his left side. He lowered his binoculars to see Sergeant Mould looking back at him.

'We need to check out and rig those bridges tonight.'

'Indeed. If we get any trouble, we need to delay them long enough to get the hell out of here.'

Into the late morning, both Mortens and his guest, Walter Roche took coffee and enjoyed each other's company. They spoke of home, their exploits to date, and to Mortens admission, Roche's anecdotes were far more interesting than his. Waiting for an audience with the rather illusive Chief Surgeon, Roche ventured outside to have his men relax and go grab coffee. All of this under the ever-watchful British Commandos across the lake.

'Rather casual, don't you think?' Mould offered, now in place of Neame, who dozed in his sleeping bag at the rear of the observation post. W-W, reluctant to rest until he saw all that he could possibly observe shrugged, eyes remaining in the optics.

'No worse than our lot.'

'True enough.'

Both men observed with interest as the Zundapp riders dismounted, before shedding their riding gear. Once done, they bundled into one of the Mercedes that pulled away and slowly made its way north through the grounds of the sanatorium.

'Wonder where they're going?' Mould muttered as the car, keeping to the road, weaved in and out of view before halting outside the largest of all the buildings. With the occupants climbing out of the vehicle, both W-W and Mould watched as they ascended the broad stone steps ups to a large set of doors. The lead German gingerly opened the door before stepping in, the others following. As the last one disappeared from view, the door closing behind them, W-W looked to Mould, a satisfied look on his face.

'They've gone for coffee, I'm betting.'

'You reckon?' Mould challenged, to which the captain nodded as he consulted his sketch map.

'I do. Other ranks cookhouse. That's the Soldier Ward. Building three. Your man Arens won't be in there.'

'Thank heavens for that,' Mould snorted, 'bloody thing is huge.'

'Yes it is,' W-W returned to where the other Mercedes sat among the now vacant Zundapps.

'We just need to confirm where the officers live.'

'Shall we call it in?' Mould offered as he looked for the Morse key. W-W shook his head.

'Not yet. Let's see what develops before we send anything through. We will call in at last light anyway.'

The remainder of the morning passed without incident for W-W and his team. The Zundapp riders, along with the Mercedes drivers had returned from the large building only to mill about where they had parked previous. The German Shepherd appeared from the building and was made a fuss of by the bored troops. Sticks were thrown to satisfy the relentlessly energetic dog, until the soldiers climbed in or on their respective modes of transportation and began to do what soldiers have done since ancient times, doze.

After having their fill of watching the enemy sleep off their coffee, the commandos watching them were then blessed with another distraction, engine noise.

Aircraft engine noise was correctly identified by one of the men chewing unexcitedly on ration biscuits. Despite the lack of leaves, the naked branches above the observation post where too clustered for W-W or any of his men to locate the noise as it grew louder overhead.

'You don't think it's our guys?' Neame offered, fully awake, for he was experienced enough to know that stranger things had happened since he joined the unit. Mould pulled a face at him.

'In daylight?'

Neame merely shrugged in response before looking up through the canopy again. Rolling on his side, W-W joined in.

'Engine pitch is too low for ours.'

A shadow flicked across them as the aircraft flew south to north before banking off to the east. As he rolled back on his front, he put his binoculars back up to his eyes. He was greeted by the same German peering in their direction through his own once more. Stomach turning, he suddenly realised that perhaps the Germans had spotted something in the wood line across the lake and had an aircraft come check it out. He could not discount it. As he scanned about where the German stood, he received a nudge from Mould.

'White coat, just come out of Building Four.'

Chief Surgeon, SS-Obergruppenfuhrer Karl Gebhardt strolled through the grounds from the Officer Ward towards the administration building. Having received word that a representative from Ravensbruck had come to speak with him, he felt it better to have the conversation away from where he led his 'Live Tissue Training.' A professor of Sports Medicine before the war, Gebhardt was appointed as Director of the Hohenlychen Sanatorium and after considerable sponsorship by the Nazi Party, the facility boasted that it was a leader in the recovery of athletes and celebrities from all over the world.

Gebhardt fell afoul of his Berlin masters after he failed to treat SS-Obergruppenfuhrer Reinhardt Heidrich after the assassination attempt on him in Prague, May 1942. Heidrich died of his injuries in early June. Distraught that his integrity, skill, and motives be brought into question, Gebhardt began his 'Live Tissue Training' programme. His test subjects arriving late at night from Ravensbruck.

As he made his way through the grounds, he was distracted by the Luftwaffe BV-222 roaring over at low level before banking eastwards as it made its final approach to touch down on the Zenesse. As the aircraft taxied up towards the north jetty, Gebhardt noticed the soldiers on their Zundapps and in the staff cars pulling themselves straight, before those with helmets on delivered a crisp, party salute. With his field cap in place, he returned a lacklustre response.

With the noise of engine wash making conversation difficult, one of the outriders jogged up into offices to announce Gebhardt's arrival. He ascended the stairs and strode in; he pulled his white laboratory coat straight so he could present the best image of himself. He seldom received visitors at such short notice. His first contact was with Lucy, who took his cap and lab coat before leading him to Mortens office. Declining her offer of coffee, he was eager to make it brief and get back to his work beneath the Officer Ward.

Stood at the threshold of the office, he was received by his Head of Security and a huge Hauptsturmfuhrer almost Yiddish in facial features. Both saluted him.

'Heil Hitler!' they called as one.

Without returning the salutation, Gebhardt frowned as he looked about the office. The engines of the BV-222 spluttered out, with peace returning to the lakeside facility.

'I have been summoned.' Gebhardt was curt. Both men lowered their arms. Roche stepped forward.

'Yes, Obergruppenfuhrer. I have been sent to brief you on developments from Berlin.'

Considerably shorter than Roche, Gebhardt felt the need to puff his chest out and jut his chin.

'You are?'

'Hauptsturmfuhrer Roche, Sir. Adjutant.'

Cocking his head to one side, Gebhardt failed to hide any distain for being disturbed by just the messenger.

'Haupsturmfuhrer? Why am I being summoned to speak with you?'

Mortens, arm now lowered, exchanged glances with his peer. He knew Gebhardt to be an arse, but this was not going to be pretty. Roche removed his cap.

'The Commandant sends his compliments but cannot attend due to a short notice visit by the SS-Reichsführer.'

'The Reichsführer?' Gebhardt's eyebrows peaked as his eyes widened. Both men before him nodded in response. Roche continued.

'After a conference at Ravensbruck, he is coming to take some leave here, Obergruppenfuhrer.'

'Take leave?' Gebhardt answered in surprise before rolling into a frown. 'Why is he taking leave here?'

'The Fuhrer has ordered him to rest here, before he assumes a combat command.'

'Combat Command?' Gebhardt was beside himself. Roche returned a tight-lipped smile as Mortens nodded slightly, loving how uncomfortable the Chief Surgeon was looking. His smugness was short-lived as Gebhardt turned his focus on him.

'I trust you have security issues in hand, Haupsturmfuhrer?'

Surprised at the question, Mortens looked to Roche, who looked relieved the focus was now off him. Mortens cleared his throat.

'The entire facility is far too open in my opinion. I trust the Reichsführer has a security team accompanying him?'

Gebhardt rolled his eyes, all too familiar with Mortens misgivings.

'Can you keep him safe whilst he's here?'

Pausing for a second, Mortens knew there was only one answer.

'Well, yes Sir.'

'Good.'

Gebhardt eyed him before looking slowly back to Roche.

'When is he due to come here?'

Roche let out a shrug. 'More information to follow. He's still in Berlin with the Fuhrer as far as I'm aware.'

'So...' Gebhardt snorted, 'they finally prised him out of his precious castle.'

'Castle?' Mortens murmured. Gebhardt forced a sinister leer.

'Outside Paderborn. Acts like the place is centre of the universe. Word is the Fuhrer has never even visited it. He even has his own private airfield.'

'Oh.' Mortens responded, looking to Roche for confirmation. All he got in return was a blank look. This castle Gebhardt spoke of was clearly not common knowledge among everyone in the SS. Clearly the select few. As Gebhardt turned towards the window, Mortens spoke up once more.

'Haupsturmfuhrer Roche here was updating me on redeployments from Ravensbruck.'

'Redeployments?' Gebhardt spoke over his shoulder.

'Inmates are being transferred west, and non-essential troops sent into Berlin.'

Gebhardt spun on his heels, eyes wide.

'Where are the inmates going?'

'Locations yet to be confirmed, Sir.' Roche answered rather officiously, 'Belsen will take the majority from the discussions I've been privy to. Fallingbostel will take a small labour force but other than that, details are light at present.'

'What about us?' Gebhardt asked. Mortens sensed he was growing rather anxious.

'As far as I am aware, Sir, this facility will remain. What security forces are already in place will also stay for the time being. I'm sure, if I may be so bold Sir, you'll have the opportunity to discuss the matter with the Reichsführer in person.'

Gebhardt appeared content with Roche' rationale, as he slid both hands in his trouser pockets. Mortens did have a question.

'Will the Reichsführer arrive overland or fly in?'

'Overland, given the short distance.' Roche offered which satisfied him. As Gebhardt went to leave, he suddenly looked to Roche.

'Why all the cars and bikes, if it was just you coming here?'

'Not my idea, Sir.' Roche shrugged. Perhaps to lure enemy fighters away from the Reichsführer visit. The weather is improving. Good for the enemy, not so good for us anymore.'

'Pah,' Gebhardt snorted, making Mortens and Roche flinch, 'you have a point there. Apart from those flying boats tipping up most days, I cannot remember the last time I even saw one of hours overhead.'

Still chuckling to himself, he called for his cap and white coat. As Lucy clipped into the office with the garments, both Mortens and Roche pulled themselves to attention. Perching the cap on his head and draping the white coat over the crook of his arm, be bid them farewell as the two SS captains saluted in the usual fashion. No sooner had he left the building, Lucy turned to the two men.

'More coffee gentlemen?'

30.

The BV-222 moored at the north jetty made observation rather difficult for W-W and Mould. It became clear as the day went on, that the buildings across the Zenesse from them were somewhat elevated by the very bank they sat upon. In the prone position amid the deadfall of their observation post, it became clear that the observers would have to look up, when it would be rather advantageous to look down on an enemy target. The large profile of the floating aircraft obscured in the sanatorium grounds immediately behind it. Enemy activity where the vehicle convoy had parked was difficult to make out and it was just by chance that Mould picked out the short, dumpy looking man, white coat draped over his right arm making his way back to Building Four. Stretcher parties from Building Three had emerged to meet with those who had arrived by air.

Through their binoculars, both W-W and Mould could identify stretcher cases, and a large number of walking wounded.

'Have the Russians started their offensive across the Oder?' Mould asked to which the captain shrugged.

'Not sure, why?'

'Casualties are coming in. Wasn't sure if this place was just for those fighting locally.'

'Not a clue, old man. Not a clue.'

'That guy in the white coat,' Mould continued,' he's back in Building Four.'

'How could you tell?'

'Same gait, just had the coat draped over an arm.'

'Well spotted.'

After an hour, the engines on the BV-222 cranked up and before long, it cast off from the jetty. In a wide turn to starboard, both W-W and Mould were convinced it was about to run aground right in front of them. It bore no red cross markings and bristled with machineguns. Should the gunners have spotted them amongst the deadfall, it could have spelt disaster for the British. As it increased in power and taxied back out into the middle of the Zenesse, all those in the observation post breathed out a sigh of relief. W-W turned and grinned at his men.

'That could've been cheeky.'

With the aircraft accelerating away towards the southern end of the Zenesse, W-W, his head heavy with fatigue felt now was the time rest. Having not slept properly since leaving Scotland, he knew that he would need his wits about him that coming night, for Mould would lead a small party to rig the road bridge for demolition. The two Mercedes and the Zundapp outriders were gone, and there was some human activity about the facility. Office staff having a cigarette on the jetty, white clad people coming to and from Building Four, sentries roaming in pairs, not looking particularly alert. W-W knew his men would wake him if anything of real note was worthy of his attention.

With Talbot already awake and eating, W-W shuffled back to allow the somewhat fresher man to take his place. To reduce the need for numerous people milling about, packing, and unpacking sleeping bags, W-W climbed into the bag Talbot had vacated. It was still warm, and the captain welcomed it.

'Boss?'

The words swam through to W-W as he surfaced from the depths of a much-needed sleep. Blinking hard, the features of Mould swam into view.

'How long have I been out?'

'Couple of hours, but you need to see this.'

Talbot made room for the captain as he hauled himself in between both he and the sergeant. The private handed him the binoculars.

'They are taking coffee on the terrace.'

'Who?'

'Building Four.'

Thanks to Roche, forewarned was forearmed. Mortens needed to ensure the Reichsfuhrer stay at Hohenlychen was secure and without incident. The lack of a patrol programme irked him, so he now needed to take matters in hand. He would visit the Guardroom and warn off the duty Scharfuhrer for a night security patrol across the footbridge, starting that night.

As he and Tommy walked through the grounds, Mortens was pleased the skies were clear enough for people to enjoy getting outside. All morning, the skies threatened rain, but now were looking rather pleasant. With the officers relaxing out on the terrace, Mortens straightened his cap, for he was in a good mood, despite the forthcoming visit by Heinrich Himmler, and all his hangers on. As he walked, he decided that after speaking with the duty Scharfuhrer, he was going home early. He planned to sit in his neat little garden, with Astrid and Tommy and enjoy a much-needed beer.

As he drew up to the edge of the terrace, he watched with interest his supposed elders and betters reading their newspapers, smoking heavily, and some even appeared to busy themselves with official paperwork. As if they were in fact still commanding units from their headquarters. Stewards were continuously being beckoned for refreshments, or to take a note to whoever was the recipient somewhere in the facility. They sat in clusters, discussing tactical or strategic matters. Mortens confessed to not exactly being a fighting man, but even he could safely deduce that these old soldiers were now out of the loop and who knows where their previous commands were now on the real battlefield.

Predictably, sat on his own, aloof of all the military pantomime, sat Jurgen Arens. Coffee in one hand, a cigarette in the other. Decked out in pyjamas and slippers, a clean army issued greatcoat, void of any ribbons or decorations draped over his shoulders to keep the chill off. Mortens, mindful of the senior ranks present, clipped his heels together and gave a crisp party salute. A few of the old guard looked up and thanked him for the compliment, one even hauled himself to his feet and returned the salutation in the same vigour. With that taken care of, Mortens removed his cap and made his way over to Arens, who was all smiles.

'Good afternoon, Haupsturmfuhrer. I trust you are well?'

'I am, Obersturmbannfuhrer, thank you.'

As Mortens spoke aloud, those sat clustered in their cliques looked over at Arens, their faces full of contempt. Arens, weary of the whole enterprise, raised his coffee cup in mock salute.

'Heil Hitler.'

Those glaring at him went back to whatever they were discussing. Mortens looked nervously at Arens; his voice hushed.

'You are telling me to watch what I say? I would say the same to you right now.'

'Relax, Otto.' Arens scoffed, waving a dismissive hand, 'given where this war is going, I'm far more important to the Fuhrer, I assure you.'

Mortens had to agree that the man certainly held some kudos with those in Berlin.

'Where will they have you continue your research?' he asked, to which Arens merely shrugged.

'Not a clue if I'm honest. I think we are running out of places to hide if you get my meaning. Norway is off the menu, that's for sure.'

Mortens looked about those Arens shared the ward.

'I trust you have yet to approach the subject with these gentlemen?'

'Are you serious?' Arens pulled a face, 'Hardly an after-dinner topic, Otto. Besides, even if I were permitted to discuss the reason for my work, I doubt they would have the brain capacity to even comprehend its potential. Let them play with their tanks and soldiers and leave the science to people like me.'

Mortens knew better than to enquire as to the detail of Arens work and bid the man good day. As he left the terrace, he caught sight of Tommy stood poised at the end of the jetty, barking out over the water. Walking on to the jetty, he called the dog, but to no avail. Tommy carried on barking out over the water. It was only as his master ruffled his flanks, did the German Shepherd acknowledge him. Kneeling, Mortens stroked Tommy's snout.

'What has got you all excited boy?'

Tommy sat, enjoying the attention. As Mortens stroked him, he looked out over the Zenesse, scanning the far bank. He could not see anything untoward. Tommy's barking fit did remind him however to go speak with the duty Scharfuhrer about a patrol across the footbridge after last light.

'The dog can smell us.'

'Nonsense. Just an excited dog. Don't fret.'

'I'm telling you boss, that dog knows we are here.' Mould countered, more forthright. W-W looked to him, biting his lip. In his heart of hearts, he suspected the very same thing. He then looked back out over the water. The dog and his handler were now stepping off the jetty and going about their business.

'Have we seen any other dogs yet?'

'No. Just that one. That guy likes to walk around with his dog.'

'So, a personal pet, not a working dog you reckon?' W-W put to the sergeant, who nodded. W-W scanned the terrace full of patients. White tunic stewards pouring coffee, spirals of cigarette smoke climbing about them.

'I think we have found the Officer Ward.'

'I agree.' Mould responded. 'The dog walker saluted one of those sat down.'

'Yes he did.' W-W smirked, still scanning the terrace. He lifted his head out of his binoculars and glanced right at the much larger building.

'The other ranks must relax on the other side of their building. The last thing us gentlemen want to see and hear is you ruffians larking about lakeside.'

Mould cocked the captain an eyebrow.

'Whatever.'

W-W snorted as he consulted his sketch map.

'I'm calling Building Four. What say you, Sergeant?'

Mould took the time to scan the terrace through his binoculars before consulting the sketch map. He then made eye contact with W-W and gave him a mischievous grin.

'Our man sleeps in Building Four.'

31.

Whilst Jones managed to doze, many of the men were restless. Unable to distract themselves by checking their weapons and equipment over and over, especially on Swedish soil, they had to try their hardest to concentrate on other endeavours. Some of the NCO's gathered to consult their maps, whilst others just took the time to sit alone, wrapped in thought.

The rest of the men were not that dissimilar. Along with the usual antics bored soldiers found themselves embroiled, reading books, playing chess, smoking, chatting, eating, picking noses, scratching themselves, they too had a keen interest in the geographical layout of the target and the surrounding area and would join those NCO's and their maps. It was not lost on the private soldiers that just one bullet could elevate their responsibilities and have them assume command before chaos overwhelmed them. Casualties among the Officer and NCO cohorts were high in commando operations since they had a habit of leading the assault from the front. The men knew that they had to be able to read the battle and not just their immediate situation. If all the leaders fell, the mission still had to continue, objectives secured, key phases and timings met. The mission came before the man.

This time, the mission was about a man. Jurgen Arens. The men within the ranks of Jones' company did not need to care for him in much as his politics, his values and standards. They were just to get him on one of the Catalinas and get him out of there, come what may.

Jones flinched as a firm hand squeezed his shoulder. Looking up, the face that swam into focus was that of Sergeant Major Tristan Montgomery. Blinking hard so to focus quicker, Jones let out a stretch.

'Are we on?'

'Message coming in now,' was the reply.

Bleary eyed, Jones followed Montgomery over to where the radio set was manned. As he pulled braces over his shoulders, he observed the signaller scribbling away with a pencil. With the chirping of Morse ended, Jones waited patiently as the signaller checked over his decoding before handing it to his company commander. As Jones took the log book from the man, he glanced up to see that the sergeant major had also roused Freya from wherever she had managed to rest her head. Looking a little fresher than he was, she greeted him with a warm smile. Standing next to him, they both read the message.

BUILDING FOUR CONFIRMED.

ROAD BRIDGE DEMOLITION PATROL AFTER LAST LIGHT.

JETTY CLEAR.

GOD SAVE THE KING.

Stone faced, Montgomery waited patiently for the major and the MI6 agent to absorb the message. Jones then looked to his sergeant major, handing him the log book. With a deadpan expression, Montgomery read the message before handing the log book back to the signaller, muttering as he did so.

'I'll rouse the men.'

In short order, Montgomery had the company assembled in the living room. With the aircrews informed of their impending departure, Jones took the opportunity to update his men with the confirmation.

'Building Four is confirmed.'

Jones paused to allow the NCOs to pull maps and sketch maps from their smocks. Once they were settled and looking back at him, he reminded them of the Order of Battle.

'Catalina One, carrying 1 Troop, plus my headquarters will be entering Building Four. Catalina Two, carrying 2 Troop and the sergeant majors' group will provide security south, with the sergeant major providing illumination should we need it at the northern jetty. Catalina Three, carrying 3 Troop, security north. We should all be aware that we should receive Captain Walsh-Woolcott's group from the north when we extract. We have planned for Catalina Three to lift them out, but to be honest, I don't give a shit what aircraft they get on, we just need to grab our man and fuck off.'

The unexpected profanity caused a ripple of chuckling from the men. A sideways glance confirmed that even Freya was trying her best to supress a smirk. Before the men became a little raucous, Montgomery called for order as he went through a few housekeeping points.

'1 Troop, be sure to get off the bird with crowbars and sledgehammers. Once you're in the building, ditch 'em. The Germans can 'ave 'em for all I care. The Quartermaster can bill me.'

The lads gave a low cheer. Their rebellion against the system. He raised a hand for order.

'I want morphine syrettes in your top left smock pockets. Tourniquets bottom right. Field dressings wherever you can fit 'em. That goes for everyone, understood?'

He got nods from everyone, including Jones. With a fold of his arms and courteous nod, Montgomery stepped back.

'That's me Sir.'

Jones looked to Freya as she pulled the log book from the radio set table.

'I'll speak with our American friends.'

As vague as she was, it was clear to Jones she was not going to say more. Looking about the room, he could see no raised hands for last minute questions. He slid his hands in his pockets.

'Tonight, we go. Make no mistake, we are going to where the SS convalesce. Let's grab our man before we shoot up the place. Once we have him, you are clear to engage all hostiles. Anyone in that place that is not Arens is to be regarded as hostile. We are there for one man, and one man only. We won't be grabbing anyone else. Understood?'

The men, in one fashion or another nodded that they understood. Jones did not want to get into the long grass about the fact that it was a hospital, nor speak of the note he had received from the Prime Minister himself. If the so-called 'patients' of Hohenlychen Sanatorium happened to be caught up in the middle of a gunfight with security forces, that would be unfortunate. He would leave it at that.

As the light of a long restless day began to wane, Jones looked on as his men took the time to ensure they boarded the correct aircraft. The small rowing boats that had been provided to lift the men from the shore to the floating Catalinas were in addition, invaluable in the ferrying to and fro stores and equipment between the aircraft as the men made fine adjustments to the loading plan aboard, under the guidance of the company sergeant major. Nursing a cup of tea in both hands, he watched with interest the activity within the cockpits. Warrant Officer Richard Monk and his colleagues went about their business in the best way they knew. Getting ready to fly into the heart of Nazi Germany and deliver British

Commandos into where the SS rest and lick their wounds, Hohenlychen Sanatorium.

Movement in his left periphery caught his attention. He looked up just as Freya sat down next to him. As she dropped the radio log book between them, she reached over and took the cup from his hands. The tepid dregs in the bottom did nothing to dissuade her from finishing them. She put the cup down on top of the log book. Pulling her knees up, she wrapped her arms around them and pulled them in tight. Her interest appeared to be the Catalinas bobbing out in the bay, the rowing boats moving between them.

'I'll be manning the set from when you leave, Fyn. Call me once you are on your way back here.'

'Sure.'

'You'll have to sit here for the day again, I'm afraid. Until it's dark at least.'

'Oh, right.' Jones pulled a face.' Why's that?'

'Submarines are not fond of surfacing in daylight.'

'Fair point.'

Both then sat in silence, content in each other's company. After a few minutes, Freya spoke.

'If Arens makes it difficult for you, promise me you'll kill him.'

Jones looked to the British agent, her face giving away nothing but a tight-lipped smile.

'Promise me.' She asked again. Jones fixed her a look.

'I promise. Along with the rest of those murdering fuckers malingering in that place. You have my word.'

As she looked away, she gave him a friendly pat on his thigh.

'Good man.'

As it finally grew twilight, Jones boarded the Catalina thanks to the rowing endeavours of Manfred, the teenager that had originally helped bring out the boats upon their arrival in Sweden. Looking back at the shore, he could just make out Freya making her way back up to the chalet. Casting Manfred off, he then picked his way carefully inside the crowded aircraft. Being the commander of the operation, he would enjoy the perk of being up front with Monk and co-pilot. As the engines spluttered into life, Jones accepted the headset handed to him by the Flight Engineer. It would be the live intercom among those who needed to speak and keep the Catalina in the air and on course. Knowing to keep quiet whilst those who knew better went through their repertoire of getting them airborne, Jones held on tight as Monk accelerated, the Catalina responding in kind, her huge airframe shuddering as she powered across the surface of the water. At the required moment, both Monk and co-pilot pulled back on their yokes, hauling the aircraft into the air. The jarring as she skimmed across the surface ceased instantly, yet the vibration of her engines and the relentless physics of her defying gravity remained.

They were on their way. The mission was on.

W-W and those remaining in the observation post watched with a little envy as Mould, plus his three demolition men patrolled back into the dark sanctuary of the forest. With Mould leading, he was followed by the damp Private Dobbs, still not dry from his unfortunate landing, Crossland and Peters respectively. As much as they were now up against it time wise, they could not afford to bungle straight into a German patrol.

They would first have to approach the footbridge with caution, for it funnelled them into a potentially deadly chokepoint. In order to reach the road bridge, they would have to cross it. In the gloom of the forest, Mould identified the trail that would lead them to the structure. Conscious not to walk on the trail, Mould kept his team on its western side by ten yards so cover was available should they encounter trouble. Deadfall refused to cooperate, as nature chooses its own path, causing the patrol to either veer closer to the water's edge or almost upon the very trail they were trying to avoid. Going under foot was deceiving, for no matter how carefully they placed their feet, strands of older deadfall would crack under them.

Out of the gloom, Mould spotted the on ramp of the wooden footbridge. As he moved in closer, the other three following on, he heard heavy footfall clanking toward them. With his stomach turning, he signalled his men to take cover.

The ten-man German patrol crossed the footbridge with no real tactical consideration. Why should they worry? They were well behind their own lines. With their NCOs armed with MP40 Submachineguns, the remainder carrying their Mauser rifles, the patrol strode across the bridge to begin a long night on the far bank because the new Head of Security wanted to make a name for himself. With their equipment and order of dress correct, the only thing that was off was their attitude. Once off the bridge, and out of sight of the sanatorium, they huddled under a tree before lighting their cigarettes.

Mould fought hard to calm his breathing. His heart thumped like a bass drum, loud enough he thought that the German patrol not twenty yards across the track could not fail to hear it. The last thing he could afford at that point was a gunfight. Ten against four was not good odds. Even if they got the better of them, the game would be up, for the entire facility would be alerted. The deadfall he concealed himself in, prevented him from seeing the remainder of his team. He prayed they too had the good sense to just sit tight and hope the patrol would just move on with whatever tasks it had that evening.

Mortens could tell the men were not entirely happy about the patrol he had sent them on, but he did not care. The regime at Hohenlychen up until his arrival had been a sham. Everyone far too comfortable in their surroundings, thinking they were untouchable. Sipping coffee on the veranda of the Guardroom, he watched as the duty Scharfuhrer led them away towards the footbridge. They were well fed and watered, well-armed, and possessed a radio. The NCO would have preferred to take an MG-42 with them, but Mortens felt that was over the top for a security patrol. The pleased expressions on the faces of the men were evident when he told them to leave it behind. They would only be out for a couple of hours. What harm could it do? He would remain at the Guardroom for a little while before heading home for the night.

Mould continued to count the Germans loitering about in front of him. Ten in all. He was certain of it. After what felt like an age, they began to move off, deeper into the forest. As they gained some distance, Mould ventured out onto the trail to keep an eye on them. They were sticking to the trail in single file. Content they were now far enough away, he clicked his fingers. As one, three men emerged from their deadfall sanctuaries. Moving in close to the sergeant, Dobbs gave off a toothy grin.

'Fuckin' 'ell,' he hissed, 'that was cheeky.'

The footbridge was a sturdy timber construction. Upon inspection, Mould could see that it was untreated and rough, as if it were recently built and yet to be weatherproofed. It mattered little, for they would need it either way when the time to withdraw from the target was upon them. Crossing the footbridge without incident, what Mould found rather troubling was the complete lack of cover on the far bank. With a few sparse trees and tussock grass as cover, Mould hunched low as he led the team along the far bank until it come upon the on ramp of the sought-after road bridge. With only the photographs to go on, he would first have to scout it properly before setting the demolition charges.

Even through the stereoscope, looks could be deceptive. The road bridge was not so much a bridge, but more of a culvert and causeway construction. Any lower towards the waterline, the lake would have consumed it.

Hugging the eastern bank, Mould and his men moved at a low crouch. To stand up at that point would have exposed them to anyone walking on or near the road. Darkness, and the slight camber of the bank was their only concealment. Signalling by hand for the men to remain where they were, Mould removed his pack full of demolitions, webbing, smock and ventured forward alone to the structure. Bushes, some chest high clustered about the right side of the on ramp. While they concealed him from anyone on the bridge, he eased himself into the frigid water so he could inspect the underside of the structure, puffing out his cheeks as he fought to remain silent to the sudden chill.

So much for just Dobbs getting wet.

Given that they were amid a cluster of lakes, Mould was not expecting the water to flow through at any particular rate or direction. The water was still, with clusters of reeds and deadfall protruding from below the waterline. With his right arm keeping the Thompson out of the water, he hauled himself forward with his left to get closer to the dark culvert. The bright moon, occasionally hidden behind lingering banks of cloud illuminated the area in an eerie glow but did not help Mould with inspecting the cluttered culvert. With his free hand, the first few limbs of old deadfall came free easy enough, but at the rate he was progressing, it would be broad daylight by the time they had gotten through to the middle of the culvert. Accepting the job was for more than one man, Mould withdrew.

'Culvert?' Whispered Dobbs, to which he received a nodding Mould in response.

'Culvert. Since we are both now wet, we'll crack on with that, you two…' he referred to Crossland and Peters, 'keep an eye out for that bloody patrol. We need to get on with this. Jones and the others are already on their way.'

Back at the onramp bushes, all four commandos got on with the task of rigging the bridge for demolition. With Crossland and Peters kneeling, the bushes hiding them from the road, one kept an eye on the footbridge they had traversed, whilst the other looked across the span of the bridge into Lychen village. All was quiet, save for the two men stripped down to their shirts, up to the chests in frigid water, try to haul deadfall from the underside of the structure quietly. With Dobbs doing the lion share of removing the limbs from the culvert, Mould stacked it as neat as he could out of the way, so it would not hinder a quick getaway. To all four men, it felt like they were taking far too long. Mould cursed under his breath for forgetting to bring secateurs to break up the spindly deadfall branches into more manageable lengths. Snapping them in half would only create noise that would carry on the night air, and that was bad for business. Carefully between them, they hauled the deadfall from the culvert. More than once, Mould slipped up to his neck as the lake bed gave way to a deeper gradient. Obsessed with the Colt in its holster, he dreaded losing it. When not hauling deadfall limbs, he had his hand on the canvas holster, taking comfort that it still contained the weapon. Slowly, they were making progress, and the water was not getting any warmer.

Bored of the poor-quality coffee the Guardroom provided, Mortens pulled on his cap as he called for Tommy, who had curled up amid the bunks where some of the guard force dozed. The NCO left manning the front desk got to his feet before pulling himself to attention as the officer and dog left the building. He had decided it was time to go home. He had a patrol out across the lake doing what they should be doing, and he had a suitable sized force left within the facility to continue with other security duties. Mortens was now content, for the first time as it appeared the place and its occupants were finally getting their head around what he was trying to accomplish. To keep them safe. What he was not looking forward to however, was the imminent arrival of Heinrich Himmler.

He had been in the company of the SS- Reichsführer perhaps twice in his career to date. The first was at his graduation as a cadet at Bad Tolz in 1938. Himmler just so happened to be the inspecting officer. The second was much later when he visited Army Group South in Ukraine where Mortens was part of the security company for Army Group Headquarters. As far as Mortens was concerned, Himmler seldom filled a room with his presence, but his entourage more than made up for it. It was this fact alone that made Mortens a little nervous. He knew that Himmler would want to commandeer a generous sized office in order to take care of his various commitments whilst he 'rested' and his hangers on would maraud the facility as if they owned it.

Not a good time to be Head of Security. Mortens knew he would have to impress all those who apparently had the ear of the SS-Reichsführer if he was to avoid commanding a company of old men and kids in a Berlin suburb. As Tommy cantered alongside him, Mortens checked himself for forgetting his torch. He paused to consider returning to the office to collect it. He doubted he would encounter Lucy enthralled with her young man, since it was the very Scharfuhrer that was leading the patrol across the lake. After a few moments, he dismissed the idea, the allure of a warm bed and an even warmer Astrid within it making up his mind. He spun on his heels and walked on.

As he approached the road bridge, he could see Tommy rigid as a statue, ears back, shoulders hunched as he growled in a constant low rumble out over the water. Pulling up next to him, Mortens squatted, rubbing the dogs back.

'What has you spooked, young man?' he spoke softly, as if to an irritated child. He looked over the top of Tommy's head to try and ascertain what had his undivided attention.

All Mortens could make out was an empty bridge and some bushes.

As he stood, determined to get home, he patted Tommy on the rump, but the dog would not be swayed. The growling grew a little louder. Mortens could see his boy was showing some teeth, in every sense of the word. Mortens looked to where Tommy was focused and walked forward. Without a torch, strict blackout protocol, and the moon rolling behind a thick bank of cloud, seeing much of anything was near on impossible. A slight glint of the calm Zenesse was all he could make out. The bushes were nothing more than a dark profile, with some thin limbs of deadfall drifting away from him. Certain Tommy was just getting touchy, he turned on his heels and called for him to come to his master.

The dog creeped forward, no less agitated, the growl and teeth unwavering. Mortens was now growing impatient.

'Stupid dog, 'he muttered under his breath as he removed Tommy's lead which he had draped across his shoulders, running down the front of his tunic. He rarely needed to use it, but tonight was certainly one of those nights. Slipping the clip onto the small metal loop on his collar, Tommy instantly snapped out of his aggressive state, only to look up at his master who stood over him with a stern expression of his own.

'Have you quiet finished making my evening longer than I want it to be?'

The German Shepherd lowered his head and began to head off across the bridge, slow enough that the lead never went tight, but enough to have Mortens follow on with a more purposeful pace. As they both headed across, Mortens could not help but keep glancing over his right shoulder.

Just bushes and water. He wondered what had spooked his dog. Tommy was usually so relaxed and playful. Maybe he was just tired, much like his master.

Crossland leaned out of the bushes to get eye contact with both Dobbs and Mould. He could see both men leaning against the mouth of the culvert, the water running between their legs, their chests heaving as they held their Colt automatics in both hands. He watched as Mould gingerly stepped out into the water proper, trying to peer over the bridge into the village. Reluctant to climb the structure to confirm the German and his dog had gone, Mould looked over his shoulder and could see Crossland looking back at him, relieved to see the rather dry commando give him a thumbs up.

Instantly, both men at the culvert relaxed, slumping against the structure in relief. Cuffing his face with his free arm, Mould returned the Colt to its holster. He patted Dobbs on the shoulder and waved him on to follow him back to where the other two were keeping watch. Clambering out of the water, Crossland could not help but give his thoughts on the matter.

'That was fucking close.' He hissed, but if Mould and Dobbs found it amusing, they did not let on. Instead, they took hold of the pack containing the explosives and timing pencils and began to make their way back out into the water. Crossland tapped Dobbs on the shoulder.

'Have you cleared enough of it?' Crossland enquired. Dobbs shrugged.

'Fuck knows. We'll just pack more explosives in there. After that close call, we aren't sticking around to push our luck.'

With a belly full of late supper, Tommy curled up under the kitchen table and settled down for the night. Mortens, after a much nicer coffee and cigarette to follow, lowered his tired frame into the much-promised warm bed. As he lay on his right side, naked as the day he was born, the warm smooth Astrid rolled over and tucked in behind him. Her nipples pressing into his back aroused him, so did her left-hand gliding over his hip to confirm he was hard. She squeezed him a little to show her approval. He rolled over to meet her, knowing to never waste such an opportunity.

32.

Back in the observation post, Mould gave W-W the short version of their culvert exploits. Pleased the demolition team did not initiate the attack prior to the arrival of the main group, W-W could not help but stifle a chuckle as the story was told. Their mutual concern was a number of issues.

Firstly, the timing pencils. Under his supervision, Mould had witnessed Dobbs set pencils from both batches for four hours. Known for being unreliable, the commandos could not be confident if either batch would initiate or go off too early or too late. The latter would not matter for they had every intention of not being there to care. There was also the issue of how much explosives they had put in the culvert. Mould knew too well he had over done it. They had not pulled enough dead fall from the culvert to plant the explosives under the centre of the span. W-W and his deputy could only hope the pending explosion did not wreck the footbridge before they crossed it to rejoin Jones and the others.

Secondly, and certainly worth addressing was the German foot patrol marauding in the woods to the rear of their current position. If they were discovered prior to the arrival of the main group, it would spell disaster for them as they would be landing on a target ready to defend itself. Not to mention the fact that W-W and his team would also be fighting for their lives deep in enemy territory surrounded by a hostile population. W-W would rather have the patrol return to the other side of the lake, but that would only give Jones more people to fight once the shooting would undoubtably start. The German patrol was a problem, that was for sure.

The next issue for W-W was the fact that in his current location, he could not observe either bridges. He needed to be able to observe its destruction, or direct fire support from the Catalinas into that area should enemy reinforcements arrive early. A red flare would do the trick, but they needed to be closer. With that in mind, he called the men to gather around him. Those in their sleeping bags were woken, so he did not have to relay the information more than once. Leaning in towards them, W-W kept his voice hushed.

'When the main group arrive, we are packing up our tents and moving closer to the bridges.'

He allowed those drunk by sleep to absorb what he was saying before he carried on.

'We have an enemy patrol lurking about here, and we need to neutralise them, so they don't come back to fight the main group whilst they look for our man. We will set an ambush for them to counter this.'

He paused once more before continuing.

'The road bridge is set for demolition, but just in case it doesn't go up, we need to be able to direct fire from the cats should we need it, okay?'

His men nodded as they went back to their duties, some curling up to sleep a little more before the drone of Catalinas gave them notice to get up and ready for battle.

'We're on our final approach, Sir' Monk's voice crackled through the live intercom. Jones nodded as he patted the man on the shoulder. Peering forward out of the cockpit window, Jones was in awe at the skill of Monk and his crew as they checked off navigational features in quick succession at high speed and at such low level. Since crossing over the German coast, both Monk and his co-pilot put the aircraft through her paces. Trees whipped past so close, it sometimes made Jones flinch. Flying fast and low along the many lakes that dotted northern Germany made his buttocks clench for he felt they were about to take on water at any moment. To top is all off for the commando major was the fact it was almost pitch-black outside. The only ambient light given from the moon when not hidden by cloud banks.

The moon revealed itself once more, allowing the glint of the Zenesse to come up and meet them as it raced past on their starboard side. Jones fought to get a view of the Hohenlychen Sanatorium on its western bank, but the Germans were not going to give it away that easy. Blackout protocols in Nazi Germany were enforced even harder than back in Britain. As they slowly banked to port for the final long swing to starboard to come in to land, Jones took it as his cue to pull off his headset and look to the nearest commandos crammed in behind him.

In the dull glow of red interior lights, he could just make out two of them. Their faces were smeared in camouflage face paint, their skin glistening with sweat. One appeared to be nodding a little as he dozed, the other made eye contact with his company commander. Over the din of the engines, the young man offered Jones a thumbs up gesture. Jones responded in kind, which immediately prompted the young commando to give his dozing comrade a nudge before calling aft of himself to rouse the rest. As the Catalina swung low and fast to starboard, Jones replaced the headset back over his ears as Monk, rather business like talked through their final drills with his co-pilot as they came in to land on the Zenesse. It was as they touched sound on the surface of the lake, Jones thought of W-W and his men who were already in the area, no doubt watching them come in to land.

As Monk put the Catalina on the water, the engines appeared to raise in pitch. Jones shook his head at the sheer din reverberating through the aircraft. It was just as well that the Germans were probably used to flying boats arriving at the sanatorium, or by now the facility would we very much alert. As Monk reduced speed and taxied over to where the southern jetty was supposed to be, Jones looked over his shoulder to witness his men, in their cramped confines getting ready to disembark.

'Now where is this bloody jetty?' Monk murmured as a crackle in Jones' ears. Jones squinted out into the gloom of the early German morning. The moon their friend at that point. No sooner had he spotted the long, low structure on the surface of the lake, did his stomach turn as two figures on the jetty switched on torches and shined them at the cockpit.

'Shit.' All three men cussed into the intercom. The two German sentries waved their torches about, as if trying to beckon the Catalina toward them, unaware of its true intention. To these guys, they were just more flying boats bringing in casualties from the Oder front. Monk looked at Jones, eyebrow cocked.

'Please do something about that, if you would be so kind.'

Jones pulled off the headset and looked at the two commandos stood hunched, ready to disembark. Leaning towards them, he hollered over the din of the engines.

'Two sentries on the jetty.' And then proceeded to give them the cut throat hand gesture. Both men nodded back that they understood. Jones turned back, patting Monk on the shoulder. Holding the microphone of the headset to his lips, Jones spoke with purpose.

'Keep the engine noise up whilst we take care of it.'

Monk did as he was instructed as they pulled up at the end of the jetty. As the two German sentries, one very slim, the other very stocky strode up to greet them, they crumpled into a pile as they were cut down by Colt Automatic fire. The engines drowned out the shots. The swift, violent action was over in a second, leaving Monk and his co-pilot stunned and somewhat lost for words. Patting Monk on the shoulder again, Jones spoke into the microphone.

'We're getting off now. See you soon.'

The first four commandos off the Catalina grabbed both dead Germans by their webbing straps and hauled them off the jetty, laying them under some trees. The remainder of those on the first aircraft fanned out to provide security as Monk taxied away, making room the next Catalina to off load. Jones joined the men searching the two dead bodies.

Just two sentries. Nothing of any real intelligence on them except the fact they were SS. The silver runes of the organisation on the collar of their tunics. They looked well fed, their uniforms were clean and pressed, and they were clean shaven. Their carbines were clean and well oiled. Jones deduced that the others in the facility would cut a similar bearing. They did not carry grenades, which told Jones that these men were assigned to the security of the sanatorium, and not combat drafts sent in to reinforce. There would certainly be others.

More commandos joined the defensive perimeter as the third and final Catalina off loaded. The first two had taxied out into the Zenesse to keep out of the way. With their markings difficult to identify, at least while it was still dark, Jones was quietly confident other sentries roaming the facility would assume they were German aircraft. The short headland that hid the sanatorium from view in the south jetty area would serve the Catalinas until they were called forward. As the final Catalina taxied out to join the other two, Jones stood to take in all of his company. With the three aircraft out on the water taking care of themselves, their engines feathered so they sat much quieter, it was now time to get on with what they came for.

Breach Building Four. Identify and extract Obersturmbannfuhrer Jurgen Arens.

With 1 Troop plus Jones leading the company along the water's edge, the commandos made for their target building. The Officer Ward sat almost opposite the northern jetty which suited Jones just fine as he planned to have the Catalinas lift them off from there. Should the situation prevent that option they would just have to haul themselves and Arens back to where they disembarked.

Jones noticed that the going underfoot was easy, for the grounds of the facility appeared, at least in the gloom, to be rather neat and tidy. Unbeknown to him, deadfall plagued the far side of the lake, both a benefit and a burden to W-W and his men.

The Germans had form for keeping things neat and tidy, Jones reminded himself.

There was suddenly a flurry of hand signals from those leading the group, beckoning everyone to take cover. Jones' stomach turned as he got down before crawling behind trees to join those already there. As he composed himself, his eyes and ears straining for what the issue could be, he received a thumbs down hand signal from those up ahead.

Enemy spotted.

There was little Jones could do but allow those that could see the enemy to take care of the problem. As everyone lay still, Jones could make out foreign murmuring that was getting louder. No sooner had he recognised it was in fact German, two sentries, their rifles slung over their shoulders wandered past, deep in conversation. With one hand on their rifle slings to prevent them from slipping from their shoulders, their free hand holding lit cigarettes. The aroma of their tobacco wafted across Jones and his men. The scent of the lit tobacco tingled Jones' nostrils as they wandered past. He could certainly have done with a cigarette.

As the unwary sentries continued on, along the shore line, Jones knew it would only be a matter of time before they would most likely come across their two dead comrades by the southern jetty. His concerns were short lived as a slight commotion broke out further down the company line. Jones quietly hoped the two sentries had enough time to finish their cigarettes.

A hushed voice message was passed up the line from the rear of the column.

'Enemy down. No intel on them. Just sentries.'

The British commandos rose to their feet and continued on to their target building. With two sets of sentries neutralised, he hoped that would be the last. As they approached the northern jetty, Jones was surprised that the Catalinas could not be heard, which gave him some comfort. The group went to ground once more, before whispers calling for Jones to join them up front reached his ears. As he moved off, movement in his periphery caught his attention. Montgomery and Melvin, their packs full of signal flares and a radio followed on. They were off to set up near the jetty.

As Jones crawled in next to the lead scouts, the NCO pointed out the jetty and the target in the murky blackness.

'Target building and the jetty, Boss.'

Close enough not to require binoculars, Jones studied the area before he made his move. He knew this would be the phase of the operation that he had to play by ear. Back in Scotland, when they were planning the operation, they had no idea as to the layout of the interior of the target building. Ideally, Jones would have liked to gain access from one end of the structure and sweep through, checking rooms and beds as they went. They had no idea if they could gain access at either end. They had no ladders, so they would have to gain entry into the ground floor at best. They had crowbars and sledgehammers with them, but to start bashing their way in would certainly rouse the garrison.

Jones cuffed his nose as he nudged the NCO.

'Take three men and go check out the southern end of the building. See if we can get in that way. I'd rather not go in the front door.'

'Sir.'

The NCO led three men at a half crouch across the neat grounds of the sanatorium to the southern end of the target building. In the gloom. Jones observed the men as they stood up on ledges and each other's shoulders for the ground floor windows were a little higher than anticipated. With that comedy act going on, Jones looked toward the jetty. Montgomery and Melvin were setting up, ready for the shooting to start.

Something going to plan, Jones conceded to himself.

The NCO and his men returned, at a half-crouched dash, sliding in beside the major.

'Windows are shut tight.' the NCO reported, his voice strained as he regulated his breathing. 'With the blackout curtains closed, they could all be sat up in bed reading for all we know.'

Jones agreed with the young man. Even if a window was open to them, the last thing they needed, at that early stage at least was to have the SS officer corps sat up in bed looking at them as they clambered through the curtains. Not wanting to chance his arm with the far end of the building, since he had no idea if that would bear any fruit, Jones was eager to get on. It was coming up to 0100 hours local time and wanted to be out within the hour if he could.

'Let's go for the front door.'

Whilst the four commandos looked for a way in, W-W and his men were now on the move. With their radio set dismantled and packed away, they evacuated their deadfall sanctuary and patrolled towards the bridges. With the remnants of the winter fall under foot, the pace was painfully slow so not to break strands of deadfall hidden under the mulch of fallen leaves. As W-W led them along the water's edge, the threshold of trees concealing them from any sharp-eyed Germans on the western bank, he had to concede that they were now fully invested in the operation. The cacophony that was the arrival of the Catalinas should have woken everyone between here and Berlin, yet the facility remained silent. Flying boat arrivals at all hours appeared to be nothing new to those operating the sanatorium. Through binoculars, he had witnessed Jones and his men creeping towards the target building, the two roaming sentries coming upon them, only to then disappear without fanfare.

W-W knew there had been offensive action, but it was quick and silent, to the detriment of the sentries. He had not witnessed the shooting of another roaming pair at the south jetty and was ignorant of the fact. His primary concern was getting to a position where he could overwatch the two bridges and not run into the large patrol his side of the Zenesse.

In the gloom of early morning, the two bridges presented themselves. Slipping their heavy packs from their shoulders, Mould plus two men scouted forward, looking for an ideal spot to sit in ambush for the German patrol whilst keeping an eye on the bridge. Once again the wayward deadfall refused to cooperate, making the going slow and the route risky. Mould finally came upon an area that served both purposes, but they would have to consider moving once the sun come up. Should they still be there that is. They would have good fields of observation, but with the deadfall sparse around the proposed position, not much cover from view once it was daylight. Mould accepted the situation, and now had to sell it to the captain.

W-W accepted what the sergeant was offering, for they could always move if they had to later. Stashing their packs together in the thicker deadfall, the radio remaining in its own pack, the commandos settled down in their positions lining the western side of the main track. They would be close to the road, for all they had to fight with were Thompsons, Colts, knives, and grenades. With Dobbs sat closest to the bridges, Mould ensured he had the flare gun for he would have to direct fire at the bridges from the Catalinas with red flares if he needed to. Sat in the centre of the ambush group, W-W knew it was now a waiting game. If the patrol returned to the facility before the shooting started, they would let them pass, for he did not want to kick things off too early before Jones had a chance to grab their man.

33.

The huge double doors to the target building were unlocked. The NCO who had looked for a way in via the southern end of the building gave Jones a thumbs up. Without fanfare, the major and his men moved at a walking pace towards their pre-arranged positions. 1 Troop which included himself emerged from under the shadows of trees and patrolled silently across the neat moonlit lawns, abutting themselves up along the front of the building. 2 Troop with equal elegance, glided past and established themselves on the northern side whilst 3 Troop covered the south side. With the target building isolated from any reinforcements, Jones gave the NCO the nod to make purposeful entry. The method of breaching the target was not Jones' usual signature move, for he was used to a far more dynamic and noisy arrival, but on this night, the longer he could keep from shooting up the place, the better. In fact, he would rather remove Arens from Hohenlychen without any shots fired.

He was quietly assured that Jurgen Arens, a Scientist and not a soldier would prefer it too.

The NCO peered inside the main foyer. The lights fitted to the walls were dimmed. The desk at the base of the wide spiral staircase was vacant. A cigarette sat unattended in its ashtray; the light blue smoke coiling lazily towards the plain smooth ceiling. Its owner could not be far. In the low light, the huge stain glass window that dominated the stairs was impressive. The NCO noted the parquet wooden floor. Their boots were rubber soled, not the standard issue combat boot with hob nails. They would squeak about as they walked, but not clatter like a bunch of tap dancers. The NCO stepped back out, getting the attention of the major.

Jones and the remainder of 1 Troop squeaked into the foyer. Thompsons slung, Colts and torches in hand, they took the time to get used to the atmospherics within the building. All was quiet, save a lone cough from no doubt one of the patients in their room. Jones knew he was now making this up as he went, so he needed to keep it quick and efficient. With the stairs and stain glass window duly admired, he took in his surroundings. Behind the desk as a set of plain, drab grey metal doors. Corridors ran away either side of the foyer with what looked like ablutions at the base of the stairs on the left. The lights were on constantly, giving away their white tiled fittings. Pausing to listen for anyone in there, Jones could not hear any movement, just the odd drip of a tap. Jones looked to the desk, a clipboard hanging on the wall caught Jones' eye. Pulling it off its crude nail, Jones scanned the papers under the desk lamp. His German was functional as he scoured the text. He flipped over the first page, reading on whilst his men kept their squeaky movements to a minimum as they peered down the dimly lit corridors.

The third sheet gave Jones a diagram of the building. It was the ward layout of the ground floor. Each box represented a room as far as Jones could fathom it. In pencil was scribbled what he could only deduce was the surname of the patient. The handwriting was scratchy gothic font, which Jones struggled to read. He came across Arens. To his relief, he was on the ground floor, South Wing. He tossed the clipboard on the desk.

'He's on this floor.' Jones hissed at his men, pointing down the south facing corridor. 'Far end room. Go get him.'

With torches and Colts in hand, the NCO led half a dozen men down the corridor. Despite their squeaky footwear, their confident footfall would hopefully not arouse suspicion to any light sleepers. Just staff doing their duties in the silent hours as it were. Jones moved over to the threshold that led into the corridor. He winced at the torch beams bouncing all around the farthest room. He wished the lads had a little more bedside manner, just so they could grab Arens first before he screamed the place down.

The torches then went out, the squeaking grew louder. Out of the dark corridor, the commandos returned. The NCO shrugged.

'He's not in bed. We checked the others.'

Jones frowned as he stomped back to the clipboard tossed on the desk. He was certain he had read the name correctly. As he scoured the pencilled names once more, he wondered if he had read the document correctly, hoping Arens was not upstairs. Just as Jones confirmed that the bed in question belonged to Arens, Jones got the fright of his life as the steel door behind him clanked and swung open. He spun on his heels to find himself face to face with a tall, slim, gaunt man in a three-quarter length, white laboratory coat. Both men blinked rapidly at each other, just before the gaunt man's eyes widened as he realised the man before him was not the duty Scharfuhrer. As his lips went to move, he was flattened by a right hook from Jones. The impact of the punch had him yelp loud enough for it to echo as he crashed against the outward swinging door. As the man slumped to the ground, Jones was already hauling him to his feet and dragging him around the desk, which shunted under the impact of the two men, sending lamp, ashtray and clipboard clattering around Jones ankles as the punch-drunk man whimpered.

The gaunt man, his nose and lip bleeding, shielded his face from more punches with his forearms. His wide scared eyes took in his attacker and a number of other rough men looking in at him. Jones parried the arms away and grabbed him by the collar of his lab coat, his Colt pushed roughly under his chin.

'Don't shoot. Please don't kill me.' The Gaunt, battered German pleaded.

'Arens. Jurgen Arens. Where is he?' Jones spat, his German laced with a tone that gave away the fact it was classroom taught, not native. The scared demeanour of the gaunt man was short lived. He recognised them as foreigners.

'Arens? Who is Arens?'

'Arens. He's a patient here. Where is he?'

'I have no idea…' His answer tailed off as he then focussed on something else. Jones went to threaten him but was also attracted to what the gaunt man was now looking up at.

Halfway down the first flight of stairs stood a bare headed SS Scharfuhrer. Smoke drifted up from the cigarette hanging from his lips. His torch hanging limp in his left hand. In the foyer beneath him was a bizarre spectacle. One man in lab coat was lying on the ground with one soldier knelt over him with a pistol under his chin, the foyer full of another twenty or so, all looking back at him. They all carried torches and pistols.

The Scharfuhrer, no doubt a seasoned soldier within the ranks of the SS decided to go with muscle memory, his right hand stroking the top of his leather pistol holster. His body suddenly burst a pink and grey mist as he was cut down in a hail of Colt fire. The report of the gunfire in the foyer instantly reduced Jones' hearing to a high-pitched whine, as both the Scharfuhrer and the magnificent stained-glass window collapsed under the devastating fire. The SS soldier remained slumped on the stairs; his life expired. Countless shards of brightly coloured glass coated him. His blood would soon pool, darken and clot of the very steps he died on. He may have lived if he had not touched his holster.

Holding tight to the gaunt man, his muffled hearing slowly returning, Jones looked about the foyer. He witnessed his men changing magazines before heading off back down the original corridor he had sent them down. Their torches on. The silent approach was no longer required. Feeling rather exposed, Jones hauled the gaunt man towards the threshold of the ablutions. As he did so, his hearing picked up shouting and the sporadic snap of gunfire, but not what he recognised as that of a Colt. Spinning around, he watched as his men came dashing back into the foyer, sliding across the threshold, before firing back down the corridor.

'They're fucking armed!' hollered one of the lads before returning fire, the brass casings spinning off to the right. The Colt giving off the more familiar and comforting *boom* compared to what was coming back at them. Most likely Luger fire. Jones got the attention of the nearest man, not wanting to let go of the gaunt bleeding German, himself trying to get small due to the incoming fire from his own countrymen.

'What's down there?' Jones hollered, his hearing yet to return to normal. As the commando changed magazines, he spoke aloud.

'The patients have still got their shooters, Sir. The fuckers are armed!'

The concept of hospital patients having access to firearms was alien to Jones. The very fact that the building they were in was housing wounded officers of one form or another. It was evident that the powers that be allowed their officers, should they be deemed fit to do so retain their side arms. This dynamic changed the plan there and then. He had to find Arens, in a building where everyone could now fight back.

It was as Jones' hearing became acute to the din around him, did he notice excited voices above and behind him. He was on the ground floor in the middle of the structure, with the north wing of the building running away behind him, accommodated with armed patients, plus those on the two floors above. Having pistols to contest Jones' efforts was bad enough, but he quickly dismissed the notion they had grenades to toss down upon him and his men hunkered down in the foyer.

Incoming snaps of Luger fire kept Jones and the gaunt German crouching in the doorway of the ablutions. He peered out as far as he dared to try and see who was fighting back from the dark bowels of the wing where Arens was supposed to be sleeping. A light came on in one of the rooms branching off the corridor, giving away the shadows of those moving about, before being switched off. The German officers may have been in their sleeping attire, but they were not in the business of giving themselves away to the enemy easily. Jones and his men had grenades at their disposal, but all were aware that they were there to lift Arens out in one piece if possible. Killing him with a well-placed grenade would certainly ruin their efforts for they would then have to fight their way out without the very man they came for. As his men and the Germans hiding in the dark south wing exchanged fire, Jones caught sight of his radio operator, Private Daniel Davey kneeling against the threshold to the north wing, his Colt at the ready.

'Davey?' Jones hollered as another exchange of gunfire echoed through. The man turned to look at him. Jones waved him over. As Davey got to his feet and stepped out, a flash from the north wing and a flurry of sparks from his radio set erupted as one, the force of the impact sending the radio operator sprawling on the floor. Jones feared the man at least wounded, but with the gaunt German squirming underneath him, he could not come to his aid. To his relief, he witnessed Davey scramble like a man possessed out of the line of fire and shrug the now ruined radio off his back. As Davey got up on to his haunches, he puffed out his cheeks in relief, only to catch the eye of the major again. Both exchanged a thumbs up.

Davey was fine, but his Colt remained in the middle of the foyer. Both Jones and Davey eyed the pistol before eyeing each other. Both commandos knew it could not stay there, and Davey knew he would have to go out there and recover it. Knowing Arens was supposed to be in the south wing, Davey pulled a grenade from his ammunition pouch, pulled the pin, and lobbed it down the north corridor. Despite the gunfight around him, Jones could hear the excited screams from those hiding in the darkness of the north corridor just as the grenade went off. The detonation pulsed through the foyer, taking the fight out of the commandos shooting south, for they were not expecting any grenade action. With everyone reeling, Davey dived out into the open floor plan of the foyer, grabbed his Colt and then scurried over to Jones, who was trying to restrain a very agitated man in a white lab coat.

'You've got style Davey; I'll give you that.' Jones hollered in the man's ear. Jones smirked as he pulled the top slide back a fraction to check he had a round chambered.

'They'll not want another one, the fuckers.' Jones returned as he emptied a whole magazine down the north corridor, the top slide locking in the rear position once empty. As he put in a fresh magazine, Jones indicated the German under his knees.

'Keep hold of him, I'm gonna get us some help.'

As he rose to his feet, Jones spotted another white clad man attempting to pull the metal door closed. Both he and Jones exchanged looks for a second before the British major snapped off two rounds with his Colt, sending the man flinching back into the dark recess that led to a lower floor. As if in a Rugby scrum, Jones put all his weight behind the desk and shoved it into the doorway so no one could try closing it again. As he shunted into the threshold, he could make out in the gloom of the stairwell leading down away from him, people dressed as the gaunt man dashing to and fro. He thought of sending a grenade down there but did not want to wound Arens if he happened to be cowering down there or kill him outright. He had come too far to just kill him. He could not rule it out, but he would prefer not to.

Commotion behind him made him flinch. In a melee of shouting by numerous people, Jones witnessed the gaunt man dashing for the main doors only to be cut down by Davey's Colt. Both rounds found their mark between the shoulder blades, the gaunt man dropping to the ground hard. Looking over to the threshold to the ablutions, Davey was pulling himself to his feet, rubbing his own jaw before spitting blood. The gaunt man had chanced giving Davey a clout and the result was not good. Davey, upon noticing that the major looking at him merely shrugged. Jones had more pressing issues as a volley of rounds snapped through the foyer, from the south corridor. They were up against armed patients, and they still did not have their man. He dashed over to the large main doors and peered out.

Thankfully, the north jetty where Sergeant Major Montgomery and Private Melvin sat was still in darkness. As he went to call for him, a claxon began to wind up and whine very loudly throughout the facility. It was the same used when there was an air raid underway back home, Jones thought. The noise, as much as he would rather not have it could serve them well. If the Germans feared an air raid, they could well remain where they were and seek shelter. He hollered out into the darkness.

'Sarn't Major?'

'Sir?' Montgomery returned, much to Jones' relief.

'Get those cats up here. I think they know we are here now.

34.

It was the thud of what he thought was a grenade going off that had W-W spin on his haunches and look in at the facility. Only when the wind dropped enough so he could hear gun shots inside the target building did he realise that it had all kicked off.

'I think it's all kicked off in there already.' The captain hissed to the men either side of him in the ambush party. This caused a couple of the men to steal a glance over their shoulders at the sanatorium sat across the narrow stretch of water. Very faintly, they could all now hear volleys of shots from within the target building, and then the claxon siren began. As it grew in pitch and then remained constant, W-W fought the urge to watch the facility to see what unfolded.

'Get ready lads, that patrol will be back here pretty quick, get ready.'

The claxon and a ringing telephone swam into Mortens consciousness. Then Tommy yapping in the kitchen before a nudge in the ribs from Astrid brought him back to the present. Blinking up at the ceiling, he fought to gather what was going on. Another nudge from Astrid.

'Get the phone.' She mumbled before rolling away from him, pulling the covers over her head. Mortens rolled on his side as he swung his legs out of bed. Still drunk from sleep, he took a moment to gather his senses. The phone, claxon and Tommy's barking all became acute and in focus as one. Naked, he got to his feet and made for the bottom of the stairs to get the phone. He lifted the receiver.

'Security Officer' he answered with a curt tone.

'Sir…Sir? Haupsturmfuhrer Mortens?'

'Speaking.'

'Scharfuhrer Kleppe, here at the Guardroom. We have a situation.'

'Air raid?' Mortens asked, the claxon very much dominating every aspect of the somewhat stunted conversation.

'No Sir.' Kleppe answered. 'We've heard what we think is an explosion, and what could be gunfire.'

'From where?...hang on.'

Mortens put the handset into his shoulder and hollered at Tommy to be quiet. He flinched as Astrid slipped his bath robe over his shoulders. She went on to calm Tommy who was pacing about the kitchen most agitated. Before he spoke again to Kleppe, Mortens fought his way into his bath robe, wrapping himself up tight.

'Kleppe? From where?'

'The officers ward, Sir.'

'The officers ward?'

'Yes Sir. We received a call from that ward. Something about a commando attack.'

'Commando attack?'

'That's what the man said.'

'Who spoke to you?'

'Sir?'

'The man who made the call. Did he give his name?'

'No Sir. He was rather agitated. I could hear shouting in the background and what could be gunfire.'

Mortens paused as he resisted the urge to berate the rather apologetic Scharfuhrer. He knew the officers convalescing were allowed to retain their sidearms, which was a bad idea from the start. Mortens had more of a credible vision in his mind's eye of officers being affronted at one another and challenging each other to a duel rather than enemy commandos running amok in the ward.

'Sir? Are you there?' Kleppe probed. Mortens rolled his shoulders before answering.

'Yes, I'm here. Kleppe, listen up. Have a patrol do a lap of the officers' ward, see if they can ascertain what is happening and get back to me. In the meantime, turn that bloody siren off.'

'Yes Sir.' Kleppe signed off before the line went dead.

As he replaced the handset, Astrid informed him that she had put some coffee on. Mortens stepped into the kitchen. Tommy was back in his bed, somewhat calmer than he was a few minutes ago. As Mortens was handed a mug of coffee, he let out a stretch, his robe falling open.

'I don't think we have any time for that this morning.' Astrid flashed him a mischievous smile. He took the mug with one hand and pulled her bathrobe open with the other.

'Says who?'

As she stepped in closer to him, the relentless claxon wailing faded away. Astrid had paid it no attention. Having lived in the city, she had become flak happy a long time ago, and was no stranger to raids, day, or night. As she took her husband in her hands, both flinched as a banging at the front door brought them back to reality. Tommy yapped at the intrusion.

'Get dressed,' Astrid kissed him on the cheek as she went for the door, closing her robe,' I'll deal with whoever this is.'

Mortens dressed as quickly as he could, periodically sipping at the hot coffee. Coffee and sex usually started his day off right, but given the hour, the coffee would have to do. Not sure how the day would unfold, he was not going to waste good coffee. His boots were unpolished, but that was fine, and his hair not as brushed as he would usually have had it, but given the events apparently unfolding in the sanatorium, personal grooming was not a concern. Fully dressed, his field cap in his hands, he returned downstairs to find Astrid and two almost middle-aged men, still in their own bed clothes stood within the threshold. With the claxon now silent, Mortens could hear the roar of engines. Aeroplane engines. He looked to the two men, wringing their hands.

'Haupsturmfuhrer, forgive the intrusion at this hour, but are we under attack?' The shorter, skinnier of the two, with thinning hair asked, his face full of anxiety.

As Mortens went to answer, the other man, A little taller, but barrel chested with thick forearms stepped forward.

'Is it the Soviets?'

Mortens eyed Astrid, whose arched eyebrows at the mention of the Soviets gave away she did not like the prospect. He held out his hands to pacify his visitors.

'I have just spoken with the Guard Commander, and he has reported that there could be an incident in the officer's ward. I have instructed him to take a patrol to investigate. In addition, I have a patrol on the east bank of the lake who will report back to me should there be anything untoward.'

Both men eyed each other nervously. Mortens had no idea who the men were. Given they were in their bedclothes, they clearly lived in the village and served the sanatorium in one capacity or another. He could not tell if he was to salute them, or consider them civilian medical staff employed by the SS.

'Have you informed Ravensbruck?' The smaller man asked. Mortens slowly shook his head.

'They will require far more information than I can provide at present. My patrols will be able to fill in the blanks.'

'Should we evacuate the families to Ravensbruck?' Astrid asked, clearly concerned. Mortens frowned.

'Why?'

'It could be the Soviets.'

'Let's get a clearer picture before we go running to the hills. Let the patrols do their work and I can then take matters in hand. If I need reinforcements from Ravensbruck to deal with this matter, I need as much information as I can muster. Now gentlemen?'

The two men looked at the Chief Security Officer.

'Please return to your homes.'

35.

In the dark, damp forest on the eastern bank of the Zenesse, W-W and his men sat waiting for the foot patrol to head back toward the footbridge. With the claxon now silent, the wind swirled through the canopy above them, giving off a ghostly moan as the three Catalinas motored their way towards the north jetty. The noise of their efforts to move about on the water was deafening. W-W could not help but peer over his shoulder and watch their dark sinister profiles as they spread out on the Zenesse, their machineguns coming to bear on the sanatorium. To the captain, they looked like three birds of prey, waiting to pounce on the first rodent to expose themselves to their wrath. All it would take was a red flare in the direction of their prey, and all hell would break loose.

'Enemy right!' hissed the men, causing W-W to pay attention to the task at hand. In the gloom, W-W scoured the woods and track off to the right of their ambush position. The mixed heights of the deadfall allowed him the opportunity to slowly stand so he may observe the enemy even better. The German patrol had indeed returned, but unbeknown to them, they were making a mess of W-Ws' plan.

They were not remaining on the track, for they were far more interested in the noisy aircraft floating on the lake. W-W and his men could now easily see the enemy as they moved off the track towards the shore, hunched over so they could get a better view of what was happening out on the water. W-W knew that if they allowed the patrol to continue on its present course, they would either stumble into the ambush party, or get between the ambush party and the shoreline. Before W-W could formulate a change in tact, two of his men closest to the German patrol stood up and cut the first two down with their Thompsons.

'CONTACT!' the men roared as one as the remainder stood and swung to the right as they fired short, controlled bursts at the stunned Germans. W-W dashed to his right to get a clear line of fire, fighting his way through small clusters of dead fall as he went. The Germans, caught by surprise, snapped off shots from their carbines as they sought cover behind the thick base of the trees around them. W-W needed his men to shake out to the right, for they were almost shooting over the right shoulder of the man in front.

'Peel right, peel right!' The captain roared. Instantly, his men repeated the order at the top of their voices, responding as if second nature. From the left, the British commandos moved one at a time, coming around behind all of their comrades to rejoin the ragged fighting line at the far end. Their lines of fire now open with less chance of fratricide. As W-W took up his new place in the line, he could see the Germans darting about for better vantage, shouting at each other in equal vigour to that of the British. W-W knew by their movements that the Germans wanted to gain control of the shoreline and push their enemy into the wood. Sergeant Mould, no stranger to close combat with the Germans read the battle well as he sent two grenades their way. The concussion as both grenades detonated amongst the enemy punched through, taking the wind out of W-W and those who were closer. As the captain stepped further to his right, a loud crack as a German bullet passed his right ear had him wince in pain. W-W stumbled a little, his free hand instinctively going to his face. The supersonic projectile had literally just missed his head. His right ear and cheek now thick and tender from the displaced air as the bullet passed. If he had stepped out a fraction earlier, it could have been all over in an instant. Relieved to feel there was no physical damage, his anger returned as he pulled his Thompson tight into this right shoulder and fired short, controlled bursts at the muzzle flashes in the gloom. His own muzzle flash causing red orbs to drift across his vision.

The Germans began to fall back, not in a rout, but fighting in pairs, well trained, well-rehearsed, and in the knowledge they were being overmatched, and would break clean and hopefully fight another day. As the last pair of SS troopers disappeared into the forest, W-W and his men took the opportunity to change magazines and catch their breath. Chest heaving, face and ear smarting, plus glazed in sweat, W-W looked about his men, who too were steaming from their exertions, scanning the ground ahead of them for any sign of a counter attack.

'Everyone okay?' W-W called out.

'Yep.'

'Yeah.'

'We're good.'

'Fuck!'

'What?'

'Bastards clipped me.'

'Where?' W-W stomped over to the voice. He come across Mould stood over a kneeling Dobbs, holding a field dressing in place whilst the sergeant pulled it tight and secure. Mould looked to the captain.

'Clipped his bicep, he's good.'

'Fucking hurts!' Dobbs smarted.

'If you weren't so fat, he'd have missed you.'

Dobbs got to his feet, affronted by the remark. The antagonist remained silent and anonymous in the darkness as all those stood about sniggered. W-W found it amusing but knew better than to add fuel to the fire.

'Prick.' Was all Dobbs offered as a counter.

'Right boys, let's go see who we got.' Mould took the lead as they made for where the Germans had taken cover.

The British picked their way carefully though the deadfall to where they thought the Germans had occupied in the ambush. The Catalinas were still moving about on the lake, so making a noise was not an issue, it was just the threat of stumbling into a wounded German who still have some fight left in him.

Mould headed to where he estimated the opening shots occurred, before stepping out toward where he felt the German patrol had been. In the gloom, Mould found what he was looking for, two Germans. One lay still, whilst the other writhed in agony, mouth bloodied, gritting his teeth as he tried to control his pain. Upon closer inspection, he confirmed they were both SS troopers, the silver lighting runes on their tunic collars under their great coats. With caution, the other commandos fanned out around Mould as he knelt to search the one that was very much dead. A Scharfuhrer, a Sergeant equivalent. Mould knew that the German army placed a lot of leadership responsibilities on their NCOs. The man beneath him, Mould estimated would have been the patrol commander.

Gingerly, through fear that the wounded man may have booby trapped his dead comrade, Mould searched him. He came across a luger pistol plus spare magazines, MP40 submachinegun with spare magazines. No grenades, however. A map, compass, whistle, notebook plus some photographs of a pretty young woman. His paybook and his identification disc. The disc was designed to snap the lower half off and retain for documentation. Mould did this. He may have been the enemy, but the least he could do was, should they get out of there, hand them over to the relevant authorities. In the gloom, he could not read the name, but pocketed it all the same. He put the photographs back in the man's tunic pocket, but retained the map and the notebook which he would scrutinise when the lighting improved.

As loud crack made everyone, including Mould flinch and instinctively raise their Thompsons to counter the threat. The writhing man now lay quiet and still. Stood over him, Mould watched as W-W lowered his Colt before walking over to where the other man had gathered around what turned out to be another fallen SS trooper. Casually, W-W stepped in among them before shooting the sobbing, wounded man out of hand. The Catalinas, their engines feathered, but still rather noisy, contained the report of the pistol shots. The men who were tending to the other wounded man looked up at the captain, who walked away, holstering his Colt. Mould called over to them, for he needed them to do their job, and not get all philosophical.

'Anything on him?'

They shook their heads as he made his way over, after collecting the disc half from the first man W-W had executed. As he knelt beside the second man shot by the captain, he repeated the action regarding the disc. As he did so, he spoke aloud.

'Don't be hard on the boss, lads. A V-2 almost killed his wife. Can't blame a man for being angry.'

The men remained silent as they continued their sweep for anymore dead or wounded SS men. W-W stood on his own, looking out at the Catalinas. In his periphery, he could tell Mould had joined him. Without looking at the man, he spoke.

'Anything of use?'

'A map, and a notebook.' The sergeant answered, matter of fact. W-W nodded as he continued to take in what the Catalinas were up to.

'We'll move closer to the bridges.' W-W informed him. 'I doubt hordes of SS will come screaming this way, and even less chance of them shelling us so close to their own dwellings.'

'Roger that. I'll round up the lads.'

As Mould stepped away, W-W looked to him.

'They nearly got Kaila, Ian.'

The sergeant returned a tight-lipped smile, nodding slightly.

'I know Boss. So do the boys.'

W-W was about to say something else when a volley of muffled shots within the Officer Ward reached their ears.

36.

'Man down, man down!' Came the roar from many mouths in and around the foyer. Jones spun around from peering into the south corridor to find Davey slumped on the ground, his body twitching as blood jetted from his throat. The man managed to get his own hands to his throat to try and stem the catastrophic blood loss, to no avail. It pumped out in thick streams between his fingers as he now writhed, fully aware that he was dying.

Confused as to the sudden violence inflicted on the man, Jones then realised what had happened as many of the men diverted their pistol up at the top flight of stairs. Those hiding up on the first floor were now gathering the courage to get into the fight against the enemy occupying the foyer. Jones grabbed Davey by the webbing straps and began to haul the man into the well-lit, white tiled ablutions. The pool of blood Davey was lying in followed them in as a ghastly red smear. The tiled floor made the effort of dragging him easier due to the dark red fluid that had already soaked the top half of Davey's smock. Under the deafening cannonade of Colt fire up at the suspected attackers, three of the men, one appointed as medic followed Jones in. Dressings were pulled from Davey's pockets, before being ripped open and palmed heavily onto the horrific wound under his chin. Jones, still stunned at the action, stood back as two of the men pulled Davey into the sitting position so they could pull the webbing straps and smock from his shoulders, revealing a heavily bloodied shirt beneath. With the shirt also getting ripped from the shoulders, the medic identified another entry and exit wound through the upper right chest. Facing Davey's back, Jones could see blood oozing from and exit wound about the size of an acorn. As he went to point it out to the medic, the man slapped a dressing on it as he fought to tie it around Davey's torso. Feeling that he would serve his men better getting something done about the enemy on the floor above, the major left Davey to his carers as he stepped to the ablution threshold. He needed the Catalinas to strafe the floor above.

Jones had to pick his moment before he made for the main doors. His men were fighting an enemy on three sides. Only the foyer and ablutions were lit, the top of the stairs and the corridors branching off remained in darkness, much to the benefit of the enemy. Quietly confident his sudden dash could outperform the pistol skills of a convalescing SS officer, he made for the main doors, only to get three paces into a sprint before brass casings from numerous Colt automatics had him lose purchase and send him spread eagled into the base of the main doors. Winded from falling on his own Thompson, Jones did not look back as he yanked the door open and got outside.

'Sergeant Major?' Jones roared as loud as his winded diaphragm allowed him.

'Sir?' Came a reassuring response.

'Catalina fire, first floor, now!'

'First floor?' Montgomery confirmed. Regaining his composure, Jones roared at him again.

'Catalina fire, first floor, now!'

'Roger that!' Montgomery countered, putting the radio handset to his ear, 'Catalina fire, first floor.'

Jones pushed his way back into the embattled foyer. His men were stacked up either side of the corridors, taking it in turns to get the better of those hiding in the darkness. Two men held firm at the ablution threshold. Leaning out to do the same with those firing down at anyone they could see. At a half crouch, Jones made for the ablutions, he could see the three men still tending to Davey in the bright, blood smeared room. He shouted as loud as he could over the gunfire.

'Heads down boys, heads down!'

At the north jetty, Montgomery and Melvin got onto their bellies. With the Catalinas receiving their request for fire support, Montgomery knew that all they needed at that point was some illumination to assist them in strafing the correct floor. With the flare gun ready in Melvin's hands, Montgomery flicked his head at the Officer Ward.

'Do it.'

Extending his right arm up vertical, Melvin let fly the flare with a loud pop. As it whooshed skywards, both men, feeling rather exposed on the grass bank by the jetty hunkered down as small as they could, for the angle of fire would have the marauding birds of prey out on the lake fire almost over the heads. Montgomery, the soldiers' soldier, was well aware that it was his own men manning the machineguns on the aircraft.

'Those fuckers had better shoot straight.'

Melvin's only response was to try and get smaller. As the flare canister completed its rapid climb, it then burst open, the white phosphorus contents immediately giving off brilliant white light that bathed the Catalinas, the jetty, and target in artificial light. Both men held their breath as the world around them erupted in a blizzard of red tracer bullets.

Their ears buffeted and whined as numerous, relentless streams of red phosphorus-based bullets snapped just over their heads, their destination, the first floor of the

Officer Ward. Most punched through the window apertures and decimated the fittings holding the frames in place, whilst others struck firmer parts of the façade, resulting in ricochets screaming skywards or towards the Soldier Ward to the north, fracturing tree limbs which under their own weight came down on the neat lawns of the sanatorium.

Montgomery could only marvel at the sheer firepower at their disposal for the operation. He quietly thanked the machine gunners out on the lake. Their shooting was certainly on target.

The men in the foyer all flinched as one as the floor above them erupted. The Germans at the top of the stairs, not to mention their comrades occupying the rest of their floor screamed hysterically as the immense firepower brought to bear by the three enemy aircraft out on the lake tore through them, the building, its fittings, and furniture. Heavy blackout curtains were set alight by the tracer as it punched through. Pillows and mattresses burst in a white, grey, and pink mist along with any human stood in the vicinity.

The cacophony above terrified Jones and his men as they sought to consolidate their positions in the foyer and ablutions. Jones looked to his excited men as they rose from their crouched postures to then cut down those who had survived the onslaught from the Catalinas above and made it down the stairs. The Germans felled alongside the uniformed Scharfuhrer were almost middle aged, in their bedclothes, with Luger pistols in the hands. The fire from the British was barely audible as the Catalinas strafed the floor above. Once the last German lay still after being hit by more rounds than was necessary, Jones waved to his men to stop firing.

They obeyed.

As Jones went to the stairs to check the identification of the dead men, the barrage from the Catalinas ceased. Despite his heart thudding wildly in his ears, Jones ignored the cries and sobs of the unseen enemy above him and hauled the dead over to see if Arens was among them. He was not. Not to offer the survivors upstairs an easy target, he retreated to the ablution threshold. Catching his breath, he noticed all was quiet. His men, the enemy in the darkened corridors, those above merely sobbed a little. What was noticeable was the smell of something burning. As the aroma grew more acute, so did the chatter on the upper floors. The chatter then became excited shouts. Jones needed to act fast before the Germans surrounding him gathered their senses.

'Boss?'

Jones turned to take in the men knelt over Davey, who just stared blankly at the ceiling. The pool of blood was already blackening under his inert frame. Numerous dressings had been applied, their wrappers strewn all over the floor tiles, but not enough to prevent him bleeding out. The men knelt over him looked exhausted and somewhat emotional. Bloodied up to the elbow, they reasted back on their haunches, using opened dressings to remove the worst of Davey's blood from their hands. Jones stepped in towards them, unsure what to say. He knew the boys had worked their hardest to save him, but his wounds were catastrophic. Before the scene overwhelmed him, for Jones was no stranger to such macabre outcomes, he cleared his throat. He needed to get his men out of the building that could end up as their tomb. They were surrounded on three sides and by the smell, it was now on fire. To top it all off, they had still not found their man.

As Jones removed one of Davey's identification discs from a boot lace around his neck, a scuff from one of the lavatory stalls had all those about Davey flinch and bring their pistols up, ready to shoot. Jones, holding his breath to try and detect movement in the stalls slowly eyed his men, for they too were doing the same. Jones had not imagined it. They had all heard it.

'Come out now, or we will start shooting.' Jones' German was passable enough to get his message across. It was not strong enough to engage in serious debate, but he was fine with that, because he was not in the business with debating with Germans.

'Come out now!' Jones repeated with more temper.

A shuffle within the middle stall had Jones and the men tense. They were more than happy to start shoot, given the circumstances. With three colts pointing at the door, Jones decided to put his away. He needed to be ready to grab whoever came out. The bolt on the stall door snapped open with an echo, almost inviting a hail of bullets in response. Jones held out a hand to his men as if it would calm them. He was certainly wasting his time. The heavily painted, Navy-blue door creaked open enough for a man's face to peer around it. The man's eyes looked shocked at what was waiting for him, and then blinked hard and often when he took in the dead soldier laying in a pool of dark sticky blood.

Jones eyed the drawn grey face that met his gaze. He was grateful to the MI6 man, Tim Lewis for having the images mass produced for everyone to study prior to the mission. Jones was in no doubt.

They had their man.

37.

2 Troop, under the command of Sergeant Paul Kimber, were reeling after the first salvo unleashed by the Catalinas. Guarding the northern approaches to the Officer Ward, they could not help but be distracted by the wrath unleashed on the building behind them. Whilst his men scanned the darkness for any opposition coming to counter their efforts, Kimber lay on his side under the foliage sparse trees to take in the now smouldering structure. He could not see any flames at that point but given the amount of smoke emitting from the second floor, fire had certainly taken hold.

Tracer bullets would have ignited fabrics and fittings such as bedding and the heavy blackout curtains. From his position however, he could not be sure how effective the Catalina fire had been on the enemy. He just hoped 1 Troop and Major Jones were not on the same floor. As he returned to focusing on his task, a clatter above on the smouldering floor caught his attention. A window had opened, releasing another column of smoke skywards. The men either side of Kimber rolled on their sides to observe what was unfolding above and behind them. As the smoke cleared, an interior light beamed out, though Kimber could not be sure if it were flame or interior lighting. A profile came to the window, leaning out and coughing violently. The light behind the figure gave away a bare headed man, in light coloured bed clothes. Once the coughing man had calmed and composed himself, his demeanour changed. He had noticed Kimber and his men lying prone amid the trees below.

'*Hallo.*' Hollered the man, in heavily accented English, before barking another sentence at them in German.

Kimber and some of his men frowned as they looked to each other before returning to the man up at the window. The man then barked more German at them. Kimber's German was basic at best but had no idea what the shouting man was saying. The German repeated in a more agitated tone, to which Kimber pulled his Thompson into his shoulder and fired a burst. The man yelped as bullets struck both him and the window frame, falling back out of sight. Remaining focussed on the window, Kimber was thrown a question by one of the lads.

'What was he shouting about, Kim?'

The sergeant shrugged.

'Bugger if I know.'

Titters were heard among the lads before one of them got somewhat excited.

'Here we fucking go! Soldier Ward, bottom left corner.'

Kimber rolled on his front, his focus now on the area called out. The huge Soldier Ward stood over them. The voice in the darkness spoke of the bottom left corner as they looked at it. Kimber could see the area in question but could not identify German troops. With shouting and commotion on the burning floor above them, Kimber resisted all temptation to look back. He knew he was on borrowed time remaining where he was. It only took someone else brave or stupid enough to look out and see them on their bellies under the trees. Kimber then caught sight of a head with helmet on peer around from behind the Soldier Ward.

If there was one, there was bound to be more, Kimber thought.

Transfixed on the head, Kimber watched as it now gave way to the whole profile of a soldier. The long profile of a rifle was easy to identify. Kimber stole a glance left and right of his position. In the gloom he could see most of his men lying completely still, their focus on the oncoming threat. Kimber looked back to the enemy soldier cautiously making his way forward. Another soldier came into view, then another. Their pace slow and deliberate. Kimber estimated that the German soldiers knew they were expecting trouble, but they could not be sure where from, or else they would have started shooting already. The British lay still, with darkness and vague information as their only advantage. Eight German soldiers, all armed with rifles were now patrolling forward towards Kimber and his spread-out force of twenty. Numbers were in Kimber's favour, but for them to exploit the hitting power of their Thompsons, they would have to let the Germans come in close, perhaps too close. As the enemy moved closer, no more added to their number. Kimber slowly took a grenade from his pouch and got ready to pull the pin and throw. He had plenty of men to do the shooting.

At fifty yards the three lead Germans were cut down in a hail of Thompson fire. The others hollered as they snapped off shots from their rifles and fell back to the corner of the ward in which they had come around. One more German fell as they withdrew. Kimber pulled the pin and lobbed it after them. The grenade went too far right and bounced off a window ledge before detonating harmlessly at the foot of the building.

'That's why you never get picked to play cricket, Kim.' A cheery voice came in from his right side to a round of tittering.

'Shut up, you prat!' Was his only counter. The giggles died down as they got back to business. As much as he needed to move his position to somewhere more favourable, his job was to screen the Officer Ward from the north, which he was currently doing with some success. He knew the Germans had form for coming back with gusto, it was just a matter of time. Those his men had cut down were not all dead. A couple writhed about on the ground, one calling out for medical attention. The others groaned through bloodied teeth, fearful of being finished off. Kimber was not in the habit of wasting ammunition on an enemy that was already down and out of the fight.

After a few minutes, Kimber noticed lights coming on in the Soldier Ward looking over them. Blackout curtains were pulled open, revealing interior lighting before the light was then snuffed out. A knot in Kimber's stomach was beginning to tighten. German soldiers were not about to give him an easy target, unlike the coughing man behind them.

'Eyes up fellas.' Kimber called out. The Germans now knew where they were, so the need for silence had now passed. Numerous windows dominated his position. Kimber looked over his shoulder at the smouldering building, as he tried to picture a suitable fighting position further back towards the shore line. As sparse as the trees were overhead, it was the only cover they had. His backpack lay to his right side, where just underneath the top flap sat the flare gun. With a red flare cartridge already loaded, he reached inside and ensured it remained close to hand.

The immediate area around the NCO erupted in a cacophony of loud snaps as incoming fire splashed around him and his men. Instinctively flinching at the close calls, Kimber pulled his Thompson into the aim and began firing short, controlled bursts at numerous muzzle flashes coming from windows on the first floor of the Soldier Ward. The Germans, now aware of the enemy position under the trees now sought elevation to get an advantage. Kimber's men acted as taught, firing their weapons before crawling left or right to change their fighting position. The method, especially in darkness can give the opposition the impression that they are in fact facing a far large force than originally thought.

A dull thwack against a tree gave away to piercing scream as one of the commandos was hit. Kimber needed to get his men into better cover. As he went for the flare gun, one of his NCOs to his right fired their own red flare at the Soldier Ward façade. As it bounced of the masonry and settled in the clipped grass verge at the foot of the building, Kimber and his men got what they were asking for.

Red tracer fire from the Catalinas splashed all over the façade, causing both belligerents to flinch and withdraw a little. As chunks of the façade where chipped off by the weight of fire, some bullets ricocheted off into the darkness with a loud moan. Kimber got to his knees, shrugging his backpack onto his right shoulder.

'Behind the burning building, move, move!'

The order echoed outwards as the men repeated the order at the top of their lungs. Under the weight of the covering fire, 2 Troop got to their feet and made for the east side of the Officer Ward. Their wounded man hauled along by two of his comrades. Leading the troop out from under the trees, Kimber caught a glimpse at the back side of the Officer Ward. Bedsheets, tide together were getting lowered from upper windows. The Germans caught above the burning floor, the smoke now giving way to flame, were trying to escape. Kimber had no time to be shooting half-dressed patients hanging from bedsheets, for he needed to get his men into far better cover. Reaching the north side of the burning building, he noticed a pair of sunken doors that would lead to what could be the cellar of the building. The sunken recess in which the doors sat at the bottom of some stone steps was too small and shallow for all his men to fit in and fight from, so he led them on to the lake side of the building, for the ground floor was not ablaze. Stood at the corner, looking back as his men shuffled past him, he counted them in to ensure no one was left behind. As those hauling their wounded friend came past, one of those helping the wounded man, sweating profusely, gasped at the sergeant.

'Bob and Kenny are down, Kim.'

'Are you sure?'

'Yeah,' gasped the commando, 'I saw 'em get hit.'

'Are they alive?'

'Not sure.'

'Fuck!' Kimber looked down the line of his men, all breathing hard, but now in much better cover. 'Danny?'

'Yeah?'

'Gimme that handset.'

Private Daniel French jogged over to Kimber before turning his pack towards Kimber, who reach under the top flap and fished out a handset. Peering around the corner back to where they had previously held the line, Kimber spoke into the handset.

'Zero Bravo, this is Two Zero, over…'

His call to Jones went unanswered, so he called again.

'Zero Bravo, this in Two Zero, over!'

No answer. Unaware both Davey and his radio set were dead, Kimber called the next best person.

'Three-Three Alpha, this is Two Zero, over…'

'Three-Three Alpha send…' The Company Sergeant Major hunkered down at the North Jetty answered immediately, which brought comfort to Kimber.

'We've come under contact on the north side of the target building, we've taken casualties and have withdrawn to the east side where there is better cover, over.'

'Understood, can you still cover your allotted arcs of fire, over?'

'Not as effective as before, over.'

'Understood, do what you can. What condition are your casualties, over?'

'We have one stretcher case with us, we took two more as we withdrew, but unable to confirm their condition, over.'

There was a long pause in the dialogue between him and Montgomery. For the young sergeant, it felt like he was about to receive a reprimand from the senior soldier. Montgomery then answered.

'Understood, don't risk anyone going back out there to recover them. Have your wounded man brought to me at the North Jetty and leave your medics with me. We've certainly kicked the hornets' nest tonight, over…'

Both Kimber and French smirked at each other. Montgomery would have said something far more colourful if it was face to face, but on the radio, professional as ever.

'Roger out!'

38.

As more and more men, in various stages of undress arrived on the doorstep, Astrid Mortens tried her best to calm their fears, including hers. The theme amid a constant soundtrack of engine noise and machinegun fire was that of a Soviet attack. To accompany the sound of battle, Astrid spotted an eerie glow coming from the sanatorium and the distinct aroma of burning. The men, members of staff at the facility, demanded to speak with the Head of Security, who was also embroiled in trying to find out what was happening.

With the telephone handset wedged between his right ear and shoulder, he buttoned up his tunic.

'Scharfuhrer, I can smell burning. Is that coming from the sanatorium?'

'Yes Sir. Officer Ward is on fire.'

'On fire?'

'Yes Sir. The enemy have aircraft strafing it.'

'Aircraft? But they are none flying about.'

'On the lake Sir.'

'What?'

'They are on the lake. Flying boats. The enemy have arrived on flying boats, likes ours.'

'Okay,' Mortens paused, 'hang on.'

He took a mouthful of the now tepid coffee and went back to the call.

'Who are the enemy, Scharfuhrer?'

'Sir?'

'Soviet? British? American?'

'Can't confirm, but we think they are British.'

Mortens paused as he tried to fathom what could interest the British enough to come this far into Germany. He now had more questions.

'How many are there? The aircraft I mean.'

'We think there are three. In the dark, it's hard to tell. On the water they keep moving about.'

'How many men?'

'Can't be sure Sir. We got a call from someone in Officer Ward, shouting about the enemy in the foyer, shooting the hell out of the place.'

'In the foyer?'

'Yes Sir.'

'Who called you?'

'One second…Standartenfuhrer Macht.'

'What is he?'

'Sir?'

'Staff or patient?'

'I think he's a patient.'

'Did he say how many were in the building?'

'He said at least twenty, with more shooting at them from outside.'

Mortens paused, taking notes. He mulled over the numbers. If there was that sized force inside the ward, then they were clearly looking for something, or someone. And to do that successfully, they would probably require at least the same number outside to protect them. He spoke into the handset once more.

'Scharfuhrer, are you still there?'

'Yes Sir.'

'Have a few of your men meet me at the village road bridge. I must see this shit show for myself.'

'Very good Sir. Now?'

'Right now.'

Mortens put down the phone. He had some in formation, but not much, and could not gauge how accurate it was until he saw the problem for himself. The guard force was panicked, it was dark, and the enemy had come in force for a particular purpose. He just could not fathom what they would want in Hohenlychen.

He joined the melee on the doorstep. The look on Astrids face was one of relief when she saw her husband. She was growing weary of the chauvinistic arseholes demanding to speak with her husband, since she was clearly just the wife and could not know what was unfolding in the sanatorium. Despite the senior ranks gathered before him, the Head of Security called for calm. Some of the men, not used to being spoken to in such a manner when from concerned to affronted at the mere Haupsturmfuhrer waving them down.

'Gentlemen,' Mortens opened, 'I have just got off the phone with the Guard Commander, who has filled me in with regards to the attack underway on the sanatorium.'

'Attack?' Some of them blurted. 'Why would anyone attack a hospital? This is outrageous.'

Mortens nodded in agreement, as Astrid slipped back in the house to make herself more decent.

'Is it the Soviets?' Was their main concern. Mortens shook his head.

'We think they are British. Commandos perhaps.'

'British Commandos? Are you sure?'

'We have to confirm who we are facing. In the meantime, because I don't want you or your families caught up in this, may I ask you gentlemen to take them to Ravensbruck for the time being.'

'Ravensbruck? At this hour?'

'I fear the attack may spill out of the sanatorium and into our streets. I would of course endeavour to keep them contained until reinforcements from Ravensbruck arrive.'

'Are they on their way?'

'Who?'

'Reinforcements.'

'I need a clearer picture before they will release the Quick Reaction Force. I'm heading into the sanatorium now to see for myself.'

The old men scoffed.

'Nothing quick about this reaction force.'

Mortens could not allow the mocking to go unchallenged, regardless the rank of the heckler.

'I assure you, Sir, the QRF commander will need to know who he is up against and how many. To have them bundle into here with vague information at best will only get them killed.'

The men before him mumbled among themselves, their lack of counter or reprimand served as a minor victory for Mortens, who was trying hard not to think of his failure to keep Arens safe in Norway, and was now charged with keeping an entire facility, staff, and families out of harm's way. It then dawned on him. Since Arens arrived, allied planes have taken an interest in Hohenlychen. The British clearly sponsored the terrorists in Norway and could well be here to finish the job. Maybe even capture him.

As his audience broke up, embroiled in discussion as to their mode of transport to Ravensbruck, Mortens decided to keep his theory to himself. The more he thought about it, the more credible it became.

The British were here for the Scientist.

What baffled Mortens was why Arens was so important in the first place to warrant assassination. His exile to Norway to continue whatever he was doing at the Vermork Hydroelectric Plant was somewhat of a mystery to Mortens and his men. They were tasked with keeping him safe, nothing more. Why would the British then go through so much trouble to come here and kill him?

They must be here to capture him. But why?

A lowly Haupsturmfuhrer was probably never going to get to the bottom of it. The career path he had walked for almost the last decade had not exactly been paved with gold. Promotion crushingly slow, but in a way he was grateful that he had somehow avoided a combat assignment. Security duties at Army Group South Headquarters was as close to the actual fighting as he got. For a young, keen to impress officer at the time, it was certainly frustrating, but by this stage in the war, his peers from the academy would certainly trade places with him, if they were still alive.

Arms folded, Astrid bit her lip nervously as her husband checked his pistol over before slipping it back into its leather holster. Her Otto was not a fighting man, he was a security officer, a bodyguard, a policeman if you will. The thought of him duelling it out with enemy commandos in the dark was absurd, and nothing good would come of it. She had to speak.

'Otto, must you go?'

'What do you mean?' He was preoccupied with fitting the holster to his belt. He did have another pistol in his office desk, but he did not like the idea of trying to reach it unarmed through a facility teeming with enemy troops shooting at everything. With the holster set, he looked up. Instantly, he went to his wife, for her eyes were shot and raw, her cheeks streaked. He took her in him arms, tilting her face up to his with a gentle knuckle under the chin.

'Do not fret, my love. I have no intention of fighting the British, but I need to see what on earth is going on in there.'

'But you have soldiers in there already. And what if they are not British?'

'What do you mean?'

'What if it's the Soviets?'

'I still have to see what's going on.' Mortens smiled, trying not to scoff. He could see Astrid was distraught. Throughout the war, she had grown desensitised to the bombing raids, but this attack felt so much different. Literally yards from her home, the enemy were fighting those charged with keeping her safe. She could hear aircraft, shooting, grenades thudding. She could smell the burning of something, buildings most likely. The war had now come to her home and had now become very real and personal. She knew the Soviets were on the Oder, and the British and Americans now owned the skies. She knew and hoped that it all had to end soon.

'I'll stay out of trouble, okay? Besides, I'll not be wandering about alone. I'm meeting a group from the Guardroom who will keep me safe, just while I see what is taking place.'

'What good will it do, you putting yourself at risk?' Astrid cuffed her nose and eyes with the sleeve of her bathrobe.

'I can then ask for help from Ravensbruck, and they will send more soldiers to help out here, okay?'

He kissed her lightly on the lips before stepping away. As he turned, Tommy was up and ready for the mission. Mortens shook his head.

'Stand down soldier. Not this time.'

Astrid took the whining German Shepherd by the collar as his master stepped out into the night. In the distance, a faint glow plus streaks of red tracer flicked high and random up towards the stars. Mortens deliberately refused to look back. He admitted to himself, he would much have preferred to stay home, and close to Astrid and Tommy. But if he did not try and save Hohenlychen, and survive, he could almost guarantee he would be a Company Commander dug in on the Seelow Heights by the end of the week.

Feeling somewhat exposed, he stepped gingerly onto the road bridge. A bridge in name only, Mortens conceded, more a wide causeway if anything. Out on the gloomy lake, he struggled to see the supposed aircraft the Guard Commander spoke of. Muzzle flashes out on the water, followed immediately but long streaks of red tracer bullets screaming in from left to right, crashing against buildings in the sanatorium grounds confirmed the

Scharfuhrer' estimations. Mortens was well read enough to know that the Americans had something called the Catalina Flying Boat. Used by their coastguard to rescue those at sea who needed it.

Had the Americans fitted them with machineguns? Genius. Mortens conceded.

He had to hand it to the enemy, for they had chosen their insertion method well. He recalled the lone aircraft streaking over just a few days ago. Most certainly a reconnaissance model. One of their own flying boats was sat at the North Jetty. Their arrival that night would have not roused much attention, given that the sanatorium often had flying boats landing on the Zenesse and mooring up close by.

Just another delivery of broken men from the front. Why bother to get excited?

Mortens flinched as a white flare burst open above the buildings. Instinctively, he crouched down, the footprint of light given off by the flare creeped towards the bridge where he stood. He did not want to be the focus of the enemy out on the lake, like a dragon scouring for prey. More tracer poured in from the lake, the relentless din of engines raising and dropping in pitch indicated to Mortens that they were moving about on the water, but how many he could not confirm. As the flare pot fizzled out, Mortens noticed German troops getting to their feet, having been caught in the open. They then moved in towards him.

'Hauptsturmfuhrer?' One of them asked, getting an affirmative from Mortens. The NCO plus three troopers pulled up, breathing hard.

'The British are in and around the Officer Ward, Sir.'

'Are you sure they are British?'

'Yes Sir. We assumed American to begin with, but they are certainly British.'

In the dark, Mortens eased a little. It was not the beginning of a Soviet offensive. Given the four soldiers now with him were armed with rifles, Mortens could not help but feel under dressed to repel a commando raid. With his pistol pulled from its holster, he did his best to look like he knew what he was doing with it.

'Show me where they are.' He commanded.

The NCO and his men spun on their heels, leading off at a jogging half crouch back in towards the sanatorium buildings. Sporadic fire rattled out from unknown positions, echoing off the buildings, giving Mortens the impression that they were already in the thick of it. Another white flare burst above them, drowning the area in brilliant artificial light. The NCO called a halt to the move, ensuring that both his men and their principle were not observed buy the murderous aircraft out on the lake. They all braced for another long lick of tracer bullets to come screaming into the facility, but the aircraft held their fire. Only a vicious but brief firefight between other weapon types spluttered into life before petering out as the light faded once again. The NCO then continued leading them along the western side of the Soldier Ward.

As they skirted around the annex that housed the swimming pool, soldiers convalescing were stood outside in various states of undressed. In the gloom, as they saw the small patrol approach, they panicked and dashed for cover back inside the building.

'Stay inside men, you cannot help if you are not armed, 'the NCO barked as he continued on. They relaxed a little once they saw that it was their own side lurking in the shadows. As the Haupsturmfuhrer jogged past, they nodded and gave mock salutes. Mortens nodded and smiled at the lacklustre salutations, knowing that now was not the time to start reprimanding them for their bearing and manner.

The pace of the move slowed down to a more cautious pace as they drew close to a group of uniformed men gathered at the southern end of the complex. Another white flare under parachute popped open revealing the group in more detail. Most were lined up along the wall of the ward, taking it in turns to peer around the corner. Others knelt over a man being wrapped in a field dressing. The wounded man growled through clenched teeth as they applied the dressing, any pain relief he may have been given yet to kick in. Leaning against the wall where the other fighting men gathered were a number of older men in their bed clothes and bath robes. Some coughed harshly whilst others accepted sips of water from SS troopers offering them their water bottles. Away from the building lay the inert forms of two soldiers, face down. The fallen.

The NCO halted just short of the group, all preoccupied with their fight to notice the new arrivals. The NCO beckoned Mortens forward, pointing at the group fighting the British.

'Scharfuhrer Beck, Sir.'

Mortens scanned the group as the light above them faded out. He approached the group; he could see they were somewhat animated. A torch came on, highlighting a map they pored over whilst another soldier leaned out to observe the enemy.

'Scharfuhrer?' Mortens spoke gently but was lost in the conference between the fighting men.

'Scharfuhrer?' A little louder, to no effect. Mortens rolled his eyes, holstering his Luger.

'Scharfuhrer!' This time a shout, which cut dead all conversation as the torch beam illuminated the Haupsturmfuhrer. Mortens instinctively shielded his face with his right forearm. The torch immediately went out. As Mortens regained his vision, the red orbs in his peripheral drifting down, he then saw the group stood to attention. He waved them down.

'Enough of that shit,' Mortens cussed, 'what have we got here?'

The troopers relaxed as they went back to the matter at hand. Mortens stepped in closer, he needed to know more about who they were dealing with. The Scharfuhrer beckoned him forward, cautiously leaning out from what protection the building offered. Mortens side shuffled nervously outwards, fearing that at any moment a hail of bullets would cut him down. The Scharfuhrer, apparently immune to enemy bullets stood boldly out in the open pointing at what could only be the Officer Ward.

The building had thick smoke billowing from a number of the windows on the first floor. Mortens could not see any flames, but the flicking glow from the lakeside of the building indicated to him that the fittings on that side were on fire. Makeshift ropes constructed from bedsheets draped from two of the non-smoking windows to the lawn below. As Mortens went to speak, a light clad figure emerged from one of the windows and clambered over the ledge.

'Shit, another one.' The Scharfuhrer cussed. Mortens glared at him.

'You have a problem with your superiors escaping a burning building?'

The Scharfuhrer gave him a double take, before realising his cussing had been heard.

'No…no Sir.' He appeared apologetic in the gloom. 'They won't stay in cover. Every time they make a run…'

'Go back! Go back!' The troopers gathered at the corner bellow at the man clambering to his feet after a long drop from about ten feet up. Mortens witnessed the man stagger a little before putting in a concentrated effort to make the dash to what he thought would be safety. The warnings from the troopers were unheard as the aircraft marauding out on the lake drowned out those trying to communicate with the half stumbling, half running man. Out from the bottom left corner of the Officer Ward, a red flare popped open not far from the running man. The red flare fired so low confused Mortens who was suddenly grabbed by the Scharfuhrer and hauled back behind the Soldier Ward with no warning. Winded at the sudden violence of the action, Mortens had little or no time to gather his senses as a blizzard of red tracer bullets whacked and screamed off the outside Soldier Ward façade into the darkness. The storm of fiery hornets snapped through between the buildings for what felt like an age, until it ceased as abruptly as it began. The Scharfuhrer released his grip on the officer before slumping against the wall, cuffing his face with his forearm.

'That happens.'

Catching his breath, Mortens put his hands on his knees, puffing out his cheeks.

'They're shooting the patients?'

'Anything that moves.'

'Christ!' Mortens conceded. 'Are we correct in assuming they are British?'

'We think so.' The Scharfuhrer nodded, as he went about checking on his men. All were unharmed, save their dressing wrapped casualty, for now.'

'What makes you think they're British?' Mortens had to be sure, for if he were going to ask Ravensbruck for reinforcements, they would demand chapter and verse before they made a decision.

'At first we thought they were American, but when they put their white flares up, they were dressed like British. Green soft hats, no helmets.'

'Commandos?'

'Most likely.'

'How many?'

'We encountered about twenty of them.'

'Twenty?'

'At least.'

'Where did you encounter them?'

'Out there.' the Scharfuhrer jerked a thumb at the contest gap between the buildings. 'We got perhaps two of them before they withdrew behind the Officer Ward. 'Three of my guys are still out there, but I can't risk anyone going to try and get them.'

'Good call.' Mortens nodded. Even he could see the logic in that fact. Mortens took the opportunity to steal a brief look out where the red flare came from. As he did so, he put another question to the Scharfuhrer.

'Given what you have seen, how many commandos do you think we are dealing with here?'

'How many?' The young man countered, a little off at now having to make a guess. Mortens leaned back in, looking him squarely in the face.

'I'm going to the Guardroom to call Ravensbruck for reinforcements, I need a number to put to them, because they're going to ask me how many?'

The Scharfuhrer paused for a moment, before the whole group flinched as one as a white flare popped high above them, washing the entire area in light. The Scharfuhrer sneered at the flare.

'Cunning foxes, the British. In the light we cannot make any moves, and the fools that do are cut down by them damned aircraft out on the lake.'

'So…' Mortens cuffed his mouth, 'three flying boats, like our BV-222's yes?'

'Yes.'

'Packed full of enemy commandos, here to cause trouble?'

'Yes.'

'Let's call it twenty-five men delivered per aircraft, give or take a man?'

As the fizzing flare pot pirouetted under its own parachute, the shadows cast drew longer as the pot got lower, giving the nodding Scharfuhrer a demonic look, his frown and cheek bones creating shadow of their own on his face.

'The men you've been engaged in combat with, one aircrafts worth my guess. So, we can now at least times that by three.'

The whole area went dark as the pot hit the clay tiles of the roof above them, before tumbling to earth, the naked branches capturing the parachute. Mortens looked up to see the spent flare pot swinging lazily before looking back to the Scharfuhrer.

'A Company.' The Scharfuhrer stated with confidence.

'A Company.' Mortens concurred.

Taking the greatest care not to expose themselves to not just the aircraft roaring about on the lake in search of their next prey, Mortens and his original four-man party picked their way carefully, when flares allowed back up to the Guardroom. As the building and gate barrier came into view, he was stunned to see the dark mass of Opel trucks lined up, their blackout covers on their headlamps giving off but a sliver of illumination on the road before them. Between the trucks and the main door to the building stood a group of soldiers. Most helmeted and armed, the long slim profile of their rifles easy to make out. Some of their faces glowed as they pulled on cigarettes. As Mortens party drew closer, they all turned toward them. A white flare burst high once again over the Officer Ward, lighting up the group of men who all as one pulled themselves to attention as Mortens silhouette gave way to the profile and features of an SS officer. He waved them to relax, his face full of concern. There were perhaps thirty of them. Not one of them looked over twenty. What puzzled him, was how they happened to be at his Guardroom already.

'What the hell are you doing here?'

'What do you men, Sir?' One of the bigger men at the front shrugged his rifle sling higher on his shoulder, a frown of confusion on his face. The flare distorted their faces as it drifted to earth. Mortens looked about them before he lost the light.

'How did you know to come here already?'

'Sir?' The big SS Trooper was now very confused. In exasperation, Mortens puffed out his cheeks as he looked to the stars for a brief moment.

'Are you the Quick Reaction Force from Ravensbruck?'

All flinched as one as three thin streams of red tracer bullets appeared out of the lake and smashed all over buildings down near the shoreline, many of which scream skywards until burnout. Mortens, now familiar with the threat marauding out on the lake recovered first. The soldiers regained their composure, straightening helmets, shrugging rifles, pulling greatcoats straight. Mortens asked them again.

'Are you the Quick Reaction Force from Ravensbruck?'

The big trooper looked about him for some support before answering.

'We're from Ravensbruck, but we are not the Quick Reaction Force, Sir.'

'Who are you then?'

'Sir?'

Was this young man trying to test his patience? Mortens thought.

'Who are you? What brings you here in the middle of the fucking night?'

'Oh…' The big trooper now realised what the Haupsturmfuhrer was referring to. 'We're the relief for the guard force, Sir.'

Mortens blinked rapidly for a few seconds, not really sure what to do or say next. Another white flare popped open, the group flinched again, clearly not expecting to roll straight into battle.

'What's that noise, Sir?' The big trooper asked innocently. Mortens spun on his heels to look back down at the lake. The large mechanical birds of prey enjoyed the cover of darkness as their engines pitched and feathered them about like swans. He could tell them, but that might take their ignorant edge away. He looked back at the soldiers.

'If you're the guard relief, why the middle of the night?'

'New directive Sir.' The big trooper responded. 'Enemy fighter bombers attack anything that moves in the daytime now. All road moves are now at night.'

Mortens bit his lip at the revelation. He could have done with that information himself far earlier. As he went to continue speaking he noticed another Opel arrive but park some distance from the remainder of the convoy. What caught his attention was the fact that none of those occupying the drivers cab dismounted. He knew exactly who they were, before picking his way through the throng of troopers gathered on the Guardroom veranda.

As he approached the truck, he could hear the grinding change in engine pitch as it began reversing away, back down the road towards the rail head. Determined to catch up with it, he called for it to halt. As he broke into a jog, he was then dazzled by the truck as it put on its main headlights. Blinded and reduced to a standstill, Mortens shielded his eyes as the truck, its engine wailing increased the distance between them as it backed away to such a point, it managed to make a three point turn on the road and head back the way it came, its lights returning to blackout mode, void of any tail lights.

With his night vision ruined, Mortens paced about a little as it slowly returned. The red orbs drifting out to the peripheries. With his vision partially restored, he made his way back to the Guardroom. The trooper he had spoken with stepped forward.

'Shall we give chase Sir? Who was that?'

'Don't worry about them.' Mortens waved a dismissive hand, for he would deal with that issue once he managed to contain and defeat the commando raid on his own doorstep.

'Listen up men.' Mortens called out to get their attention. The troopers pulled themselves to attention, cigarettes at various stage of consumption flicked away into the darkness. Mortens looked to them.

'We have a security situation here at Hohenlychen, and your timing could not have been better.'

He looked to the NCO who had met him with at the road bridge before continuing.

'We have enemy saboteurs in and around the Officer Ward. This is not an exercise I assure you.'

Another white flare popped above the facility, accompanied by streams of red tracer bullets arcing between the buildings, flicking, and whining high into the night sky as they ricocheted off building facades. The men flinched, but Mortens, now aware of the enemy flying boats out on the water, held firm.

He gestured the NCO stood off to the flank. The troopers looked in at him. He gave them a courteous nod.

'This young man will take you down to join with those already on the scene containing and battling the enemy. Please give the Scharfuhrer at the tip of the spear your stoic resolve as German soldiers.'

The troopers he could tell had not been baptised into battle and the looks on their faces gave that fact away from the off. He offered them what he thought would be some reassurance.

'I'm calling for more reinforcements from Ravensbruck to assist with defeating this attack, so do not feel you are alone. We must however defeat the enemy before they can either reinforce themselves or retreat into the night. Go with this NCO and he will get you down to where our comrades are currently containing the enemy.'

'Follow me!' Was all the NCO gave by way of instruction as he walked away briskly, his MP40 in both hands, towards the white flare drifting down to earth. The troopers slid their rifles from their shoulders and followed on, in a rather disorganised trickle. Working the bolts of their rifles, they chambered a round and fell into single file. As darkness returned, Mortens made his way into the Guardroom, its heavy blackout curtains containing the eerie glow of lamps.

As he stepped between the curtains to cross the threshold, he noticed a trooper manning the main desk. The young man stood up as he recognised an officer entering. Mortens waved him down as he eyed him.

'Just you?'

'Yes sir.' The trooper nodded nervously, revealing a lower limb in a plaster cast, his trouser cut just short of the knee.

'Battle wound?' Mortens was intrigued. The trooper blushed.

'Football, last week.'

Mortens snorted, and welcomed the light comedy given the situation.

'Any chance of a cup of coffee?'

'Of course, Sir.'

The trooper hobbled away as Mortens tossed his field cap on the desk before reaching for the phone. As he put it to his ear, a crackling female switchboard operator answered immediately.

'Which department please?'

'Operations Officer, Ravensbruck please.' Mortens tried his best to remain calm and professional.

'Given the hour, may I return this call once he is roused?'

'Fine, please do.'

'Who is calling please?'

'Haupsturmfuhrer Otto Mortens. Chief of Security, Hohenlychen. We are under commando attack here.'

There was a pregnant pause before the switchboard operator responded. He needed to get that information over quickly or else Obersturmbannfuhrer Frederick Platz would just go back to sleep vowing to call him in the morning.

'I'll have him on the phone to you as soon as I can, Haupsturmfuhrer.'

'Thank you.'

The line clicked off.

The trooper returned at a limp nursing a cup of coffee with both hands. As he handed Mortens the cup, the look on his face was one of concern.

'Is it the Soviets, Sir?'

Mortens took a sip before answering.

'British by the looks of things. Your comrades have only heard English being spoken by the enemy.'

The trooper limped over to the rifle rack and pulled the sole remaining carbine free. As he turned, Mortens waved the young man down.

'You have a broken ankle. You have nothing to prove to me. Put that back and sit down.'

Mortens was not sure if the trooper was actually feeling forlorn, or just putting on a show to prove he was as brave as the Fatherland expected him to be. The young man returned the carbine to the rack and returned to his seat. The relief on his face as he took the weight off his injured leg visible.

As the trooper went to speak, both were distracted by more automatic fire, most likely from the flying boats. Mortens dimmed the oil lamp and peered through the heavy blackout curtain covering the doorway. Another white flare hung high above the sanatorium with red tracer flicking high and wide. Mortens had to concede that if the enemy had anything going for them at that moment, it was firepower.

Mortens was finishing off the mediocre coffee when the phone rattled an incoming call. Putting the cup down, he allowed it to ring a couple of times. He needed to appear calm and in control. He then picked up the handset.

'Head of Security, Hohenlychen.'

'Mortens?'

'Yes.'

'Haupsturmfuhrer?' An irritated Platz opened, 'why am I woken for the second time in less than an hour?'

'Sir?'

'I have already deployed the Quick Reaction Force; they should be with you momentarily.'

Mortens frowned at the trooper massaging his leg.

'Troops have arrived Sir, but they are the relief for the guard force.'

'What?' Platz scoffed, 'have the halftracks arrived?'

'One moment please.' Mortens put the handset down and stepped through the curtains. In the eerie glow of flares, he walked about the trucks sat in front of the guardroom. He could not see any halftracks. He returned inside and took up the handset again.

'I have three trucks only Sir.'

'Right...' Platz yawned in Mortens ear, 'I've deployed a company of troops, they are in half a dozen trucks, and two halftracks. I think we are talking about two separate groups here.'

Mortens tried his best not to be confused. If Platz had deployed the Quick Reaction Force, he was trying to fathom how Platz knew to send them. He had to ask.

'Excuse the question, Obersturmbannfuhrer, but how did you know to send them here?'

'Standartenfuhrer Wolf called it in.'

Mortens took a breath. He had no idea who this Wolf was.

'I have no idea who that is, Sir.'

'For fuck's sake,' Platz snapped, 'Wolf called me in a panic earlier, something about British Commandos in the foyer beneath his ward, and the fact he had been strafed and his room was on fire.'

'He's a patient?'

'He's a fucking patient, who I actually know personally.'

'I see. Thank you for your time, Obersturmbannfuhrer. Apologies for rousing you.'

Without salutation, Platz rang off. Mortens replaced the handset, more annoyed than embarrassed. Since when did patients take it upon themselves to call out the Quick Reaction Force? It was bad enough that the sanatorium had a rather lacklustre attitude regarding security and were now paying for it. Now he had patients, senior or not, calling who they liked. Mortens was now in a limbo. He had men fighting what has been assumed to be British Commandos in and around the Officer Ward, and he was now waiting for the supposed Quick Reaction Force to arrive and assist. He had no idea where they were, or how long they would be.

39.

To Jones, the man stood in the cubicle in bedclothes and slippers appeared not very impressive, but it was the man they had come for. At a limp, the man shuffled forward out of the cubicle, his hands open and raised to show he was not armed. The three soldiers had pistols pointed at him. What shocked the man was the dead fourth soldier lying in his own blood, the detritus of field dressings and wrappers all about him. A vicious exchange of gunfire in the foyer had him retreat back into the cubicle. As he stumbled back, sitting back on the toilet, one of the soldiers stomped forward into the cubicle, grabbing him by the bathrobe before yanking him back out onto the slippery tiled floor. The man slumped to his knees, the blood on the tiles already soaking into his pyjama trousers. The soldier released his grip and stepped back.

The soldier not covered in their comrades' blood stepped forward, his pistol at his side. The man looked up at his prospective executioner.

'Doctor Jurgen Arens?'

Arens blinked hard at the question given to him in English. He was relieved it was not Norwegian or Russian. It had no American twang to it either. The soldier prodded him in the shoulder with the pistol.

'Are you Jurgen Arens?'

Arens nodded nervously, not entirely sure if his acknowledgement would have him shot on the spot.

'Obersturmbannfuhrer Jurgen Arens?'

Arens stomach turned since the soldier sneered as he spoke his honorary SS rank. He was now at the mercy of a man that clearly despised all that he stood for. Arens stuttered a response.

'It's just a rank they give me for administration purposes.'

The fearsome looking soldier stood over him looked to one of his comrades as he holstered the pistol.

'It's him. Let's get ready to move.'

Relief washed over Arens as the bloodied soldiers gathered up their weapons and equipment and moved to the threshold. The remaining soldier hauled him to his feet. Arens instinctively grabbed the man's forearms as he steadied himself in the blood. He looked the soldier squarely in the face as the man spoke.

'I'm Major Fynlay Jones. You are coming with me, dead or alive, which do you prefer?'

'The latter if I may.'

'You are limping, yes?'

'Yes,' Arens nodded, 'I was shot in Norway. I have a cane.'

Jones released Arens so he could return to the cubicle and fetch his cane. As he remerged, gunfire erupted out in the foyer once more. Hand on his holster, Jones eyed the bloodied men at the threshold.

'We must get out of here. The floor above us is on fire and everyone is this place is armed.'

'I'm not armed.' Arens felt the need to make that known. Jones glanced at him.

'You're not a soldier, Doctor. Yet your peers apparently are.'

'That's true.' Arens looked down at the dead man. 'I've felt like an outsider ever since I got here.'

Uninterested in Arens story, Jones made for the threshold. He could see out across the foyer one of his men applying a dressing to another. They had to get out and over to the jetty for pickup. With the crackling of fittings above them, and the relentless drone of Catalina engines out on the lake, they needed to make their move. As two of his men went for the main doors, both were cut down in a hail of bullets. As Jones and the two men in the threshold flinched, the commandos in the foyer diverted their fire, now a combination of Thompson and Colt up at those on the staircase. The enemy upstairs had now organised themselves and were getting bolder and more accurate. Jones stepped out into the foyer. With the main doors under withering fire, the enemy hiding in the dark corridors grew bolder, and fired volleys into the foyer. With the open floor plan now a killing area, Jones made a snap decision.

'The cellar, go! Get in the cellar!'

Bursts of Thompson and Colt preceded the men as they vaulted the desk holding the cellar door open. Jones turned to Arens who held his cane in both hands as he was manhandled out into the foyer. His shoulders hunched as high as they could go as bullets snapped past him, fearing being hit at any moment. Amid the cacophony of gunfire, he could hear shouts in both English and German. To add drama to the already outrageous situation, the huge chandelier came loose from its anchor point and crashed to the floor, bursting all over the dead and dying British caught on the open tiled floor. Before Arens could take in the scene, Jones had him by the back of the neck, bending him over the desk as he tumbled him over into the arms of two soldiers just inside the entrance to the cellar. The assault on his senses flashed him to anger, for he had never been treated this way before. He knew better than to protest, except for his cane to be picked up where it had cartwheeled out of his grip during his chastisement. Hauled to his feet, his cane was shoved into his chest, taking the wind from him as they brought him down into the cool, white tiled cellar.

Breathing hard, Jones looked up at the door held open by the desk. About him was the majority of his unit that had entered the ward. He had casualties to consider, but he could not guarantee those remaining up in the foyer were dead. His stomach turned at the thought of them falling into the hands of an angry enemy. They had attacked an SS facility, so could expect no mercy.

The stark contrast of their new surroundings from the previous was evident. Jones and his commandos now found themselves in a brilliantly lit, white tiled arrangement. The layout almost mirrored what the ground floor offered. A foyer, not as big as upstairs, with off shoot corridors, only these were well lit. Fresh blood was smeared on some of the tiles, which alarmed him. He looked to his men.

'Someone's wounded, check for wounds, lads.'

Whilst a few kept their weapons covering the door, others began to pull off smocks and shirts. One or two had indeed been clipped in the gunfight, but not enough to warrant such bloodletting. Jones then noticed the smeared blood was in fact from the two lads that had tried to save Davey in the ablutions.

'Relax.' Jones called out those feverishly check each other over. 'It's not from wounds. It's Davey's blood.'

'Davey?' A voice murmured, to which Jones nodded. As the men redressed themselves, one of the NCOs snarled at the pathetic little man nursing a cane.

'Hey, you!' The commando sneered, which got Arens attention.

'You had better be fucking worth it.'

Arens wrang the cane hard, his knuckles white as he looked forlorn at the tiled floor. Jones made no attempt to come to his defence, nor reprimand the soldier. The major was no fan of the scientist, and just wanted to get their mission over with. Whatever their mission was exactly eluded Arens. He chose to keep his mouth shut and do as he was told.

'Boss, we've got people down here.' Came a call from a room that did not branch off from a corridor, its threshold abutted against the small foyer. Jones, his rubber soled boots squeaking on the tiles made his way in, leaving Arens to fend for himself amid the bloodied wolves.

Six men, clad in white lab coats stood in the far corner, their hands tucked in their pockets. The one at the front, a tall, premature grey man sneered defiantly at the intrusion, whilst those clustered behind him feigned hardiness or displayed genuine fear. Jones stood before them.

'Who are you?'

They only looked back at him. Jones was in no mood to drag this out.

'Arens?' he bellowed over his shoulder. The good doctor would have a chance to prove how useful he could be.

Arens sheepishly peered in the room, only to have those in white look at him in a mixture of surprise and disgust. Jones sensed the man loitering in his periphery. Arens shuffled in closer. As he drew close, gunfire had them all flinch. The enemy now occupied the foyer.

'Ask who they are.'

Arens spoke in German. The white coated men remained silent. Arens then tried again in Norwegian. No answer. Jones took a deep breath, pulling his Colt from its holster. A sharp intake of breath from some of the white coated men as he cocked the hammer back had their formation loosen as those at the back begin to shuffle outwards. Jones had raised the ante; he could not afford to back down.

'Try again, if you would, Doctor.'

Arens asked the question once more in German. The big, silver man lifted his chin as he slowly crossed his arms, as he hissed something spiteful at Arens. Those stood behind him gave off a mixture of defiance and apprehension. Not taking his eyes of the front man,

Jones cocked an ear for Arens to enlighten him. Arens let off an apologetic cough.

'They don't answer to the enemy or traitors.'

Jones turned to Arens with a frown. In return all he got in return was a forlorn shrug. Rolling his eyes, Jones pointed it at the face of the defiant German and fired.

Instantaneously, the Germans head and the wall tile behind burst with a sharp crack and a pink, brown and white mist. The gunshot was deafening in the confines of the small lobby. The other white clad men staggered outwards; faces winced as they covered their ears. The surprise gunshot had Jones' own men reeling. The body dropped like a puppet with its strings cut, with what remained of its face bouncing off its own jack-knifed knees before toppling forward, coming to rest in a wet thump on the floor, its backside remaining propped up in the air. As the pulp that was his face let out the pooling dark blood, Jones returned the hammer to its forward position under pressure with his thumb and placed the Colt back in its holster. Given the sudden trauma of the execution to those around him, Jones was calm.

He had his man, everyone else was expendable.

The remaining men in their blood speckled lab coats appeared now in a far more cooperative mood. All began speaking at once, to which Arens struggled to make sense. Slowly, Jones put a finger to his lips, which immediately brought silence from the scared, jabbering men. They did not want him to present the pistol again. Jones looked to Arens to begin. The old man hobbled forward a little.

'Who are you?'

The scared men sheepishly looked to each other before one gathered the courage to respond.

'We are scientists.'

Arens translated. Not taking his eyes off them, Jones began to engage in dialogue.

'What do you do here?'

'We treat wounded men from the front.'

'The east?'

'Everywhere.'

Jones went to ask his next question when he heard commotion from one of the corridors behind him. Turning with Arens, Jones could see two of his men leaning against the tiled wall, one dry heaved whilst the other openly vomited. Instinctively, Jones spun on his heels to look at the white coated men, who now looked nervously at one another, whilst wringing their hands. He stepped off towards his sick men, jerking a thumb over his shoulder as he spoke to others.

'Watch them fuckers.'

'Sir.'

As Jones drew near his sickened men, the one that had vomited cuffed his chin, his sweat beaded head leaning against the cool white tiles. The other leaned back against the wall, puffing out his cheeks, his face glistening. As Jones looked to them, other commandos ventured forward to peer into the ward where the men had just been.

'Holy shit.' One of them gasped, his eyes flicking up to meet Jones' who was not sure who to tend to first. The soldier that had dry heaved slumped forward, his hands on his thighs.

'Fucking rough in there, boss.'

'What?'

'Never seen anything like it.'

'What?' Jones raised his voice.

The soldier stood himself straight, the other who had vomited waved himself a time out, he was not going back in there.

Jones and Arens followed the soldier into the ward. It was high ceilinged, brightly lit and tiled throughout. A large, metal examination table stood in the middle, with a small table to one side. At the far end of the room stood another table covered in pristine tools worthy of a surgeon. On the examination table heaved a woman. A pregnant woman covered in thin, white bedsheets. As Jones stepped closer, he could see she was gagged with a thick stick and leather strap. Her head shaved roughly. Her arms were restrained out to her sides in a cruciform with leather straps, a number crudely tattooed on her left forearm. Her swollen belly appeared deflated and off centre.

It was as Jones stepped around to look into the large kidney dish, did his stomach turn and take his breath away. Turning his back on the woman, he fought hard to keep himself from vomiting. Arens and those who had dared to venture in, stepped back, not wanting anything more to do with the macabre scene. Composing himself, Jones noticed Arens shuffling back towards the threshold. Jones allowed it. The man was a Doctor of Nuclear Physics, not this barbarity. Arens was just as horrified as he was. He let him be. Taking a breath to compose himself, Jones realised he was the only one stood with the woman. Clearly too much for the others to take in. Turning back around, Jones forced himself to look in the large kidney dish.

The infant, umbilical attached lay still in whatever fluid occupied the dish. Tubes protruded from the tiny lifeless body, running off to various bags of fluid hanging from different hooks over the examination table. The woman looked to Jones, her eyes wild, her face smeared in dribble from the wooden bit which forced her jaw wide open. Jones pulled a sheet gathered around his boots up and over the kidney dish. He knew the poor woman had laid there for some time whilst they used her unborn infant as a lab rat. Time to give the poor little soul some dignity.

He pulled his knife from his belt kit, which had Arens and those commandos' stoic enough to remain in the ward to gasp. He made short work of the leather strap and removed the wooden bit from her mouth. She gasped at the air, her pale bare cheat heaving heavily. She began to mutter, over and over again something Jones could not understand.

'Doctor Arens?'

'Yes?' a meek voice responded. Jones waved him over.

'If you please.'

Unsure what Jones wanted of him, Arens shuffled over, his resolve improved with the sheet now over the kidney dish. Jones looked to him.

'What is she saying?'

Arens shrugged a little.

'It's Polish, I don't have a clue.'

Jones looked to the woman, whose eyes welled up as she managed a smile. What she was saying appeared to be soothing, no panic in her tone. She clearly knew her baby was dead and was resigned to join them. Jones lifted the sheet over the kidney dish ever so slightly to cure his curiosity.

It was a boy.

'Is she in pain?' Jones asked as he stroked her shorn head. Arens shook his head a little.

'I doubt it, given the trauma to her abdomen. How long she remains pain free is anyone's guess.'

Jones reached inside his smock, his fingers fumbling around his shirt collar. He then pulled clear the loop of bootlace that was around his neck. Along with his identification discs came two 'Monoject' syrettes of morphine, taped to the lace. Slowly he pulled the first syrette free, before pulling the long black rubber cap which protected him from the needle away with his teeth. As he did so, Jones noticed the woman remained calm, as if at peace. Respectfully, Jones exposed her pale white thigh, and gave her the morphine. Throwing the spent syrette over his shoulder, he then pulled free the second and last syrette. As he put the syrette to his lips to pull free the black cap, one of the NCOs stepped forward.

'Boss, what if you need it?'

Jones eyed him long enough to have the NCO break his gaze and step back. The major then went about administering the last of his morphine to the poor wretch on the table. With the second empty syrette sent the way of the first, he held her hand whilst stroking her head. Her eyes widened as her breathing became more rapid and desperate. Jones felt the least he could do was take her out of the cruel world as elegantly as possible, not taking his eyes off hers. In his periphery all his men, even Arens looked away as the woman's breathing then became slower and shallower until her chest came to rest and her pupils dilated for the last time. As he covered her over, he spoke aloud.

'Get them in here.'

For a moment, the commandos looked to each other, not quite sure what the major was asking. The penny dropped with one of the NCO's who then stormed away, out of sight. Resting his hands on the table, Jones looked to the brilliant white tiled ceiling. His eyes glazed as he swallowed hard to fight off the rage that was consuming him. The din of both battle and blaze raged above him as he stood with the inert body of a woman and her infant whose only crime was that they were not part of the Nazi ideal.

Commotion out in the foyer grew to a pitch as the white coated men were hauled into the room. Gripped by the scruff, the chastised men held up their hands to shield their faces from assault. Looking to them, Jones cocked his head, indicating the sheet covered bodies.

'Is this the same in the other rooms?'

Arens translated. The white coated men looked sheepishly at each other. Jones pulled himself straight from the table, which prompted them to begin speaking, all at once to begin with. Jones held up a hand in an attempt to calm them.

'Just one speak, if you please gentlemen.'

The hubbub of German chatter calmed to where only one spoke. Jones looked him up and down. He clearly enjoyed the catering at the sanatorium for he appeared overweight, his lack of height no doubt making him appear rather rotund. Bespectacled and thin side combed hair had him look older than the others, perhaps in his late fifties. With hands wringing, he spoke directly at Jones, not in the usual manner where everyone had a habit of speaking to the translator. This man had travelled and was used to translators. He spoke calmly, and at a pace that allowed Arens to keep up.

'In the other rooms you will find similar scenes. We are tasked with conducting 'Live Tissue Training' so my learned colleagues can return to their home cities and do good in the wake of your bombings. Many German citizens have perished under your bombs.'

As he stopped speaking, his so-called colleagues winced as they tried to side step away from him. The commandos stood alongside restrained them once more as Jones gave the orator a murderous glare. If the little man's explanation was designed to move him, it did not work. Instead, the fearsome looking major stepped towards him, never taking his eyes off him. Arens shuffled a little, unsure what the major was going to do next.

'How many more do you have down here?'

Arens translated. The German frowned a little, as if unsure what Jones was referring to. Jones pointed to the woman and her infant. His eyes never leaving the little man.

'How many more?'

'Three. All unsuccessful trials.'

As Arens finished translating, Jones blinked hard for the little man before him displayed not an ounce of emotion in his description. Before the rage overwhelmed him, he glared at Arens, whose eyes widened fearing retribution was about to be directed at him. Jones looked back at the little man.

'You will take my men to these people, and they will administer morphine to those that need it.'

'Your morphine will most certainly kill them.' The scientist countered. 'They are already heavily sedated.'

'I know.' Jones responded, looking to his men.

'Please use your morphine, boys.' He implored to his men. 'They cannot remain in a place like this.'

The commandos nodded, knowing what was being asked of them was most unorthodox, not to mention, against their better judgement. Under guard by those spared having to go find other victims of their ghastly experiments, the white coated men were herded against a wall in the corridor, their hands now tucked in their coat pockets. Jones stood before them with Arens, as the echo of his men coughing and vomiting rolled through. Jones did not think less of his men. They were tough to a man, but this situation required a man to go deep into his own soul and seek reason. No one could prepare them for what they had stumbled across, but as far as Jones was concerned, he was kind of glad that they had. He could have grabbed Arens and in a different situation have fought guns blazing back to the jetty and escape. By having come down into the cellars of the Officer Ward, whose patients probably had no idea these 'trials' were taking place under them, those poor women strapped to the tables with their unborn infants in kidney dishes besides them would not have had the morphine induced salvation.

'Boss?' called out one soldier, 'Come see.'

Jones followed the corridor to where he thought the voice had come from, with Arens following on, for the Nazi Scientist felt somewhat safer in the British officers' company than his own countrymen. As they walked past the open thresholds into other examination rooms, Jones could see his men at the side of the tables, either pulling sheets over the dead wretches prone upon them or leaning against the walls trying not to be sick. It was not lost on Jones that by a sudden turn of events, he had led his men into a hell he was not prepared for. Only this hell was bright, tiled, and cold.

At the end of the corridor, a large heavy set of double doors barred him from going any further. Just beyond, he could hear the battle raging outside. The chatter of Thompsons, accompanied by English shouting of orders, not to mention a fair helping of profanity. He recognised one of the more dominant voice amid the chaos. Sergeant Paul Kimber.

Instantly relieved to hear that 2 Troop were still in the fight, Jones looked about at those that had now gathered in the corridor behind him. If he could get the doors open, and assuming Kimber and his men did not cut them down at the surprise of the action, he could link up with 2 Troop and fight their way down to the jetty for extraction.

They had their man, why stick around any longer?

Across an open threshold to his right stood two of his men, Corporal Roy Gale, and Private John Thatcher at an open, single heavy steel door. Stood on the threshold, the breath of the two commandos could be easily seen. The cellar facility was not particularly warm, but they must have opened up some kind of cold storage room. Both caught Jones looking at them inquisitively. One of them shook their head slowly.

'I've not seen anything like it.'

Intrigued, Jones stomped over to them, to which they parted to make way. Arens followed on behind. As he went to step on through, a large thud above them had everyone flinch. Whatever was happening up on the ground floor was not good.

Stepping through, the sharp cold took Jones' breath away. Most certainly a cold storage room. Moving on inside, he noticed the room was large and bare. No shelving, the kind that would allow a restaurant to keep its foodstuffs in order. All there was on the floor in the middle of the room was two piles of what looked like rolled up carpets or rugs. Both stacked neatly, the pile on the left considerably bigger than the other. Stepping in closer, Jones cocked his head over his shoulder. Arens had not followed him in. Not overly concerned at the man's absence, he continued on. As he pulled up in between the piles, he noticed that there were white sheets, wrapped around what initially looked like animal carcasses, like you would see hanging in a butcher's shop. As his eyes adjusted to the gloom, his stomach turned when his identified the profile of a human body on top of the stack.

The discovery, as macabre as it was, failed to deter the officer from investigating further. From what he had already seen in the first examination room, he kind of expected it. Leaning in closer, he could tell the body was that of a pregnant woman. Her naked form wrapped in a white sheet, all nice and neat, as the Germans liked things, ready for wherever they were to go next. Stepping back from the larger stack, he looked over the other.

Children. The larger ones nice and neat at the bottom, the dead infants perched on top.

Jones spun on his heels, pulling the Colt from its holster. At the threshold, Arens' eyes widened as he stepped away, to avoid Jones' wrath, tucking himself in behind Thatcher. Gale stepped in to see his commander, Colt in hand, eyes full of hate.

'Get them in here.' Jones snarled.

Gale could handle himself in the worst of situations, but even he knew better than to challenge the major at that moment. He turned and bellowed for the laboratory staff to be brought forward. Gale then stepped in and gingerly approached the major. He said nothing, for he knew exactly why the man was angry. About a minute later, the white coated Germans appeared at the threshold, their escorts not realising what had been discovered. If they had known, the Germans would have most certainly been chastised into the cold room. Thatcher, well informed as to the contents, kicked them into the room, those at the front sliding painfully to their knees before the others tumbled over the top of them.

'Get on your feet, you murderous fuckers.' Thatcher hissed as they untangled themselves. Getting to their feet, they glared back at Thatcher, not used to such treatment. In defiance, most pulled their lab coats straight just before the lead one was gripped hard by Jones who, with all his strength hauled the unfortunate German onto the pile of dead woman. Momentum sent the unwary man cartwheeling over them, before coming down hard on the stone floor beyond. The assault had the others step back in shock, only to be jostled forward by

Thatcher, sending some of them sprawling on the ground at the feet of the Colt wielding, furious Jones.

'What the fuck is this?' Roared Jones, the Colt pointing to the pile of dead children, before flicking back to the face of the nearest German, who flinched instinctively, fearing immediate execution.

'Is there any humanity left in you barbarians?' Spit flew from Jones lips as he hissed in their faces. At his feet they remained. Pathetic and resigned to their fate. Standing straight, Jones snorted.

'The master fucking race. Is this what you cretins stand for? Women and children for heaven's sake.'

Gale stood off as he could see not only anger rising in Jones, but also emotion as the man's eyes became raw and shot before welling. He knew he needed to keep a lid on things, but was unsure how to step in. He looked at the German who had been thrown across the frozen bodies. He was on his knees, his right arm in front of his face as if it would afford him protection. It was as Jones pulled the hammer back on the Colt that served as his cue.

'Boss. Don't do it.' Gale stepped between Jones and the kneeling men. 'We are better than this. Better than them.'

He indicated the men at their feet, who dared not move. Jones sneered at Gale.

'Get out of my way, Corporal.'

'Boss. Don't do it. Don't be like them. It's not what we do.'

Gale took a chance and held out a hand for the Colt. Jones frowned as he looked down at the open palm. It dawned on him that he was stood on the precipice. His war had been long. His war had been bloody. His war had been cruel. It could be so easy to join the madness, and twice as hard to stay above it. Jones lacked the humility to hand over his sidearm to the NCO, and opted for releasing the hammer slowly forward, before putting it back in its holster. Gale let out a sigh, content that the Colt had at least been put away. Jones stepped back before walking around the kneeling men, his hateful glare not leaving them. He joined Arens at the threshold, beckoning both Gale and Thatcher to follow on.

'Let's get the fuck out of here.'

Slowly, Gale and Thatcher obeyed, with Gale looking at both the kneeling men who shuffled on their knees to look around and Jones at the threshold. Gale locked eyes with Jones, who returned an irritated glare.

'Let's go, Corporal Gale.'

Relaxing his demeanour, a little, Gale nodded slightly as he cast a last glance at the kneeling Germans. He knew it was time to leave.

As he stepped past Jones, he began to hear protests from the Germans. He turned to see the major taking hold of the door. Arens began to translate what they were saying but was cut short by Jones raising a hand.

'I don't care what they are saying. Step back.'

Arens glanced at Gale, who showed no sign of intervening. He did as the officer ordered and made way as Jones slammed the door shut, before pulling the two bolts across.

40.

From his position across the Zenesse, Captain Matt Walsh-Woolcott watched the company sergeant major and his man, from their position near the north jetty send up another white flare. As the flare burst open, it gave the restless captain a grandstand view of the battle raging between both the officer and soldier wards. The flare added to the glare of flames emitting from the first floor of the Officer Ward, the tracer ignited curtains and fittings well and truly taking hold. Smoke billowed from the top second floor of the structure, with little sign of activity on the ground floor. What W-W could observe was what must have been 2 Troop gathered at the bottom right corner, engaged in trading fire with an enemy out of sight to those across the lake.

The relentless drone of Catalina engines off to his left dulled the sound of gunfire, save for their own .303 Vickers machineguns which sent streams of red tracer bullets arcing into the sanatorium grounds whenever 2 Troop fired a red flare.

The fire control rehearsals in Scotland had certainly been valuable, W-W confirmed.

With each white flare, W-W took the time to scan the frontage of the Soldier Ward, looking for enemy troops who may be trying to outflank 2 Troop, who were fixed on the lake side of the Officer Ward. He could not see any. He was hardly surprised, given the intense fire coming from the Catalinas. He did not envy any German patrol caught in the gunsights of the marauding black swans on the water. W-W was itching to join his company in the thick of it but knew too well it was not his job on this mission.

With himself and his men set ready to ambush what remained of the German patrol they engaged earlier; he noticed the men spent more time looking over their right shoulders at the battle across the lake. He did not blame them, for they were all in the commandos for the action, not the prestige. They all understood that their role in this particular mission was just as vital as any other phase, but at some point they would have to pack up and join the main force for their extraction. A green flare would signal the start of the extraction. So far, all they had seen were red and white.

Another consideration entered his conflicted mind. The timing pencils set to blow the road bridge. He only hoped that Mould and Dobbs had set them correctly. What did concern him was the fact that Dobbs put near on all of the explosives under the bridge. W-W knew enough about demolitions that such an amount would most certainly make a hole in the planet when it went up. It was a mathematical challenge as well as a tactical one when it came to explosives. You only needed enough to fracture any structure, and let its own weight bring it down. Dobbs had form for over-cooking his tasks, and knowing him, when the bridge went up, bricks would land in Berlin.

In W-W's mind, the most dangerous part of his particular situation, would be rejoining the company within the sanatorium. He had three scenarios that could get himself and his men killed in short order. Firstly, once across the footbridge, he encounters a large enemy force, who will no doubt, shoot first and worry about questions later. Second, getting mown down by the Catalina gunners, and lastly, 2 Troop shooting them as they try to link up. He would be sure to send a radio message to the sergeant major at the north jetty, to be mindful of his men coming down the shore line from the footbridge.

It would all be a question of timing.

As he went to grab some chocolate from his pack, Mould gave the far bank a double take.

'Whoa, whoa. What the fuck is this?' His voice muffled from another volley of Catalina strafing. W-W turned in time to get somewhat of a fright.

Rattling across the road bridge into the open grounds of the sanatorium came two German Zundapps followed closely by two halftracks. About one hundred yards behind them came a convoy of six canvas covered Opel trucks, with two more Zundapps at the rear. Forgetting the chocolate, W-W bellowed to his men.

'Get on to the sergeant major now!'

As Neame put the handset to his ear, both W-W and Mould moved toward the shoreline, which remained outside the glare of the white flares drifting above the sanatorium. With the artificial light making the use of binoculars unnecessary, Mould called back at the radio operator.

'Two halftracks, six trucks, four Zundapps. North side. Most likely enemy reinforcements.'

For all his best efforts, Neame squinted as he leaned in to hear what Mould was shouting. Catalina engines raising in pitch as they manoeuvred made it difficult to catch all of it. Before getting the chance to call for the information again, W-W spun on his heels and went for his pack, relaying the information again as he did so.

'Two halftracks, six trucks, four Zundapps. Enemy reinforcements.'

Neame got the information this time and went about calling Montgomery at the northern jetty. Whilst he did so, W-W pulled the flare gun from his pack, and fumbled through the flare satchel to ensure he loaded the correct coloured flare.

'Troops!' hollered Mould as he watched the six trucks disgorge countless German troops. W-W, kind of confident he had the right flare for fire control staggered back out onto the shoreline. He aimed high above the cluster of German vehicles now stationary on the south side of the road bridge and fired. As it popped skywards, W-W was relieved that it was in fact a red flare. The pyrotechnic arched beautifully before bursting open under its small canopy. Its journey to earth was short as it landed between the Zundapps at the front of the convoy. Mould cursed the Catalinas.

'Please see the flare, you fuckers.'

Nothing.

W-W fired another. As the second red flare burst open, another streaked skywards from the north jetty and burst white directly above the enemy convoy. Montgomery had gotten the information. No sooner had the light washed over the convoy, its troops still jumping free from their canvas backs did their world erupt in a blizzard of red tracer fire. The Catalinas were on them.

W-W and Mould, their tactical acumen lost in the moment, stood like spectators at a firework display as the Catalinas shredded the trucks, which to their credit made every effort to try and make for the safe side of the Soldier Ward. Tracer bullets that went wide or through their targets skimmed off hard surfaces before finishing their flight in the village of Lychen itself. All four Zundapps remained where they were. Their riders and sidecar gunners nowhere to be seen. The halftracks however, somewhat hardier to machinegun fire reversed and manoeuvred to then return fire at the aircraft out on the dark lake. Both got into position and began to fire long streams of their own tracer back at their attackers. From what W-W could see from his vantage point was an instant reaction from the Catalinas as they seemed to direct all their fury onto the halftracks. One halftrack crept forward, its machine gun letting off rippling bursts right up until it was safely out of the line of fire behind the Soldier Ward, whilst the other, now reversing bore the brunt of overwhelming British firepower. With the reversing halftrack creeping ever closer to the stretch of water in which the road bridge spanned, the other halftrack behind the Soldier Ward reversed back out and gave the Catalinas a long strafing, which had an immediate effect on their attackers. With the exposed halftrack rattling to a standstill by the bridge, W-W noticed none of the crew bailing out. The vehicle had been pulverised.

The active halftrack made a quick move forward behind the Soldier Ward just as return fire from the Catalinas splashed all over the far-right façade of the building in reprisal. W-W needed to warn Jones that one halftrack plus a company's worth of enemy infantry were now in the sanatorium grounds.

As he went for Neame to pass the message, a loud thud echoed through. Mould grabbed him by the arm.

'Shit, look at that.'

The captain spun on his heels to see a sight that he could have done without.

One of the Catalinas was on fire.

41.

With troops apparently containing the attackers down at the Officer Ward, and the pending arrival of reinforcements, Mortens felt it only served to be more productive by waiting for them at the Guardroom. With the blackout curtains in place, he paced about the veranda in the darkness, which, despite the white flares drifting above the sanatorium, and the furious gun battle down at the shoreline, he felt somewhat safe. The patients that had made it out of the Officer Ward were now resting in the Guardroom cells, a little worse for wear considering having to escape a burning building only to then be shot at from multiple directions as they gathered their senses. A few of the patients that were senior in rank were somewhat affronted that there was no one at the Guardroom on hand to tend to their every whim. Merely a soldier with his leg in a plaster cast.

They were welcome to rest in the cells at the back of the building. Not exactly mess standards of accommodation, but certainly safe from the fighting. A general found it rather improper to share a cell with a captain, which proved most troublesome for the Head of Security. Mortens had already blackened his name with a couple of his half-dressed superiors who felt it was their place to coordinate the defence of the sanatorium from the Guardroom. After being polite and cordial to no avail, he reprimanded them and ordered them to rest in the cells. If the attack on the sanatorium had not already earmarked him for an Oder front command, his tone and curtness with the patients probably would.

He would worry about such outcomes later.

As the gunfire petered out for the briefest of moments, he could hear the drone of an engine, along with the squeal and rattle of metal on metal. Unsure of where it was coming from, he stepped off the veranda, only to get a fright as a lone halftrack lumbered out of the gloom from the direction of the lake, not the main western approach road into the facility. It lurched to a halt, its gunner up in his weapon station waving at Mortens.

'Sir. Help us please.'

A little confused, Mortens made his way to the rear of the vehicle and was greeted by the shell-shocked machine gunner in the rear of the halftrack stood among a clamour of wounded soldiers slumped in the back. All were groaning and bleeding. Some wore crudely fitted field dressings, others winced and grimaced through bloodied clenched teeth.

'Help me get them inside.' Implored the trooper. As Mortens went to take the first wounded man from the halftrack, movement behind him made him panic. Looking around, he could see more soldiers emerging from the gloom. As another white flare burst above the facility, the light revealed to Mortens mixed relief that they were in fact German. He stepped aside as the soldiers hauled their wounded comrades from the halftrack. As they began setting them down on the veranda, Mortens stepped through into the Guardroom and barked at the football injured trooper manning the desk.

'Call for medics, we need medics.'

The young man nodded as he lifted the handset on the telephone. Mortens stepped back out onto the veranda, allowing the curtains to remain open a little so the soldiers could see what they were doing as the shadows grew longer with the descent of the flare. Just as all appeared to be in order, a Scharfuhrer presented himself to Mortens. No salute, just polite.

'Scharfuhrer Lette Sir. We were deployed from Ravensbruck to assist.'

'QRF?' Mortens wanted to confirm. Lette shrugged, looking to his wounded men.

'What's left of it. We came through the village, and before we knew it, red flares landed at the front of our convoy, before we got strafed by whatever is out on the lake. Gunboats I think.'

'No,' Mortens shook his head. 'Flying boats.'

'Flying boats?' Lette pulled a face. 'The British came in flying boats?'

'Looks like it.'

'Well...' Lette tailed off a little, 'we've damaged one of them. Before we came up here with our wounded, I saw one of them on fire.'

'Really?' Mortens was both surprised and impressed. Lette nodded.

'Yes, Sir. But they really gave it to us before we could get into cover. What you see here is all that's left.'

'Fucking hell.' Mortens murmured, looking about the veranda. Besides the wounded, he could only count about twenty men fit to fight. He needed to get on top of the situation.

'Get the halftrack back down there and keep shooting at them fucking things on the lake. We'll get these men down to where we have the British contained. Around the Officer Ward.'

'Yes, Sir.' Lette agreed as he went to brief the halftrack crew. As Mortens went to rally the men able to follow him down to the Officer Ward, the limping soldier manning the desk leaned out through the curtains.

'Sir, phone for you.'

'Who is it?'

'Mrs. Mortens.'

'What?' Mortens spun around. Astrid would never usually call the Guardroom. His office now and again, but never the Guardroom. The trooper's face was one of concern.

'Your house is on fire, Sir.'

Mortens scrambled past him so hard, the trooper had to keep himself from tumbling over by grabbing the curtains, which held firm. Mortens clamoured for the handset on the desk, shoving it to his ear.

'Astrid?'

'Otto. The village is under attack.' The woman was hysterical. 'Our roof is on fire. Our house is on fire, Otto.'

'I'm coming. Get you and Tommy out of the house. I'm coming.'

Mortens slammed down the handset and made off out into the night, leaving his field cap on the desk. As he ran past Lette, the Scharfuhrer called out to him.

'Where do you want us Sir?'

'Soldier Ward, south side.' Was all he hollered over his shoulder as he ran home. His thoughts now full of nothing but Astrid and Tommy.

As he made for the road bridge, he gave the marauding swans on the lake spewing tracer into the sanatorium no consideration at all as he dashed through the sorry remains of the QRF convoy. He gave no thought to the dead men strewn about the trucks. He noticed a halftrack smouldering by the bridge, but it mattered not to him at that moment. What he did pay attention to was the flames licking skywards from houses in the village. One of them was his apparently. With his lungs burning he cleared the bridge in a matter of seconds. As he made the meandering left turn through the village, he was punched flat as the road bridge was blown sky high.

42.

On the south side of the Officer Ward, 3 Troop could not help but look over their shoulders at the battle raging just the other side of the building. With flame and smoke billowing from the upper floors, Sergeant Sam Wilson commanding the troop felt as if he was letting the side down by not coming to assist in the fighting. His orders were clear. 3 Troop were to protect the target building from a southern attack or reinforcement. During the operation to that point, Wilson and his men had not seen so much as a sentry wander across their frontage. It was all happening to the north. If there was one thing going for his troop at that point, they had not been fired upon, which meant the Germans did not know they were there.

Wilson was now second guessing himself. He listened to the vicious exchanges between the Catalinas, 2 Troop and the enemy. The snap of a German carbine, the distinct chatter of Thompson. The unmistakable long chugging bursts of multiple Vickers machine guns mounted on the Catalinas. Up until that point, he had faith in the fact that his comrades in 2 Troop, supported by the Catalinas overmatch whatever sorry excuse for opposition the Germans presented in Hohenlychen. What did unnerve him was another soundtrack to an already chaotic exchange, MG42 fire. He feared for the safety of 2 Troop, but also aware at the lack of radio chatter from 1 Troop, who were in the burning building, somewhere.

The distinct rippling bursts of MG42 reached his ears about the same time as he cast a glance out onto the lake to see tracer bullets splash all over one of the Catalinas. Fixated in horror, he watched it happen again and again, until a dull thud resulted in the aircraft catching fire. The Germans had now recovered from the initial assault and were now fighting back. It was at that point in the battle, Wilson felt that 3 Troop could be of more use to their comrades.

'Spin around!' Wilson hollered as loud as he could, whilst doing exactly what he ordered. For a few seconds, there was no follow-on repetition of the order down the line so the rest of the men could comply.

'What?' A lone voice challenged. Wilson rolled his eyes as he repeated the order.

'Spin around. We're no bloody good to anyone laying here.'

The order to 'spin around' was hollered down the line. To the ear, it sounded more like a question than an order. After a minute or so, 3 Troop were facing the opposite direction. Wilson slowly raised himself to the kneeling position and took in what was before him. The right half of his troop were out of line of sight from the backside of the Soldier Ward, thanks largely to the target building. Wilson could see, due to the white flares drifting back out over the lake, German troops gathered at the bottom left corner, taking it in turns to shoot at whoever they could see. Most likely 2 Troop. He watched as a red flare skimmed of the façade high above them, which prompted them to duck behind the building as tracer spewed from the Catalinas, delivering a long, masonry smashing lick before they gingerly ventured out from behind the bullet scarred Soldier Ward.

What decided it for Wilson was when a fresh white flare, subjected to a fresh wind, drifted over the lake, revealing a potential disaster with their extraction plan. The stricken Catalina, flames easily seen licking the sky from a large hole in its fuselage powered away toward the far bank, with people leaping into the water. A second aircraft followed on, probably to rescue those in the water. With one aircraft no longer fit to fly, it could only encourage the Germans to exact their revenge on the remaining two, leaving the commando company stranded deep behind enemy lines. Clambering to his feet, Wilson began to jog toward the south facing side of the burning Officer Ward.

'Follow me!' he roared, not looking back. As he slowed to a walk at the base of the building, he was pleased that his order had not been ignored or misconstrued. The remainder of 3 Troop jogged in toward him, most coming in at a wide left hook to get behind the building, out of the line of fire. As the men gathered against the building, Wilson looked to the floors above. The fire had yet to take hold immediately above them, but smoke managed to find its way out. Stepping away from the wall, he looked to his men.

'Boys, we can't sit here holding our dicks any longer. One of the cats is on fire. If we lose one more, we are walking home.'

A few of the men frowned as they looked out over the lake to confirm. They received a shock. One on fire, one rescuing crew, the other providing fire support. Not good.

Wilson was faced with two options. Skirt around the lake side of the building and join 2 Troop at the far end, or fan out on the western side and draw fire away from 2 Troop that way. Peering around the corner toward where the Germans gathered on their corner of the Soldier Ward, he witnessed the appearance of a halftrack behind the German troops. That fact alone made his mind up for him.

He would join up with 2 Troop. With only one Catalina in the fight at present, and nothing else to fire at the halftrack, it would be suicide to put his men out in the open. He rejoined his men.

'The fuckers now have a halftrack, and we all know what that means.'

The men did not say anything, but by their facial expressions, they did not fancy their chances with a vehicle fitted with an MG42. Their Thompsons would not be much good, not at range anyhow. Wilson peered around the lakeside corner of the building. It appeared free of enemy troops, only its upper floors now licking flames and smoke. At the far end he could see a cluster of men gathered on the corner. Wilson hoped it was indeed 2 Troop. A white flare shot skywards from the northern jetty. Wilson was pleased to know that the sergeant major was still in the fight. With the flare bursting high above, illuminating the far side of the Officer Ward and casting his intended route in artificial shadow, Wilson looked back at his men, who were ready to react. Private Sandford, his radio operator was tucked in behind him.

'Call 2 Troop. Let 'em know we are come around to join them.'

As Sandford went about his radio duties, Wilson looked out on the lake. The darkness in which the Catalinas enjoyed up to that point was now begin interrupted by licks of flame erupting from the furthest aircraft, its ammunition and fuel cooking off as they succumbed to heat and flame. From his vantage point, Wilson had no idea as to the fate of the stricken Catalina crew. He could only hope that they managed to be rescued by the others. With the burning aircraft almost run aground on the far bank, the remaining two increased engine pitch and returned to the fight, keeping in darkness as best they could.

Sandford patted him on the shoulder, before giving him a thumbs up. Wilson then waved his men on.

'Let's go, follow me!'

As Wilson came up level with the main doors, he noticed one of them slowly opening. Standing still, his sudden action almost had his men concertina into each other. Waving his men down, they all took cover wherever they could, the open lawn not giving them many options. In the gloom, Wilson and his men witnessed a head appear before disappearing back inside. Wilson had no idea if it was friend or foe. He gave the two men immediately behind him a look, to which he only received a shrug in return. The men at the tail end of 2 Troop were also looking back at the door. With a slow right arm signal, Wilson had his men fan out away from the building. He did not want 2 Troop opening fire on those trying to leave the building and his men be stood directly in the flight path of their bullets. Movement at the door again had him focus there once more. A man appeared, dress as if he had just gotten out of bed. The man had a pistol in his hand. Two more men appeared dressed and armed the same. Just as two more emerged from the building did the two lead men realise they were stood right in front of enemy troops, who were dressed and armed much better than they were. It was, however, the last man to leave the building that ruined any good intentions.

He aimed and fired at Wilson and his men who responded in kind in a blizzard of Thompson fire. Some of 2 Troop also joined the fray. In less than two seconds it was over. The short, violent action prompted Montgomery to fire another flare high and close to illuminate the area. As the light washed over Wilson and his men, both he and the sergeant major could see each other clearly. They waved to each other as the shadows lengthened. With darkness returning, their night vision ruined. Wilson and his men took their time making their way past the doors to join up with their comrades in 2 Troop. The men they had just killed lay sprawled all over the steps, their blood pooling beneath them, and their pistols still in their hands. None of the Troop reported any wounds from the few shots fired at them, which was a relief to all.

'Let's get moving boys.' Wilson waved them on. Their link up with 2 Troop was complete. It was quick, crude, and violent. But a success all the same. With the corner of the building already cluttered with 2 Troop, Wilson ordered his men to take cover and wait for further instruction. He needed to speak with Paul Kimber, 2 Troop Sergeant.

With both 2 and 3 Troop now located together, it was evident that both parties were pleased to see each other. Those not engaged with shooting at the Germans behind the Soldier Ward shook hands with their comrades, happy in the knowledge they were still many in number. Even those who had been slightly wounded in the exchanges gave a thumbs up where they could. Wilson picked his way through to the corner where the action was happening. He was yet to come across Kimber.

'Where's Kim?' He called out to no one in particular. A private soldier leaned out and pointed to the sunken steps that led to a set of cellar doors.

'Down there.'

The latest white flare provided by Montgomery allowed him to see a number of heads bobbing around within the intimate confines of the steps. As the shadows cast by the flare grew longer, and the gunfire eased a little, Wilson took the chance and made for the stairs, vaulting over the nearest low concrete wall that then had him drop half a dozen steps to the damp floor that was the threshold to the metal doors. His acrobatic arrival gave everyone, including Kimber a start. The flare allowed Kimber to see Wilsons cheeky grin emerge from under his blacked-up face, his teeth glistening. He returned a frown.

'Sam? What the fuck?'

'Shut up and listen. You've a halftrack sat just around that corner. Picking its moment to come and give us trouble. Thought you ought to know.'

'Oh right.' Kimber climbed the stairs, hunching low near the top. 'Good to know. Cheers.'

'You are welcome.' Wilson replied sarcastically. With his focus on the Germans that kept leaning out and shooting at them, Kimber spoke over his shoulder.

'Thought you and your lads were covering the south side.'

'We were. Since we lost a Cat we…'

Just as Kimber spun on his heels at the revelation, a biblical thud of an explosion rocked them all. Enough for both the British and the Germans to stop firing, even for just a few seconds. Over the relentless drone of Catalina engines, Kimber and Wilson could hear material clattering to the ground, some debris even splashing into the lake near the north jetty. Wilson grabbed Kimber by the forearm as he leaned in to speak.

'I think that was the bridge.'

'What do you mean we've lost a Cat?' Kimber was clearly more interested in the news of their precious fire support and ride home.

'They managed to shoot one up enough for it to catch fire.' Wilson jerked a thumb over his shoulder. 'We now only have two. We need to find the boss and get the fuck out of here, or else we could end up walking home.'

Ash and embers rained down on them constantly from the fire consuming floors above. The crash of fittings collapsing within the structure had all those on the sunken stairs flinch.

'Well, he's in there somewhere. I hope he's found our man.' Kimber returned to the fight. Wilson looked about the two other men stood with them. The radio operator did not carry any, and the other was stripped of equipment, except his weapons and magazines. A field dressing wrapped around his head. He climbed the stairs high enough to peek over the low concrete wall.

'We need crow bars and sledgehammers.' He hollered, before a bullet struck the wall next to his left ear, sending a small chunk of it into his face, his left ear ringing instantly. Collapsing heavily at the bottom of the stairs, Wilsons punch drunk mind did not register pain at first, for he felt like he had just taken a heavy right hook to the side of the head. Head swimming, he noticed Kimber and the wounded private soldier sitting him up straight. He could hear nothing but feel the thud of something on his left side. The thudding sensation was not just in his battered mind, for it had Kimber stop tending to him and look to the door. In the melee of the soldier wrapping a field dressing around his head, Wilson caught glimpses of Kimber standing back as one of the doors opened. Looking up and around the soldier tending to him, he recognised straight away Jones peering out from behind the door. Just as Wilson managed a numbed smile, the battle returned to him like a screaming locomotive.

'Halftrack!' shouted the radio operator, who ducked down just in time as tracer bullets smashed above and around the sunken stairs. The snaps came rippling through, so close, it buffeted ears. With both Jones and Kimber crouched over the top of him, Wilson drunkenly fished in his smock before pulling out his bulky flare gun. Kimber grabbed it with both hands, broke it open and confirmed it was indeed loaded with a red flare. Shuffling up one step at a time, Kimber kept low for the halftrack was having a time of it by spraying the commandos' position with long rippling bursts of MG42. He did not want to risk getting hit, so had to gauge where the apex of the building was by looking to the upper floors of the Soldier Ward. With no white flare for illumination, not to mention the long, naked, spindly fingers of the trees looking to ruin his idea, Kimber would have no choice. The firing let up as the halftrack crew became bolder and pulled out further, which also enticed the infantry accompanying it to follow on. Standing up straight, Kimber fired the red flare directly at the halftrack, the fizzing canister deflecting off the nose of it before landing at the feet of German infantry as they sought cover behind trees. In awe of his own shot, Kimber turned smugly just as Jones grabbed him by the smock before they dove back into the sunken stair well.

Catalina fire pulverised the infantry who felt they were safe behind the trees. Trees collapsed as the scythe of incoming fire laid waste to most of those not afforded the armour plate of the halftrack, which itself was smouldering and punctured as it reversed hastily, its transmission screaming, back behind the Soldier Ward. As the Catalina fire let up, a white flare arrived, washing the shattered trees in an eerie glow. Jones and Kimber stood up to examine the devastation.

The halftrack was gone. Wounded German troops rolled about and tried their best to crawl back to where they had come from. No one fired upon them, for there was no need. Their fight was over. The fact that they were wounded would continue to serve Jones and his men for they would now be a burden on those still in the fight. Jones looked to his Troop sergeants.

'I heard the bridge go up. How much bloody dems did they use?'

The question raised a chuckle from those who heard it. Jones glanced over where the German assault had been halted. All was quiet for the time being. If he knew the Germans, they would not be silent for long. He pulled out his own flare gun, breaking it open before sliding in a flare canister.

'It's time, gentlemen.'

Jones pointed the gun straight up and fired. As the flare whistled skywards, the dazed but alive Wilson called out to Jones, his hearing yet to recover properly.

'Did we get 'im?'

As the flare popped high above them, all the British commandos looked skywards as a green glow washed over them.

It was time to leave.

As the green flare drew long shadows, Jones jerked a thumb at the open cellar door. Wilson gingerly got to his feet and shuffled to his right to peer around the door. On the threshold, bathed in a green glow, stood Corporal Roy Gale, filthy and exhausted. His right hand gripping the left bicep of an older, dishevelled man that looked ready for bed. Cane and all.

At a trot, with 2 Troop covering the move to the north jetty, the remainder of the company made their way down to join Sergeant Major Montgomery and young Melvin, who was now firing one green flare after another. As the Catalina's manoeuvred for pickup, one coming to the jetty whilst the other remained out on the lake to provide fire support if needed, Gale walked Arens out on to the jetty. As the principle, all Jones had to do, should the Germans intervene once more, was get Arens out of there, come what may.

As the first Catalina pulled up at the end of the jetty, 2 Troop joined the rest of the company in a protective half circle. Once the Catalina was moored, its engines feathered back a little despite throwing spray everywhere, Jones ordered 1 Troop to board with Arens. As they began the British tradition of queueing on the jetty, Jones suddenly realised that all was not well.

'Is Captain W-W's team here?'

Before an answer came to him, all hell broke loose. Tracer screamed just over those on the jetty, whilst some hit the fuselage of the Catalina moored in place. Jones and the men dropped to their bellies as they crawled off the exposed wooden structure. Concerned for getting Arens out of the area, Jones waved for those nearest the aircraft to get Arens aboard. The scientist had the common sense to not remain standing as tracer bullets smashed into the jetty and aircraft. As his men got off the jetty, Montgomery put up another white flare towards the northern end of the Soldier Ward. A rippling muzzle flash at the far end of the structure was soon bathed in white light, revealing the troublesome halftrack that had survived the most recent strafing from the Catalinas. Around it emerged infantry, who snapped off shots from their various weapons. The British commandos defending their extraction point crawled outwards in a fan, determined to defend their position, as exposed as it was.

There was no need for a red flare. Thanks to the white flare drifting out over the lake, it cast the shadow of the halftrack and German infantry well against the façade of the Soldier Ward. The Catalina gunners wasted no time in dealing with the problem as they poured tracer at the enemy. Sparks rippled off the armour plate as the halftrack attempted to reverse its way out of the maelstrom, running over a number of infantrymen taking cover behind it. Fist sized chunks of masonry were chipped out of the façade whilst soldiers caught in the open burst in a pink and grey mist as they were mown down. The halftrack, now beyond use, lurched to a standstill. Jones could see what remained of the smashed wooden footbridge beyond the ward. The demolition charges had wrecked both the road bridge, and W-W's means of re-joining the company. He knew it would be far too dangerous to try and have them board from the far bank. He refused to give the Germans anymore chances to right off another aircraft. They had planned for such a situation and would owe the captain dinner once they all got home.

As the flare faded out, Jones got to his feet. He could not confirm if the crew managed to bail out. It did not matter, as far as he was concerned. They were not going to fight back now.

With darkness returned, Jones hollered for the men to get aboard. As they staggered onto the jetty, Jones made his way back to where the sergeant major was located. With the untethered Catalina still strafing the northern end of the Soldier Ward, Montgomery went to fire another flare, but Jones caught him in time.

'We need the darkness, Sarn't Major. Get ready to move.'

Montgomery readied his pack and weapons whilst the men boarded the moored aircraft. Remaining standing, Jones watched as his battle-weary men clambered aboard. It was going to be a squeeze. They had taken casualties, and those that were wounded were all walking wounded. They did not need stretchers. He had men that had been killed and would have to be left behind. He was confident that those who had fallen would have ensured that only their identification discs would be on them. Nothing more. Not even a wedding ring.

Give the enemy nothing.

With 2 Troop aboard, the sergeant major nominated half of 1 Troop to also get aboard, for they had less men to load due to casualties taken in the Officer Ward. With the first Catalina now filled to the point of bursting, Jones assisted the men casting off so it could taxi away and resume fire support duties. As the second aircraft came in to moor up, a great crashing sound caught everyone's attention as the roof of the Officer Ward collapsed within the outer walls. The flames, now exposed to the sky, illuminated a wide area, making those still yet to board the second Catalina feeling rather vulnerable. There was nothing they could do about it. Just get on board and get out of there.

'Look!' One of the men on the jetty pointed to where the sunken stairs were located. As Jones turned to see, people began to emerge out into the open. The brilliant glow from the fire revealed them to be the patients that had fired down at him, and his men caught in the foyer. As they emerged from the building, some of them defiantly stood with their arms folded, staring right back at the commandos gathered at the jetty. Jones looked to Montgomery.

'Sarn't Major?'

'Sir?'

'Get the lads aboard, there's something I need to do.'

Before Montgomery could fathom what that could be, Jones walked through the men, back towards the shore. When he reached the threshold where the jetty abutted the bank of the lake, he pulled his flare gun from within his smock. He broke it open to confirm it was indeed loaded before snapping it shut. With all of what remained of his company now on the jetty, clambering into the Catalina as quickly as their bulky frames allowed, Jones counted over a dozen people gathered by the sunken stairs. Hands on hips or arms folded, like they were allowing the enemy to depart unhindered. Jones pointed the flare gun at the sparse tree canopy above the patients that had gathered.

He fired.

The red flare popped just as it began its quick return to earth landing just to the right of the intended party. Jones turned and walked back along the jetty, with all those gathered before him flinching as the Catalina out on the water erupted in a furious display of firepower. The strafing lasted all of thirty seconds. As the cacophony of machinegun fire echoed away, leaving only the comforting drone of aircraft engines, Jones found himself reflecting on a particular sentence in the note presented to him in Edinburgh.

Grab your man and destroy that nest of vipers with extreme prejudice.

He had grabbed his man, but at a cost. He had dead and wounded to contend with. He would not know to which extent until W-W and his team were recovered. He had nothing but extreme prejudice for that nest of vipers.

Now it was time to leave.

W-W watched as the two Catalinas accelerated south, away from the devastation they had left in their wake. W-W took in the panorama of carnage. The Officer Ward was now just a blazing shell. Its fiery glow illuminated German troops, who cautious at first moved out from behind the Soldier Ward which had also taking some punishment during the raid. Smoke emitted from the south side of the huge complex, most likely the result of tracer bullets setting fire to fittings, or a well-placed flare through a window.

W-W looked to the north side of the facility. The German convoy sat shredded with no sign of life around the punctured, sorry looking trucks. Both halftracks were now just pulverised wrecks. Dwellings in the village were now on fire. Thanks to the Catalina fire punching through the convoy, their lethality not wasted as they found the village beyond. W-W cared little for the occupants. They worked for the sanatorium, and in his mind they were no better than the patients that malingered in the facility.

They got off lightly, he concluded. They were not the target of a V-2 rocket.

Both bridges were smashed. Dobbs had certainly made a hole in the planet. At his right shoulder he could feel the presence of someone. As W-W slid his hands up onto his hips, they spoke.

'Sorry about the footbridge, Boss. Too much of a bang perhaps.'

The captain turned to the forlorn Dobbs. His overzealous demolitions not lost on the man. He could have berated him, but there was no point. He cut a disapproving look at Sergeant Mould, who was with Dobbs when the charges were placed. Mould was too busy assisting Warrant Officer Monk become more familiar with the functions of a Colt Automatic pistol. Monk had just managed to escape being burned alive in just what he was wearing. His own personal weapon, a Thompson for this particular mission remained in the smouldering cockpit. It was Monks Catalina which took the brunt of the Germans return fire. With his crew rescued by another Cat, save his Co-Pilot who was killed as the Germans strafed the cockpit, Monk powered the stricken aircraft away to the far bank. With the aircraft run aground, Monk still managed to end up in the water as ammunition began to cook off due to the heat, which almost blew the Catalina in half. Her burnt-out shell still let off a loud crack as something else combusted. The Co-Pilot still aboard. The Germans would no doubt have his remains handed over the Red Cross in due course.

With his back to the burning sanatorium, W-W addressed his men.

'Gentlemen. Well done.'

All, including Monk stopped what they were doing and looked to him. He continued.

'We did our job and did it well.'

As he tailed off, he glanced at the smashed footbridge.

'A little too well, some may argue, but there you have it.'

He gave Dobbs a mischievous wink as the lads began to chuckle at Dobbs misfortune. The unfortunate Dobbs returned a smile, knowing that the boss was not going to let him forget it any time soon, but he still had a home in the commandos. W-W concluded by rubbing his hands together.

'Right then, let's gather up our monkeys and parrots and make our way back to our drop zone. We'll have to sit tight until tonight, but we can hopefully rest a little better. My only concern is that patrol we bashed up earlier.'

As the men pulled the packs onto their shoulders, W-W noticed Monk looking rather damp and under dressed for a mission behind enemy lines.

'Sergeant Major?' As a Warrant Officer, W-W could address Monk as such. The pilot looked to him.

'Sir?'

'Sorry about your man. We all are. Are you fit to travel?'

'Yes Sir.' Monk nodded. W-W returned an approving nod, jerking a thumb at Dobbs.

'Stick with young Dobbs here. If we get into any bother, just get down and let us deal with it. You okay with that?'

The pilot, now pressed into infantry work nodded, feeling very much out of his comfort zone. With his own pack pulled in tight on his back, W-W took a firm grip of his Thompson.

'Corporal Fletcher?'

'Sir?'

'Since you did such a sterling job getting us here, would you be so kind as to get us out of here?'

With Fletcher leading, the cold, tired and hungry commando team, along with a damp Catalina pilot, patrolled away in single file, through the maze of deadfall.

43.

Torso Bay

Sweden

It was dusk when, out in deep water, the American submarine broke the surface. They had been waiting submerged merely hours before Jones and his victorious men returned to the small, unremarkable fishing port. To hand Arens over in daylight would be pushing their luck. Officially, the Americans could not afford for their submarine and crew to be interned in Swedish custody, because that would take some considerable statecraft to unravel. They had approval to be there to collect the principle, but to openly flaunt their presence in Swedish waters would make for an uncomfortable summons should the American ambassador be called to explain why. They were to be out of sovereign waters by dawn the next day.

Jones took coffee with Freya on the breakwater as Arens was taken out to the awaiting submarine in a small rowing boat. He was accompanied by two of Jones' men, one rowing, the other ensuring Arens did not decide to do something foolish. Humans were prone to desperate measures when in a desperate situation. Anchored on the outside of the breakwater bobbed the two Catalinas. Their bullet peppered fuselage and blood speckled interior spoke of a battle that would have to be explained in Jones' post-operational report. He knew that Lewis and his department would insist on chapter and verse regarding the mission to grab a key Nazi Scientist deep behind enemy lines. He knew Colonel Hook would also want his pound of flesh in writing. Some serious homework was due once they got back to Scotland. But for now, he enjoyed the peace. He would spar with the typewriter soon enough.

Arms folded, nursing a cigarette between thumb and forefinger, Freya nodded towards the little boat as it made its way towards the impressive silhouette of the submarine.

'Do you think he's pleased?'

'Who?' Jones replied, lowering the cup from his lips. Freya jabbed the air with her cigarette.

'Arens. Do you think he's pleased he's off to America?'

'Not sure.' Jones shrugged. 'He doesn't really have a say in the matter.'

'True.'

'The Advance Team,' Jones offered, changing the subject, 'They'll be taken out tonight?'

'Yes.' Freya let out a light grey mouthful of smoke. 'A Halifax is tasked with getting them out. A solo pick up, so they need some guns on them should they get into a trouble.'

'Does W-W know he's expecting a Halifax, he'll need to know how big a strip to recce and prepare.'

'He's been informed. Nothing he cannot handle I'm sure. They'll return to Glasgow.'

'I trust Colonel Hook and Lewis will be there to meet them? I feel rather bad for leaving him behind.'

'They'll be there. Relax.' Freya smiled reassuringly before frowning a question.

'Why did you leave him behind?'

Embarrassed to admit that his men blew both bridges instead of just the one, he opted for the more a macho reason.

'Enemy strength was too great for him to re-join us as we extracted.'

Silence returned between them. A flock of gulls squawked overhead. The wind picked up a little, sending a chill rolling through the exhausted commando officer. Rolling his shoulders, he used his free hand to pull his collar up. Freya handed him her cigarette, which he took gratefully. As he took a pull on it, footsteps behind them caught their attention. Both turned as one to receive the Company Sergeant Major. As he pulled up, Montgomery pulled a small notebook from his smock pocket. He opened it before peeling off a page and handed it to Jones.

'Those confirmed killed at present Sir. Not including the advance team of course.'

Jones looked at the page. The list was mercifully short. Six names, two included gunners from Monks Catalina, who was also unaccounted for. He folded the page.

'Our wounded?' Asked the major.

'They're okay. They're sore and beaten up, but they'll live.'

Montgomery nodded a smile at Freya.

'Thanks for getting doctors and nurses down here. Our training only goes so far.'

Freya returned a smile.

'No problem. We can't afford for any of you to be in a hospital here. So, we had to bring Mohammed to the mountain as it were.'

'Well, the lads sure appreciate it. I'll leave you folks be. I've allowed the men a couple of beers. I think they've earned it.'

'They sure have.' Jones smiled. 'I'm gonna hold off till the Advance Team are back.'

'Sure.' Montgomery took his leave and walked away. Turning back to the submarine, Jones unfolded the page once more, taking in the names. It was some time before he murmured his question.

'Is he worth it?'

'Huh?'

'Arens.' Jones spoke up. 'Is he worth it?'

Freya let out a sigh. 'I sure hope so.'

Jones nodded a little as he put the paper in his pocket.

'He'd better be, for I would not trade him for any of those on this list.'

44.

Wittenberge

66 Miles West of Berlin

Nazi Germany

1st May 1945

In the shadow of a badly damaged railway bridge, Astrid sat scolded, blood spattered and numb at the side of the road with her semi-conscious husband and a worn-out Tommy. They waited, like hundreds of others for the overworked, under powered ferry to take them across the strong currented Elbe to the west bank, away from the Soviets not far behind. Mortens could not manage the rail bridge for the sheer effort of walking had him swoon with extreme nausea.

Severe concussion, along with a head wound that gave Astrid the initial impression that her husband had been scalped, seeped through the bandages. The explosion that almost killed Mortens wrecked not only two substantial bridges, it also rendered the dwellings closest unhabitable. The large fragment of cobblestone that nearly took his head off ended up killing a horse tethered in a stable.

God certainly favoured Otto Mortens, Astrid deduced. Her husband was a party member, but still tended church, much to the bewilderment of some of his peers.

Neighbours had found Mortens on the road and got him to a car heading for Ravensbruck. As the car followed in convoy, along with other cars and trucks that evacuated Lychen village, Mortens lay sprawled across the back seat, with Tommy draped across him, keeping off the early morning chill. Astrid rode up front, with Doctor Klaus Berbett behind the wheel. Berbett was a neighbour, home alone as his wife and daughter were away visiting family in Celle when word got back to him that the British had overrun Celle, trapping Ursula and Laura behind enemy lines. Berbett fretted, but Ursula wrote to him, reassuring him that Celle was largely undamaged, and all was well. The British stayed outside the town for the most part. Food was in short supply, but the British were trying their best to help with the issue. Berbett relaxed in the knowledge that his wife and daughter would be spared the wrath of the Soviets. He acknowledged that the British were somewhat more refined, and less likely to harm his family. With the blackout protocol still strictly enforced, the SS physician crept along with the convoy as it slowly made its way to Ravensbruck.

It was not until early dawn, did the evacuees from Lychen reach the final approach up to the gates of the camp facility. With Mortens dozing from the pain relief given to him by Berbett, Astrid found the scene before her rather eerie. The watchtowers were unmanned, the security barriers locked in the raised position. The convoy crunched past the Guardroom; Astrid could not see anyone.

Not a soul.

As the convoy meandered along the main road through the facility, it came upon a large open area festooned with SS troops, some of them attempting to wave them away. Astrid wound down her window so she could hear what the Haupsturmfuhrer was shouting.

'Turn around. Turn around now. We have a Typhus threat. You must leave. Leave now!'

The cars continued to roll past them, fanning out as they made their long wide turns to go back the way they had come. The soldiers became more agitated as the convoy broke up, arcing left and right under their own accord.

'Get out of the camp, now! There is Typhus here. Get the hell out. Now!'

As Berbett swung wide to the left, something at the base of a large, long brick wall caught Astrid's attention. She patted Berbetts gear changing hand.

'Stop the car.'

'What?'

'Stop the car. What is that?'

The car rolled to a stop. Astrid was halfway out when soldiers jogged over, their arms out to corral her.

'Fraulien, it is not safe. You must leave.'

As she was chastised back into the car, she was certain the darkened mass at the base of the wall was bodies. Human bodies. The door was slammed hard after her. The roof was banged incessantly by the soldiers.

'Let's go, let's go. Quickly now. It's not safe.'

Astrid looked to Berbett, who looked rather eager to leave the scene. If he were an SS officer at all, he could have alighted the car and reprimanded the soldiers, for he was an Obersturmbannfuhrer. As they sped away, Astrid turned to get another look at the wall through the back window. The soldiers obscured her view. She glanced down at her drug induced husband, bleeding through his bandages before sitting back around, he eyes on the road as they sped out of the open gates.

'Those were bodies, Klaus. I'm sure of it.'

'Where?'

'By the wall.'

'Are you sure?'

Astrid looked to her wringing hands.

'I'm not sure.'

Berbett, well in the knowledge of what took place in the facility allowed the conversation to wither on the vine as he sped along to catch up with the other vehicles evicted from the camp. Astrid looked to him.

'Where are we going now?'

'Not sure.' He shrugged. 'West I suppose.'

'Towards the British?' Astrid's eyes widened at the realisation. Berbett gave her a sideways glance, his attention on the cars in front more paramount.

'Would you rather sit at home and wait for the Soviets?'

As darkness gave way to the twilight of dawn, Astrid dozed as the car rocked her gently. Only now and again did the groaning of her husband rouse her. When the pain relief wore off enough to the point of severe discomfort did Berbett pull out of the convoy and stop only long enough to administer more morphine.

It was during one particular halt did Astrid stir from her slumber. Climbing from the car, the chill of early dawn took her breath away before she let out a much-needed stretch. Rolling her shoulders, she pulled her winter coat tighter around her slim frame. Eager for coffee, she knew there was no time, so instead, rummaged through her pockets for tobacco, only to be disappointed in discovering she had pulled the wrong coat from her burning home. It was the pile of rags at the side of the road not fifty meters from the car that caught her attention. Whilst Berbett tended to her husband, she ventured forward, as other cars and trucks crept past. Drawing up closer, she was shocked to see the skeletal face of a human being. The body was in the foetal position, bare footed yet clothed in an oversized filthy army greatcoat. Their short, cropped head showing a neat hole behind the ear. It suddenly dawned on Astrid the situation presented to her. The starved creature before her had been executed.

Shocked at first, she stepped back, only to then notice another body not more than twenty meters further on. This time however, the body was face down, the body straight, their bare feet almost getting run over with every passing vehicle. The profile, however, was similar to that of the body at her feet. Skeletal, short, cropped hair, bare footed, dark, filthy oversized clothing. She could not see a hole in the back of the head but did not wish to investigate further.

'Astrid, we must go.' Berbett snapped her from her macabre trance.

Stepping back, she forced herself to look away and make for the car. The warmth from the heater within was welcoming. The morning was indeed bitter.

As it grew lighter, Astrid struggled to sleep. All she could do was look out of the grimy window and observe more and more bodies lining the road. Most lay at the roadside as individuals, some were grouped in twos and threes.

'Klaus?'

'Yes?'

'We are in the middle of nowhere, yet dead people line the road. Why?'

A long exhale of breath from the doctor had Astrid glance at him, eager for an answer. As the car rolled on, Berbett could see her in his periphery looking to him for an answer. He knew she was no fool and would not settle for the Typhus ruse. He blinked slowly; the woman deserved an explanation.

'Ravensbruck has been evacuated.'

'Evacuated?'

'Yes. The Soviets are not far away, so we must relocate further west.'

'But why are there dead people all along this god forsaken road?'

The car rocked harder than usual, causing Mortens to groan, and in turn it encouraged Tommy to lick his face. Berbett stole a glance at the woman, still looking at him.

'There is not enough transport for the inmates, so they've had to walk. If they cannot keep up…'

Astrid looked out of the window. She did not need to press the man any further.

By late morning, the slow-moving column halted. Astrid was not keen to get out of the car for it was very cold and the warmth within made her doze. She was exhausted. They were all exhausted. The dead lining the road had now numbed her. She had no idea why they came to being there, or what their crime was, but one thing she did know, is that Berbett and his colleagues were well informed as to the circumstances behind why they were there. She looked over her shoulder at her unconscious Otto. Was he party to it? He spoke little of his work, and it had never really occurred to ask what he had done prior to Hohenlychen. He was stationed in Norway, that much she did know, and before that, a spell in Russia. As far as she was aware, he was part of a security team protecting a headquarters, and then a factory in Norway. That was all Otto would say.

A clatter of metal on metal caught her ear. Through the condensation on the windscreen, she could see two soldiers coming down the line of cars, speaking with each in turn.

'What is this?' Berbett murmured before climbing out into the cold. Pushing the door shut behind him, he went forward to the soldiers, who were hauling between them what looked like a milk urn. As they opened it, steam rose from within. Astrid looked in with interest as Berbett conversed with the soldiers before returning with a cup of something steaming in each hand. Hands full, he stood back from the door as Astrid leaned over and push the door open. He leaned in, a wide smile on his face. Astrid instantly recognised the aroma of coffee.

'It's not much, my dear, but I've put enough sugar in it to make your teeth fall out.'

Astrid gratefully took one of the tin cups in both hands and brought it up to her nose. It was indeed coffee. As she put it to her lips, she gingerly tasted it. It was hot. Very hot in fact. As she savoured the first sip, she then went in for her second. As she withdrew the cup, the smiling Klaus Berbett popped in a loud crack all over the interior in a grey and pink mist. Her face seared in coffee and peppered in cadaver; Astrids hearing was so muffled in the sudden violence that she did not even register the Typhoons screaming through the column. The thud of detonations rocked the car, which gave her brain the signal to evacuate the Typhoons prey. Scrambling from the car, a barking Tommy not far behind her, she made for the trees in which she could hopefully find sanctuary. Under the canopy, she gasped for breath. Looking left and right, she could see the sorry demeanour of those that had made it clear.

The Typhoons had gone. Cars burned, the dead and dying littered the road. The dying would have to wait a little longer before the living was brave enough to venture out and tend to them.

With the drone of aircraft fading to nothing, Astrid looked to the sorry looking parade of cars and army trucks. Limp, punctured, with most smouldering on the verge of bursting into flames. As she took a moment to gather herself, Tommys whining brought her back to the present, her husband.

Clambering to her feet, she then staggered out of the treeline to a chorus of shouts and screams from men and women, respectively. With Tommy in the lead, she made for the car which, hopefully, her darling Otto was alive, and no worse for wear. The low, sleek car sat heavy at the back, the suspension shattered, neat holes where cannon shells had punctured the engine block. Already, oil dripped heavily into the ditch that ran alongside. Thankfully, the car was not on fire. As she peered into the blood-spattered interior, she caught sight of Otto moving, which brought relief. As she leaned in, her wounded husband hauled himself into the sitting position. He looked, wide eyed around the car, unsure what to make of the scene. Their eyes locked, her expression one of relief, whilst he just looked confused.

A horse drawn cart was requisitioned to carry the wounded onwards. Everyone else would have to walk. Mortens was crammed onto the cart with the others. His bandages now long overdue changing. Astrid, Tommy, and the others shuffled along, forever looking skywards for the marauding Typhoons. They had nothing to bury the dead with in the way of picks and shovels, so were instead pulled to the side of the road and covered over as best they could. Astrid could not bring herself to haul what remained of Klaus Berbett free of the strafed car. Three men from the column, all of which knew the doctor took care of the macabre duty. Berbett took his place in the line of dead. Some of those killed were women, their husbands knelt with them, holding their hands as they wept. Astrid was relieved to see that the children had been spared. Not by design, since the Typhoons seldom cared for those they attacked, but by just a game of chance. Astrid and Otto never had children, and in a strange twist of fate, she was glad that she did not have to exhaust herself with keeping them alive. The little ones were carried in their parents' arms, whilst the older ones either skipped alongside or rode on the cart where there was room. Astrid could feel the war was nearly over, one way or the other. She had long passed caring who won. With the Soviets on the Oder, and the British coming up on the Elbe, if the rumours were correct, she knew the outcome, but did not have the courage to voice them in her present company.

By mid-afternoon, Wittenberge emerged on the slate grey horizon. Its suburbs looked remarkably untouched by the war, yet suffered more damage as they closed on the rail bridge which spanned the Elbe. A checkpoint was established across the main boulevards. SS Officers, looking fresh and yet to see battle inspected each transport for fighting aged males to join their ranks. They even considered teenage girls to take up arms against the oncoming Soviets. Astrid watched as mothers dressed their teenagers in bloody bandages to ensure they were not pressed into service at gunpoint. The far younger children looked on confused as to why their older siblings were now dressing up. The real men folk in the battered convoy were middle aged if a day, and Mortens, an actual officer in the SS was far too wounded to fulfil any combat capacity. The press gang, after close scrutiny of the convoy allowed it to pass into the sorry looking town, the fresh looking Hauptsturmfuhrer conceding that the doctors were of far better service to the Reich in their medical capacity, not in a combat role.

Whole streets were smashed, and the air was filled with the sickening aroma of damaged sewers. The occupants, much to their credit had cleared the streets, and busied themselves amid the ruins of what was most likely their dwellings and boutiques. The children of Wittenberge were true to form. Running about in packs, some even laughed as they played, the much smaller ones gripping the skirts of their mothers, who looked on as the sorry looking convoy shuffled through, hoping to find sanctuary on the far bank.

Mortens gathered his senses enough to be able to sit up under his own effort. Astrid helped him get comfortable and regretted not having anything for him to drink. The citizens of Wittenberge had been generous with what they had, and so would no doubt offer more in the way of refreshment when it became available. She put her arm around his shoulders, with Tommy putting his head in his master's lap.

'How are you feeling, Otto?'

'Like I've hit the schnapps too hard.'

Astrid snorted, instantly putting her free hand to her mouth apologetically. Her husbands' humour was the very tonic she needed and felt lighter for it. He gingerly put a hand up to his bandaged head.

'The British almost got you.' Astrid rocked a little with him. He returned a confused look.

'What do you mean?'

'You were on your way home, when they blew up the road bridge.'

Mortens winced as he felt the bandages. Astrid lifted his free hand to her lips and kissed it.

'I'll get you some fresh bandages once we've crossed.'

Mortens looked to his wife.

'They're going to arrest me when we get across, you know that right?'

'Who?'

'The British.'

Astrid took in her husband's attire. His blood speckled greatcoat, not to mention his tunic sported silver SS runes on the lapels and collar, respectively. She gave off a slight shrug.

'Throw them in the river.'

'No.' Mortens shook his head gingerly. 'I'm not a coward. And besides, it's bloody cold this morning.'

'What happens to Tommy and me when they come for you?'

'Go to Emma. She'll have room for you both. The British are there, but other than that, her place appears to be peaceful now.'

Mortens sister, Emma lived in Soltau. A widow since 1940, after her husband fell in France. Her two boys, thankfully too young to fight remained with her. Astrid agreed with his idea.

'The boys will enjoy playing with Tommy.'

Both looked out onto the wide, fast flowing Elbe. Its grey, threatening current did not look at all inviting. The ferry, underpowered and well past its prime chugged back to the east bank in a wide berth to prevent it from drifting under the bomb wrecked rail bridge. Its superstructure was warped and crumbling, with clumps of brick and masonry falling away under the weight of human foot traffic shuffling across it towards the west bank. Astrid knew that to take the bridge was risky, but her Otto was far too unstable on his feet to make the walk. She was surprised he was sat up cracking jokes, never mind walking anywhere. As the ferry made it to its mooring, an officious old man with a clipboard, jabbed a pencil at those he felt should go next. Astrid and Mortens were among those selected to go next. As she helped him to his feet, Tommy circled them, tail wagging. The ferry master in response wagged his pencil.

'Not the dog. We've not the room.'

'I'm sorry?' Astrid looked to him as he began to walk away. The old man turned; a nod of his head indicated Tommy.

'The dog stays. We don't have the room.'

As she went to protest, Mortens pulled himself to his full height, and looked the man up and down.

'Old man, you have a decision to make.'

'I have a what?' The man turned square on to the SS officer, the bloody bandages fooling him in to thinking he had the last word. Mortens jerked a thumb at Tommy.

'If the dog stays, you'll be joining those manning the checkpoint, ready to repel the Soviets when they get here.'

'What?'

'You heard me.'

The old man allowed his arms to fall by his side. A stern look drawn across his face.

'I'll have you know, Haupsturmfuhrer, I've eaten more mud at Verdun than you've had hot meals.'

'Then you are no stranger to combat. They will certainly benefit from your wise council.'

The stand-off had all those about them in a trance. Their eyes shifted from the stocky, barrel chested Great War veteran and the younger, badly wounded SS officer. Astrid could hear her own heart beating like a drum, for her husband refused to give up Tommy. The old man eyed the dog as he nodded a little.

'Keep that dog under control. This ferry had seen better days. I need to get you all away.'

Mortens made an effort at a smile.

'Thank you, Sir. And my compliments to your endeavours as a younger man. You have my admiration.'

The old man snorted.

'Lot of fucking good it did. Come on. We can't waste any more time.'

The ferry was open to the elements, save for a small, raised wheel house on its right side. It was designed more for moving freight, not passengers. Dangerously overloaded, the ferryman cast off and gave a thumbs up to the young man in the wheelhouse. Crammed into the centre of the open deck, Mortens and Astrid had to stand with their feet wide apart whilst leaning on each other to remain steady. Sitting down was not an option. Tommy fidgeted between their legs before curling up for the journey. Mortens concussion quickly made his head swoon with sea sickness, not that he had anything to bring up, for he had not eaten properly for some time. Other passengers looked wary at the sorry looking SS officer. As the ferry engine chugged away against the relentless flow of the Elbe, people spoke in hushed tones, their eyes forever darting at Mortens. Astrid could not hear what they were speaking of and was past caring. If the British were on the west bank, her husband would be most likely taken into custody. It was just a matter of time. He needed a hospital sooner rather than later. He would most certainly require stitches, and his current dressings looked ghastly.

Out in the middle of the wide Elbe, the young ferry pilot fought hard to keep the ferry from drifting towards the bridge supports. As the pathetic engine raised in pitch, screams rang out around Astrid and Mortens. With those around her looking up, she looked up to see what warranted such a response. To her horror, the centre span of the bomb-damaged bridge gave way under the weight of human traffic and swung down, the humans upon it, man woman and child cartwheeled screaming down against the exposed upright and bashed into the water. As the swinging span gave way altogether, it toppled over, landing on those trying to swim away. As the ensuing tsunami rolled outwards, it lifted the ferry, causing all those aboard to fall in the direction of the wheelhouse. The sudden shift in weight had the overloaded craft pass the point of no return and roll over, casting Astrid, Mortens, Tommy, and every other passenger, old and very young into the dark, frigid, unforgiving river.

Two men swam into focus. One was a young, trim, bareheaded Haupsturmfuhrer, the other was an older bespectacled man of similar height, thinning hair, and a neat, trimmed moustache. The latter was wearing a white physicians coat with a stethoscope around his neck. As Mortens gathered himself, the older man spoke in English.

'Haupsturmfuhrer Mortens, my name is Major Charles Walton of the British Army, do you require this young man to translate?'

Mortens blinked hard as the SS officer translated. He then looked immediately around the two men stood over him. They were under a canvas roof which billowed a little from a light breeze. The walls around him were of brick and plaster, the canvas roof, supported by metal poles allowed the damaged structure to become habitable once more. A log stove crackled in the middle of the large space, its chimney rising up through the canvas. The fire was effective, for Mortens face and bare chest were warm, which had Mortens take in the fact that he was lying naked under clean sheets and blankets, his pillows were soft, the slips crisp, laundered and white. To either side of him were empty beds, all made up, ready to receive those who needed them. He peered around the men, to see that none other the beds other than his own were occupied. He then looked back at the men speaking to him.

'Are you German, Haupsturmfuhrer?' Walton asked, the young SS officer translating without being prompted.

'Where is Astrid?' Mortens croaked in German, blinking hard in the confusion, his head throbbing under fresh dressings. The uniformed young officer translated the question to the British major, who remained tight lipped at the question for a few moments before responding. Not used to employing translators, he spoke to the uniformed man and not directly to the one lying in the bed.

'People are still being brought in.'

As the young man translated, Mortens attempted to sit up to which Walton stepped forward to assist.

'Please take care, your stiches are fresh. That's quite some head wound you have. Amazed you survived whatever did that, never mind your unplanned dip in the Elbe.'

The SS officer began to translate in haste when Mortens raised a hand.

'I can understand you Major. The good Haupsturmfuhrer can return to his duties.'

Both men looked to each other, each a little flushed in the cheeks at what Mortens assumed was an inert situation. After a tight-lipped smile, Walton called over his shoulder.

'You can take him back, thank you.'

Mortens observed two British soldiers enter the room armed with rifles. They both looked fresh, clean shaven, and rather young. The SS officer nodded to Mortens before being led away. Watching the three of them leaving, he then looked to the major.

'Where am I?'

'You are in British custody young man. I can't tell you where, security and all that.'

'Security?'

'Yes.' Walton nodded. 'Can't have you escaping and reporting where you have been, that would be very bad indeed.'

'But...' Mortens tailed off, looking about the room, shifting higher in the bed. As he did so, the effort made his head swim. 'How did I get here? Where's my wife?'

'Our chaps pulled you from the river. Ghastly thing, with that bridge collapsing. They are still bringing people in,

I'm sure she'll be along shortly. How anyone managed to get to the bank is remarkable.'

'Remarkable?'

'Indeed. The current is strong, so I'm told. We had one hell of a job cutting your uniform off and cleaning you up, especially that terrible head wound of yours.'

Mortens went for his bandages a little too heavy handed, which caused both men to wince.

'Careful young man. Don't tear the stitches. They can come out in a few days. After that, I'm afraid your accommodations may slip rather. You'll be questioned before you join your comrades in the main cage.'

'A cage?' Mortens looked concerned. Walton waved a dismissive hand.

'Not literally a cage, it's just a term for a prisoner facility. In the meantime, rest. Enjoy the bed, and if you need the toilet, give one of the orderlies a shout, they'll take you where you need to go.'

'My uniform?'

'Cut off and incinerated. You'll be given plain field grey to wear going forwards. We have your paybook drying out in my office, and you have your identity disc. The Red Cross will come and chat with you before they take you to the cage. Make sure we are holding up our end.'

'Your end?' Mortens was confused. Walton dropped the friendly village doctor demeanour and looked the SS man squarely in the eyes.

'Yes Haupsturmfuhrer. Make sure you are not on the verge of starvation, or Typhus.'

Walton fixed Mortens a glare. The SS man sank back in the bed, knowing exactly what the British officer was alluding to. Mortens knew he had no defence and accepted that the British could well have left him on the river bank to die from either blood loss or hyperthermia, whichever came first. Walton then put on his charming bedside manner once again, for he had made his point. He broke into a warm smile.

'Now then. I'll have one of the orderlies bring you some coffee. Not exactly Fortnum and Mason, but certainly better than that ghastly crap you fellows have had to suffer with for heavens knows how long.'

As Walton went to leave, another man entered the large room, he approached Walton, before the pair of them wandered towards the door, speaking in hushed tones. Mortens heart sank.

Walton returned to Mortens; a mournful look written across his face. The other man, head bowed left the room altogether, hands wringing as he went. Walton reached out, his hand giving his former foe a gentle squeeze of the shoulder.

'Only a handful of men made it to the bank, I'm sorry.'

The End

Printed in Great Britain
by Amazon